First published in Great Britain by HarperCollins Children's Books in 2014
HarperCollins Children's Books is a division of HarperCollinsPublishers Ltd,
77-85 Fulham Palace Road, Hammersmith, London, W6 8JB.

The HarperCollins website address is: www.harpercollins.co.uk

2

Copyright © Robin Jarvis 2014
Illustrations copyright © Robin Jarvis 2014

ISBN 978-0-00-745130-2

Robin Jarvis asserts the moral right to be identified as the
author and illustrator of the work.

Printed and bound in England by Clays Ltd, St Ives plc

Conditions of Sale
This book is sold subject to the condition that it shall not, by way of trade
or otherwise, be lent, re-sold, hired out or otherwise circulated without
the publisher's prior consent in any form, binding or cover other than
that in which it is published and without a similar condition including
this condition being imposed on the subsequent purchaser.

MIX
Paper from
responsible sources
FSC
www.fsc.org   FSC C007454

FSC™ is a non-profit international organisation established to promote
the responsible management of the world's forests. Products carrying the
FSC label are independently certified to assure consumers that they come
from forests that are managed to meet the social, economic and
ecological needs of present and future generations,
and other controlled sources.

Find out more about HarperCollins and the environment at
www.harpercollins.co.uk/green

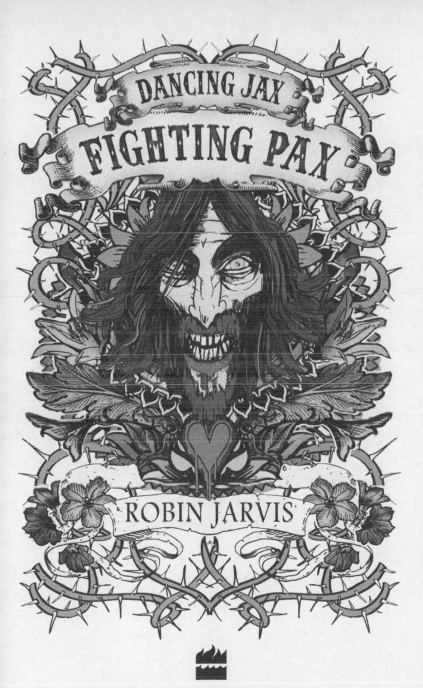

DANCING JAX

FIGHTING PAX

ROBIN JARVIS

HarperCollins *Children's Books*

"All this – this insanity, the terror and the hellish creatures everywhere – it's all because of a book, a kids' book, called *Dancing Jax*. It was written back in 1936 by... I don't know what you'd call him there, but I'd say 'occultist'. Do you know what that is? But he was and is much more than that: Austerly Fellows – the most dangerous and evil man to have ever lived – and he's still very much alive. The book wasn't published until late last year, by a man who Austerly Fellows has completely taken over. The guy was just some layabout chancer who broke into the wrong place and that was the end of him. He goes by the name of the Ismus now, after the main character in the story, and the world hangs on his every word.

"So many people have died, so many lives torn apart, so many more are suffering right now, but what really scares me, what keeps me wide awake, well into the night, is not the fear of him and his foul creatures finding me: it's wondering what he's got planned. What next? This isn't it – this won't be enough. Austerly Fellows is working to a plan, something even more terrible than what we've already seen. No, I have no idea what it is. How could I?

"Look, I'm nothing, a nobody – this isn't political. That – all that – is history now; it doesn't exist any more. I'm just a maths teacher from a tiny place in England called Felixstowe, and I'm tired and desperate. Why else would I be here, begging for your help? You've got to believe me, *Dancing Jax* is coming – and not even you can shut it out. You've been cut off from the rest of the world for a long time, but that won't help you now. Nothing can stop it! Nothing... except just maybe... one of those kids back in the UK. He just might be the answer to our prayers and that's why you have to help. It's the only hope we have."

The video message ended and the TV screen went blank. The Marshals turned to the figure in black seated between them.

"Do what he asks," their Supreme Leader said quietly. "Instigate the rescue – immediately."

1

ACROSS LONDON, COLUMNS of dark, oily smoke rose high in the still air. There were always fires now: cars, homes, people. There was always something to burn. The mirrored towers of Canary Wharf flashed with the apricot light of an evening in late summer. Although many of those windows were now shattered or smeared with the filthy trails of bloated creatures that crawled down at night, there were enough panes left for the setting sun to dazzle and flare in.

The Thames was high. Its surface was unmarred by river traffic, but fouled by scum, creeping weeds and long waving chains of jelly-like spawn. The water moved thickly around half-submerged wrecks of lorries and buses. They had been torn from the bridges by things that made their nests in the shadowy arches beneath, where great clusters of leathery eggs hung in webbed nets.

A teenage couple strolled along the deserted South Bank, heedless of the ruined city, eyes only for each other and the occupant of the buggy pushed by the boy. It was one of those overdesigned three-wheelers that looked like it should be roving the surface of Mars. But garlands of fluffy pink feathers had been twined about the handles to soften and personalise it and a foil Garfield balloon bobbed above.

Lee Charles smiled down at the infant secured safely in the seat. A knitted hat, shaped like a cupcake, with pink woolly icing and a glittery cherry on top, sat lightly on her small sleeping head. The biggest grin in the world lit up Lee's face whenever he looked at her. She was the most precious and beautiful baby he had ever seen. He lived for her smiles, and her innocence lapped around her like a flame. He would surrender his life to keep it burning. By his side, arm linked through his, the girl called Charm rested her chin on his shoulder.

"Aww," she said. "What is you like? What a softy. Some gangsta you is."

Lee planted a chuckling kiss on her lips.

"You two's my gang now, Sweets," he told her, his nose pressing against hers.

The girl kissed him back then glanced across the river at the once grand buildings, now derelict and unsafe.

"Were it worth it though?" she murmured. "I mean... all that. All what went on. Were it worth what you did?"

Lee pushed his fingers through her long hair and guided her lovely face back to him.

"For you to be here with me, right now? For our little angel? You messin' with me? It were worth it all. I'd do it again a million times over, babes. Don't you never think otherwise. You hear?"

Charm lowered her gaze and nodded.

Lee gripped the handles of the buggy once more.

"Time we got back," he announced. "Be gettin' dark soon. We don't wanna be out when the big things start movin' and the sky gets busy."

"Where we goin'?"

"Back to our place, babes. You know."

"Our place?"

"Yeah, the rad warehouse makeover, with steel shutters, gun emplacements and trick flame-throwers – all that good stuff."

The girl's forehead puckered slightly as she struggled to remember.

"I don't... is me ma there?"

"Let's get goin'," Lee urged softly.

"Well, is she or what?"

"She ain't there."

"Where then?"

"I told you, babes."

"If you did, I forgot. Why ain't me ma here to share this? Why ain't she wiv her granddaughter? She'd go freakin' mental for her she would."

"Your mother ain't around no more," Lee said, walking off. "She's gone. I told you."

Charm hesitated and put a hand to her temple in confusion. "Gone?" she repeated. "Where'd she go? I can't fink straight. When were this? When did you tell me?"

Lee halted, left the buggy and came back to her. Cupping her face in his hands, he looked into her eyes.

"She's dead, hun," he said gently. "When she found out what happened to you, it were too much. She couldn't face it and had to bail. Man, I almost caved too. Your mother was strong and fierce – you should be proud. She got the rest of us outta that hellhole, but she couldn't hack it out here without you. She thought you was dead forever. She didn't know what I had planned, how I was gonna go fetch you from that Mooncaster place. I'm gonna make sure our angel don't never forget she had a lioness for a grandma."

Charm blinked her tears away. Lee stroked her cheek. She never remembered. Perhaps it was best that way. Perhaps he should stop reminding her. The horrors of that camp, where children immune to the effects of *Dancing Jax* had been interned, were best forgotten, especially by her. She moved away, towards the railing, and stared down at the cloudy river. Lee followed, drew the girl close and held her tightly. As long as they were together, nothing else mattered. He would do anything to keep her in his arms forever. Sometimes he couldn't believe what he had already done.

And then that sudden sense of dread tore at his stomach, as it did every night. Still wrapped in his embrace, Charm raised her eyes and screamed.

Running along the path towards them were a dozen hideous little hunchbacked men, with hooked noses that curved down to meet the upturned tips of equally grotesque chins. They were Punchinello Guards from the pages of that evil children's book, ugly and brutal creatures that had crossed over into this world. They were dressed in the yellow and crimson livery of Mooncaster, with large velvet bicorn hats on their deformed heads and spears in their fists.

Lee grabbed the girl's hand and the couple ran back towards the buggy. But the guards were already upon them.

A savage kick knocked Lee's legs from under him. His knees crashed on to the concrete. Charm's hand was torn from his fingers and his face slammed against the ground. He roared in pain and rage as a steel-heeled boot stamped on his shoulders. His arms were yanked up over his back until he thought they would snap or be ripped from the sockets. His joints felt on fire. He tried to struggle, but a brass knuckleduster crunched into his ribs and a pinched, nasal voice squawked in his ear.

"Goody goody!" it screeched. "Oh, goody goody! You twitch again, Creeper, and me smash bones. Me likey hear them splintery crack, splintery crack."

The boy could only stare as three of the Punchinellos bounded after Charm, squealing and quacking with cruel delight.

"Get away from her!" he bawled. "Don't you touch her!"

Even as he yelled those words, the girl was dragged to the floor by her hair and powerful hands clamped over her mouth, smothering her terrified shrieks.

Then two more guards came waddling up. Between them they carried a large leather suitcase. It was so long it required two handles and, when Lee saw it, his eyes widened in horror. The suitcase was shaped like a coffin.

"No!" he bellowed.

The guards set the macabre case down and skipped around it, flicking the catches open. Then they threw back the lid. Charm was hoisted into the air and flung inside.

"We had a deal!" Lee cried. "I did what your Ismus psycho wanted. We had a deal!"

The Punchinellos ignored him. They hopped and danced about the suitcase, tormenting the petrified girl within, jabbing and prodding her with the tips of their spears.

"You hurt her and I'll kill you!" Lee thundered.

"Prick the squassage!" they taunted. "Prick it, poke it, make it spit, make it sing and squeal in the pan."

"Girl no belong here," the evil voice hissed in the boy's ear. "You not done what Ismus want."

"I did!" Lee protested. "I did it and damned myself to Hell. But I didn't care! Don't you take her from me now!"

"You liar. You no do it. Girl stay dead till you does."

Lee watched them reach for the lid of the suitcase and looked on Charm's stricken face one final time.

"Don't you be scared now!" he shouted across to her. "I ain't gonna lose you again! Wherever you is, I'll find you! I promise! I promise!"

The lid snapped down and quick, dirty fingers locked it. Then the suitcase was snatched up and the two guards went scurrying away with it. Charm's muffled screams faded in the distance.

The crushing weight of the boot lifted from Lee's shoulder and the owner of the voice stepped before his eyes. There stood Captain Swazzle, chief warder of the castle guards. He was dressed in the same absurd outfit as the last time the boy had seen him, back at the camp. The pinstriped, 1920s, Al Capone-style suit, complete with pearl-grey spats and white fedora, was still in place and a stream of pale blue smoke curled up from the fat cigar in his mouth.

"You want see girl again?" he snarled, tapping ash down on to the boy's face. "Do what Ismus say."

"Big mistake messin' with me!" Lee thundered back. "You know what I'm capable of. You know why your head guy is so scared o' me. I am gonna make it my personal business to take you right outta this world and scrub you from that book forever – like you never was – an' there ain't nuthin' could..."

The threat died on his lips. The other Punchinellos had started to squawk.

"Oohhhh, a baby! Look at the baby! Looky – looky!"

They gathered round the buggy and began pawing at the infant inside.

Lee roared at them to get away, but they paid no attention and fawned over the baby, distorting their misshapen features even more by pulling faces and sticking their dark tongues out. A moment later, the child was crying and the guards started squabbling.

"You woke the baby!"

"No, you woke the baby!"

"You did!"

"You!"

Bickering, they jostled for possession of the buggy, wrenching it from one another's greedy grasp.

Lee bawled at them. The hands gripping his arms gave them a sudden, violent twist and his face smacked the ground.

"Please stop," he begged fearfully. "Don't do this. Don't hurt my angel. I'll do whatever you want."

Captain Swazzle cackled and swaggered across to join the others.

"I make baby sleep," he declared. Grabbing the buggy's handles, he rocked it roughly from side to side. Leering down, he brought his hideous face close to the child's and blew a smoke ring. Then he began to croon a foul Punchinello lullaby.

"Halt your wailing temper or you shall earn a clout,
only bitches whimper, only cats mew out.
I'll pinch and pull your nose to grow,

I'll give your chin a curl.
Dream of stunted legs that bow
and be a humpbacked girl."

While he sang, another guard took hold of the front wheel and, together, they swung the buggy in ever-increasing arcs.

Lee tried to break loose, but every movement was rewarded with a vicious wrench on his arms and a violent stamp on his legs.

"Stop!" he pleaded. "Stop!"

"More!" Captain Swazzle squawked. "Up she goes!"

The swings became wilder. The buggy swept higher and higher into the air until it was level with the Punchinellos' hats. If the baby hadn't been secured in the seat, she would have fallen out. Then it went higher still. Captain Swazzle's yellow eyes bulged in their sockets and he hooted repulsively.

"Up and down!" he screeched. "Up and down – up and down... that's the way to do it."

The rest of them joined in the familiar chant, stamped their feet and flourished their spears.

"That's the way to do it, that's the way to do it!"

Lee couldn't bear it. Hot tears streaked his face. He prayed and he shouted, but there was nothing he could do.

"Aaaaaand... up she goes!" Captain Swazzle shrieked one last time. As the buggy went higher than ever, he let go of the handles and the other Punchinello released the front wheel. The buggy continued sailing through the air. It flew up and over the railings, then down again.

Lee squeezed his eyes tight shut. He heard the splash, followed by the trampling of the guards' boots as they charged across to watch the buggy sink into the river.

"Oooooh, what a pity," Captain Swazzle cried, staring down at the cloudy waters where a woollen hat, in the shape of a cupcake, floated on the scum. "Oh, what a pity."

Lee's scream ripped across the Thames.

The pain bit deeply into his wrists and he lurched upright.

His face was dripping, drenched in icy sweat that stung his eyes. He wrenched at his arms, but they were still held firm. His despairing yell filled the room.

"Mr Lee Charl," a calm, female voice soothed. "You fine, you safe, you not worry, please."

The boy's frantic, heaving breaths continued and his heart pounded as his eyes stared blankly around. The river was gone. The Punchinellos had disappeared. He was in a dimly lit room with blank walls and no window. A hospital bed was before him, surrounded by monitoring equipment, and four men in smart olive uniforms, armed with AK-47 rifles, were standing impassively on either side. There was a figure on the bed, sitting bolt upright, with wires attached to his forehead. A petite woman, wearing a white lab coat over her army uniform, crossed to the door and snapped on the main light switch. Overhead, a fluorescent strip began to stutter. Lee now saw that the eyes of the patient were wide and the stark, traumatised expression on that face was painful to witness. Then something pink glinted under the clinical light. It was a diamanté stud in the patient's ear. With a jolt, Lee remembered he was staring at a large mirror covering one entire wall and the pitiful figure on the bed was him.

Repulsed, he looked away and the calmly efficient female doctor consulted his case notes.

"You want sedative, Mr Lee Charl?" she asked with crisp politeness.

"Hell, no," he answered thickly. "I slept plenty already – and they make the dreams worse."

"Same dream, please?" she asked, ready to jot his words down.

"Pretty much."

"Was Ismus in dream?"

"He's never in them, Doctor Choe. They're just dreams. It's not like the other thing. I'm not sneakin' off and going to Mooncaster, you know that. They're just bad dreams. I ain't havin' no secret cosies with that mad son of a..."

"Detail of dream, please."

He shook his head. "Laters – I'll save it for the shrink session."

"You might forget detail," she said a little more forcefully, though the smile didn't slip from her face. "Detail important."

"Fat chance of that," he uttered bitterly. "Now can I hit the shower and get me some dry clothes? Feels like I peed in these. Is there hot water today?"

Doctor Choe Soo-jin put the notes down and reached for a syringe.

"First I take bloods," she told him.

"More? You supportin' a family of vampires at home or somethin'? You've had enough juice outta me since I got here to fill a hot tub."

"Not so much," she said through her implacable smile. "We need to test, Mr Lee Charl. Test important."

"So you says, but I can hardly find a vein no more. My arms are worse than a dead junkie's. Gimme a break, yeah? If it ain't the red stuff, you're moochin' every other damn thing I got."

Doctor Choe Soo-jin proceeded to take the sample. Lee gazed around at the four young soldiers flanking the bed. They might have been shop-window dummies for all the expression on their features. None of them spoke English, or at least had never acknowledged that they could. Sometimes he wondered if they listened to what was said when he was in the company of his friends and then reported everything to Doctor Choe, or their commanding officer, afterwards.

Lee cast a piercing glance at the mirrored wall. He was sure it was one of those two-way numbers; probably a video camera behind there taping it all anyway.

He looked back at the two grim-faced men on his left. There were three different sets who 'nannied' him in rotation, with a changeover every four hours. He'd given each group a name to amuse himself. This quartet were the Sex and the City women, because his mother used to enjoy that show, and they'd taken over from Take That (minus Robbie) sometime during the night when he was asleep. His grandmother had been a big fan of "that nice Gary Barlow". Soon it would be the turn of the Spice Girls (minus Geri). He didn't know anyone who had liked them, but it cracked him up to call these stern guards Sporty, Posh, Baby and Scary.

His eyes dropped to the aluminium chain threaded through their belts. The pair on the right were joined in the same way. Both chains ended in a set of steel handcuffs, locked round Lee's wrists. He blew on them gently. He'd been pulling on them in his sleep and the skin was raw and broken.

"Just another day chained up in North Korea," he murmured. "Can my life blow any more? How the hell did it get to this?"

2

THE SECRET STRONGHOLD in the northern region of the Baekdudaegan
Mountains had taken seventeen years to excavate. From the outside
there was no evidence of the extensive tunnel system in which 7,500
members of the People's Army were stationed at any one time. The
largest terraces and balconies were built in the style of old temples,
with sagging tiled roofs, artificially distressed to appear ancient and
neglected, while others were simply cut horizontally into the slope and
disguised with camouflage. The two helipads and missile silos were
similarly obscured. The single road which zigzagged up to the main,
but discreet, entrance was constantly monitored by sniper outposts.

Beneath the pagoda-like roof that sheltered one of the terraces,
Maggie rested her elbows on the low wall and pulled the fur-lined

collar of the greatcoat round her chin. The biting December air was sharp in the fifteen-year-old's nostrils and she buried them in her mittened hands. She couldn't remember ever being warm and, to make it worse, there was no hot water in the showers. The primitive plumbing had broken down again.

The usually breathtaking view was hidden today. Beyond the wall, the grey slopes of the mountain dropped steeply into a thick white mist that filled the valley, blotting out the dark forests and surrounding snowy peaks. It was like staring into a universe of nothing, an endless blank canvas waiting for the first mark or stroke of colour to be applied. It was almost hypnotic and Maggie's mind drifted.

She thought back to that July night, when they escaped from the prison camp in England — how she and the other aberrant children had crowded into a military helicopter, with no idea where they were being taken. Through the darkness, they were flown across the Channel to a private airstrip in France, where a jet was waiting to whisk them on across the world.

At the time it felt so unreal, like an adventure happening to someone else. They didn't question anything. The elation of having got out of that horrendous place alive, combined with the food provided on the journey, drove all other thoughts out of their heads. They didn't care where they were going. They were finally safe from Punchinello bullets and starvation. Each new day would no longer be a hopeless struggle for survival. Even when they touched down and sleepily discovered just where this sanctuary was, it didn't really register.

North Korea, or 'the Democratic People's Republic of Korea' as they swiftly learned to call it, had shown them its most benign and welcoming face. The children of the camp had been fêted as honoured guests and, for the first week, enjoyed the best that this secretive and isolated corner of the world could offer. After the privations and sadistic treatment they had suffered back home, it was like a surreal holiday.

They were given grand tours of the capital city, Pyongyang, and the surrounding provinces. They were bussed to old Buddhist temples, imposing monuments and battle sites, and attended a banquet at which the Supreme Leader, Kim Jong-un, was present, surrounded by an austere array of Generals and Grand Marshals. They were even ushered into the palatial mausoleum where the embalmed corpses of Kim Jong-un's revered father and grandfather were ceremoniously displayed in glass cases. Maggie and the other refugees filed past them in disbelief: what sort of a country was this? A girl called Esther threw up on the steps afterwards.

A crew from Korean Central Television, the only news broadcaster, followed them everywhere. Just three channels were available to the people of Pyongyang and the rest of the country made do with one. There was no satellite TV or Internet for ordinary citizens: such things were forbidden. Every TV set was configured to receive only these official channels and regular checks were made to ensure they were not tampered with.

The rescued foreign children became instant celebrities. They were interviewed together, in small groups of three or four and individually. North Korea wanted to know the exact nature of the madness happening outside its borders. How could a mere book of European fairy tales be the cause of so much turmoil and confusion? Viewers watched with horrified fascination as the youngsters recounted frightening stories of the camp and the rejection by their own families.

Maggie lost track of the times she had repeated the same information.

"No, it's not a normal book," she had said, struggling to explain the unexplainable. "It sucks you in and you really believe you're one of the characters in it and all this, the real world, is just a dream. Honest, that's what it is – and you wear a playing card to show who you are in that story! No, it didn't work on me, or any of the others here. We don't know why, it just didn't. That's why they locked us up and treated us worse than animals. We were rejects. You wouldn't believe what they did to us."

The interviewer pressed for details and the interpreter had difficulty keeping up with the barrage of questions. Maggie was shown footage, gathered by the Research Department for External Intelligence, of foreign cities where protests against *Dancing Jax* had escalated into violent riots. Bookshops and publishers were firebombed. Civil war had burned fiercely but briefly until everyone was under the book's spell.

"Same happened in Britain," she said, watching a pitched battle storm through the streets of Moscow, between those who had read it and those who hadn't. "We went through all that. You can't fight it. It's too strong. Then there are the... things."

The microphone almost poked her in the nose as it was pushed closer.

"Somehow things are coming through, from the book," she said. "It sounds mad, but it's true. Nightmares, monsters in those fairy tales, are becoming real. I've seen them, I've fought them. I thought the Punchinello Guards were bad enough, but then there were... I dunno what they really are, but they're called Doggy-Long-Legs in the book and all they want to do is eat your face. One of the guards had his nose chewed right off. Then there was the... we never found out what it was – all giant worms and tentacles. It killed my... a friend of mine. It got him – it got my Marcus."

Maggie fell silent. The interview had then cut to a segment of an American news report from several months ago, back when America was wondering what was happening in the UK. It was second- or third-generation video, again acquired by the intelligence department. The reporter was Kate Kryzewski, speaking from Kew Gardens, investigating a previously unknown invasive shrub with pulpy grey fruit, called minchet. Eventually she too had fallen victim to the power of the book.

When the news cut back, Maggie had been replaced by a self-conscious, bespectacled boy wearing a cowboy hat. "Er... yes," he said. "That stuff grows everywhere now and it stinks. The creatures from the book eat it, as well as other things... and the Jaxers use it to heighten the reading experience. Makes it better... sharper somehow. It tastes worse than it smells though and gives you gut ache."

"Gives you the trots!" Maggie's voice shouted off camera.

The picture cut to an army scientist holding a single horned skull, fixed to a stout stick. The austere, shouting voice-over told the audience it had been thoroughly examined and undergone testing. It was not a hoax; this was a genuine unicorn skull. In North Korea they called it a *kirin* and its appearance was seen as an auspicious sign, for these mythical creatures only appeared during the reign of wise rulers. But where had it come from? None of the children seemed to know and the boy in the Stetson only admitted to bringing it from the camp.

Another strange item was held up for the viewers. A long, crooked silver wand, tipped with an amber star. The interviewer waved it around, pulling comical faces. Maggie said it belonged to the retired Fairy Godmother character, but didn't say how it came to be in the camp. Both it and the skull were confiscated.

"I don't want my damn face on TV!" Lee had growled, among other things that didn't get translated.

"What they do to you?" he was badgered. "What they do?"

"You really wanna know?" he snarled back. "They dragged my girlfriend to an abattoir and slaughtered her like a pig, that's what. Then those sick bastards fed her to us. You got that? You comprende that? Yeah, you heard right – they fed her to us!"

And so the Democratic People's Republic of Korea learned about *Dancing Jax*. For once the ceaseless, bombastic propaganda machine didn't need to exaggerate the evils of the imperialist Western aggressors; in fact, it concentrated its efforts in downplaying the dangers to dampen the mounting sense of panic. Yes, it was a state of emergency and they stood alone against the entire world, but that was nothing new. Such a crisis is what their founder, Kim Il-sung, foresaw in his great wisdom and why they would survive even this. Whatever threatened their borders would be dealt with. They had no need to fear. Kim Jong-un, the founder's grandson, would ensure no harm would come to his people. They would remain isolated from the world and stay safe.

But the presence of the foreign children was a constant reminder of the outside danger and so, when that first week was over, the special treatment, the visits, the interviews stopped. Then the only adult female, Mrs Benedict, was found dead in the bathroom of their hotel. She had killed herself and the euphoria of having escaped the camp died with her. Two nights later, they were all removed from Pyongyang.

Maggie recalled that less comfortable journey in the back of military trucks through rugged, hilly terrain and seemingly endless forests, along rudimentary roads until, finally, they reached this secret base built into the mountain. The holiday was over. They had swapped one prison for another.

"Your face will freeze and drop off out here," a friendly voice declared.

The teenage girl blinked. She had stared into the fog too long and her eyes ached. Turning away from the blank void, she saw a neat, elderly gentleman approaching along the terrace.

"Morning, Gerald," she called, glad to see him. "I was miles away."

"A chon for your thoughts?"

"Oh – I was thinking back to when we first got here."

The man clapped his gloved hands and shuddered inside his overcoat.

"All those months ago," he said. "When you piled out of those wagons. It was like something from *Oliver!* I almost started singing 'Consider yourself' and giving you my Artful Dodger."

He gripped his lapels and did some nimble footwork. Maggie laughed.

"More like an Artful Codger nowadays, mind," he chuckled.

"I wish I'd seen you back when you were performing," Maggie said. "I bet you were amazing."

Gerald Benning put his arm round her. He never really spoke about his show-business past, but somehow word had got around the children here, probably via Martin, and they liked to ask him questions about his former life. Gerald always answered with good humour, but usually steered the conversation around to other things and asked them about themselves. He thought it was important to remind them, especially the younger ones, what their world was like before all this had happened.

He got them talking about the little aspects of that time, the simple things that they'd forgotten: family holidays, best birthday presents, favourite movies and songs, names of pets and who they'd sat next to in school. He didn't promise them that, one day, those things would return and everything would be as it was. That would have been cruel. They wouldn't have believed him anyway. But those memories told them they weren't just refugees dependant on the charity of a suspicious nation, and that there had been goodness and love in their lives, and they shouldn't hate their parents for rejecting them. It wasn't their fault. *Dancing Jax* was to blame.

Maggie smiled at him. "God knows what we'd have done without you," she said. "All these months, stuck away up here with less freedom than we had in the camp and nothing to do, day in, day out, but snipe and bitch. We'd have probably killed each other by now. I was ready to strangle that Esther first thing today. She's worse than she ever was. What a spiteful cow; she's really doing my head in."

"She's difficult to like, that one," Gerald conceded. "And, since she went all limpet-like on Nicholas, he's developed full-blown annoyingness too. But we're none of us perfect and you've all been through enough to send most people round the twist and back again. Being cooped up here like battery hens doesn't help. Don't let it get to you. Rise above it, my dear."

"You always make it seem better somehow. Even in this miserable place..."

"Titipu," he interrupted with a wink. Gerald had mischievously christened the mountain base after the fictional town featured in *The Mikado*, which was a huge insult to their North Korean hosts. There was nothing but enmity between them and Japan, where *The Mikado* was set.

"See, all the kids call it that now. They dunno what it is, but it sounds funny. You've given them something to laugh at, as long as the Generals don't find out. You make it bearable and keep us busy with daft schemes. Look how you wangled your way into the kitchens to make that birthday cake for Lee last month."

"He'd have been happier if I'd managed to get him some ciggies."

"Oh, don't expect him to show gratitude, he's never been the demonstrative type, but that meant a lot to him that did. He's not the same since Charm... since she died."

"Poor girl," Gerald said sadly. "That was horrific for all of you. I'd like to have known her. She sounds dazzling."

Maggie lowered her eyes. "Best friend I ever had," she said. "Not a day goes by when I don't think about her – and my Marcus – and miss them. After all these months, it still hurts."

"Course it does. And it always will, but it won't always be as sharp and you'll remember how good they made you feel more often than the pain of losing them. Takes a long time though."

Maggie bit her lip guiltily. She had forgotten the Scottish boy, Alasdair. He had lured the Punchinellos away so that the rest of them could escape. They had all heard the ferocity of the gunfire in those dark woods and understood what it signified. His body was probably still in the New Forest, unburied and picked at by birds and animals – or worse.

And then there was Mrs Benedict...

"I should've done more to help Charm's mum," Maggie said unhappily. "That first week, after she found out what happened, I should've..."

"There was nothing anyone could do," Gerald told her firmly. "Mrs Benedict just couldn't live with her grief. Not everyone can. Don't you ever think you could have stopped her. Despair is a terrible thing, the absolute worst."

He blew on his gloved hands as if to dispel the sadness and the vapour cloud melted into the fog.

"But it's no use dwelling on the past, young Maggie," he declared breezily. "'Turn, oh turn, in this direction,' as the chorus sing in *Patience*. Worse things are undoubtedly just around the corner and we've got to be ready for them. But, in the meantime, 'Let the merry cymbals sound.' We're not at home to Mr Despair and we've got to ensure your friend Lee doesn't slip down into that dark pit."

The girl agreed. "He's not about to join your choir though," she told Gerald. "I don't know how you roped the rest of us into it either. My voice is never going to be mistaken for Adele's. And then there's the music lessons you do, way more popular than Martin's boring maths classes. You really do keep our spirits up, not to mention the stuff you coax out of the guards for us. I've no idea how you manage that. I can't get a smile out of the surly buggers."

"I let them slay me at chess," said Gerald, waving the compliment aside. "They're mad about it. Now, glad you mentioned the choir because I've decided it's going to be Christmas carols all this week – and not just the obvious ones. There'll be no jingle bells, Batman smells or shepherds' socks from you lot. Let's show these gloomy Titiputians what they're missing."

"They're not going to let us sing Chrimble songs, are they? I thought you said they were anti the whole thing in a mega way?"

"Oh, they are. Before this madness happened, the South Koreans used to put lights round a tower near the demilitarised zone so it looked like a Christmas tree and this bunch always threatened to fire rockets at it. They didn't want their hoi polloi getting any fancy ideas. So what we're not going to do is tell them we're singing carols. I know some lovely old ones that aren't too specific and I can tweak the words in others. They won't cotton on; they'll just think we're doing our usual practising. I might even get the interpreters and guards joining in – now there's a challenge. If I could get them to warble a wassail, or 'The

Coventry Carol', that would be my Christmas present to myself. How hot do you think their Latin is?"

Maggie laughed. "About as good as mine – which is non-existent."

"Fab, I might see if we can get away with a bit of 'Quem Pastores'. That should fox them."

"Feels weird talking about Christmas here where they don't believe in anything but the party and their precious leader," the girl murmured. "I used to love it: tinsel and telly, parties and the food – specially the food. I used to really wind up my stepmum by pigging out. Seems like another life now; so much has happened since."

Gerald gave her shoulder a gentle squeeze. "You've grown up, that's what's happened to you," he said. "You've realised you don't need to live up to anyone's expectations but your own. That stepmother was a monster, trying to make you anorexic, and, of course, you being you went and did the exact opposite – you barmpot. But look at you now. How much weight have you lost since you got here? Not that you needed to: you were lovely as you were. The other kids have managed to put some on, but you must've trimmed down by a couple of stone at least."

Maggie looked back into the fog. "I didn't need to be big any more," she said. "And, one thing the camp taught me, there's a better chance of survival if I can run a hundred metres without collapsing. That's why I jog up and down here every morning; besides, there's not much else to do."

"Yes," Gerald agreed. "And the running isn't done with yet. This place has lasted much longer than I expected. Austerly Fellows must be saving it for the very end."

"When do you think that will be?"

"Not long now." He turned to glance back at the female soldier who had followed him out on to the terrace and gave her a cheery wave. Their ever-watchful hosts were never far away. "They're extra nervy lately," he muttered, just loud enough for Maggie to hear. "Haven't you noticed? There's rumours about all kinds of things happening near the demilitarised zone in the south. Quite a lot of them have families back there you know; you can learn a lot whilst twiddling with your bishop."

"If they ever find out you're picking up the lingo, you'll be in serious trouble."

Gerald grinned. "I'm not about to give myself away," he said. "And my best teacher is General Chung's youngest daughter, little Nabi. It's just a game to her. Besides, I'm only picking up the odd word here and there, although the Korean for 'piano' is exactly the same as ours. Who'd have thought that? But, from what I gather, there's been books smuggled in across the frontier and unnatural creatures have been sighted in the woods there."

"It's started then," Maggie said flatly. "Soon it'll be the helicopter fly-pasts with readings over loudspeakers. Not that they need them in Pyongyang: the whole place is wired up to that annoying PA system. But where do we go from here? There's nowhere left to hide. We're trapped in the last corner of the world. What'll happen to us then?"

"Anything that comes flying into this airspace won't last long," Gerald reminded her. "The Marshals are itching to launch their missiles as it is, specially Tark the Shark. He's a blood-soaked devil, that one, and just back from the south. He'd have pressed every red button already, given half the chance. That's probably why the Chinese haven't tried the old helicopter routine around here. They're only thirty or forty kilometres behind these mountains don't forget. No, I think Mr Fellows is going to try a different approach. After all, we've got the two things he desperately wants."

"Lee and Martin."

"Yes, Lee and Martin. For two very different reasons."

They fell silent and huddled together, facing the featureless mist.

Gerald and Maggie had clicked the moment they met and greatly enjoyed one another's company. The fact he was almost seventy years old and she only fifteen didn't matter. She was not only the granddaughter he had never had, they were also firm friends and laughed at the same things.

"Time to go," he announced presently. "Martin and I have got another of those useless coffee mornings with the big hats in half an hour. Get in out of this cold and tell everyone choir practice at the usual time later. Oh – and remember: 'tis the season..."

"Fa la la la la," she sang after him as he departed along the terrace, followed by the female soldier.

Maggie turned back to the fog. The last time she had sung a Christmas carol had been back in the camp, over the fresh grave of a young boy killed by one of the Punchinello's spears. Maggie was ashamed to realise that she couldn't even remember his name now. Too many faces had gone from her life. But one she would never forget belonged to a girl called Jody. She shuddered in horror whenever she recalled what *Dancing Jax* had done to her. Jody had been caught between the two worlds. Here her eyes turned to blue glass, while in Mooncaster she had become a hollow glass rabbit, filled with a virulent plague. The memory of that would haunt Maggie for as long as she lived.

"Which probably won't be too much longer," she murmured softly.

Peering into the thick white vapour, Maggie thought over what Gerald had said, about the creatures sighted in the far south. What if others had started to creep across the nearby Chinese border? The wooded valleys and mountain slopes could already be crawling with them, invisible in the concealing mist. This disturbing thought caused her to jump away from the wall and she hurried back inside the military base. The metal door clanged shut behind her.

IT WAS ONLY marginally less cold inside the mountain. Martin Baxter
was waiting on the concourse, behind the main entrance. It was a huge
imposing space, where five of the key tunnels converged. The facility
was so large and rambling it required transport to travel from one area
to another, and each of those routes was wide enough to accommodate
two lanes of traffic. One of the tunnels even had rails laid down to
convey heavy equipment and munitions. The walls of this man-made
cavern were bare rock and the lighting was basic and functional,
connected by hanging wires and cables.

Dominating the central area was a scaled-down version of the
twenty metre-high bronze statue of Kim Il sung in Pyongyang. Even
though it was smaller, this was still seven metres tall. With its right arm
outstretched, it looked as though it was directing the vehicles driving
around it. Above the entrance to each passage hung the red starred flag,
and the same design, with its blue borders, had been worked into the
mosaic floor.

The first time Martin had set eyes on this impressive interior, it
reminded him of early James Bond movies, with those amazing sets

of the villain's lair designed by Ken Adam. The geek in him had gone a step further and couldn't help imagining daleks gliding around, instead of the old jeeps and bicycles that the base used, and robot Yeti lumbering around outside. But he hadn't mentioned that to anyone. Only Paul, his partner's twelve-year-old son, would have appreciated it. But Paul had been one of the first victims of *Dancing Jax* and was now part of the Ismus's entourage, together with Carol, the boy's mother. Martin missed them both desperately.

That morning he was agitated and annoyed. These weekly meetings with the Generals were pointless. They never listened to what he had to say and barely concealed their contempt at his presence. Since the rescue of the children from England, absolutely nothing had been accomplished. He couldn't understand it. They wouldn't even discuss a campaign against the Ismus. Their policy was to wait and gather as much information as they could, which, more often than not, they didn't share with him. Martin decided that today he was going to get some answers. They owed him that much. He wasn't just anybody. He was the thorn in the Ismus's side, the man who had denounced him from the start, who had spent the best part of a year trying to warn the rest of the world.

A tinny voice barked and crackled from the tannoy system and went echoing through the tunnels. The language was Korean, but it was so distorted that, even if it had been in English, Martin wouldn't have been able to understand what was said. Just the usual announcements and orders of the day, he supposed.

A veteran jeep pulled up alongside. The North Korean war machine was a curious hotchpotch of new technology and relics of the past.

Although it had almost a thousand missiles trained on South Korea, possessed ZM-87 laser weapons, was nuclear capable and had an active space programme, most of its other arms and vehicles dated as far back as World War Two.

An even younger female soldier than the one that had been shadowing Gerald was at the wheel and a grim-looking guard with an AK-47 sat beside her. She directed a stony-faced expression at Martin and the former maths teacher clambered in beside Gerald who was sitting in the back.

"Piccadilly, please, cabbie," Gerald quipped. "And don't go the long way round or you won't get a tip." These trifling games were what got him through his time here. Life inside this mountain was barely tolerable, so he embraced every opportunity to tickle it along. At times his teasing attitude infuriated Martin, but the children adored him for it.

The girl betrayed no sign she had heard and drove on. Her name was Chung Eun-mi, eldest daughter of General Chung Kang-dae.

When he first arrived in the country, Martin's irrepressible sci-fi self had noted that, just like the Bajorans in *Star Trek*, here the family name preceded the individual name.

Conscription at seventeen was mandatory for everyone, but, for Eun-mi, there was no other possible path. This was a vocation. It was her life's dream to wear this uniform. She was everything her father could have wished for in a son. Perhaps, if she had been a boy, their relationship would have been different.

Eun-mi was passionately loyal to the state, determined to devote herself to the People's Army, and strove to be the best in all she did, pushing herself to the limit at the expense of everything else. She had trained harder than any cadet in her unit, could strip a rifle and put it back together faster than the rest and was fluent in Russian, Mandarin and English. She and her young sister, Nabi, had been assigned to the Western refugees, to serve as interpreter, guide and companions. Maggie and the others knew they were also reporting back everything that was said. Well, perhaps not Nabi, who was only six and, unlike Eun-mi, appeared to enjoy spending as much time with the English children as she was allowed.

Gerald had grown very fond of little Nabi and had learned many Korean words from her, but he had no such affection for her older sister. Those beautiful yet flinty features gave nothing away. However, he could see the disgust glittering in her eyes whenever she addressed him or the others. Like everyone else in the country, she had been raised to distrust the West and she, being a General's daughter, magnified that into rabid hatred. She genuinely considered these Europeans to be an inferior race and would've preferred to have been given other duties away from them, but she was fiercely obedient and it never occurred to her to even think about questioning her orders.

As the jeep skirted the bronze statue, Eun-mi and the guard bowed respectfully until they passed into one of the tunnels. Martin and the others were only permitted access to a small fraction of the base. Dormitories and an exercise area had been allocated for them in the medical centre. Everywhere else was forbidden. The personnel they were allowed contact with were also restricted and they ate in their own separate refectory. Even some sections of the medical centre were out of bounds and doors to mysterious rooms were either locked or heavily guarded, or both.

The room where these weekly meetings were held was located in the northernmost section of the base. It was one of the most secure areas, where intelligence was gathered via spy satellites, and row after row of computers were manned round the clock by teams of hackers leaching data from foreign security systems. Neither Gerald nor Martin saw any of that. They were always guided from the jeep to the meeting room without deviation and, once inside, weren't allowed to leave, not even to use the toilet. Once the meeting was over, they were shepherded straight back to the jeep again.

Gerald always found this journey interesting. The installation was constantly bustling with activity and the ting-a-ling of bicycle bells. He wondered what everyone did, and why they were in such a hurry the whole time. Whatever it was, they were very serious and intense about it. Sometimes he tried to make the guards laugh, but the most he had achieved was a triumphant grin when they checkmated him.

The jeep came to a stop before a set of red double doors, blocked by two hefty sentries bearing the familiar Kalashnikovs.

"A wandering minstrel I," Gerald sang softly to himself as he got out, waving a hanging wisp of exhaust fume away from his face. The ventilation system had broken down again in this tunnel. That was the third time since September.

The soldier next to Eun-mi took her place behind the wheel and drove off. The girl spoke to the sentries and they stood aside to let the three of them pass.

"And I shouldn't be surprised if nations trembled," Gerald continued in a low, lilting murmur. "Before the mighty troops, the troops of Titipu!"

The meeting room was another space designed to impress. It was what every supervillain's war room should look like: oval in shape, with low-level lighting around the walls that accentuated the texture of the roughly hewn rock. A print of a vibrantly colourful, highly idealised and flattering painting of the three presidents, from Kim Il-sung to his grandson, hung in the centre of the longest wall. Sticking with his *Mikado* theme, Gerald called them the Three Little Maids and, whenever he saw one of these paintings, which were all over the place, sang a line from the song that seemed appropriate.

"Nobody's safe, for we care for none."

A large, elliptical table, made from cherry wood, dominated the centre, with a massive TV screen at one end. At least it was warmer in here than out in the tunnels. Three incongruous electric fires, the old-fashioned sort often found in pensioners' front rooms back in the UK, had been brought in to lift the temperature and all their bars blazed brightly orange.

The Vice-Marshals and Generals were already gathered and waiting; they rose from the table when the two Europeans came in and bowed.

Martin and Gerald returned the bow and cast their eyes over who was present. These fourteen middle-aged men were the most powerful in the country, under the Supreme Leader. The Chief of the General Staff was here, as was Eun-mi's father, General Chung Kang-dae, who made no acknowledgement of her presence. Then there was Marshal Tark Hyun-ki or, as Gerald called him, Tark the Shark. His sour face was half hidden behind large mirrored sunglasses as usual. He never attempted to disguise his hostility towards the English refugees. Martin despised him.

When they first arrived and Lee's incredible ability had been thoroughly discussed, Marshal Tark Hyun-ki had demanded they send the boy into Mooncaster, strapped to an atomic warhead. Upon its detonation, everyone on the planet who was under the book's spell would be wiped out, leaving only this glorious nation in command of a depopulated earth and finally safe from foreign aggressors.

Some of the other officers supported this efficient method of genocide and were only dissuaded when the practicalities were debated. The sudden death of entire populations would have serious consequences. How could they make safe and maintain every nuclear facility, chemical plant, gas field, oil refinery, pipeline and the innumerable other toxic industries around the globe? It would be physically impossible. And what pestilence would billions of unburied human corpses produce? What guarantee did they have that the monsters from *Dancing Jax* would also be killed?

Marshal Tark Hyun-ki refused to listen to the counter-arguments. He was adamant it was the perfect moment to settle accounts with the hated West. The time of empty rhetoric was over and they would be triumphant.

Lee's reaction, when he heard what they'd been planning, was nuclear in itself. In ferocious language he yelled that anything he took to Mooncaster was only a copy; the original objects always remained with his unconscious self in this world and so any bomb would blow up in both places. In spite of this raging outburst, it took a phone call from Kim Jong-un himself to dissuade the Marshal. After that, there was no more talk of sending Lee to Mooncaster and the boy had been chained to four guards, day and night, to keep him anchored here.

As a consequence, at these meetings, Tark the Shark's bow was always the curtest and he showed his displeasure further by never facing the two Englishmen. Ever since his grotesque proposal had been rejected, he had brought his aide along and communicated only through him.

The aide, a good-looking twenty-year-old called Du Kwan, was the one person who smiled when Martin and Gerald entered, but the friendly greeting was not for them. Over the preceding months he had grown to admire the beauty and composure of Eun-mi. He longed to speak to her privately, but such contact was forbidden. He was anxious to declare his affections, but how could such a thing be? Was she even aware of his existence? Her lovely eyes never strayed in his direction; she was focused solely on her duties as interpreter and kept her gaze fixed on the centre of the table. It was making Du Kwan despondent. Just one look from her would bring him joy.

Also present in the room that morning was Doctor Choe Soo-jin, clutching an overstuffed folder. She was due to deliver the report on her findings so far and the results of the tests she had been running. She cast a quick, sly glance at Martin. She also had certain recommendations to make that she would instruct Eun-mi not to translate.

"Good morning," Martin said in his no-nonsense schoolteacher's voice.

Gerald scattered friendly smiles left and right. He was always amused by the oversized hats the top brass wore here. They all looked like army pillar boxes and the medals that studded their jackets were like magnified milk-bottle tops.

Everyone sat down and those with briefcases placed them on the table as they took out laptops or files or sheaves of paper. The Chief of the General Staff chaired the meeting and he called on General Chung Kang-dae to relate the most recent intelligence.

Eun-mi's father opened a file. He was a smallish man and marginally younger than most of the others in there. Under his hat the hair was thinning, but his eyebrows were thick and black like caterpillars. It was not an unpleasant or harsh face, but laughter had been an infrequent visitor to his lips since the death of his wife, soon after the birth of Nabi.

Before he could speak, Martin interjected.

"I need to know what's being done about the Ismus!" he said firmly. "Where is he, what is he doing and why haven't we come up with a plan of action to deal with him?"

The officers glowered in surprise and anger. How dare he interrupt? He was only here out of courtesy. He had nothing to contribute. They stared at Eun-mi and waited for her to translate.

The girl did so dutifully. She was also angered by Martin's outburst. Her role as interpreter meant that she too had interrupted her father and the colour rose in her cheeks as she felt his disapproval.

"All this time and you've done nothing!" Martin continued. "Every day you hesitate it gets worse and worse out there. God knows what abominations are crawling through the streets now. If you allowed me access to the Internet, at least I'd be able to see for myself. The one thing I do know is that Austerly Fellows has something far more evil planned than anything we've seen yet. The last I heard he was writing a second book, a sequel to *Dancing Jax*. He may have even completed it by now. When that gets published, what's happened already will pale in comparison!"

He paused as the girl repeated his words in Korean. When she finished, she dared to raise her eyes and saw the icy fury on her father's face. She looked away quickly and caught sight of Du Kwan. The aide was smiling shyly at her, giving her gentle encouragement. The unexpectedness of that flustered her. She snapped her attention back to the centre of the table and her cheeks burned redder.

"And then there's the items the kids brought with them from England," Martin pressed on, before they could stop him. "Where are they? The wand and the skull? What did you do with them? They should be monitored constantly. And what about the kids in those camps set up in other countries? Why haven't you done anything to help them escape? There must be hundreds if not thousands of them out there, suffering God knows what, and nothing's been done.

"Look, you've got this boy, Lee, who has this miraculous power to enter the world of that book and not be taken over by it. The Ismus is terrified of him. That lad is the one thing that can turn his madness against him. You should be thanking me for bringing him to you. Using him to our maximum advantage should be our top priority and I don't mean as a method of bomb delivery. But all you've done is kept him chained up like a veal calf since he got here. What sort of a strategy is that?"

The Chief of the General Staff slammed his hand down and called for silence, flecks of spit flying as he yelled.

"You listen, you learn," Eun-mi translated rapidly. "You have no voice here. The Democratic People's Republic of Korea shows you kindness and good will. You nothing, you Western beggar. This emergency the blame of imperialist weakness. Your peoples dirty and corrupt. You spread sickness over whole world. The Democratic

People's Republic of Korea will find solution. Wisdom of Supreme Leader Kim Jong-un will protect us."

Martin slumped back in his chair. It was no use: he couldn't make them understand the urgency. Austerly Fellows was going to inflict something new and unimaginable upon everybody and here they were building sandcastles, believing they could withstand the tide.

The Chief of the General Staff bowed to General Chung Kang-dae. Eun-mi's father took up his files once more and began his report.

Gerald folded his arms and listened politely. He'd had no idea Martin was going to blow up like that. He should know by now it would be a waste of energy. Nobody could comprehend the horror of *Dancing Jax* until they had witnessed its effects first hand on people they knew.

General Chung Kang-dae listed the fresh information gathered that week. The poorer African countries were now completely under the influence of the book and powdered minchet was being added to baby-milk formula for the remote villages where missionaries were spreading the words of Austerly Fellows. From the smallest fishing communities in Greenland, to the nomadic tribes of Afghanistan, *Dancing Jax* was supreme. All fighting, all disputes over territory, drugs, race or religion had been forgotten. For the first time in history, the world was at peace.

A murmur of sneering distaste rippled round the table.

The General continued. Many major cities were being abandoned. Satellite images disclosed streets empty of traffic as people sought a more rural, simpler existence to match the one in the book that they believed to be their true lives. Fires were raging out of control in Sydney, Berlin and Tokyo, while pollution clouds over Chinese factories producing components for iPads and Samsung tablets had increased to extremely toxic levels. In spite of the global desire to live medieval, Mooncaster-themed lives, the production of such electronic devices was at a record high. Of more immediate concern, however, was the fact that more and more footage of unnatural creatures was coming to light on CCTV across the world.

Flame-throwers and chemicals were being deployed near the border with South Korea to sterilise the ground so that the minchet plant could not take root and citizens had been commanded to be vigilant. Any sighting of the invasive shrub had to be reported immediately. They were forbidden to approach it themselves.

Gerald's concentration wandered. It was pretty much the same report as last week and the week before that. He wasn't sure why he was required at these meetings. They never asked his opinion on anything. He gazed distractedly about the table and pined wistfully for a tall gin and tonic.

Marshal Tark Hyun-ki hadn't taken any notice of Martin's tirade. The Shark sat there with his face turned resolutely aside, palms down on his briefcase. Gerald couldn't begin to guess how much blood was on those hands. He suspected that man had overseen the torture of many. Brutality was graven into his face, with its cruel, downturned mouth, framed by deep creases. It was a blessing those pitiless eyes were concealed behind sunglasses. He was too sinister to be given any name from *The Mikado*, even 'the Lord High Executioner' wasn't adequate, as that was a comic role and the Shark was anything but funny.

Gerald's attention shifted to the young aide.

Gerald's people radar was highly developed. Not much got past him; he could read the intricacies and dynamics of strangers' relationships with just a few moments' study. People interested him; his talent for observation had been put to expert use during his former career as an entertainer and then as the proprietor of the most select guesthouse in Felixstowe. He knew the main reason Eun-mi pushed herself so hard was to earn her father's admiration and he also knew that she would always be disappointed. The General favoured his younger daughter, Nabi, over her and the more Eun-mi tried to get him to notice her, the more he found to praise in her sister. Family troubles were the same the world over.

For some time now Gerald had been perfectly aware of Du Kwan's feelings towards Eun-mi, and that it was a futile infatuation. But now, suddenly, that granite maiden had noticed Kwan, and Gerald was fascinated to see the bloom on her cheek and how often her eyes flicked back across the table.

"Here's a pretty how-de-do," he told himself. "This is a story that can only end in tears." But his estimation of Eun-mi thawed a little. She wasn't just a robot of the party; there was a flicker of human feeling in there after all.

With a final disparaging word about the progress of the full-scale replica of the White Castle of Mooncaster that was being built in England, General Chung Kang-dae came to the end of his report and the Chief of the General Staff bowed to Doctor Choe Soo-jin.

The doctor rose from her seat.

"Medical analysis of juvenile group now complete," Eun-mi translated. "Or complete as possible within restriction. When arrive, health poor, malnutrition. Physical and mental stress level high, test result not reliable not consistent. Good diet, good rest, thanks to generosity of Democratic People's Republic of Korea, they improve. Now final result ready."

"You're wasting your time," Martin said impatiently. "This phenomenon isn't something you can explain away with science. You can't point a microscope at it and understand what's going on. Don't you think others haven't tried? Every country I've been in since this thing started has had their top people on it, with better technology, better scientists than you have here! They found nothing because this is bigger... it's older than that."

The doctor ignored him as she consulted her notes.

"It my conclusion," she declared, "nothing unique in any aberrant. Abnormality in blood – none. Immunology studies say no antigens present."

"Ha!" Martin said.

The doctor carried on as if he wasn't there.

"DNA profile: chromosomal analyses inconclusive. Cannot rule out they carry homozygous recessive trait, need more positive control tissue samples. Neural activity, cognition, ECG – also inconclusive and compare to People's Army subject volunteer test group. Nothing to suggest medical reason for resistance to influence of book. None I can find, under restriction. Further examination of immunity not possible under restriction. Search for viable vaccine against book influence therefore not possible under restriction."

The Generals and Marshals muttered in disappointment while Martin and Gerald wondered what on earth she meant by "under restriction". What restriction?

"Male subject sixteen year, Lee Charl," she continued. "Subject continue experience nightmare, but it normal and consistent with psychological trauma. No biological reason for remarkable ability. Further study necessary. Most strongly recommend lifting of restriction only way forward."

She looked directly at Eun-mi and told her to stop translating. Then she made a direct appeal to the Chief of the General Staff.

"What was that?" Martin asked when nothing was repeated in English. "What did she say?" He hated it when they shut him out like this.

"Business of state," Eun-mi had been instructed to reply and she did it with cold finality and controlled relish.

Gerald regarded her. The stony mask was back in place, but he thought he had marked the slightest tremble in her eye when the doctor said a certain word and then when the Chief of the General Staff said it again. He made a mental note of it and wondered what they were talking about. Doctor Choe was beginning to lose her cool, professional manner. It was turning into a bit of an argument. The Chief of the General Staff was refusing to agree to her request and she was brandishing her notes at him in frustration.

Presently he slapped the table and practically screamed at her. The doctor collected herself and sat down, defeated.

Martin and Gerald exchanged glances. Whatever she had been insisting upon, they were relieved it had been rejected.

But now Du Kwan had been invited to speak.

The young aide rose and bowed. With a hesitant, secret smile in Eun-mi's direction, he explained that Marshal Tark Hyun-ki had been making a nine-day tour of inspection in the three provinces divided by the demilitarised zone. He had also overseen the destruction of the incursion tunnels leading to South Korea that were excavated by the People's Army underneath the border during the 1970s.

"People near zone are afraid," Du Kwan said. "They hear of monsters breaching fences. They hear of farmers finding book out in fields and whole families fall under its spell."

"Is this true?" the Chief of the General Staff asked.

The young man bowed. "Soldiers of Marshal Tark Hyun-ki discover seven farms where families think they live in fairy-tale land. Marshal Tark Hyun-ki order families shot. They no in fairy tale now."

The Chief of the General Staff nodded with satisfaction. Martin and Gerald turned away.

"Border guards also need be shot," the aide continued. "Many loudspeakers across checkpoints; many bad Korean brothers and sisters read from book beyond fences. Border guards, they listen and believe in fairy tale. They shoot at soldiers of Marshal Tark Hyun-ki. We lose twelve men in battle. Now new guards at checkpoints wear ear defenders. Reinforcements needed. Marshal Tark Hyun-ki demand three thousand men go to south with tanks."

The Chief of the General Staff laced his fingers together and considered this.

"Marshal Tark Hyun-ki also find monster," Du Kwan added quickly. "Spider big as dog making nest in thorn tree. Marshal Tark Hyun-ki shoot and kill. Marshal Tark Hyun-ki most brave."

"Where is spider?" Doctor Choe asked. "Why you not bring here?"

Du Kwan bowed to her. "Monster on way to medical centre," he explained. "Marshal Tark Hyun-ki gave order when we arrive."

The doctor wrote something at the top of a sheet of paper. An examination of this creature could be invaluable. She wanted to race off now and start working on it.

Du Kwan was about to say something more when the Shark stirred at his side. The young man turned to him in some surprise. It wasn't like the Marshal to speak to him during one of these meetings. Everything that was to be said was planned in advance. The aide listened to a whispered command then sat down sharply.

The mirrored shades of Marshal Tark Hyun-ki reflected everyone around the table as he shifted to address them.

In the locked darkness of a steel box, inside a metal vault, behind one of those forbidden doors of the medical centre, a pale amber glow began to glimmer. A pulse of light flared within the star on Malinda's wand.

"Gangle not all I find," the Marshal announced, removing his palms from the briefcase and flicking the catches open. "I find also – blessed truth."

Reaching inside, he brought out a book covered in plain green paper. With an expression of ecstasy on his face, he began to read aloud from it and rocked backwards and forwards in his chair.

"Beyond the Silvering Sea," Eun-mi translated, puzzled by his actions.

Martin and Gerald sprang up.

"Stop him!" Martin yelled. He threw himself across the table and tried to snatch the book out of the Shark's hands. But the Marshal slid sideways out of the chair and carried on reading.

The other Generals had leaped up and were shouting in fear and confusion. Suddenly the room was full of noise as four shots exploded.

Marshal Tark Hyun-ki was catapulted backwards in a grotesque ballet as the bullets ripped through him. Three in the head, one through the heart. He was dead before he crashed to the floor and his mirrored sunglasses went skittering across the carpet.

Everyone's ears were ringing. The gunshots were deafening. Gerald looked away from the Shark's body and down the table. Pistol in hand, General Chung Kang-dae stared dispassionately at what he had done. Then he turned to the young aide.

Du Kwan was stammering with shock. A speckled mist of the Marshal's blood was sprayed across his face. He raised his eyes, aghast. Then he saw how everyone was looking at him.

"I... I did not know!!" he protested. "Marshal Tark Hyun-ki said nothing of this to me – I swear it. I did not know. I have not read the book! I swear – I swear!"

"What are you doing?" Martin cried when he saw General Chung's grim face. "The lad hasn't been affected. Look at his eyes. They're normal! He's not a Jaxer!"

He rounded on Eun-mi and begged her to translate. The girl wavered. Then she hurriedly beseeched her father to listen.

The pistol fired two more bullets and the handsome young man joined the Marshal on the floor.

Eun-mi gave a horrified gasp.

"Animal!" Martin bawled at the General. "That poor lad was one of us! He wasn't any threat. You just murdered an innocent boy!"

General Chung didn't understand what he said. He merely smiled and gave a little bow as he returned the pistol to its holster.

The meeting was over. A short while later, an ashen-faced Eun-mi drove Gerald and Martin back to their section.

"They're all innocent, Martin," Gerald reminded him gently, "Don't forget that. Even the Shark, vile devil though he was, wasn't responsible once the book got hold of him. If you start thinking the Jaxers are anything but victims then what does that make you? Think of Carol and Paul: they're innocent too."

Martin Baxter said nothing. He was sick to the stomach by what had just happened, but there was something more. Gerald's words had touched upon a very raw nerve and he couldn't think about it right now.

Back in the meeting room, the Chief of the General Staff had just taken a phone call. The entire meeting had been transmitted via webcam to the palace in Pyongyang. The order from the Supreme Leader was very plain.

"Tell Doctor Choe Soo-jin the restriction is lifted – with immediate effect."

4

LEE WAS IN the refectory that also served as the refugees' common room. He was sitting at one of the long tables, with his feet up. The four guards he was chained to stood stiffly either side. It was the Spice Girls, four young men in their early twenties. They had taken over from the Sex and the City quartet under an hour ago.

Many of the other children were there, because their dorms were small and cell-like and unheated. Here there was a wood-burning stove, but the logs were rationed and their daily allocation lasted only about four hours.

The children were wrapped in rough blankets or oversized military greatcoats. Having escaped from the prison camp in England with nothing but the rags they had on, they now wore clothing generously donated by the People's Army and looked like the destitute outcasts that they were. Most days they sat, clumped together in small groups, either playing the Korean board games also given to them by the military or whispering among themselves.

Maggie was a dab hand with a needle and thread, so Gerald miraculously scrounged the rudiments of a basic sewing kit for her, including a small pair of scissors. She happily filled her hours adapting the cast-off uniforms, cutting them down for a snugger fit or turning them into completely different garments. Spencer's Stetson had been confiscated as being too strong a symbol of the US, so she had made him a cowboy-style waistcoat with a star on it like a sheriff's badge to compensate.

She paid special attention to the group of girls who had been in Charm's hut back in the camp. Her late friend had asked her to look out for them so she made sure their requests were dealt with first. Western dress was forbidden in North Korea so the guards raised their eyebrows at the home-made fashions. It was the closest Maggie ever got to making them smile. With the remnants, she created small dolls and animals, initially to keep herself occupied in between alterations and to put around the dorm and refectory to cheer the place up. But they turned out so well every girl wanted one, except Esther who said they were "fugly".

That afternoon Maggie sat across from Lee, stitching eyes on to a bear with coloured thread. It was a gift for little Nabi, who spent as much time as she could in the company of the English aberrants. Maggie found it hard to believe she was Eun-mi's sister. The two were poles apart. Six-year-old Nabi was a lively, excitable, curious child whose laughter could be heard ricocheting down the long, bleak corridors. Her raven hair was tied in bunches and her face was almost always scrunched up in a toothy grin that swallowed her almond eyes. She was nearly too cute at times and Maggie jokingly suggested Nabi had slid off one of the chocolate-boxy propaganda posters.

The six-year-old was besotted with Lee. He was something new and amazing to her. Black people were extremely rare in the Democratic People's Republic of Korea, usually embassy staff and diplomats who lived separately in gated communities. They had all been ejected from the country many months ago, so she had never seen anyone like him before. For the first few weeks she'd followed him around with an open mouth and bulging eyes. When he touched something, like a door, or set a cup down, she would pounce and inspect it to see if his colour came off. To begin with he yelled and roared at her and she would run and hide like a terrified hamster. But, eventually, she would come stealing back for more and gaze at him with those bright, worshipping eyes.

Even though he was still numb with grief and raging against his chains, Lee found it impossible to take his anger out on Nabi. He knew exactly what Charm would do if she was still alive. She would have befriended and loved the child and so he tolerated her.

That morning she was sitting next to Maggie, watching the bear take shape and insisting it look fiercer by making savage faces and growling. Her English consisted of the few words and nursery rhymes Gerald had taught her and several other pieces of choice language that she had picked up from Lee, which always scandalised her sister, if her vocabulary stretched that far. Then there was that infamous occasion when Nabi had squealed, tunelessly, in front of their father, "I see you, baby, shakin' that ass, shakin' that ass." For three weeks after that she was forbidden to visit the refugees, but had finally managed to bring the General around, as she always did.

Outside the refectory, in the long, gloomy corridor painted a bilious green that was blistered and peeling, Spencer waited for Martin and Gerald to return. There was nothing else to do; besides, he liked being on his own. In this place there was little privacy. The dorms were smaller and more cramped than the huts in the camp had been and the toilet facilities were basic and communal.

He scuffed the worn heel of his shabby shoes across the concrete floor and the sound went echoing eerily up and down. Five small dorms, the refectory, the shared bathroom, the stone steps to the terrace and Lee's hospital room were accessed by this broad yet claustrophobic passage. Further on it turned a sharp right corner into the prohibited area with the mysterious doors they weren't allowed to enter.

Spencer glanced towards that corner and squinted at the armed soldier standing rigidly still there. It was impossible to be alone anywhere here. If it wasn't the guards, it was the other children, or visits from that overzealous, pushy doctor wanting to do more tests. The boy craved a bit of solitude. He yearned for the desolate stretches of sand dunes in his home town of Southport and missed the lonely walks he used to take there out of season, when he could roam all day and not meet another soul. Everything about this place was so oppressive, at times it made him breathless. It wasn't just the joyless regime and the fear of what lay ahead, but the mountain itself. He tried not to think about the millions of tonnes of rock that surrounded him, but was constantly aware of them and could almost feel them pressing down.

He would often lie awake in his bunk, listening to the distant noises of the base and the eerie sound of the air coursing through the vents and tunnels. If the main entrance was open, and the wind came squalling in, it howled through the connecting passageways. When other unknown and distant doors were unbolted, it could be like the whispering of ghosts. Spencer wondered how frequent earth tremors were in this part

1. Balcony
2. Dormitories
3. Refectory
4. Toilet and Showers
5. Lee's room
6. Forbidden Area

of the world. One slight judder would be cataclysmic and the mountain would come crushing down. When he did sleep, it was fitful and shallow and the faintest creak or scratching of mice caused him to lurch awake.

Unlike the other refugees, he didn't call this place Titipu. Instead he preferred 'the Hole-in-the-Wall' after the Wild West hideout of outlaws. But that didn't help much. Passing a hand over his bare head, he tried to suppress the anxiety he could feel rising in his chest. The loss of his Stetson had been like a kick in the gut. It was his comfort object and he felt bereft without it. In the camp, when the Punchinello with the silver nose had swiped it from him, at least Spencer knew where it was. These people had probably burned it and that likelihood distressed him deeply. Maggie had been extremely sympathetic, but the waistcoat she had made was no substitute for his beloved hat, although he secretly liked it when Lee called him "Sheriff Woody".

Spencer turned his unhappy face to the other end of the corridor, where it opened out on to one of the main tunnels. Digging his cold hands into his pockets, he leaned against the rocky wall and waited.

"It really Christmas already?" Lee asked, back in the refectory.

"At the end of the week," Maggie answered. She had been telling him Gerald's plans for the choir.

"Dunno how or why you bother keepin' track. Ain't no point no more."

"I bother because it helps," she said.

"One day's like every other in this dump. Could be Pancake Tuesday for all the difference it makes. Those things mean nuthin' now. Sooner you stop pretendin' they does, the better."

Maggie didn't let him nettle her. She had got used to his attitude and temper. After all this time, they were like background noise, but he was getting worse and not many of the others talked to him any more. Today he was particularly volatile and ready to kick off. She didn't know the details of his nightmare, he never shared them with anyone but the doctor, but everyone could hear his screams.

"Gerald says he makes fantastic mince pies," she rattled on, "with chocolate in. They must be gorgeous. Suppose it'll be same old kimchi and rice or noodles here on the day."

Nabi's ears pricked up. "Kimchi!" she repeated, patting her stomach and nodding. "Good yum."

Lee curled his lip at her and she squirmed with pleasure.

"Long as it's not no more of those thin spicy soups," he grumbled. "Thought we'd done with that kinda slop when we left the camp."

"Don't suppose I'll ever so much as sniff another roast potato," Maggie said mournfully.

"Girl, you ain't never gonna do a whole mess of things again. This, right here, this is your life now, till the Jaxers catch up with us – and that can't be far off. After that, you won't have no life no more. Think they're gonna keep you as a pet or somethin'? The lot of you'll be lined up against the wall and be a bullet buffet."

"'The First Noel'," she declared, switching back to the subject of the choir. "That's my favourite carol. I'd rather sing that old Slade song though. Bit too obvious what they're about I suppose, so we probably won't be singing either of them. What's yours? You must have one, even if you won't join in with the Wenceslassing."

He threw her a disbelieving 'WTF?' glance. "You think you pierced my brain when you did my ear?" he snapped. "I ain't forgot the last time we sang 'Silent Night', over the grave of that crazy kid Jim, who thought he was a superhero and got himself stuck in the guts. Have you?"

"Ah, of course – his name was Jim. Poor lad."

"And there's no way I'm ever gonna forget what that Ismus guy wants outta me. Don't you remember what he said when you, me and Spence went to Mooncaster that time? I do not want to hear no songs about no towns in Bethlehem or herald angels bein' noisy in the neighbourhood and I specially don't wanna hear nuthin' about no shepherds. You got that? I am gonna be spending that entire day hooked up to my bleepy machines in my hospital bed – Scroogin' it large."

Maggie had forgotten nothing about that, how could she? But she had hoped he'd stopped brooding by now. She was wrong. That time when Lee had accidentally dragged her and Spencer to that other fantastical realm, the Ismus had proposed a disgusting bargain that she had never been able to get her head around. That evil man had promised Lee could be reunited with Charm, there in Mooncaster, but only if the boy did something for him, only if he killed someone – someone very special.

"That was just mad talk," she said with a frown and a shrug. "He was screwing with your head. I don't believe it; it isn't possible. There's no way she can come back, not even there. You know what he's like, all filthy lies and nastiness. What he says eats at you because that's what it's meant to do. Best to shut it away and not think about it – ever. Drive you nuts that will."

Lee swung his feet off the table and pushed his chair away. Not think about it? It was the only thing that kept his heart beating throughout the day, and what fuelled his nightmares. He gave his chains a sharp tug and one of the attached guards blurted an angry protest. If he hadn't been tethered in this way, Lee would have returned to Mooncaster long ago. His mind was made up. He was going to accept the Ismus's obscene offer. He would do anything to have Charm back in his life, even if it meant spending the rest of their days in that extreme world of castles and monsters. He had to be with her.

He was about to leave when the door opened and Spencer entered. His spectacles misted over as they encountered the warmer air. Some of the girls sniggered idly.

"Er... Martin and Gerald are back," he announced, wiping the lenses. "The jeep's just pulled in."

"Woohoo," Lee uttered woodenly. "Break out the Pringles and party dips."

"Ohhh... Pringles," Maggie breathed dreamily.

The other children stopped what they were doing and faced the door. Those weekly meetings were their only source of outside news and they looked forward to them with an intense mix of curiosity and dread.

"They don't seem happy," Spencer warned everyone.

"When is Baxter ever happy?" Lee asked. "He gets off peddlin' the-end-is-nigh stuff."

"Shh," Maggie hissed.

The door opened again and the two men came in. A shocked murmur escaped the children's lips. Spencer's warning had been a huge understatement. They looked terrible. Maggie rose and tried to take Gerald's hand, but he said he was fine and eased himself on to a chair. It was the first time he had looked his age. Little Nabi pattered over and rested her head on his arm.

Perching on the edge of a table, Martin considered what to tell them. There was no point concealing what had happened and these kids had been through too much already not to know the truth.

"No easy way of saying this," he began solemnly. "And maybe I should wait till you're all here, but you've a right to be told straight away. Now I don't want to alarm you..."

"Spit it, Baxter," Lee heckled. "You ain't on TV now, no need to milk your moment. Get to the point."

"One of the Marshals, Tark Hyun-ki, had been turned," Martin continued. "He started reading from it in the meeting."

The children uttered cries of dismay. They all knew exactly what 'it' was and they also knew this day was inevitable, but it was still an appalling jolt.

"Oh, game over!" Lee snorted with a twisted grin. "Why'd it take so long?"

"What about the others in the meeting?" Maggie asked. "Are they Jaxers now as well?"

Martin shook his head. "The Marshal was shot, killed before he could turn anyone else."

"What?" Lee roared in disbelief. "You know better than that! It don't take more than a few lines to sucker some people in. You, me, we both seen that happen."

"No one else was affected," Martin repeated firmly.

"You is talking pure, unrefined, steamin' straight from the sphincter BS and you know it!" the boy countered. "This is how it starts. Every damn time! Them words is in this base now. No way that guy was the only one. It's gonna be all round this place like the flu, come tomorrow.

You can say goodbye to playing hide-and-seek. We been busted and that Ismus is gonna be poncin' through this ass end of nowhere any day, rubbin' his greasy mitts together."

"There is no immediate danger of that happening!" Martin stated, raising his voice. "This facility is still the safest place for us and will continue to be defended for some time."

Lee jumped to his feet. He couldn't believe what he was hearing.

"Listen to you!" he shouted. "Who does you think you is? You don't have no special handle on this. You know nuthin'! You is nuthin'!"

"Sit down!" Martin told him.

"What? You don't get to order me around, Baxter. You ain't in no classroom no more and you sure as hell ain't the boss of me. I'm outta here – can't stand the stink of stoopid in the morning."

He yanked on the chains and the guards marched with him to the door.

Martin ground his teeth. That lad was impossible. He took a calming breath, but, as Lee left the room, he heard him growl the word "Loser" and Martin boiled over.

Racing into the corridor after him, he surprised the four guards when he grabbed hold of Lee's shoulders and pushed him against the wall. The Koreans shouted and brandished their rifles to make him back off, but Martin was so incensed he didn't hear them.

Lee yelled fiercely and lunged at him, but the chains stopped his fists flying. It took all four guards to restrain him.

"Touch me again and you're dead, Baxter!" the boy raged, kicking out.

"What is your problem?" Martin shouted. "From the minute we met you've done nothing but antagonise and undermine me. So you've had it rough. Big deal. There's not one of us who hasn't. What makes you different, what makes you so special?"

Lee raised his hands and rattled the chains, almost proudly. "Is you dumb or what, Mr Maths Teacher?" he sneered. "These make me special. I'm the Castle Creeper – I'm the most special and coolest thing there is."

A slow, mocking grin appeared on his face. "Yeah," he said. "That's what this is about, ain't it? You can't stand that you're just another nobody now. All that TV you used to do, telling the world how bad that book is, all them shrill blogs and runnin' from country to country, tweetin' and preachin' – pushin' your own brand of panic an' drama at anyone who'd listen. Thinkin' you're the leader of some sort of resistance, what a joke!"

"Oh, you really are a piece of work," Martin growled in disgust. "You make me sick. And to think, at first, I couldn't wait to meet you. You were going to be the answer to this madness. I honestly believed you were going to turn it around. Well, more fool me!"

Lee laughed at him. "Don't feed me that. You're the one who thought he was somethin'. Austerly Fellows' great nemesis, the badass Martin Baxter, the saviour from Suffolk who tried to save humanity single handed. You got hooked on bein' famous, dintcha? Man, that is pathetic. While the rest of them out there got addicted to the book, you became a fame junkie – just another media ho. 'Loser' don't even start to cover it."

"Shut up. You have no idea what you're talking about."

"I know them Generals all laugh at you. You got nuthin' worth sayin' to them at their meetings, you deludenoid. You ain't no leader, no hero, just another sad reject what got caught up in this at the start an' don't know when it's over."

"And what are you? Council-estate scum! I've taught hundreds of identical no-marks, who can't even spell 'GCSE'. They drift their way through school and can't wait for it to be over so they can start claiming benefits and sponge off the rest of us."

"Yeah, the likes of me is what your taxes kept in flat-screens and Nikes. Real generous of you, thanks. And guess what, soon as this place gets Jaxed, I'm headed to Mooncaster to live it up as a prince."

Martin stepped back. "You'd really do that, wouldn't you?" he said in disbelief. "Kill the Bad Shepherd, even knowing who that is. You'd sell out everyone, just so you could get back with your girlfriend."

"Hell, yes! If you hadn't grassed me up and got me cuffed, I could've gotten there months ago. And don't tell me you wouldn't do exactly the same to get your old lady and her kid back – even though the Ismus has been bangin' her this whole time and got her knocked up."

Martin flew at him. Before the guards could intervene, he punched the boy in the stomach and cracked him across the chin. Lee crumpled to the floor, but he was laughing, knowing his words had hurt the man far more.

Martin would have waded in again, but the rifles came jabbing at his chest and Gerald's hands were pulling him away.

"Leave it," the old man said. "Grow up, the pair of you. I could knock your heads together, squabbling like toddlers. Martin, you go get some fresh air and you, Lee, go cool off somewhere else."

Lee looked up at him. He had a wary respect for Gerald. That old guy had seen it all and had faced more discrimination, suffered more hate and prejudice from society than anyone he knew. Back in Peckham,

Lee's gang never messed with people like Gerald. They couldn't be intimidated and fought vicious and dirty.

Rising, he was about to give Martin a parting snarl when a military ambulance braked at the end of the corridor and Doctor Choe stepped out, yapping instructions and slapping the vehicle's side. Two soldiers jumped from the back and together they hauled down a stretcher bearing the body of Marshal Tark Hyun-ki.

The children had crowded out of the refectory to watch Lee and Martin's fight and the few in the dorms had come to their doors to do the same. Now they watched in silence as the Shark was carried past. A blanket had been thrown over him. Doctor Choe guided the bearers down the corridor. They passed the guard stationed beyond Lee's room and disappeared round the corner, into the prohibited area. When they had gone, the teenagers noticed a trail of blood dotting the concrete floor.

They stared at it in thoughtful silence. Lee was right: the power of the book had infiltrated the base and the clock was ticking. They weren't safe here any longer.

"Never saw Doctor Frankensoo so stoked," Lee observed dryly. "Like she got a whole new set of sticky toys to play with."

"I wonder who the Shark thought he was in Mooncaster," Spencer mused aloud.

"Hope it was the dung guy," Lee said. "Nobody's gonna waste no tears over him. That piece of crud wanted to turn me into a suicide bomber. Sizzle in Hell, you sorry-assed douche."

The others began filing back into the refectory and the girls from the dorms hurried across to join them to find out what had been going on. Maggie went in search of a mop and bucket.

"So here it is, merry Christmas," she muttered under her breath with heavy sarcasm. "Everybody's having fun. Look to the future now, it's only just begun... not."

Little Nabi wanted to take a closer look at the blood, but Gerald led her back inside instead. There was something he wanted to ask her. Doctor Choe had just used the same word he had noted earlier in the meeting.

"Nabi," he began with a friendly, coaxing smile.

"Itsy bitsy!" she demanded, pouting because he had denied her young bloodlust. For a little girl whose name meant 'butterfly' she took great delight in the gruesome.

"Later," he promised. "I want to know, what does *pookum* mean?"

"Itsy bitsy!" she said, stubbornly folding her arms and glowering.

The old man realised he'd get nothing out of her until he complied. It was one of the nursery rhymes he had taught her. She enjoyed it because there were actions. She loved making spider legs with her fingers and miming raindrops and sunshine. Gerald spoke the rhyme with her and then she insisted he do it a second time.

"She's got you well trained," Spencer commented.

"Now *pookum*," Gerald asked her again. "What does it mean?"

The six-year-old laughed and shook her head. "Nabi no no," she gurgled.

"Maybe you're not pronouncing it right," Spencer suggested.

Gerald tried again, using the same inflection he had heard in the meeting earlier and just now in the corridor. Nabi put her head to one side attentively, but smiled ever wider.

"No!" she declared.

"Never mind," Gerald sighed. "You're probably too young to know anyway."

"What do you think it means?" Spencer asked.

The man shrugged. "Probably just me fretting over nothing as usual. Evelyn's always telling me—" He broke off, startled at himself. He tried not to talk about 'Evelyn', having suppressed her since leaving Felixstowe with Martin a year ago. But her name had been on his lips more and more recently. It was as if she refused to be forgotten. That was so like her.

Spencer noticed Gerald was disconcerted, but he didn't like to pry. He fiddled with some snippets of olive-coloured cloth lying on the table and waited. He was slightly in awe of Gerald, ever since he discovered the old man had once worked with the legendary John Wayne on a movie, in London, back in 1975. Gerald's part only amounted to one line that had been cut from the final edit, but he had still shared the screen for a few seconds with 'the Duke' and that elevated him in Spencer's eyes to some stratospheric level way above 'cool'.

Nabi gave a small exclamation of understanding and pulled at Gerald's arm enthusiastically.

"Boo gum!" she cried. "Boo gum!"

Grabbing the discarded stuffed bear, she laid it on its back with its legs in the air. Then, using the scissors, she mimed cutting it open.

"Boo gum!" she said gleefully, her eyes vanishing in her expansive grin.

"What was that?" Spencer asked, mystified.

"I think she's just demonstrated an autopsy," Gerald murmured faintly.

"Oh, well, that makes sense," the boy said, not sure why the old man looked so afraid all of a sudden. "That's what Choe's going to do to the Shark, isn't it? Although I'd have thought cause of death was pretty obvious, what with it happening right in front of you all."

The old man made no response. He didn't want to tell Spencer the doctor had used that word long before the Marshal had been shot. A ghastly chill crept along his spine and he shivered.

"I need to talk to Martin," he said quickly. "We can't stay here."

Doctor Choe Soo-jin dismissed the stretcher-bearers and her technicians from the laboratory, which also served as an operating theatre, and put on a plastic apron.

The lab, like much of this base, wasn't furnished with the most up-to-date equipment, but what it had still did the job efficiently. It was vaguely reminiscent of an old-fashioned, large and sinister kitchen and smelled sharply of antiseptic. Yellow tiles covered the walls, one of which was taken up by four great ceramic sinks. A blood analyser that looked more like a bulky photocopier stood in one corner and a cream-coloured refrigerator, showing signs of rust, occupied another. Cylinders of gas stood in a row like the artillery shells in the munitions section of the base. Electrophoresis apparatus, microscope, centrifuge, organ bath, steriliser and other instruments were stored neatly along two Formica counters, as if they were food appliances. Then there were metal trays containing surgical saws, serrated knives and scalpels, drill bits, retractors, clamps and rasps. Beneath the counters were built-in cupboards that housed the beakers, test tubes, flasks and Petri dishes. The glass-fronted cabinets fixed to the walls contained drugs, medicines and chemicals that were kept under lock and key.

Two stainless-steel examination tables, with leather restraints, were in the centre of the room. The body of Marshal Tark Hyun-ki occupied one of them; a cardboard box containing the remains of the spider creature he had shot near the demilitarised zone was on the other.

The doctor hooked a paper mask over her nose, mouth and ears. Her excitement caused her hands to tremble slightly. At last she would have a subject to study, in forensic detail. She needed an affected specimen such as this and she had never liked the man. He had been more than vocal in his scepticism of her competence and had insulted her more times than she cared to remember. Medicine was not considered a suitable occupation for women and she had worked and studied three times as hard as any man to get to where she was.

But there was no sense of triumph or acrimony involved as she looked forward to dissecting him. Her scientific hunger pushed any personal feeling aside. The Marshal was merely a resource now, an object to document and label. She was eager only to discover answers to this mystery. The power of that book simply had to change the biology. She had a theory about the hypothalamus that she was keen to explore, and other investigations would prove invaluable. She was glad also that the restriction had been lifted and she would presently be able to test those same theories on the English refugees.

Moving to the table, she lifted the blanket and extreme disappointment registered in her eyes. As a result of the gunshot wounds, there wasn't a hypothalamus to examine. Letting the blanket fall once more, she looked up and her glance rested upon the cardboard box on the other table. Curiosity dispelled her frustration. The box had arrived in her absence and she approached it with interest.

A copy of the Newspaper of the Workers, *Rodong Sinmun*, covered the dead creature inside. Cautiously, Doctor Choe Soo-jin removed the paper and peered down.

Her surgical mask distorted as she inhaled sharply. The thing was unlike anything she had ever seen. It was the size of a small terrier and its eight spidery legs were wrapped in a tangle round a body covered in matted black fur. The repulsive face with its wide mouth, crammed full of sharp fangs, was upturned and the round, glassy eyes seemed to be staring straight at her. She couldn't help shuddering and she wondered how it was possible – how could this have come from a book of children's make-believe?

Her thoughts returned to the meeting and those introductory words the Marshal had read out. She recalled that they had sounded pleasant at the time. What was there to fear in them? A wide sea, dappled with silvery light, sparkled in her thoughts, giving way to a green land of thirteen rolling hills and, in the central plain, rising over a quiet, sleepy village, the turrets and high walls of a beautiful white castle.

Inside the vault, in the room adjacent to the lab, the wand of Malinda began to glimmer once more.

The doctor shook herself and her training regained control. She would record everything: tissue samples, blood, musculature, skeleton. This was a totally new species. A series of photographs would have to be taken before any examination could take place, however, and there simply wasn't time for that at the moment.

Lifting the box and shying away from the pungent odour rising from the Doggy-Long-Legs within, she carried it to the fridge and deposited it inside. She would attend to this monster later. But first she had other experiments to conduct.

Pulling the mask under her chin, she went to the door and spoke to the guards outside.

"Bring one of the Western children," she commanded, "immediately!"

The guards bowed smartly and hurried up the corridor.

Doctor Choe returned to the metal trays and began selecting the knives she would need, a razor to shave the child's head – and a surgical saw.

5

GERALD HAD HASTENED out on to the terrace to find Martin. The thick fog had lifted a little and the bluish-grey blur of distant peaks could be glimpsed through the shifting vapour. Martin wasn't wearing a coat. He'd been too wrapped up in his angry thoughts to feel the cold, but now it was beginning to bite. The dense mist drank up the noises of the base, distant voices sounded small and lonely and a truck departing down the rough mountain road was remote and strange. He was astonished to hear a helicopter landing on one of the pads. Even that sounded weirdly unreal and he found himself thinking it was a cretinous risk to fly in this sort of weather.

Gerald hurried past the female guard who was watching at the entrance and took his friend by the arm.

"We have to get out of here," he told him urgently.

Martin looked at him in astonishment. "What's happened now?" he asked.

"I know what that doctor is planning. She's been impatient to do it since we arrived, the sadistic maniac."

"Slow down. What are you on about?"

"Her argument with the Chief of the General Staff earlier: I understand what got her so irate. She's done all the tests she can on us and found nothing."

"So? We knew she wouldn't find anything."

"Exactly! Now she wants to take it further. She wants to have a go at some post-mortems. She wants to cut us up, to prove there's a medical reason for the book not working on us. That's what the restriction was: they wouldn't let her."

Martin almost laughed. "You're imagining it. Look, it's been a really bad day; we're both strung out."

"Martin! I'm serious. Don't let your pig-headedness lead you into making another fatal mistake. Look what happened the last time. If you'd have believed Paul when he came to you, right at the beginning... well, that's in the past, no use dredging it up again. What's vital right now is we need to get out and quick, before that doctor gets all Sweeney Todd on us with her snickersnee. How long do you think the restriction is going to last after what happened to the Shark today? Those Generals have finally witnessed what that book can do, at close range, and they won't want to be next. If they can turn on their own, like they did with that poor aide, they're not going to give us a second's thought."

The other man began to listen. Gerald wasn't one to panic unnecessarily. Throughout all of this he had been the solid foundation that Martin depended on, the one who had stopped him giving in to black despair, time and again, and kept him fighting. If Gerald Benning suspected something then, for him, that was as good as proof. He didn't question his assessment of their situation again.

"OK..." Martin said. "But you're forgetting two important things.

There's no way out of here. Even if there was, there's nowhere to run to."

"We'll worry about that second little detail later," the old man told him, brushing it aside as if it didn't matter. "Our first priority is escape. I suggest we get the kids out here on the terrace and scramble down the mountain. It's not as ludicrous as it sounds; it isn't quite as steep over at the far end there. We might be able to make it to the valley and the shelter of the trees. It's a bit too like *The Inn of the Sixth Happiness* for my liking, but there's no other option."

Martin spluttered. "What? I thought you meant steal a truck and smash our way out the main entrance. We'll break our necks climbing down there; not only that, but there's guards with machine guns stationed all round."

"And in this fog they couldn't see the cast of *Show Boat* promenading underneath their sentry posts. But it's starting to thin so we don't have much time."

"Wait, you mean right now, this minute?"

"Absolutely. These military types aren't going to mess about any longer. They'll be more desperate to find this mythical vaccine than ever – and Lee was right: the power of the book has arrived. This place is done for. We've seen it time and again everywhere we've been. You know how fast it takes over."

"But how? I mean... what about the guards here in the medical centre? We can't get past them. They're not going to let us bring the kids outside en masse. They'll know we're up to something."

Gerald's jaw tightened. "We could if we were armed, Martin," he said bluntly. "They won't be expecting that; we'd take them by surprise."

"What? Guns! Are you... how are we going to get hold of them?"

"Quite easily. I've been thinking it might come to something like this for a long while. I know just where we can lay our hands on four rifles. We're going to need weapons once we leave here anyway; there's no knowing what we'll encounter out there."

"God, Gerald," Martin breathed. "You'd have to be prepared to use them. Actually shoot someone."

"I know. But the alternative is too horrendous to think about. In difficult times there are no easy choices. It's them or the children, Martin."

"They're not kids any more, not after everything they've been through, everything they've seen. But yes... you're right. So where are these rifles? Have you got them stashed away someplace? You're amazing."

The old man gave him a grim smile. "No," he replied. "Four very generous guards are going to give them to us."

"Sorry?"

"Our young friend Lee's entourage. We're going to snaffle their rifles."

Martin finally understood. "No," he said firmly. "That's madness! He'll never agree for one thing and, even if he did, we can't trust him. You know what he's going to do when he gets there!"

"We need those rifles, Martin. This is the only way. Lee is going to have to perform that special hoodoo he does and go into the world of that evil book, taking the souls, or whatever you want to call it, of his guards with him. What's left behind of them here will fall down in a faint and all we have to do is relieve them of their weapons. It's so simple, it's frightening."

"No, what's frightening is what Lee intends to do once he gets there."

"Let's deal with one crisis at a time, shall we? What Lee does, or doesn't do, will be up to him. I don't believe he's the vile scum you think he is."

Martin could feel his temper rising again. "You don't?" he hissed. "Really? That lout in there – that selfish, idle thug – is going to Mooncaster for one reason only: to do Austerly Fellows' dirty work. He's the one person in all creation with the power to kill the character called the Bad Shepherd who, according to Maggie and Spencer, is some warped manifestation of none other than Jesus flaming Christ! And you don't think that lad is scum? He's worse than that; he's itching to be a second bloody Judas!"

"That isn't the real reason he wants to go, Martin. He's been torn apart by grief and horror. He wants to be reunited with that lovely girl. So no, I don't think he's scum. He's just a person in pain."

"Don't give me that. He's chucking the whole of humanity over for the sake of a dead chav who, from what I've heard, was so dumb she thought Jane Eyre was a cheap airline to Ibiza for hen parties – and that toerag is laughing in our faces about it."

"Martin!" Gerald snapped angrily. "You disappoint me sometimes, you genuinely do. You can be such an elitist snob! Lee is the way he is because people like you made him that way, long before Jax happened. Outside of his family, Charm was the first person to reach out and love him for who he was – is it any wonder he's so churned up about her? Neither you nor I met the girl, but she sounds magnificent. I know what's really biting you; it's what he said about Carol. I've told you before, she can't help what's happened to her. She's a victim."

"Is she? She knew what the book was capable of, yet she read it deliberately. She wanted to get turned. That's what I can't get out of my head and what eats me up inside. She wanted it."

"She only did that so she could find Paul! Remember how distressed she was when he became the Jack of Diamonds and disappeared. She was beside herself; she had to find her son. Why is that so impossible to understand? She sacrificed her own identity, everything she was, for her child's sake. That's what every mother does. How can you hold that against her? She wasn't to know she'd become the Labella character."

"She didn't have to do it. I would've found him."

"And a fat load of good you were when you eventually did. But that was then and this is now and we need to act. We've got to persuade Lee to take those guards of his into Mooncaster. Whether you like it or not, he's our one and only chance to get the rest of these kids out of here alive. We're all dead if we don't."

"Then God help us."

The water in the bucket had iced over. Maggie cracked through it with the handle of the mop then began swabbing the bloody traces from the floor. The young refugees were not given work to do, but they were expected to keep their areas clean. Sometimes they almost wished they did have some sort of duties to keep them busy, but they never found themselves missing the minchet harvesting they'd been forced to do back in the camp.

Maggie couldn't understand why Lee hated Martin so much. OK, so he was a bit up himself, thought his opinions were more important than everyone else's and slipped back into teacher mode too regularly, but hadn't he been proven right all down the line? If the authorities back in England had taken him seriously at the start, the horror of *Dancing Jax* might have been averted.

Working her way down the corridor, she didn't notice the guards sent by Doctor Choe emerge from around the far corner. The men stared at her and exchanged glances. That girl would do. One of them opened his mouth to call out when Spencer came from the refectory to join her.

"I'll finish that off if you like," he offered.

"Nah," she said, thanking him with a smile. "I might as well do it now. Not as if I'm missing anything."

"Gerald was a bit weird just now. Said we couldn't stay here."

"What did he mean by that?"

"I dunno. Something Nabi said spooked him."

"Oh, blimey, what else has Lee been teaching her?"

Before Spencer could reply, the guards began to shout. The teenagers looked back at them in surprise. The men were pointing at Maggie and beckoning.

"What's up with them?" the girl asked.

"They want you to clean their bit as well."

"But we're not allowed over there."

"They just don't want to have to do it themselves. It's women's work, you know."

The guards became impatient and started to advance down the corridor towards them.

"Well, they can sod off," Maggie declared through a phoney smile. "I'm not cleaning a floor I'm forbidden to walk on. The lazy, sexist buggers."

Spencer took the mop and bucket from her. "I'll go," he said. "You find Gerald and see why he was so rattled."

"All right, I'll ask Nabi what she's been saying first. She's a right little madam that one. Her dad's going to have his hands full when she gets older. Can't see her being a party drone like her sister. She'll probably be leading the revolution single-handed."

"It wasn't like that," the boy tried to tell her. "It was to do with cutting up the Shark or something." But Maggie had already breezed back into the refectory.

Spencer approached the guards, whistling a few bars of *The Good, the Bad and the Ugly* theme to himself. They seemed a bit put out that Maggie had gone and barked at one another.

"I can handle a mop," he assured them when it looked like they were about to follow her into the refectory. "It's not gender-specific you know."

They regarded him for a moment then nodded and led him away. Spencer smiled to himself. With the rest of the world in chaos, it was almost funny, perhaps even comforting, to encounter this unyielding chauvinism.

A bitter draught blew down the stone steps that led to the terrace on the left. Spencer shivered and glanced in at the last door on the right before the corridor bent sharply. This was Lee's room. He was slouched on his bed, glaring down at the steel cuffs on his wrists. When he was in that mood, he was best left alone if you didn't want your head bitten off. Spencer had never been the most socially adept person. Even before the Jax phenomenon, he'd been a loner at school and at home. Back in the camp, Lee had been the first to stick up for him, and accepted him and his oddball devotion to that Stetson. Spencer had never forgotten that and, as he set the bucket down, he determined to brave the boy's temper and go talk to him – as soon as the floor was clean. After all, even if he did get his head bitten off, it was no big deal; there was no hat to put on it.

But now the guards were shouting again.

"All right!" he said. "I'm doing it as fast as I can. What's the hur—?"

Without warning, one of them snatched the mop away and threw it to the floor. The other covered the boy's mouth with his hand. Crying out was impossible and there was no time to struggle. Startled and fearful, Spencer was dragged further into the prohibited area. Locked doors flashed by and he was hauled into the lab where Doctor Choe Soo-jin was waiting.

"On the table," she ordered severely.

The guards slammed him on to the gleaming metal surface. He barely registered his surroundings, but he saw the body of the Marshal covered in the blanket and, suddenly, he understood why Gerald had been so alarmed. The shock of realisation was like a violent punch.

"You're not serious!" he yelled when the guard uncovered his mouth and began fastening the restraints about his wrists. "You can't do this! You're crazy!"

Terrified, he began to yell at the top of his voice and twisted and kicked, hitting one of the men in the face. A brutal fist struck him in return and Spencer shouted even louder.

"This room soundproof," the doctor said. "No one hear you."

Spencer continued to fight frantically. They caught his right foot and strapped it down. Doctor Choe moved closer to check the strap was secure and he booted her in the shoulder with his left. The woman went reeling sideways. She crashed against the other table and fell across the Marshal's corpse.

Springing back, she snapped at the guards and they hastily buckled the other foot down.

"Make final strap tight!" she commanded. "Then wait outside. I am not to be disturbed, by anyone or anything."

The last restraint was pulled under Spencer's chin and over his throat, almost strangling him and flattening his windpipe. He choked and gasped and his cries were crushed into desperate croaks.

The guards bowed smartly and left the lab. Spencer was pinned fast to the table. He could only turn his head around a fraction before the thick strap bit into his neck. Struggling for breath, he watched the doctor move in and out of his line of sight and heard the ring of metal against metal as she sorted through her instruments. When she crossed his vision again, she was holding a syringe.

"You can't do this!" Spencer rasped, sweating in horror. "I'm not a specimen you can cut up and examine. When Martin finds out, he'll tell the Chief of the General Staff. They'll have you shot – you're raving mad!"

Doctor Choe disappeared again as she moved to the drugs cabinet and unlocked it. He heard the door open and the clink of small bottles as she examined the labels.

Spencer wrenched and heaved on the straps. He contorted his hands and feet and tried to slip them free, but the restraints were too strong and tight. There was nothing he could do. He turned his face as far to one side as he could, only to find himself staring at his dead neighbour. The boy grimaced and peered through his spectacles at the macabre sight. When the doctor had fallen against it, she had displaced the Marshal's arm and it was now hanging over the side. Tark the Shark was still clutching a green book in his hand. Even in death the Jaxers didn't let go of it. His blood dotted the cover.

Spencer's mind was racing. He couldn't break free, he couldn't call for help, what else could he do? What else? He remembered back in the camp, when he'd been at his lowest, and had wanted to run outside after curfew so the Punchinellos would shoot him. Marcus had saved him then and made him realise that you had to keep battling, you had to keep looking for chances – you never gave up. But what chances were there here? Unless someone came barging in to the rescue, he was done for.

"Was Chief who lift restriction," the doctor's voice informed him. "Martin Baxter, him only important for study. His brain should be most interesting. Reason for immunity must be found. Democratic People's Republic depend on my skill to find answer. I must create vaccine."

"Brain?" the boy gasped. "You want our brains? You really are sick in the head. It's your brains what need bottling! You're out of your ruddy skull!"

"Brain of subjects only first avenue of study," she told him. "Other organs may also hold clue that is vital."

"There is no cure, you silly cow! It's not a disease. When are you going to start listening to us? It takes you over. It's evil – full stop. You get possessed. There's no vaccine for that."

He heard her flat heels turn on the tiled floor and, moments later, she was leaning over him. The syringe was no longer empty and a bead of clear liquid glistened on the needle's tip.

"Lethal injection?" he asked, almost hysterical with fear. "That's just wonderful that is. You're putting me down like Old Yeller!"

"No lethal," she corrected coldly. "Enough barbiturate to induce sleep or coma only. Point three five gram for now. Lethal dose might damage brain."

"Oh, gee, bless you. You're not going to kill me until after you've scooped out my skull. That's really considerate."

Her hand reached for his face. She wasn't going to inject straight into his head, was she? He flinched as much as the strap across his throat allowed. He closed his eyes, expecting to feel the needle's sting, but Doctor Choe was only removing his glasses. He felt them pulled from his nose and heard them being set on the counter. Then her gloved fingers pushed the cuff of his overcoat up his forearm as she selected a vein beneath his pale, European skin.

And then a wild and crazy idea flashed into his mind.

"Beyond the Silvering Sea!" he said, as loud as he was able. "Within thirteen green, girdling hills, lies the wondrous Kingdom of the Dawn Prince."

Back in Britain he had been forced to read that book so many times he knew most of it by heart.

Doctor Choe Soo-jin blinked at him in surprise and annoyance. Above the surgical mask her eyes narrowed.

"No speak," she ordered.

"Yet inside his White Castle, the throne stands empty!" he continued defiantly. "For many long years he has been lost in exile and thus the Ismus, his Holy Enchanter, reigns in his stead."

The woman felt a strange prickling sensation crawl up the back of her neck. She gazed about the lab and it seemed to darken. Deep shadows crept out from beneath the counters and behind the sinks, seeping up through the floor. The dead fingers of Marshal Tark Hyun-ki quivered as the book they held twitched and tugged to get free.

In the vault, the metal box containing the wand of Malinda began to tremble and judder. On a shelf close by, the jaw of the unicorn skull opened slowly and the darkness seethed and breathed around it.

"Till the day of his glorious returning," Spencer persisted, almost spitting the words out, "and the restoration of his splendour evermore!"

Overhead a fluorescent strip popped and the lab dipped into deeper gloom. Another bulb began to flicker. The syringe fell from Doctor Choe's grasp. It dropped to the ground and she gripped the metal table for support as her head swam. The paper mask blew in and out of her mouth. A fresh morning breeze seemed to be moving through her hair. Sunlight was filtering through the fresh green leaves of spring. It was another ravishing day in Mooncaster and she had come to the bluebell woods with the other young girls from the village to wash her face with dew...

"For that day approaches," Spencer recited, and now his voice was strong and reverberated in her ears. "The Lord of Rising Dawn is drawing nigh. He is returning to the land that was his. His light shall crown the hills with crimson flame and we shall bow before his unmatched majesty."

"No!" the doctor declared vehemently. "I am Soo-jin!"

The spring light faded and the creeping shadows in the lab retreated. Breathing hard, she ripped the mask from her mouth and turned a stern, vengeful face on Spencer. The boy's voice had dwindled back to a compressed whisper.

Doctor Choe stooped to retrieve the syringe. As she crouched, she heard something drop to the floor. Glancing under the table, she saw that the book had fallen from the Marshal's hand. It was splayed open, white pages facing the ceiling. As she looked, one of them curled over, disclosing a black and white illustration of peasant maidens gambolling through bluebells.

The doctor straightened and hurried around. But, when she reached the space between the tables, the floor was empty. The book had gone.

She glared at Spencer suspiciously. The boy was still strapped down. He couldn't have moved it. Her doubtful glance darted aside to the Marshal's body. She scowled, angry with herself for even thinking such a thing was possible. So where was the book?

Beneath one of the sinks came the sound of rustling paper. The doctor drew back. Spencer fell silent and their eyes locked. He had only tried to get her hooked on the words of Austerly Fellows. He had no idea what forces he had awakened. Reading her concern was gratifying though and he couldn't stop a smirk stealing on to his face.

There was another dry fluttering of pages. This time it was behind the blood analyser.

"Big mice you've got here," the boy said mockingly.

Doctor Choe stepped away and went to the tray of surgical knives. She took up the largest scalpel and held it out in front as she approached the analyser. Cautiously, she leaned over and peered down into the gap between it and the wall. There was nothing there.

Suddenly one of the cupboard doors flew open. Test tubes, flasks and beakers exploded out, smashing on the floor. The doctor jumped back in alarm. Another cupboard was flung wide and Petri dishes came spinning into the lab like Frisbees.

"Vaccinate that!" Spencer taunted as the contents of a third were violently ejected.

The woman clasped the scalpel more tightly and went crunching over the powdered fragments, staring inside each cupboard. They were all empty, but the final one was still closed. Moving nearer and nearer, she reached out to yank the door wide and was primed to lunge the sharp blade at whatever was revealed within.

Holding her breath, she snatched the door open and stabbed wildly. The thin blade lacerated the melamine shelving then snapped. There was nothing in here but boxes of surgical gloves, masks and disposable aprons.

Her tense, squatting frame relaxed. But it was not over yet.

There was a clattering din. One of the metal trays came shooting off the counter above her head. It struck her temple with force and the instruments it contained showered down as she fell backwards. Sterile blades sliced her cheek and skewered her lab coat. Her skull smacked the tiled floor and she cried out. Her head thumped and for several moments she lay there in a shocked daze. Razor-sharp knives had kissed through her skin and rivulets of blood had begun to flow. Yet none of that mattered. As she blundered back, she'd caught a glimpse of something up on the counter, where the tray had been. It was the

Marshal's green book.

The doctor raised her head to look again. It was no longer there. Then she saw it. The book was now lying on the floor, by her feet. As she watched, the book raised itself upright.

"Not possible!" Doctor Choe exclaimed, shaking her pounding head. When she looked again, it had clambered on to her legs. Tilting diagonally, it balanced on one corner and swung the other forward, waggling itself along her body.

The doctor tried to hurl it away, but her arms were unnaturally heavy and she couldn't move them. Her legs were the same. She was as helpless as Spencer on the examination table. Throwing back her head, she yelled for help then sobbed as she recalled the lab was soundproof.

Dancing Jax continued its relentless, shuffling progress until it came to a stop on her chest. With slow menace, its pages opened and her eyes were compelled to gaze.

Strapped to the table, unable to see what was happening, Spencer could only listen and try to guess.

"Doctor?" he ventured. "Doctor Choe?"

There was no reply. Spencer breathed a sigh of relief. He had saved himself, invoking the power of the book to ensnare her. But the real peril was only just beginning. The force he had unleashed was unstoppable and would sweep away everyone in the base. There was no escape now.

Minutes edged by, in which the only sounds were the woman's soft, trance-like murmurs. Then, abruptly, she rose from the floor, appearing behind the Marshal's body. A far-off look was in her glassy eyes and *Dancing Jax* was clasped to her bosom.

"I am the Four of Clubs," she announced ecstatically. "I am Dulcie, the innkeeper's daughter. All the boys and menfolk do like to kiss me, for I have ale on my ripe cherry lips, the tints of a warm summer evening in my golden hair and my pretty duckies do fill my bodice most bounteous. Blessed be."

6

EVEN AS THE guards dragged Spencer into the lab, Martin and Gerald descended the steps from the terrace.

"You!" a severe voice shouted.

The two friends halted and looked down the corridor. Three soldiers were striding purposefully towards them from the main tunnel where a jeep was waiting.

"You, quick!" one of them ordered. "You needed."

Neither Gerald nor Martin recognised them. They were dressed in the usual olive uniform of the People's Army, but they had not seen their faces in the base before. Perhaps their duties kept them in the prohibited areas; those units never had cause to come here.

"You, come!" the same man called again. From the four stars on his uniform they could see he was a *daewi*, or captain.

"What is this?" Martin asked uncertainly. "What do you want?"

"Chief want see!" the Captain shouted fiercely. "You not keep wait!"

Martin's and Gerald's faces fell. Their desperate, reckless scheme was collapsing before it had begun. What was going on? Martin had never been summoned so brusquely before.

"Quick! Quick!" the Captain insisted.

"I have to go," Martin whispered. "There's no knowing when I'll get back – or even if I will."

"Don't say that!" Gerald hissed.

"Whatever happens, the fog won't last so you're going to have to do this on your own. Get Lee to do his thing and you take those kids out of this place. I'll try and keep them as busy as I can in here."

The old man's eyes glistened and he gave the slightest of nods. They both knew they probably wouldn't see each other again.

"And you... look after yourself, you wonderful, dotty old gentleman. Good luck – it's been an honour and a privilege."

"Quick!" the Captain snorted for the last time. He grabbed hold of Martin's arm and pulled him towards the jeep.

Gerald Benning watched them get into the vehicle. He couldn't bring himself to shout goodbye. Instead he raised a hand in farewell and, under his breath, sang, "Hearts do not break! They sting and ache."

The jeep roared off into the tunnels. Gerald turned his back and ran to Lee's room. There wasn't a moment to lose.

Lee was still sitting on the bed, staring at the steel cuffs. He didn't look up when the old man entered, but recognised Gerald by his brown brogues.

"This is not a place you wanna be," he grunted. "I ain't got nuthin' to say. 'Cept Baxter is a ass, I feel like crap, an' if you think I'm gonna join in with your Christmas glee club, you is missing more than a tinselly tree – but I knows where you can shove one."

"Never mind about that now," Gerald said urgently as he cast a wary glance at the four guards chained to the lad's wrists and prayed they didn't understand English. "I'm taking the kids out of here, but I need your help."

Lee raised his eyes.

"You what?"

"Things have changed – drastically," the old man told him. "That doctor is planning to experiment on us."

"She already does that, man. She's got enough out of me to build a spare."

"I mean she's going to dissect us."

"Get outta here."

"I was never more deadly serious. I'm taking the kids and I'm taking them now, but I can't do it without you."

Lee could see he wasn't joking, yet he still gave a snort of laughter. "You're hardcore crazy, guy," he said. "You got no place to go and zero chance of getting there and you're sayin' all this right in front of my big mirror here, behind which, I am damn sure, is a camera. That's so lame-ass dumb it deserves its own reality show."

"Will you help us?"

"Help get you killed? You doesn't need no help from me. You is on to a sure thing there."

"Lee," Gerald insisted. "It's weapons we need, not attitude." His eyes flicked either side, to the guards, and he said pointedly, "Those weapons."

"What you sayin'?"

"I want you to go to Mooncaster and take your friends here with you."

Lee shook his head. "My posse ain't goin' no place," he said flatly. "Bad enough they have to stalk me here. I ain't invitin' them to no twisted Disneyland for an outing. When I go there, it's gonna be a single one-way ticket."

"You can't be that selfish."

"Watch me."

"Don't you care what happens to Maggie and Spencer?"

The boy returned his reproachful stare. "I already gave," he said quietly. "You're all deadsauce anyways, you know that – why you draggin' it out? You're good as ghosts already, hauntin' this sad dump day an' night. This ain't no life and you got nuthin' better in front. Get some smarts and give it up. Show's over for you, been over since we got here."

"You're not that bitter," Gerald replied, refusing to believe him. "I've heard and seen how much you adored that shining girl. A heart so full can't become that callous."

"Don't presume to know me."

"I don't, but I know what love is like and, from what I hear about Charm, she wouldn't want you to be this way."

"End of conversation, old man. My services are not for hire. I ain't no black cab. Now go get yourselves all killed and leave me be. I got a gut ache. When's lunch comin'?"

Gerald eyed the rifles one last time and his hopes of escape plummeted. It was no use. The boy couldn't be persuaded. Was Martin right about him after all?

In the dark, narrow space behind the great mirror, Eun-mi had been watching everything. She checked the video camera was still recording and picked up the old-fashioned base telephone to call her father. A look of gloating satisfaction soured her young features.

At that moment the lights in Lee's room sputtered and the boy doubled over. He cried out, clutching his heart. His guards began to yell as the chains yanked at them when Lee rolled wildly from side to side. Gerald sprang forward and was shocked to see sweat pouring down the lad's face.

He dashed into the corridor, but there was no guard on duty at the corner of the prohibited area.

"We need the doctor!" he shouted, trespassing into the forbidden area. "Quickly! I think Lee is having a heart attack!"

Down the passage he saw a discarded mop and bucket and, further along, two soldiers stationed outside the lab. The old man shouted again, but they aimed their Kalashnikovs at him and yammered excitably. Gerald swore at them and hurried back to Lee's room.

The boy was shivering and writhing in pain. His four guards were shouting and shaking him roughly.

"Get off him!" Gerald snapped, pulling them clear. "Lee, can you hear me? Lee?"

He took hold of the boy's hand. It was freezing. Above them sparks began to spit from the cables connecting the strip lights and the room skipped in and out of darkness. Lee swung his head round and his eyes bored into Gerald.

"Let go o' me!" he hissed through clenched teeth as he pushed him away. "You's gonna get your gats after all. Someone real close by is readin' the book an' goin' to that place for the first time. It's draggin' me with it. Don't you touch me or you'll be comin' too. Damn! It never hurt like this before! It's ripping me apart!"

Gerald jumped back. The boy clawed the air as his stomach kicked inside him. The breath was slammed from his lungs and his eardrums screamed as if they were going to shatter. He gave one last agonised shout, then his arms dropped and he became as still as death. At the same time, his guards uttered wails of dismay and fear. Then they too crumpled, falling where they stood, either to the floor or across the bed.

Gerald could hardly believe it. Their minds or souls, or whatever it was, had gone into the world of *Dancing Jax*.

Behind the mirror, Eun-mi was urging her father to come at once. Then the line went dead. She looked into the room beyond and saw the old man approach the collapsed figures. Reaching down, he took the rifles from the unconscious guards then hastened to the door. Pausing, he said a grateful farewell to Lee.

"Good luck. I hope you find what you're looking for in that place. Just don't disappoint that dazzling girl. Don't do what Austerly Fellows wants. Be the person she fell in love with. You're far from scum, Lee Charles. Goodbye and thank you."

Eun-mi watched him leave. She tried the phone again, but the earpiece was full of wails and crackles. She threw it down in anger and took her pistol from its holster.

The secret observation area was a thin, L-shaped space that hugged two sides of the medical room. The entrance was in the prohibited area and she groped her way through the narrow darkness to find it. When she emerged, she looked for the guards, but those outside the lab were nowhere to be seen. Pistol in hand, she ran round the corner – ready to shoot at anything that moved.

The corridor was deserted.

She looked fleetingly into Lee's room and regarded the unconscious men with disgust. They were weak and would be punished for allowing their rifles to be taken.

Silently, Eun-mi proceeded, checking the dorms as she passed them. They were empty. The refugees were probably all gathered in the refectory, waiting to be fed. So much the better.

"You must be mental!" the girl called Esther scoffed when Gerald had hastily explained his escape plan and the reason for it. "They wouldn't operate on us and cut us up. They're not Jaxers here, they're normal."

There wasn't time for Gerald to go into just how wrong she was.

"I'm not going to argue with you," he said impatiently. "If you come now, there's a chance, but if you stay you'll end up in more jars than a range of jams in Sainsbury's. The rest of you will need to wear as much clothing as possible, everything you've got basically. It's going to be bitter out there in the fog and we'll be sleeping rough for a while. Also we can't carry anything: you need both hands to climb down the mountain."

"Stupid old git," Esther butted in. "You've got no idea where to go out there and we'll be frozen solid by morning, if we don't get blown up by landmines. I'm not listening to some senile geriatric who used to prance about in frocks."

"Oi!" Maggie shouted her down. "Shut it. No one's listening to you. You did this last time, in the camp. Dithering until the last minute and almost getting Lee killed. Just button it or I'll smack you one. Gerald knows what he's talking about. You can stop here for all I care, but I'm going to risk getting away. It's Lee I'm pig sick about, having to leave him behind."

There were eager noises of support from the girls who had been in Charm's cabin back in the camp, which prompted hesitant, uncertain murmurs of agreement from the others. They were all horribly frightened, but they trusted Gerald completely. If he said there was no other choice, they believed him.

Little Nabi was still seated at the table. She was watching the hurried discussion with wide eyes. The unexpected shock of Gerald's announcement had made everyone forget the six-year-old was even present. She couldn't quite understand what was happening, but she knew her English friends weren't supposed to have weapons. Imagining her father's fury when he found out made her anxious and afraid for them.

"Give me one of them Kalashnikovs," Maggie said to Gerald. "I won a cuddly rabbit at the fair once. That was a scary night. For one awful minute I thought I'd been shot in the bum, but it was only a packet of moist handy wipes that'd burst in my pocket when I bent over."

Gerald passed her an assault rifle. It was lighter than she expected and she struck aggressive poses as she handled it.

"Commando girl," she purred. "And no, that doesn't mean I'm not wearing pants."

"Don't touch that lever on the right-hand side there," Gerald warned. "That's the safety catch. Up is safe, down isn't, so let's keep them up, OK? I don't anticipate having to use them, not in here anyway, they're just in case. I don't even know how much ammunition is in the magazines, so no one get any ideas. I don't need to tell you they're not toys or replicas. These are lethal, so treat them with respect."

He looked around for another he could entrust one to.

"Nicholas, how about you? Do you think you could?"

The boy shifted uncomfortably and looked to Esther for his answer.

"He's not having anything to do with it," she stated, arms folded tightly. "You walk out of here with them guns and you're all going to get shot – and rightly so in my opinion."

"I'll have one," the lad called Drew piped up.

"You're mad, the lot of you," Esther said, cracking her knuckles nervously. "It'll be a bloodbath."

"Where's Spencer?" Gerald asked. "He's handled a firearm before, hasn't he? Didn't he shoot one of those Punchinellos at the camp?"

"He's mopping up in the no-go area," Maggie told him.

"No, he's not. The mop and bucket are there, but he isn't."

"Someone go fetch him from the loo then, quick."

A girl called Sally jumped up to get him. Before she reached the door, it was kicked open and Eun-mi was standing there, arm outstretched, pointing the pistol, finger on the trigger.

"Drop weapons!" she shouted. "Drop or I shoot!"

Shocked, the refugees stared at her for several moments.

"Told you so!" Esther said.

Eun-mi moved her aim slowly across the astonished faces.

"I say drop!" she repeated.

Gerald was the first to comply and he told the others to do the same.

"She means it," he said. "She wouldn't hesitate."

"Nabi!" the girl called to her sister in Korean. "Bring the weapons here. Be careful. Don't let them take you and use you as a shield."

Little Nabi gawped at her and had to be told again, more forcefully.

"Anyone moves, they die!" Eun-mi warned as her sister slid

reluctantly from the chair and started collecting the AK-47s. "I aim for head. There will be no error."

"You don't have to do this," Gerald tried to reason with her. "You can let us go. Just give us this one chance. You know what Doctor Choe Soo-jin is planning to do. You heard her at the meeting. You can't want that on your conscience. It's inhuman."

Eun-mi tilted her head back proudly. "Doctor will be hero," she declared. "She will find cure. She will save Democratic People's Republic from Western sickness. Doctor Choe Soo-jin is pioneer and scientist most brilliant. Lives of European refugee little price to pay. Then Supreme Leader will save rest of world. Everyone will praise Kim Jong-un."

"What about the life of Du Kwan earlier?" Gerald asked. "Was that a small price to pay? He didn't need to die and nor do we. There is no cure to be found because there is no sickness. It isn't physical. You can't inoculate against the Devil."

"Doctor Choe Soo-jin know best!" the girl shouted, refusing to listen. "Now no speak or I fire!"

Nabi placed the rifles at her feet and stared up at her miserably. "Do not hurt my friends," she begged her sister in a forlorn voice that was close to tears. "Please. They are kind and nice. I like them, they are good."

"They are enemies of our Republic!" Eun-mi answered. "You do not understand, you are too young. We have given them everything; food and shelter – when our own people are starving in the provinces. We give them asylum from their own degenerate kind and they show us only disrespect and bring disease. The Supreme Leader has demonstrated his great benevolence and mercy in saving them, but these are bad people. They have no gratitude, no discipline; their island is the corrupt puppet of America. They would have killed our soldiers to escape this base. They would have killed you too. Would you take their side against your own people? Would you betray our father and dishonour the memory of our mother?"

Nabi stared at her feet and shook her head.

"Go, now!" her sister ordered. "Fetch more guards and wait for our father – hurry."

Nabi cast a wretched glance back at Gerald and Maggie. Her bottom lip quivered. Wiping her eyes, she ran from the room.

Eun-mi's hand was steady. She almost wished one of the refugees would try something and give her a reason to fire. She had endured their offensive company for too long and had no qualms about pulling the trigger.

Nabi stumbled out into the corridor, tears streaking down her scrunched-up face. She cast around for any sign of the guards, but there was no one in sight and the long, empty passageway was unnaturally quiet.

"Help me!" she called out and her wavering voice ricocheted down the walls. The shadows lay deep in the recesses of doorways and the little girl wrung her hands together.

"Help us!" she called again.

No answer came. She took several apprehensive steps towards the forbidden area, but it was so dark down there she grew even more frightened.

"Hello?" she murmured.

From somewhere around the corner, she heard a door clang shut, followed by the sound of footsteps striding briskly over the bare concrete floor. But there was something else – a strange clip-clopping. It was very like the hooves of a large animal.

Nabi peered into the concealing darkness and backed away. She didn't like it. Turning, she began to run towards the junction with the main tunnel.

"Chung Nabi!" a voice rang out behind her.

The child stopped and spun round. Doctor Choe Soo-jin was there, stepping from the shadows – a welcoming smile on her Band-Aid-patched face. In one hand she held a green book; in the other was a long silver rod, crooked at one end, and tipped with a glimmering amber star.

"Come here, dear one," the doctor said, beckoning. "I have a blessed gift for you."

7

MARTIN SHIVERED, WISHING once again for the overcoat he had left on his bunk. He hardly gave any attention to the Captain and the two other men who had whisked him away in this jeep. His thoughts were with Gerald and the rest. He wondered if Lee had agreed to the request and if the English guests of the Democratic People's Republic of Korea had managed to escape. Were they clambering down the craggy mountainside at this very minute? He hoped fortune smiled on them and they could disappear into the fog before the alarm was raised. Where they would go after that was up to Gerald, and providence. Driving through the tunnels, everything seemed business as usual and Martin took that as proof their exodus was still undetected.

He recognised this journey, it was the same one he had taken earlier that morning, and guessed rightly they were heading for the meeting room. He had no idea why he was wanted so urgently, but that didn't really matter. His own safety was right at the bottom of his list of concerns.

Suddenly he heard the rumble and roar of four other vehicles approaching at speed. Their headlights swept the poorly illuminated gloom before them. Voices were barking commands and, as the lead car drew closer, he made out the thick black eyebrows of General Chung Kang-dae.

Martin uttered a dismal cry. They knew! They were making for the medical centre. But it was so soon. Gerald and the children couldn't have got very far. They probably weren't even hidden by the fog yet. They'd be sitting ducks on that mountainside. Martin didn't know what to do. He couldn't just sit here and let it happen.

The four jeeps raced nearer. They were only moments away from passing when Martin threw himself forward. He dived between the Captain and the driver and wrenched at the steering wheel. The vehicle swerved sharply into the other lane and the approaching headlights dazzled him.

Horns blared and startled yells shrieked out. The tunnel was filled with the screeching of brakes and the reek of scorched tyres. The oncoming jeeps veered aside, while Martin's scraped along the tunnel wall, showering him and the three soldiers with fiery sparks.

Suddenly it was over. The four jeeps thundered on and Martin's skidded to a standstill. He couldn't believe he had survived and despaired that he hadn't been able to stop them. The Captain and the other two were bawling at him and he was wrestled back to his seat. One of them hit him, but he barely noticed.

"I'm sorry, Gerald," he muttered, staring after the receding lights. "I've let you down."

"You no do that again!" the Captain was shouting in his face. "You crazy UK!"

The engine started once more and the scarred and dented vehicle spluttered on its way, rattling and juddering until they reached the red double doors of their destination.

Martin stepped out and the armed guards stood aside. The Captain pushed him forward and he entered the meeting room for the second time that day.

The Chief of the General Staff was waiting, standing stiffly by the table. Martin thought he looked faintly embarrassed, almost shamefaced, as he bowed in greeting.

"What do you want?" Martin asked. "Why am I here?" Then he realised there was no interpreter present.

The Chief bowed again. There was something awkward, even shifty, about him. Martin saw his eyes slide over to the high back of a chair that was facing the large TV screen at the end of the room. Someone was sitting in it: Martin could just see the top of their head.

The Chief mumbled something that sounded like an apology, then strode past and left the room.

Martin didn't understand. He looked across at the chair back, but he wasn't in the mood to play these sorts of power games. Remembering he was cold, he moved over to one of the electric fires and held out his hands. Over by the far wall, the carpet was still dark with blood. He was just wondering where the young aide's body had been taken to when the chair swung round and Martin had one of the greatest surprises of his life.

"Hello, Baxter me old mucker!" said an extremely familiar voice. "What's all this then, a sabbatical? Or are you playing truant or what?"

Martin couldn't believe it and his mouth actually fell open.

"Barry?" he cried. "What the hell...?"

The former headmaster of the school he had taught at in Felixstowe was grinning at him across the table. He was the last person Martin had expected to see here. Barry Milligan was now part of the Ismus's inner circle and travelled the world with him and his Court. Way back, so long ago now, when the book had been distributed to the unsuspecting inhabitants of that quiet seaside town out of an old camper van, Barry had been one of the first to be possessed. He had become the mischievous character of the Jockey and had fooled everyone until the very last moment.

He was a middle-aged, squarely built man, with a face florid and craggy from a lifetime's overindulgence in salt, saturated fat and whisky. His pot belly was a testament to the same.

"Is that all you've got to say, Martin?" he asked, laughing and slapping the table. "Here we are in a top-secret bloody military base, dug into a mountain – in North Korea, with China breathing down our necks – and that's the best you can manage? That's just rubbish that is. The thickest yobs we used to try and teach could've come up with something better than that."

Martin regarded him uncertainly. His former boss was wearing a large black overcoat and he could see there was a blue tracksuit underneath. Where was the Jockey's signature caramel leather outfit?

"What are you doing here?" he demanded. "That was you on that helicopter earlier, wasn't it? Makes sense now: no one in their right mind would risk flying through this fog. Shouldn't you be skipping around the Ismus, amusing him with puerile tricks and scaring the rest of them with jokes that only you find funny?"

Barry shook his head gravely. "I'm not part of that no more," he assured him, putting his hand on his heart.

"Pull the other one."

"It's true, I swear! I don't know why or how, but a few months ago the effects of that book simply stopped working on me. I think it's because of something that Ismus geezer was writing on his laptop. I caught a glimpse of it over his shoulder one day and... I dunno, the bit I read made my old head feel like it was about to split wide apart. After that, I stopped believing in it. Everything I thought was real – that mad, medieval place and the plonker I was supposed to be there – had gone. There I was, finally wide awake, and wondering what the hell had been happening. It's like waking up from the longest pub crawl with the rugby lads. There's a lot of it I can't even remember."

"Don't do this," Martin said. "Don't lie to me."

"Honest, Martin! I'm out of it, and today I managed to get away without them even suspecting I was back to normal. I just had to find you. I know how to get Carol and Paul out of it. We've got to get that laptop and make them read it. Just think – if we could email that file to everyone, this huge sorry mess would be over."

Martin staggered and steadied himself against the table. Could it really be that simple? His heart began thumping with excitement and his eyes started to swim. The horror, the anguish, the horrendous loss of life, was the end of all that so near? Was he going to see the two people he cared most about in the world again? Was it possible?

A flame of hope spluttered in his heart and a tear ran down his face. In that brief instant of blazing joy, he totally forgot about the plight of Gerald and the children.

"Oh, thank God!" he uttered. "Oh, thank, thank God!"

Barry rose. He clapped his hands and cheered, as if his favourite team had just scored a try.

"We're going to save the world, old son!" he shouted.

Suddenly Martin's elation perished and the light that had flared so briefly in his eyes was quenched. When Barry moved, he could hear the creak and squeak of leather beneath his clothes. Martin stumbled back and gave a howl of anger and frustration.

"You evil, evil freak!" he raged.

"Haw haw haw!" the other man crowed. "I teased you, I tricked you, I taunted you and played you. What a bad boy the Jockey is. How he rides them all."

Throwing off the coat and tracksuit, he revealed the toffee-coloured costume underneath and hopped around in a triumphant circle.

"But you were too easy, Mr Baxter," he scolded, wagging a finger. "You wanted it to be true so much you quite took the pleasure of my game clean away. I was expecting to have to work much harder at the dissembling. Gullible chumps like you are no fun."

The bitterness of Martin's disappointment was almost unbearable. He felt utterly crushed. To have that sparkling hope dangled in front of him, only for it to be snatched away, was a pain he didn't think he could endure.

But he had to.

"So what are you here for?" he asked, broken. "You've found me, you've won. What are you going to do now? I'd have thought your precious Ismus would want to be here and gloat in person at the finish."

"Hoo hoo hoo!" the Jockey guffawed. "I'm not here because of you! You really do have an inflated view of your significance, even worse than that charlatan, Old Ramptana. No, we've known exactly where you've been skulking from the beginning. You just weren't important enough to go chasing. Did you honestly think you were? Haw haw haw – that is very funny. Wait till I tell the Lady Labella; how she will laugh."

"How... how is Carol? Is she OK?"

"The Lady Labella," the Jockey rebuked him, "is in the pinkest of health. Since the advent of the Holy Enchanter's son, she has been as radiant as the morning."

Martin closed his eyes. Hearing that revolted him.

"And Paul?" he asked. "I mean the Jack of Diamonds, how is he?"

"The light-fingered doings of Magpie Jack are none of your concern, Martin Baxter."

Martin gritted his teeth and fought the urge to smash the other man's face through the large TV screen. It wasn't easy.

"What about this new book?" he asked instead. "Was that part true? Is the Ismus writing a sequel?"

"Oh, most assuredly so. Wherever we go in this silly dreamland he has been tappy-tappy-tapping on his laptop, late into the night, shunning company and comforts. But it is not a sequel, for how can there be such a thing? 'Tis a furtherance of our merry lives in the Realm of the Dawn Prince. We of the Court are agog and breathless to be granted even so much as a fleeting glimpse of it, but that is forbidden for the moment, yes, for the moment."

He gave a twitch of agitation and Martin guessed correctly that the Jockey had already tried and failed to read the manuscript.

"All will be revealed betimes though," the Jockey continued. "A declaration shall be made this very day and the whole of this grey drabbery will know of it. Oh, such plans are a-place, such excitement there shall be for you all, yea, even the aberrants. We genuinely do all we can to make this drudging gloom more sprightly for you – perk it up and keep it lively, keep it bright and frolicsome."

"You really shouldn't bother."

"Now, now, don't irk. Let us not curdle this jolly day with your vinegary humour. I have come to rescue you from these dank grots and caves, fit only for worms and pin-eyed bats. You should be glad and singing."

"You've already said it wasn't me you've come for. So who, as if I didn't know?"

The smirk slipped from the Jockey's face. "My Lord Ismus wishes the Castle Creeper brought unto his presence," he told him with great solemnity. "There is a covenant between them he is most keen to pursue."

"I know all about that. It's his maddest, most disgusting scheme yet. What I don't know is how you persuaded the North Koreans to let you come here."

The Jockey threw back his head and let out a throaty laugh.

"Persuade them?" he hooted. "They really aren't in a position to deny me. When my Lord Ismus tells them to hop, they leap like hares from a burning field. Dear me, Mr Baxter, you cannot truly believe your raggle-taggle band of aberrants have been their guests these many months? You silly, dolting muttonhead. This impecunious country is on its knees and the people are suffering. Famine bites hard and their children are stunted and starving. Though they are friendless in this silly world, they are dependent on foreign aid, even from the West whom they despise. You and your young vagabonds have not been guests here, you have been hostages – and used as articles of barter for an increase in that aid. What wily hagglers they are. They have done well from the bargain. My Lord Ismus has been sending them oodles of food and fuel – such munificence! 'Tis a marvel their trousers still fit."

Martin finally understood why the North Koreans had not explored ways of utilising Lee's gift. They were too busy profiting from keeping him here. They hadn't wanted to attack the Ismus, because they were accepting aid from him and now it was time for their benefactor to collect. This was why the Chief of the General Staff had looked so ashamed a few minutes ago.

"And have they also done a deal to keep their republic free of *Dancing Jax*?" he asked.

The Jockey tittered behind his hand. "Of course they have! The Holy Enchanter has given his word not to distribute the hallowed text within these borders."

The sentence had scarcely left his lips when the lights began to flicker.

"Oh, the Ismus is such a rascally swizzler!" he giggled. "His promises are spun of the most brittle, sugary strands. Now I am charged to fetch the Creeper. You are to be taken to the whirlycopter. There are some surprises and japes in store for you, Martin Baxter. What a thrilling Christmas you'll have in this tedious sleep world this year."

"Wait," Martin called as the Jockey brushed past him. "I just want to know... is there anything of the Barry Milligan I worked with for over twenty-five years still left inside you? Was that only an act before? Is there no trace of that rugger-loving sod anywhere?"

The Jockey stared at him in puzzled amusement. "We are the Aces," he explained slowly, as though to a simpleton. "We do not have to pretend to be who we are not, in these shabby dreams. I am, and forever was, the Jockey. The man you thought you knew as Barry Milligan was but a pretence of my invention because the jest suited me. No more than that. There was never a drunken headmaster, there was never a school nor a mirthless place called Felixstowe – there is only Mooncaster. That is the one reality. How pitiful it must be to be an aberrant and not know this plainest of truths."

Martin looked away and the Jockey scampered out of the room.

In the tunnels, the lights were exploding and panic and chaos had started. Harrowing cries were echoing through the passageways. The Jockey clambered into a jeep, his pinching caramel outfit squeaking and creaking. Then he was driven off, towards the medical centre.

The Captain and two soldiers who had brought Martin here marched him in the direction of the helipad. Gunfire crackled in the distance. Martin hung his head. It was over. *Dancing Jax* had finally conquered everything.

8

EUN-MI WONDERED WHAT was keeping the reinforcements she had sent her sister to find. It had been too long. Where had Nabi gone? What was she doing? Had she betrayed the Republic in favour of her new Western friends after all?

The young English refugees didn't dare move or utter a word. They couldn't take their eyes off the barrel of the gun that continuously switched aim from face to frightened face.

"Do you want to shoot us?" Gerald asked quietly. "Is that it? You want to punish us? What crime do you think we're guilty of?"

"You steal People's Army weapons!" Eun-mi reminded him.

"That's not the reason," he answered. "That's the excuse. Your hatred goes back much further. You just don't like us, it's as basic as that – xenophobia. How very sad in one so young to be so completely brainwashed into despising and persecuting the unlike. But then that's why we're here, isn't it? Because my young friends and I are different. The rest of the world has the Ismus to tell them that; you have your Supreme Leader. Pogrom is pogrom, no matter who's behind it."

"I shoot you first!" the girl threatened, aiming between his eyes.

"Human nature really is so depressing," he replied. "I could almost wish you would."

"Gerald!" Maggie exclaimed anxiously. "Don't say that."

The old man gave her a gentle smile. "And then," he said, "I remember that there are people like my dear friend Maggie here. Lovely, joyous souls with open hearts, brimming with kindness and affection, and I know we're not so bad after all. But then you wouldn't understand that, would you, Miss Chung? I don't suppose your life has been a particularly happy one."

Without taking her eyes off the Westerners, Eun-mi leaned back, into the corridor. It was deathly quiet. Scowling with impatience, she called for her sister. Where was Nabi?

"Of course," Gerald continued fearlessly, "what you loathe most of all is yourself, isn't it?"

Eun-mi's face didn't betray the fact that his remark hit home. If he was trying to provoke her, to get her to release them, it wasn't going to work. Her self-control was impervious to his clumsy psychology. She prided herself on her detachment.

"I shoot," she repeated implacably.

"That won't make your father love you," he told her. "The great General Chung – just what is it makes him so... indifferent towards you? You might as well be part of the furniture as far as he's concerned."

"No more talk."

"Why is he so cold to you, but lights up whenever he's with little Nabi? Why does he cherish and adore her, but treats you like something he's trodden in? What did you do?"

Eun-mi pulled the trigger.

The air exploded. The teenagers shrieked and covered their ears. Most of them dived to the floor. The gunshot seemed to shake the room and Eun-mi's nostrils flared with exhilaration as she kept the pistol level.

Gerald let out a staggering breath. For all his bravado, that had shocked and frightened him. Looking at the solemn-faced girl with the gun, he knew she had missed deliberately.

"Next time I kill," she said coldly, the ghost of a smile pulling the corners of her mouth. "Next time you dead."

Overhead the refectory lights crackled. Everyone glanced upwards. The fluorescent strips were flickering. Out in the corridor it was the same. The lights there were dying. A fizzle of sparks ran along the cables like a firework. Then the passage was engulfed in the supreme darkness that is only found underground.

The refugees murmured dismally and Eun-mi looked annoyed. She believed the generators were breaking down again. Too much of the machinery and equipment here was out of date. Too many elements had been repaired and jury-rigged far too often. It was infuriating that the power should fail at this critical moment.

Suddenly there was a snap of electricity from the wiring above their heads and the refectory was tipped into darkness too. The only light was an infernal orange-red glow from the grill of the wood-burning stove. It threw ominous black shadows around the room, leaping up the walls like tormented souls.

"I don't like this," one of the younger girls whimpered.

"Don't be scared," Maggie reassured her, trying to sound as if they weren't being held at gunpoint, deep inside a mountain in North Korea, where the lights had gone out. "It's just a glitch. They've probably not paid their leccy bill."

"Be silent!" Eun-mi commanded. "People's Army engineers will fix."

"That wasn't a surge or a blown fuse," Gerald told her. "Something else is happening here, can't you feel it?"

"It's getting colder," Nicholas said, huddling up to Esther.

"Nobody move!" Eun-mi demanded. Then she too shivered and the gun trembled in her hands.

A blast of freezing air had squalled in from the corridor. They heard a door slam, followed by echoing footsteps.

"It's just the door to the terrace," Maggie said, although it sounded nothing like that door.

Even Eun-mi held her breath as they waited and the steady, measured footfalls drew closer. There was a predatory menace to those steps.

"Who's out there?" Sally asked fretfully.

Eun-mi wanted to twist round and look, but she felt the threat of that approach and the hairs on the back of her neck lifted as gooseflesh spread up her spine. For the first time since the death of her mother, she felt afraid and didn't know what to do.

Then, very softly, in the corridor, a voice began to chant. It was a young child's voice, slowly reciting the first two words of an English nursery rhyme.

"Itsy bitsy..." it repeated over and over. "Itsy bitsy..."

"Nabi!" her sister declared with overwhelming relief. "Nabi!"

Taking her eyes off the refugees, she stepped back through the doorway and looked along the corridor. Maggie and the others watched a furrow form across Eun-mi's forehead. Something was wrong.

"Itsy bitsy…" the voice continued.

Eun-mi saw the six-year-old walking slowly from the prohibited area. Before her, she carried a silver wand as though it was a standard. Her face was lit by the pale golden light radiating from its amber star. When she passed the door to Lee's room, she halted. Her large eyes were glinting but glassy – and so were those of the creature that sat upon her head.

Eun-mi caught her breath. It was a large, spider-like shape, its fang-filled mouth resting on Nabi's brow.

"Itsy bitsy…" the little girl intoned.

At first Eun-mi thought it was alive, and she nearly sprang forward to tear it away. But then she saw its spindly legs dangling limply around Nabi's shoulders and knew it was dead. That made it worse somehow. Nabi had placed it there willingly. It was macabre and repulsive. Before Eun-mi could think of what to say, other figures emerged from the darkness at the end of the corridor.

It was Doctor Choe, her two technicians, the guards, and the female who had been stationed on the terrace. Behind them came something else.

Eun-mi's lips parted and she cried out in horror and disbelief.

"Nabi!" she called urgently. "Come here, hurry! Get away from that!"

Within the refectory, the Westerners had no idea what she was seeing. They had never known her react to anything like this before. It alarmed and unnerved them more than staring at the barrel of her gun.

"What is it?" Gerald asked. "What's out there?"

She did not hear him and a new sound prevented him asking again. It

117

was the clip-clopping of hooves on concrete. Eun-mi swung the pistol round and aimed it down the corridor.

"Nabi!" she cried again. "Move away! Come to me."

"Chung Eun-mi," a female voice called to her. "Put away your gun. There is naught to be afraid of."

The refugees recognised it immediately.

"Doctor Choe," Maggie whispered.

"Yes," Gerald breathed. "But listen. She doesn't have an accent any more. Her English is perfect."

Eun-mi stared at the doctor incredulously.

"What is that?" she demanded, shaking her head in confusion at the shape that walked beside her. "What is it?"

"A wondrous beast from the true Realm," the doctor answered. "It has come to guide you, to guide us all there. This is but a dream and we have tarried here too long. Nabi has seen the blessed truth, now you shall also."

The doctor began reading the familiar opening paragraph of *Dancing Jax*.

"Oh, God," Maggie uttered. "DJ's here. It's got her."

"Don't let her read to you!" Gerald shouted to the girl in the doorway. "Stop her!"

"Put book down!" Eun-mi ordered fiercely. "Down or I fire!"

The doctor ignored her and the guards and technicians joined in, their voices filling the corridor. Little Nabi added to the intoning chorus.

Maggie and the others looked at Eun-mi anxiously. How long could she hold out against the power of Austerly Fellows' infernal words?

"Do not make me do this!" Eun-mi warned.

The chanting and the menacing advance of the hooves continued. Eun-mi closed one eye and fired the gun. The shot thundered throughout the corridor, followed by a weird, unearthly bellow that made every heart thump faster.

Unable to sit still any longer, Gerald leaped up and ran to the door. He had to see what was happening out there. Maggie tried to call him back, but the old man joined Eun-mi and gasped at what he saw. Another bestial cry trumpeted and the other refugees scrambled to the furthest corner of the refectory and hid beneath the tables. With her heart in her mouth, Maggie edged to the doorway.

Gerald was reaching down for one of the rifles. Eun-mi didn't stop him. Peering past them, Maggie had to fight to stop herself screaming.

"The Ismus said Malinda's wand wouldn't work in this world," she cried fretfully. "'Just a pretty stick,' he said."

"Austerly Fellows and the truth don't mix," Gerald told her, grimly flicking up the safety catch as he took aim.

At that moment there came a roar of engines, and four military jeeps sped in from the main tunnel. Their headlights flooded the corridor with harsh light and General Chung Kang-dae jumped out, pistol at the ready. Yet the orders to his men died in his throat when he beheld the scene before him and he struggled to take it in.

There was Eun-mi, pointing a gun at her own people. The white-haired Englishman was next to her, an automatic rifle in his hands. Beyond them, in the line of fire, were his beloved six-year-old daughter, Doctor Choe Soo-jin and five base personnel. Had Eun-mi gone mad?

He was about to scream at her when another bellowing screech resounded and he finally realised what the strange shape next to the doctor actually was. At first he'd thought it was merely the peculiar skull on the stick, but now he realised it was more than that, much more.

Caught in the dazzle of the headlights, every shiny bone was gleaming. Vertebrae had replaced the stick.

"*Kirin*," he whispered.

Behind him, the General's men uttered cries of dismay when they too saw the unicorn's complete skeleton pawing at the ground with dainty, bony hooves. The dark, empty sockets of the grinning skull angled round to gaze at them and the teeth champed together, causing the tuft of reddish beard still attached to the jaw to flick and swish.

Then it bellowed again.

Gerald opened fire.

The rifle sprayed light and noise. Eun-mi rushed to drag her sister to safety against the wall, swiping the dead Doggy-Long-Legs off her head with the back of her hand and wrapping her arms round her.

The horned skeleton reared, paddling the air with slender forelegs. The bullets bounced off the white bones like dried peas. Then it stamped and kicked and gave an unearthly scream as it charged. Gerald leaped aside, but he wasn't quick enough. The unnatural creature crashed into him. The old man was flung into the air, as easily as one of Maggie's stuffed toys, and hit his head on the concrete when he fell. The unicorn galloped over him, stampeding towards the General's stupefied troops.

With its macabre head lowered, it rampaged into their midst. Screams and shots erupted as the unicorn slaughtered every soldier in its path. The single, tapering horn went slashing through the uniform of the People's Army, impaling hearts and ripping out lungs.

The bravest tried to surround it. They wrenched at the exposed ribcage, shoving their rifles inside, using them as levers to try and snap it apart. But the ferocious skeleton was too strong for them. Its limbs lashed out and it spun round wildly. Moments later, those men were on the floor, their heads torn from their shoulders. Hooves kicked out and headlights smashed. The corridor collapsed back into gloom and Doctor Choe Soo-jin continued reading aloud.

The surviving soldiers drew away from the unicorn, retreating between the jeeps. It went stalking after them. Then, one by one, they dropped their weapons and began rocking backwards and forwards, their lips mumbling in time with the doctor's. The skeleton tossed its blood-dripping head and tapped the ground as if applauding.

Standing in the centre of all this, General Chung stared around, aghast. He saw the dismembered bodies of his men and the nightmare apparition now dancing over them. He saw the entranced, smiling faces of the doctor and those with her. Then his dumbfounded gaze took in the old Englishman, lying deathly still, with Maggie crouched at his side, tearfully calling his name. Finally he saw Eun-mi, shielding her sister from the surrounding horrors.

Shakily, the General stepped towards them. His head was buzzing and felt light and giddy. A cold breath blew on the back of his neck and the corridor seemed to peel away, revealing the blue sky of a summer day where the towers of a white castle rose tall and majestic.

General Chung yelled in protest and he was in the corridor once more. The words of the book were burning inside his mind, consuming his will and strength. He clenched his teeth and swayed unsteadily. He had to fight it, he had to resist. He had to stop the destruction of everything he was, stop that overwhelming, leaching force.

Raising a quaking hand, he shot Doctor Choe Soo-jin through the head. She dropped like a stone. At once, and without blinking, one of the guards with her picked up the accursed book and continued reading from where she had left off.

Shafts of sunlight came breaking through the crackled paint of the ceiling. Birds were singing in the trees. The General's shoulders sagged and his legs bowed. The infernal words were raging through his brain.

His thick eyebrows clashed and he snarled in agony. The torment of resisting was unbearable. Shrieking, he snatched up Gerald's discarded rifle and emptied the magazine into the guards and technicians. He had to silence the words. He had to save the Republic from the contagion of this foul, Western disease.

Breathing hard, he let the AK-47 fall. But the words had not been silenced. A single voice was still reciting the opening passage from *Dancing Jax*.

Once more the paint flaked from above and sunlight came streaming in. He heard a lute playing and happy voices singing.

"No!" he raged.

The General threw off his hat and clawed his scalp. He would not be able to resist much longer. Desperate and driven half mad, he turned to that one remaining voice and raised his pistol to silence it.

Still held tightly in Eun-mi's arms, Little Nabi's glassy, doll-like eyes stared back at her father as she chanted Austerly Fellows' bewitching words.

General Chung lurched forward and pressed the gun to her young forehead.

"Stop!" he ordered. "Stop!"

Eun-mi could not believe what he was doing.

"No, Father!" she begged.

"Stop!" he repeated when the six-year-old continued as if he was not there.

Terrified by his insane, murderous expression, Eun-mi covered her sister's mouth and implored him to put the pistol down.

The General glared at her. There was a demented light in his eyes and she hardly recognised him. His nostrils quivered and he sniffed her suspiciously. Why was she not affected? Why was she still in control? Couldn't she hear the songbirds? Couldn't she feel the sunshine beating down? How could she stop her feet from skipping to the merry tune of the minstrels? All the other young maidens were cavorting on the green with their gallants. What was she? Why was she different?

"Ab... b... aberrant," he stuttered thickly and he began to growl.

"Father!" Eun-mi wept.

"I am the Six of Clubs – head bowman of the outer wall!"

"No, Father! Come back to us!"

The sunlight dimmed and the man shivered. He moved the gun from Nabi's head and put it against his own. This was the only escape for him.

"Don't!" Eun-mi yelled.

Reaching out to him, her other hand slipped from Nabi's mouth. The six-year-old instantly resumed spouting *Dancing Jax*.

General Chung's face contorted. In an unhinged fury, he rounded on Nabi again. The barrel of the gun pushed against her temple and his finger closed over the trigger.

"Father!" Eun-mi screamed.

A single shot blasted out.

Cowering with terror and filled with despair, Maggie was nursing Gerald's head in her lap. He was deathly pale and it was too dark to tell if he was breathing. With jittery fingers, she fumbled for a pulse, but couldn't find one. The gunshot cut through her desolate sobbing and she turned to see General Chung Kang-dae slump lifeless to the floor. A thin wisp of smoke was rising from Eun-mi's own pistol.

Eun-mi's eyes were wet and sparkling, but she appeared frozen and unaware of what she had done. Then, slowly, she tilted her head and stared at the weapon in her hand. At that moment nothing else existed for her, just the gun and the painful scratch of her own voice as it tried to howl.

Nabi disentangled herself from her grasp and stepped casually over their father's body.

"I am the Five of Spades," she chirped dreamily. "I am naughty Posy, the Constable's daughter. I spy on everyone in the castle and know all their secrets. Blessed be."

The six-year-old retrieved the copy of *Dancing Jax* from the dead guard then strode past her trembling sister, to join the unicorn and the soldiers who were anxious to hear more of the sacred text. Little Nabi greeted them with a gurgling laugh. Cheering, they lifted her on to the skeleton's back and she rode haughtily through the tunnels – towards the main concourse and the booth that housed the microphone for the tannoy system.

In the refectory, the other refugees finally dared to creep from under the tables and ventured to the doorway. With horrified faces, they looked out at the carnage in the corridor.

Maggie was huddled over Gerald, stroking his forehead – bereft and grieving.

"In fields where they lay," she sang in a halting, tuneless whisper, "keeping their sheep. On a cold winter's night that was so deep."

The girl wiped her streaming eyes.

"Goodbye, Gerald," she sniffled. "You're safe now. Safe from DJ. Reckon I'll be seeing you soon. We'll have a merry Christmas then, won't we, eh? Me, you, my Marcus and Charm. Give them my love and don't start on those chocolate mincies till I get there. Promise me now."

Throughout the mountain base the tannoy crackled into life and little Nabi's voice began to read...

9

LEE WAS JOLTED AWAKE. His four guards were yelling and shaking him roughly. He looked up and found himself lying on the ground, with them standing over him. Their young faces were angry, fearful and wrought with panic. Shouting at him in Korean, they pulled on the chains attached to his wrists and forced him to sit upright.

"Quit that!" the boy barked at them, giving the chains a vicious tug back that almost wrenched the nearest guard off balance. "Give me a second to wake the hell up. I feel like crap."

Ignoring their continued cries, he looked about. It was a deliciously warm afternoon and they were in a forest. All around them, the leaves were intense shades of gold, red and orange and the sky was an unbelievable blue. Beneath the branches, fallen chestnut casings were in abundance, split open – displaying cream-coloured flesh and the fattest, shiniest, chocolaty-brown fruits. A faint and delicate scent of sweet-smelling woodsmoke laced the air, combining with the damp must of rich, fertile earth. Early autumn in Mooncaster was a ravishing feast for the senses, just like every season here.

Lee felt nauseous. This time the crossing had been different. He still felt groggy and exhausted and bile burned the back of his throat. Remaining seated, he shifted around and saw that the trees stretched far into the distance in every direction. Whatever forest this was, they were deep in the middle of it. He had no idea exactly whereabouts in Mooncaster they were. There was no landmark in sight to help him.

"Don't matter," he told himself. "We ain't hangin' here longer than we have to." But he wasn't looking forward to the trip back if it was as rough as the journey getting here. His innards felt like they'd been put through a blender.

Looking up at the guards' rifles, he hoped Gerald had removed the real versions from their sleeping selves back in North Korea and was making good use of them this very minute.

"Tough if he ain't," Lee said aloud. "Cos we is outta here."

Rising to his feet, he tried to get the guards to calm down.

"Hey, Sporty!" he said, calling them by their Spice Girl nicknames. "Enough with the whinin', and Scary, if you nudge me with that rifle butt one more time, I is gonna leave you here, I swear to God."

The guards waved their arms and continued to shout.

"Yeah – yeah," Lee said. "It's mad, it's off the hook, but stressin' out and boohoos won't do no good, ladies."

Suddenly, close by, there was a furtive rustling. The guards leaped around in alarm and 'Baby Spice' opened fire. The autumnal peace erupted with a blizzard of bullets that went ripping through the undergrowth and a tree trunk splintered as lead hammered into it. A red squirrel fell from a branch and another half-dozen shots made it jump and twitch before the nervous guard realised what it was and ceased firing.

The others stared across at the thoroughly dead animal, then began to snigger in embarrassment. Their shared tension had been released and they gave Baby teasing punches on his arm.

Lee shook his head at them. "You all got that outta your systems now, yeah?" he asked warily. "That weren't cool, you assholes. That furry bullet bag coulda had somethin' to say – you have no idea what the zoo life is like round here. That coulda been anythin'. That was dumb, guys – real baseline dumb! Trigger-happy ain't the word; trigger-hysterical is what you is. You need to frost up, right now, 'fore one of us gets capped the same way."

The guards had no idea what he was saying. They pointed at the squirrel and laughed. It was the only time Lee had ever seen them display any jubilant emotion. Their relieved, joking chatter sounded weird in this place. One of them, the thinnest, and usually the surliest, was the first to become grave once more and lifted the chain that tethered him to Lee's wrist. Then, with urgent gestures, he mimed the boy taking them away from here.

"You got it, Posh," Lee agreed. "That's what I is 'bout to do – take us back over that rainbow. This messed-up Oz has got enough crazy muthas in it already; it don't need four more with guns, what don't speak local."

After several frustrating minutes in which he tried to indicate what he was going to do, he finally had them lined up on either side of him. They were on an overgrown forest path and, by scissoring his forefingers, managed to demonstrate that they were going to run along it a little way and wake up back in the medical room.

"In North Korea," he said, nodding his head slowly. "DPRK – yeah?

That crap heap, ass end of nowhere. We go back there, mkay?"

"Kay!" affirmed Scary and Posh Spice on his right.

"Kay!" chimed in Sporty and Baby on his left.

Lee took a moment to compose himself and crunched his neck muscles a few times. Glancing along the forest path, he reckoned they'd be back in the mountain base before they made it past three trees. What they'd find waiting for them back there, however, was an entirely different matter.

"You'd best be long gone when we get back, old man," he muttered. "These ladies is burnin' to shoot something bigger than squirrels."

Closing his eyes, he tensed and then ran forward. The chains rattled and the four guards ran with him.

After passing at least ten trees, Lee slowed to a stop and took deep breaths as he gazed about, frowning. Why were they still here? What had he done wrong? He didn't understand it.

The guards looked at one another uncertainly and voiced their confusion.

"I know, I know," the boy said. "I got me no idea neither. We go again, yeah?"

"Kay!" they said in military unison.

Lee closed his eyes again and concentrated harder than before. He thought of the familiar room, with its monitors, wall mirror and hospital bed. That's where he was going to find himself this time. No doubt about it.

With a grunt, he ran along the path, leading the eager guards.

When that attempt also failed, followed by a third, fourth and then a fifth, during which they'd held hands, the guards' keen anticipation had gone and they had reverted to shouting at him angrily.

"We should be gone by now!" Lee declared, holding his hands up. "We should be back in that dump you call home. This is not my fault."

Posh Spice had run out of patience and he turned his rifle on the boy, prodding him in the stomach to get this most basic threat across in no uncertain terms.

"Hey!" Lee yelled. "You do somethin' crazy an' there's no way you're gonna get back, stupid."

The others seemed to agree with him and they shouted at Posh in Korean, pushing the barrel of the Kalashnikov away.

Posh railed back at them and Lee let them bawl at each other. He tried to work out what he was doing differently. There'd never been any trouble getting back to the real world. He had flitted in and out of this twisted place at will. Mind you, he'd never had to take four adults with him, but there hadn't been a problem bringing them here in the first place.

"Yeah, but that weren't down to me," he told himself. "I was dragged here, like when I brought Spencer and Maggie back in the camp. Maybe I got me a two-person max limit?"

"Hey, ladies," he called, interrupting their argument. "Let's try this again, but different this time. Just two of you come with me. I'll bounce straight back for the others, yeah?"

He tried to show them this new idea by pretending to remove one of the cuffs from his wrists and leaving with just two guards. The four men scowled at him, perplexed, as he repeated the actions again and again. It was Scary who grasped his meaning first and he rapidly explained it to the other three. The proposal was not met with joyous approval and they shouted at Lee louder than before. None of them wanted to be left here, even for a short while.

"Then we is stuck!" he told them fiercely. "I can't think of no other way."

Lee kicked the top off a toadstool that was growing at the side of the path. Perhaps he was just too damn tired. Maybe, if he gave it a bit more time, his mojo, or whatever it was that made him the Castle Creeper, would be back to full strength and there'd be no problem. He hoped that's all it was.

"Listen up," he announced. "We need a time out. I gotta park and recharge."

But the guards wouldn't let him sit down. They had got it into their heads that the only way to get home was to keep moving and he couldn't make them understand that wasn't how it worked. They were determined to march down the track and see where it led to. Chained to them the way he was, there was nothing Lee could do except be pulled along.

"This won't get you no place," he objected, trudging along unwillingly, "'cept mebbe dead. This neighbourhood is full of monsters you never dreamed of. We're gonna end up toasted if you don't stop – right now!"

They refused to listen. He had had his chance and failed. Seeking refuge in the familiar, they started singing 'No Motherland Without You', the signature song of Kim Jong-il, at the top of their voices in Korean.

"You pushed away the severe storm.
You made us believe, General Kim Jong-il.

We cannot live without you.

Our country cannot exist without you!"

They marched as if they were on parade and Lee groaned. He hadn't realised just how accurate he had been, referring to this place as a messed-up Oz. Here they were, prancing through the forest, singing and looking for a way home. All they lacked was a yellow brick road. Even their number tallied with the characters in that old movie.

"As long as I'm the dog," the boy grumbled. "No way am I one of them other suckers. Woah, am I glad no one I know can see me right now."

When the guards had finished that song, they began another. It bolstered their confidence in this strange place, but Lee's unease mounted. Whatever lived in this wooded corner of Mooncaster was more than aware of their presence. He was sure they were being watched, but by what?

The third stirring, patriotic song came to an end. The North Koreans were in a better humour and they debated what to sing next. Scary Spice turned to Lee and invited him to start one, signalling that they would join in. The boy shook his head in disbelief.

"You yankin' me?" he cried. "Ain't no way..."

Then, in spite of their predicament, or maybe because of it, he was struck by a sudden notion and a slow, mischievous grin spread across his face. He wondered if he could remember the words...

Presently he was leading the guards in an excruciating, out-of-tune rendition of the old Spice Girls song, 'Wannabe'.

"You wann be ma lovah, you got get wi' ma frenn," the guards sang heroically, repeating what he had taught them, but not understanding any of the words. "I wann-ah, I wann-ah, I really really really wann-ah zig ah zig hah!"

Lee was in creases. He couldn't believe he had got them to do it. It was so surreal and he wished Maggie had been able to share this; she would have got such a kick out of it, seeing them march in their uniforms, mangling those lyrics. No one would ever take his word for it. But then he probably would never see any of the other refugees again. For all he knew, they might be dead by now. Gerald's pathetic escape plan never had a chance.

"Hell," he hissed, pushing that thought away and returning his attention to the guards. "This makes me Geri, don't it? Man, that blows!"

The meandering path gradually began to take a steady downward course as the land dipped into a valley. Lee guessed they were skirting round one of the thirteen hills, but he was completely lost. Along the edge of the track, the toadstools now grew in dense clusters. They were large and ugly, with greyish-brown, leathery caps, dotted with pale spots, and, as the terrain sank lower, the toadstools grew taller.

A glimmer of recognition sparked in the back of Lee's mind. He was sure he had read about this in Austerly Fellows' book. This exact place was mentioned – but he couldn't recall why or what happened here.

"Where is you when I needs you, Sheriff Woody?" he muttered, knowing that Spencer would have remembered without hesitation. Geeks really had their uses. But Spencer was probably lying face down on the mountainside back in the real world, his body peppered with bullet holes. Lee ground his teeth together. There was nothing he could have done to stop that. He just had to keep focused on what he wanted.

Some of the toadstools were as high as his waist now. Up ahead, they loomed over the pathway. The afternoon was slipping into evening and, beneath the trees, the shadows deepened.

The guards stopped singing. They too were growing uncomfortable and they stared at the oversized fungi with suspicion. Sporty raised his rifle and tapped one tentatively. A cloud of bloated flies came buzzing from the gills beneath the cap and everyone sprang back.

"We come the wrong way," Lee declared. "This ain't takin' us no place good."

He was about to signal the others to turn back when a high, squeaky voice began to sing.

"Tra la la, tra la lee.
Who is this that I can see?
Five fine fellows on a strolling spree,
finding their way to merry me."

On to the path leaped
a strange little
creature. It was
a long-legged
goblin, wearing
striped woollen
stockings under a
soft leather tunic,
over which was a

waistcoat of orange velvet. A hooded cape was fastened under his chin and a pair of pince-nez was balanced on his sharp nose.

It was like an Arthur Rackham illustration come to life. Both eyes were bright green, but one was larger than the other. They gleamed in the gathering dusk and the golden buckles on his pointed brown shoes glinted as he capered in a dainty, twirling dance.

"We shall play some games, but I shall win,
for my name is Nimbelsewskin.
I like to snip and stitch and mend.
Each of you I shall make my friend..."

The four guards opened fire simultaneously – yelling as the AK-47s blasted the goblin back down the path.

When the shooting was over, they were out of breath and smiling at a job well done.

"Oh, you dumb, dumb asswipes," Lee uttered in shock and disgust.

The guards pulled him over to where the goblin's body lay across the path and they stared at it with intense curiosity, prodding and nudging it with the toes of their boots.

"Hey, the guy's dead, OK?" Lee said, suspecting that if one of them had a camera they wouldn't waste any time in getting snapshots of themselves with their fresh kill. They were so excitable they'd be plastering any such photos all over Twitter and Facebook. But social media didn't exist here in Mooncaster – or back in North Korea.

"Silver linings," the boy commented dryly.

He glanced down. The goblin had been about the same height as little Nabi and there was a look of blank surprise on its face. He felt sick and wanted to get away, but the guards were still gawping.

"*Dokkaebi!*" they exclaimed several times over. "*Dokkaebi!*"

It was the Korean word for a mischievous sprite. Posh was sceptical, but Sporty whistled through his teeth and his eyes opened wide with amazement. He had always loved those old stories his grandmother had told him when he was very young.

He and the others pointed to the uncanny features, the like of which they'd never encountered, then scrutinised the clothing. The waistcoat lapels were stuck through with a collection of threaded needles of different shapes and sizes and, strapped to one knobbly wrist, was a large and crowded pincushion. Cotton bobbins of various coloured twine had tumbled from the waistcoat's many pockets and a tiny pair of scissors was strung across the stomach, looping about the gold buttons on a fine chain. A silken tape measure was draped round its neck.

"Congratulations," Lee said bitterly. "You done murdered some kinda tailor. Guess that explains why you people dress like crud. We done here now? Show over, yeah?"

The guards were satisfied and Sporty was still grinning. They were about to retrace their steps along the path when a new sound came bellowing through the trees.

"What the hell is that?" Lee whispered.

It was a deep, baying howl. None of them had ever heard anything like it before. Some large beast was crying mournfully, back there, behind them.

Even though the efficacy of their rifles had just been proven, the guards didn't like the sound of whatever this new creature might be.

There it was again – a bass lowing like a nightmarish mongrel of cow and bear.

"I don't think we should go back after all," Lee said quietly. "Your gats work just fine on midgets, but that thing out there – that sounds way bigger. I don't wanna be around when you find out there's some things in this place tougher than Kevlar."

The guards appeared to understand and agreed, with worried nods.

Leaving the dead goblin behind, they hurried on down the sloping path. The toadstools soon towered over them and mossy roots crisscrossed the way, forming a natural, uneven staircase as the ground sloped ever more sharply. Then, abruptly, the trees and the toadstools opened out and they stumbled down into a wide, grassy glade. The sun was hanging low in the autumn sky, just dipping behind the surrounding treetops, its slanting light drenching everything in a deep amber glow and vibrant purple shadow.

"This damn place is made of weird," Lee muttered, staring ahead at what stood in the centre.

The guards gripped their rifles a little more tightly as they exclaimed in wonderment.

In the middle of a closely clipped lawn that was freckled with daisies and buttercups, bordered by the vivid colours of hollyhocks, lupins, foxgloves, snapdragons and loosestrife, was a picturesque, circular cottage made from woven hazel twigs and roofed with bark. It was built around three enormous toadstools that reared up between two stone chimneys and whose broad, domed caps provided extra shelter from bad weather. The chimney pots had been fashioned in the form of comical, expressive faces and the smoke that curled from the top of their terracotta heads was pale green and smelled of burnt sugar and fried onions. At the front was a low wicker door and here and there were little windows of leaded glass, whose diamond panes winked in the sun's failing rays. It was an idealised, child's vision of a fairy dwelling.

Behind this twee building rose a gnarled and ancient oak, the greatest in the Realm of the Dawn Prince. Its serpentine boughs twisted over the tops of the three toadstools and were heavy with golden leaves. But other things were hanging from those branches. Bundles of garments of every sort – jerkins, hose, scarves, kirtles, cloaks, tunics, hoods and hats – dangled down like cloth fruit.

"Must be laundry day," Lee muttered. "But that's gotta be a year's worth of wardrobe up there."

He lowered his head, remembering that Charm's mother had been a laundress in this world. He wished he hadn't been so consumed by grief after escaping the camp in England. If he had only taken time out to help her deal with her despair, Mrs Benedict might still be alive. Even though he'd dreamed about it most nights since, it was going to be real tough to finally tell Charm her mother was gone, when they were reunited here.

The North Koreans were hesitant about stepping out on to the lawn and venturing near the strange cottage, but they stared, entranced, at the abundant flower borders. They were the loveliest they had seen. Even in Pyongyang there were no blooms to match the intensity and perfect beauty of those growing here. A sea of heavenly perfume flowed out from them and the four members of the People's Army breathed deeply as memories of their childhood began to stir and they recalled things that had been suppressed or forgotten and dreams that had been forbidden. Even Posh's perennial scowl lifted.

Another roar behind them wrenched them all back to the present and they hurried over the grass.

Lee wasn't happy about approaching the cottage either. There was no telling who or what might live there. The woods in this Kingdom were full of peculiar creatures that weren't even mentioned in Austerly Fellows' book and he'd learned that the most innocent and sweetest-looking places could harbour the worst dangers. But what other choice was there? As they crossed the lawn, he strained and concentrated, trying once more to return them back to the real world, but it was no use.

Stepping on to a central path made from wide, flat stones, they passed beneath the shadow of the radiating oak branches and moved cautiously closer to the cottage.

There was no movement behind those leaded windows; no sharp little face peered out through the half-open door. The stillness and silence were even more unsettling.

"Hey!" Lee called. "Anyone in there? We just wanna find out where we is. We got ourselves lost."

There was no answer. Sporty Spice was gazing up at the laundry dangling down from above. He said something to the others and they too stared upwards.

"Is you in there?" Lee continued. We ain't lookin' for no trouble or aksin' for nuthin'."

He waited but there was still no reply. Turning to the guards, he found them pointing and chuckling at the branches.

The boy frowned at them. What were they staring at? He glanced up.

What he had taken to be drying washing was nothing of the sort. Suspended from those branches were scores of dolls, or puppets, he couldn't tell which. The oak was crowded with them. They were all shapes and sizes, but they were crudely made, with large stitches and deformed faces and misshapen limbs that didn't match or line up with one another. Several held musical instruments; most of them were supposed to be children or odd, gnomish folk with long beards, but there were also rabbits and dogs, squirrels and badgers, and the occasional maiden with long golden tresses and painted red lips.

"I never even liked the Muppets," Lee said. "But them things is ugly as."

The way they twirled and twisted in the slightest breath of wind was creepy. They looked like they'd been hanged and the tree was an enormous gallows. Turning away, he spat on the grass.

"I don't think no one's home," he said, nodding at the cottage. "And we ain't gonna find out squat stood here. Dammit."

He led the guards to the wicker door and pushed it warily.

The interior was snug and cosy and cluttered. Just inside the entrance was a cloak rack, with upturned hooves for hooks and a different hooded cape on each one. The floor of the main room was bare earth, strewn with rosemary and rushes and circular rag rugs. Scraps of fabric of various colours and quality were scattered all over and tucked into every corner. Patchwork quilts covered the walls and kept out the draughts, and a pair of embroidered portraits of two elderly goblins hung above the stone fireplace in oval frames. The brass coal scuttle by the hearth contained balls of wool instead of fuel, and oversized knitting needles, one of them made of gold, were in place of fire irons.

The room was dominated by the three toadstool stalks, rising from the soil like stout woody pillars. A great worktable took up half the space, on which the latest puppet was being made. The half-finished, understuffed head was waiting to be completed and the cut-out panels to make its arms, legs and body were in a neat pile close by. Next to them was a large glass jar brimming with beads and buttons, ready to provide the eyes, and a sack of hay and straw was there to fill it all out.

Lee's eyes fell on the gleaming array of tools that had been ranged with obsessive precision along the table's front edge. There were three pairs of scissors of different sizes, four silver knives with bone handles, a golden buttonhook, a piece of blue chalk and a row of thimbles.

Beside the table was a strange chair. It was crafted from a honey-hued wood, but the turned struts that supported the arms ran through a collection of reels holding rainbows of coloured cotton. Attached to the back was a spinning wheel, worked by a treadle beneath the foot rail, and a spindle holding a tall bobbin of pink wool spiked up at one of the corner stiles. Set into the arms were little drawers with brass handles. Lee pulled one open. It contained rolled-up ribbon and the next held brass buckles and tiny bells. He closed it with a tinkling jingle.

"Explains why no one's home," he said. "This crib belonged to that tailor guy you dumb ladies gunned down back there. Poor sucker."

The guards didn't understand. They were fascinated yet still half afraid of this place. It smelled strange. Beyond the logs that crackled in the grate, giving off the green, scented smoke, there was a sickly, rotten musk on the air that increased their fear.

Then Baby held up one hand and shushed the others.

A slow, steady dripping could be heard somewhere nearby. It wasn't outside, it was in here, but where and what was it? They looked under the table and up at the rafters, but couldn't locate the source. Finally Scary moved closer to one of the quilted wall hangings and gave a hiss. It was behind there.

The Kalashnikovs came jabbing forward and Scary drew the hanging aside.

An instant later, Lee was yelling in shock with them and they all jumped back at what had been revealed.

"Hell!" the boy yelled. "That is hardcore sick!"

Behind the quilt was a second smaller room. Large iron meathooks were fastened to the ceiling beams and knives and saws were ranged across two walls. It was a slaughterhouse.

A hoard of bones, not quite picked clean, was stacked to one side like a gruesome log pile and, suspended from one of the hooks, was a little wizened creature with a long grizzled beard. He was a gnome from the copper mine in the neighbouring hill. His face was grey and drained. His throat had been cut and the blood was collecting in a large earthenware basin below, with drips as regular as the ticking of a clock. A watering can, also filled with blood, was beside it.

The guards shook their heads and backed away, muttering in horror. They didn't want to stay in here a moment longer. Outside the cottage, the shadows of night deepened and things began to awaken in the swelling dark.

10

Any sorrow Lee had felt for that goblin tailor flipped 180 degrees.

"That crazy wack-job!" he uttered, stumbling against the table. "What the actual hell? Was he some psycho-ass serial killer? Man! It never gets any better in this damn stinkin' hole. They got every sort of Jack in this place, including their own Jack the Freakin' Ripper!"

Reeling from the harrowing sight of that corpse, he leaned on the table and caught his breath as the guards jabbered in shrill voices. Then Lee's revulsion was swept away as a ghastly chill washed over him. He'd been staring down at the unfinished puppet and suddenly realised the carefully cut-out pieces were not made of cloth.

It looked like thick parchment, but a glance at the half-stuffed head, with its sewn-up eyelids and real hair, told him the macabre and sinister truth. This wasn't an ordinary home-made doll or a puppet in the normal sense. It was the skin of one of the goblin's victims, preserved and tanned using bark from the huge oak tree. From the size, it looked like this victim had been a young one.

What had that monster sung, just before the bullets cut him up?

This is what he had intended to do to them: lure them to the cottage and kill them, then carve them up, flay their skins and make life-size dolls with the remnants. That's what all those other things hanging in the branches outside were – the stuffed trophies of the people and creatures he had killed.

"Sweet God," Lee whispered in disbelief. "He musta been clean outta his dome."

Suddenly he clamped his eyes shut. He didn't want to see any more. There was something about the face of that incomplete head lying there...

In spite of the stitching that ran across the features, puckering one brow and part of the nose, and even though it was inadequately stuffed, and the skin was distorted, the face seemed familiar.

Lee's stomach churned and he began to breathe hard as he dared to open his eyes again. He had to be sure. Swallowing nervously, he directed his gaze towards the tidy stack of pieces waiting to be sewn up to create the body.

One of the guards was shouting at him, urging him to follow them outside. He pulled on Lee's chains and the boy roared back.

"Gimme a minute! Just one goddamn minute – you hear?"

Reaching out with trembling fingers, he touched the foul segments of skin and began sorting through them.

The guards glared at him, impatient to leave. This was an accursed, evil place. They yelled at the English boy and Posh banged the table with his fist.

Lee shuddered. He had found what he dreaded would be there. One of the largest pieces had a ragged hole in the middle, but around that tear he could still make out the silvery scarred lines that made up a capital letter J.

Jim, the poor insane boy back in the camp, who had believed he was a superhero, and whom the Punchinellos had killed with a spear, had made it to Mooncaster after all – and Nimbelsewskin had found him.

"Sleep in heavenly peace," Lee muttered with rancour. "What a joke."

He had seen enough, too much. He needed to get outside – into the fresh air before he threw up – and he let the guards tow him towards the door. Before they reached it, they heard something thud on the roof overhead. There was a scuffling sound on the bark tiles, then there was another thump and another and another. A fine rain of dust came drizzling from the rafters. Lee and the guards halted and stared up. There was more scrabbling and more bumps. What was happening?

Then shapes began dropping past the windows.

The North Koreans shouted in alarm and gripped their rifles in readiness.

"You gotta be kiddin' me!" Lee snapped. "Don't it ever let up? What now, huh?"

They edged warily to the door.

Beyond the windows, more shapes fell.

Scary was the closest to the doorway. He leaned out and his mouth gaped wide. Then he began shooting wildly. The others heard a clamour of dismayed cries, followed by an almighty, rumbling din as if an avalanche was thundering against the roof. The cottage quaked and the two framed portraits fell into the hearth. Thimbles went rattling along the table and the dead gnome swung on its hook. Scary was bawling defiantly, blasting whatever was out there.

Then the ammunition ran out.

He stared down at the AK-47 in shock. Panicking, he tried to snatch Posh's rifle off him. Posh refused and the two wrangled and argued over it as a crowd of deformed hands came reaching over the threshold. Strong fingers clutched the ankle of Scary's right boot. The man shrieked and tried to kick them away, but their grip was too strong. He hit them with his rifle butt, but that only maddened them. There were savage snarls and they pulled hard.

The guard was flung off balance and he hit the ground. More hands came grabbing at his leg, squeezing and clawing as they tore at it. Howling, he was hauled through the doorway, his fingernails scoring the earthen floor.

It happened so fast, the others couldn't stop it, but they were still chained together and were dragged after. They slammed into the doorway and uttered horrified shouts at the scene that met their eyes.

Scary's howls turned to screams.

Every one of Nimbelsewskin's victims that had been hanging from the oak tree was there – moving and yet not alive. They were animated corpse shells, driven by unclean forces that made them so much more than poorly executed taxidermy. They had detached themselves from the branches and, if Lee thought they were ugly from a distance, up close they were terrifying.

The goblin had set a devilish enchantment on them, embroidering a powerful necromancy with every stitch, singing an incantation with every fistful of straw. He reanimated them with his own malevolent will and was their master. Absolute obedience and devotion were at the very core of their unnatural being. They were his companions, his attendants, his accomplices, his servants, his slaves. There was always work for them to do. He made them toil in the garden, feeding the flowers with a mulch of their own blood and ground-up bones. They kept the windows gleaming and clipped the lawn velvety-smooth with the smallest scissors. They cured and cooked their own flesh for him and joined in the slaughter of fresh victims. In the evenings, he commanded them to play music, then he had his pick of partners to dance and cavort with.

Their faces were nightmarish. Each one was fiendish and repulsive. Paint had been applied, post-mortem, to the maidens' faces, giving them the seductive smiles of she-devils, or heart-shaped pouts, with splodges of rouge over their badly stuffed cheeks. Lashes of dark wool surrounded the glass beads and buttons of the eyes – and, due to the goblin's dark crafts, those shiny embellishments were not sightless.

All of them were attired in whatever grotesque whim had delighted him. Even the dead animals had been dressed up, decked out with bonnets and shawls and frilled aprons, which heightened the horror all the more.

The people and gnomes were creeping abominations, and they had been furnished with the power of rudimentary speech. Threats and disgusting oaths came grunting from their mouths and their filleted bodies were unnaturally strong. Scary had shot holes through a dozen or more, but to no effect.

Bawling through the gaps in their loosely sewn-up lips, they surged forward and Scary disappeared beneath them. Then they ripped and tore at his uniform.

Ramming their heels in the dirt, Lee and the other guards tried to pull him back. Clinging to the chain, in a desperate tug o' war, they trawled and strained, putting their backs into it, but they were no match for the goblin's hideous servants.

Scary's screams changed to fitful gargles and, without warning, the chain came loose. Lee and the other three tumbled backwards, into the cottage. Posh was the first on his feet and stormed over to close the door.

The others stared at the end of the aluminium chain. It had been bitten through, and was wet with blood. The sounds outside made their own blood run cold. Shaking, Sporty began to shuffle away from the entrance, throwing down his rifle, for what use was it against them? Posh thrust it back into his hands, but he pushed it away again and tears welled in his eyes. Posh shouted at him and slapped Sporty across the face, then hoisted him to his feet.

Lee blew on his wrist. The steel cuff had scraped it worse than ever.

"Hey!" he barked, holding his hands out. "Time to bust me free, yeah? We don't stand no chance leashed up. C'mon! Get me outta these!"

The guards needed no translation. They knew too well it was suicide staying like this. But there was one small problem.

"You jerkin' me?" Lee snapped when he realised what Baby's flustered mime meant. "You tellin' me the key to these is back in Korea? You dumb bitches! We is gonna die – you comprende that? We is gonna get our heads ripped off by them killer zombies out there!"

He gave a shout of frustration and kicked the wool scuttle across the room.

"No way!" he bawled. "I will not be totalled cos of you sorry-ass grunts."

Posh saw the solution and spoke rapidly to the others. Hurriedly, they unbuckled and removed their belts. The chains that looped through them dropped to the floor. Now they were free.

"What?" Lee demanded, raising his fists, dragging the chains with him. "What about me? Is that it? You gonna leave me with these?"

There wasn't time to answer. Already the disgusting rending noises had ceased outside and gore-soaked fingers were pushing against the wicker door. Posh took command. He ordered Sporty and Baby to drag the worktable over, to use as a barricade. Then he dashed into the other room and grabbed the knives and saws from the walls. If bullets were no good against those devils then perhaps old-fashioned steel would prevail. He threw the weapons down and told his men to take one in each hand. Then he turned a determined face to Lee and nodded for him to do the same.

Lee had wrapped the chains round his arms to stop them trailing and being snatched at. Seizing two vicious-looking knives, he threw his weight against the table with the guards and they waited.

The door was bowing inwards as many dead fists beat upon it. The hazel withies were snapping and the heavy table juddered.

In a small voice, Baby began to sing 'No Motherland Without You', but his two compatriots didn't join in and the words faded. Any moment now the wicker door would split apart and the goblin's reanimated victims would come bursting through. Sporty bowed his head and offered up a prayer so that the spirits of the dead would not harm them. Posh regarded him with disdain; he had always suspected that one to be tainted by the old Korean belief in shamanism. The whole family was questionable. If they ever got back home, he would report him.

Something smacked against the nearest window and Lee saw a horrendous face pressed against it. The button eyes were leering in at him and the stitched lips uttered threatening growls. The face was smeared with Scary's blood and it rubbed a scarlet streak across the leaded glass. Eager fingers started to claw and scrape at the woven walls. Animal carcasses that had kept their teeth were chewing their way in and more were pulling at the bark tiles on the roof. They were going to rip the cottage apart.

"This is so not what I had planned for my first night back here," Lee said bitterly.

With a splintering crash, the top half of the door came smashing in and Nimbelsewskin's slaves swarmed through the breach, in a murderous, unstoppable tide.

The guards sprang back and the knives slashed and stabbed. In an instant the cottage was a seething mass of flailing arms and ferocious shrieks. A knight, whose legs were too long for the armour he had worn in life, led the attack. The sword he wielded was rusted but lethal enough and it bit deep into the table, missing Baby by a fraction. As the knight wrenched the blade free, three fearsome and repellent hounds leaped in and launched themselves at Lee and Posh.

The boy swung out with his arm, and the teeth that had been left inside the dog's harrowing snout clamped ferociously about the wound chain. Lee yelled in pain. He couldn't believe the power of those dead jaws. Staggering sideways, he drove the dog against the stone fireplace. But the vice-like grip remained and it hung on. Though Lee hacked and chopped at its neck, he could not shake it loose. Another of the hounds came snapping for his legs, its mummified ears flattened against the mottled and threadbare fur of its head.

Posh was fitter and better trained than the lad from Peckham. Within minutes, the hellish dog that came ravening for him was on the ground, in twitching segments. But they were swiftly trampled as other larger things came rampaging. Roaring, Posh cut through seams and stitches, severing limbs and tearing off heads. Such was his ferocity, he drew the main force of the onslaught to him. When the knight came bearing down, sword raised, Posh's wild blows were no match for that tarnished armour. The knives glanced off and one of them twisted out of his hand. He was driven back, through the hanging quilt – into the other room, where the dead gnome was swinging on the hook. Posh dodged round it. The sword came sweeping across and the gnome was sliced in two. The knight advanced, kicking the basin of blood aside. Braced against the wall, clutching his one remaining blade, Posh tensed for a last frenzied defence.

By the toadstool stalks, Sporty had cut through half a dozen marauding corpse skins, when he was confronted by one of the dead maidens. The apparition tilted its revolting face, causing the flaxen tresses to fall across its blue bead eyes. The painted mouth buckled and issued a dismal, wretched howl. It was like a tormented plea for mercy and the Korean guard hesitated in striking out. Seeing his indecision, the maiden lunged forward and caught hold of his throat, shaking and throttling him. More of Nimbelsewskin's slaves came piling in. Holes were torn in the ceiling and smaller horrors dropped down. A freakish rabbit, wearing a little doublet and feathered cap, dived on to Baby's head and swiped at his eyes with a tiny knife sewn to its paw. The man cried out as it missed and sliced his cheek. He grabbed at the thing and hurled it away, only for it to come bounding back and leap on to his thigh.

Then, in the midst of this clamouring battle, a trumpeting bellow boomed in the forest. It was filled with anguish and distress and went echoing up into the wooded hills and across the rolling fields far away.

The effect on the attacking skins was astonishing. They fell back immediately. Uttering bewildered groans and whines, they scrambled through the broken door and rushed across the lawn.

Lee was lying on the ground; a corpse dressed as an old woman in a shawl had thrown him down and the second hound had leaped on to his chest to bite away his face. But, the moment that dreadful noise came blaring into the cottage, the dog whimpered and its lumpy tail flicked between its legs as it slunk away. The one still biting down on his arm let out a piteous whine and fled, leaving several teeth embedded in the chain.

"Dora..." the old woman moaned fretfully, dropping the knitting needles that were about to be plunged into Lee's windpipe, as she shambled to the door. "Dora...."

The same name was on many other withered lips. Even the knight hissed it as the armour went clanking out of the cottage.

What was going on?

The attack was over; only Lee and the guards were left inside.

Lee turned to them. They were cut and battered, but still alive and couldn't believe it. Posh emerged from the slaughterhouse, clutching the knight's abandoned sword. They stared at one another in confusion. Sporty closed his eyes and offered up a prayer of thanks as he rubbed his bruised throat. Baby looked searchingly at Lee for an answer.

"Don't 'woot' or wet your frillies too soon," the boy warned. "No way this is ended. You better stay on point."

Rising, he winced and swore under his breath. His leg was bitten and bleeding. He hobbled over to one of the windows and stared out.

The goblin's dead servants were moving away, over the lawn – towards the steps leading to the forest path. The guards exchanged wary glances and hurried to the doorway. Why had those terrors left so abruptly? It made no sense – and what had made that terrible din? It was the same, fearful beast they had heard earlier, the one that had driven them to this place. Were the corpse slaves frightened of it too?

Lee was just as much in the dark. Peering through the glass, he saw them congregate at the bottom of the mossy steps, where they waited, swaying from side to side, groaning and wailing.

Then something began descending. The thronging cadavers parted and Lee saw her. He saw Dora and his mouth went dry.

She threw back her frightful head and let out another bone-shivering bellow. The three Koreans trembled and felt faint. If Spencer had been there, he could have explained all about Dora. But even Spencer's knowledge, informed by descriptions in the book, would not have prepared him for the full horror of Nimbelsewskin's greatest achievement.

She was the goblin's magnificent protector, his bulwark against all enemies. In life she had been the daughter of the blacksmith in

Mooncot. Even then she had been a giant of a girl, with a hulking frame and the strength of three men. Everyone in the village was proud of her and treated the hefty girl with the utmost respect, but no boy courted her and they baulked at the very idea. One fateful, heartbreaking day, she overheard the one she was sweet on declare he would rather kiss Dung-Breathed Billy full on the lips than peck the back of her ogre-like hand.

The cruel words smote deep into her tender heart. So, at first light the next morning, she set off in search of Malinda, to beg for a love philtre or a magick glamour that would make her beautiful. But Dora soon lost her way in the great forest of Hunter's Chase and the mazes of enchantment that Nimbelsewskin had woven between the trees turned her broad feet this way – towards his cottage. It had taken all of his servants to overpower her and the result was his most splendid triumph.

What he created from her empty husk was truly monstrous. He poured his blackest, most heinous arts into every stage of her construction and, when he was done, he skipped around her, clapping his hands, overjoyed at his accomplishment.

During the tanning process, Nimbelsewskin had taken great pains to stretch and pull and tease and cajole the scraped and salted hide. So, when it was all stitched together and overstuffed with straw, the Dora slave was larger than she had been when she was alive. She was too large to hang from the oak during the day with the rest. Her place, when she was not roaming the forest with her murderer and creator, was outside the cottage, standing like a sentinel before the door that was too small to let her pass.

"Holy crap," Lee whispered to himself. "Game truly over."

The thing that stepped down on to the lawn was almost twice his height. It was wider than a bull and the arms were stout as pigs. The face was a masterpiece of vileness: a coarse, uneven jigsaw of tough, leathery patches, with a wide slit for a mouth and iron pot lids for eyes. The flattened nose was spread to one side and hanks of dark hair hung in tattered clumps about the solid, packed neck. A simple smock of calico covered the bovine frame and Nimbelsewskin had snickered and cackled with mocking glee when he embroidered a floral border along the edge and added fussy bows of pale lemon ribbon down the front. What a sublime finishing touch of irony, that something so feminine should clothe something so repugnant. He never tired of admiring his handiwork and chuckled foully to himself, praising his own consummate artistry.

But today Dora had discovered the goblin's bullet-riddled body, back there on the path, and was carrying it home. In those massive arms, Nimbelsewskin looked like a limp rag doll that had been emptied of stuffing.

When the other dead servants saw what had happened to their master, they shrieked and screamed, crowding round him, pawing and lamenting. Dora let loose one more ear-splitting howl, then bent her loathsome head down and began quaking, gulping out jarring bass sobs, until the shambling skin of the old woman spoke into one of her stretched ears and pointed an accusing finger at the cottage.

Dora's deranged sobs ended and the iron eyes glowered at the splintered door, where the North Koreans were standing, their faces graven with fear.

"End of," Lee said with flat finality.

He backed away from the window and the guards retreated from the door. They stared around helplessly. They were trapped in here, with nowhere to hide and no time to cut a way out of the back of the other room.

A rumbling snarl vibrated across the lawn.

Dora laid the body of Nimbelsewkin gently on the grass. Then she reared up, screeched in vengeful fury and charged.

Inside, Lee and the others felt the pounding of those elephantine feet.

Suddenly chaos and destruction erupted. The front of the dwelling was ripped right off and sent crashing into the flower beds. Dora exploded into the cottage with the unstoppable violence of a hurricane, pushing the rafters out of the way and toppling the chimneys. A fist, like a boulder with fingers, snatched up Baby. He was dashed against the fireplace then catapulted outside where the other servants pounced on him and tore him to pieces.

Dora's awful face swung round as the others ducked and darted aside. Diving behind the stems of the toadstools, they pulled the quilts from the walls and threw them over her head as they tried to dash and swerve past her.

Dora dragged the hangings from her eyes and uprooted one of the toadstools. There was an almighty rending of wood as the roof was ripped away with it and she sent them crashing over her shoulder, cutting off any escape. The golden leaves of the oak tree rustled overhead and the branches creaked as a strong wind came gusting over the forest. The circular walls of the now lidless cottage shook and a feral growl emanated from deep within Dora's throat as she spun round and toppled the two remaining toadstools.

Posh gave a fierce war cry and took a flying leap off the sewing chair. Brandishing the sword over his head, he brought it down on Dora's neck and chopped a notch in her thick hide. Dora screeched at him. Grabbing the weapon, she ripped it from his hands and bent it like a blade of grass in her fingers. Then she hurled him through the air. The pile of bones broke his fall, as well as his arm, and the stacked ribs, tibias, femurs and loose vertebrae collapsed on top of him.

Sporty ran to help. Dora's fist lashed out, delivering a horrific, skull-crushing punch. Sporty smashed through the back wall and was already dead by the time he smacked against the oak tree.

Dora rounded on Lee and both of those horrible hands came reaching.

Lee bared his teeth and gripped his knives for one final rumble. "Sorry, baby," he shouted above the rising gale as he thought of Charm. "Ain't gonna be with you after all."

Dora lurched to catch him. At that same moment a blizzard of autumn leaves came slamming in. It was as if they were directed by some greater power. In a thickly twisting tempest they whirled about Dora's immense bulk, blinding her and beating her back. The posts of the ruined cottage were plucked from the soil and Lee had to fling himself to the floor as the splintered walls tipped and tumbled across the lawn. A jag of lightning blasted the centre of the garden where the knight had been standing, leaving only a smoking pit. One of the dead maidens and the old woman had been standing close by and they burst into flames. The other servants of Nimbelsewskin shrieked in dismay and fled. The smaller animal skins were caught up by the sudden cyclone and went spinning over the forest, while the rest were driven into the trees.

Dora thrashed her arms and leaned into the hammering wind. It pushed and pummelled her out of the wreckage. Though her powerful legs strove against it, she was forced back and back, and baying howls were torn from her wide lips.

Lee watched her stumble away, arms flailing wildly. Then, as quickly as it had begun, the uncanny storm dropped. The swarm of leaves around Dora's head fluttered to the ground and she tottered unsteadily. Her pot-lid eyes stared up at the night sky and she let out a lowing cry of fear and doubt.

Lee rolled over to see what had scared her. Something was floating down from the darkness above.

"Get you gone, abhorrent slab of walking skin!" a severe voice called out. "Too long have you plagued the Dawn Prince's Kingdom. Your reign of horror is ended. The depraved enchantments that bind and compel you, and the rest of your filthy kind, will be undone."

Dora wavered as the figure descended. Her slow, rudimentary wits groped at the meaning of that warning. She saw the long silver wand gleaming in the newcomer's hand and heard a clap of thunder in the cloudless sky. A streak of lightning travelled across the stars and smote the oak tree. Suddenly the night was bright with flame as the remaining leaves burned furiously on the branches.

That was enough. Gibbering, she blundered away, pausing only to claim Nimbelsewskin's body. With him clamped under one arm, she went crashing into the forest and was never seen again.

The figure with the wand alighted on the ground. He turned his pale, gaunt face towards Lee and his dark eyes glinted.

"You really do get yourself into the most foolish scrapes, Creeper," the Holy Enchanter of Mooncaster greeted the boy.

Lee managed a grim, arrogant smile.

"What the hell kept you?" he demanded.

11

"OH, PLEASE," THE ISMUS said sarcastically. "Don't gush and go overboard with the gratitude. I get more than my fill of grovelling and scraping."

Lee glared back at him. "Took your time getting here," he said. "Thought you could always feel when I snuck on to your turf."

"Snuck? Ha! My dear Creeper, you practically used a wrecking ball to cross over this time – and then all that gunfire. We could hear that in the Great Hall. Old Ramptana thought one of the spells he had left cooking had gone sour and hurried to his tower in a state of near apoplexy. He was in such a fright, the Lady Labella did fear for his safety on those uneven stairs."

"Whatever. So where you been? How come you didn't show till now?"

"Because of Jangler," the Ismus retorted, and the glib, bantering tone had left his voice. "I haven't forgotten what you did, that you removed him from both worlds as if he had never existed. I thought you deserved a little of what you might call 'payback'. I trust it has been sufficiently testing and disagreeable."

"That sick asswipe earned what was comin'," Lee spat. "If I coulda made him suffer ten times over, I woulda done it with a sunny smile and my boot in his face."

The Ismus regarded him for a moment, then approached – picking his way through the debris of the cottage. The glare of the fires overhead flared and shone in the broken glass and shattered fragments of glazed pottery and dented brassware.

"What a sorry shambles," he declared, setting the sewing chair back on its legs. "I've been meaning to deal with this irksome goblin for some time. Neighbours can be such a nuisance. But you know how it is, always something else to attend to. He really was a busy little necrodancer. What a lot of grisly skin puppets he made. Dolls are so 'other', aren't they? It was rather an impressive collection and it seems almost a shame to destroy the rotten fruits of his labours, but I'll dispatch Captain Swazzle and his fellow warders tomorrow to hunt those frightmares down. The Punchinellos will enjoy that. Be a jolly outing for them."

As he stepped through the rubble, silhouetted by a flurry of burning leaves and glowing embers, he cast his eyes over the broken bric-a-brac, stooping to search for the scattered fire-iron knitting needles until he found the one made of gold.

"Nimbelsewskin's wand," he announced, twirling it in his hand. "Most careless of him to venture out without it and leave it lying around – very sloppy. I shall give it to Malinda; she simply hasn't been herself since you stole hers. Sank into quite a depression, the poor old twinkler. A Fairy Godmother isn't much without her magick wand, specially a retired one. I don't suppose you brought hers back with you by any chance?"

He took Lee's stony silence as a negative.

"No, I didn't think you had. Not the most intelligent decision. That wand can only do damage in your world, serious damage. It really isn't just a pretty stick, you know, in spite of what I may have told you."

Lee's brow lifted in pretend concern. "Oh, shame," he said. "Why don't you fetch it here yourself?" Then he laughed harshly. "Oh, yeah, I forgot – you can't do that stuff, can you? There's only me what can UPS from here to there and back again."

The Ismus directed a look of wry amusement at him, then continued, holding up the golden knitting needle. "No matter, perhaps this will put a smile back on her..."

His words ended abruptly as a knife came singing through the air. Blazing with reflected flame from the crackling fires, it barely missed his head before stabbing deep into the ground some distance behind.

Unruffled, the Ismus turned. Lee did the same and was astonished to see one of the North Korean guards standing in a slew of bones, breathing hard and in obvious pain.

Through grinding teeth, Posh swore that he would not have missed if his arm had not been broken.

"How fortunate for me then," the Ismus replied in perfect Korean. "But how very unlucky for you."

He retrieved something else from the floor – one of the discarded AK-47s.

"Dear me," he said. "Such a number of hazardous things left unattended around here."

Posh made to run, then changed his mind. He was no coward; he was a soldier of the People's Army. He would not show his back to the declared enemy of his nation. Not wanting to die unarmed, he took up one of the leg bones and stood his ground, proud and defiant.

"Wait!" Lee shouted to the Ismus. "You don't need to do this. Let me take the guy back. He don't belong here."

"Take him back?" the Ismus repeated with a snorting laugh. "You still don't fully understand, do you? Haven't you worked it out yet? You can't take him back. This time you bulldozed your way into the Dawn Prince's Realm, and broke the bridge behind you. There's no going back for you – ever."

"Bull!" the boy said. "I'm the Castle Creeper. I can duck out whenever I want."

"You could flit between your world and that of *Dancing Jax*, yes."

"That's what I just said."

"Except this isn't *Dancing Jax*, not any more."

"Huh? What you sayin'?"

"You've barged your way into the furtherance I have written, the new text that shall expand and enrich that earlier work. Rules and laws are slightly different now, and so are many other things that you may, or may not, find amusing. Think of it as an upgrade. This is the land of *Fighting Pax*, and you've hacked your way in several days ahead of release. No one is supposed to have access to this yet and, as a result, I'm sorely afraid, there's no returning for you. You're locked in here – for good, as they say."

Seeing the blank surprise on Lee's face as this sank in, the Ismus chuckled.

The Korean chose that moment to rush at him, brandishing the leg bone and yelling at the top of his voice, praising the revered memory of Kim Il-sung. He knew what would happen and he ran to embrace it.

The automatic rifle pumped out death and the guard was cut down – an exultant expression on his face. The Ismus tossed the Kalashnikov away.

"The Punchinellos in the other place do adore those noisy toys," he remarked mildly.

"You just wasted Posh Spice," Lee muttered in a stunned monotone.

The Ismus's smile grew even wider. "Speaking of happy homicides," he said, getting down to business, "the last time we met, I proposed a certain bargain and you were imprudent enough to refuse it. I hope that was mere reckless bravado and you've changed your mind. Your stay here will be extremely brief if not."

Lee closed his eyes. It was no use dwelling on the dead guards. Their comrades back in the mountain base were probably responsible for the deaths of his friends. He told himself these were not people he should mourn. He was right not to have learned or even asked their real names. His jaw tightened and he mentally closed the door to any feelings of sympathy and sadness. He couldn't afford to be weak here. He had to stay focused, remember what he wanted most of all, the person he would sacrifice everything for.

His eyes opened.

"Take me to her," he demanded.

"Now, now," the Ismus chided. "You have to perform that certain task for me first. You have to kill the Bad Shepherd."

"I know what you want me to do," the boy answered. "But I ain't doin' nuthin' till I know you ain't lying. I want to see her 'fore I do another damn thing."

"Do you doubt I am able to uphold my side of the contract? I find that vaguely offensive."

"Just do it!"

The boy struggled to his feet and almost fell down again. He had lost a lot of blood from the bites in his leg.

"We should get you to the Court Physician," the Ismus told him. "Those wounds need attention and the blacksmith can remove the cuffs from your wrists. Just don't mention anything about Dora. I don't think he'd be able to concentrate on the job if he knew what had happened to his daughter."

"No!" the boy shouted. "I gotta see her, or there is no deal and you might as well empty the rest of them bullets in me. Take me to her now – take me to Charm."

The Holy Enchanter frowned with annoyance, but there was no way around it. Even so, the boy couldn't walk anywhere with that leg. He gazed over the rubble and saw the perfect thing.

Returning to the sewing chair, he brushed the dust and dirt off the seat and invited Lee to get on.

"I don't need no rest!" the boy told him angrily. "I said take me to her."

"That is what I am attempting to do. I am not, however, going to carry you all the way. Battle Wood is many leagues from here."

"Don't you got no horse you can whistle up?"

"That would be useful certainly, but it wouldn't address the problem we'd encounter upon our arrival. The fortress in which she sleeps has no entrance. This really is the only way; now do please sit down."

Lee still refused. The Ismus shook his head wearily and took a small jar from a pocket of his velvet tunic. It contained the yellowish-grey minchet ointment and he spread a little over the chair arms and around the spinning wheel at the back. Then he gave the spokes a push and set the wheel in motion.

The wheel revolved with a *clackety-click* and the treadle beneath the seat see-sawed. Almost at once, the whole chair began to shudder and it jerked and tilted along the ground before giving small hops, as if it had the hiccoughs. Then it rose into the air and the Ismus had to catch hold to stop it drifting out of reach.

"Get on," he repeated.

Lee almost laughed.

"Shut up!" he said in disbelief. "You 'spect me to get on that fool granny ride and look a dick? No way!"

"Then you will never see Charm," came the flat response.

Lee swore but he had to submit. He limped across to where Nimbelsewskin's chair was bobbing above the ground and planted himself on the seat. The chair bumped back to the floor, then rallied and floated up again.

"Hold tight," the Ismus advised.

With his own silver wand in one hand and the goblin's in the other, he spread his arms wide and glided effortlessly upwards.

Lee gripped the arms of the chair and it rose swiftly. The wreck of the cottage, the blasted garden, the wind-torn flower borders and the bodies of the North Korean guards were left far below.

The spinning wheel on the chair's back clacked and whirred and the strange conveyance flew up in front of the burning oak tree. The heat was blistering and, for one suspicious moment, Lee wondered if the

Ismus had tricked him and was going to pitch him into the flames. But the chair continued to soar. It passed through the pall of black smoke and glimmering ashes and the tree was soon a beacon in the distance behind them.

Drenched in cold sweat, Lee glanced at the Ismus. The Holy Enchanter was some distance ahead, flying fast and steady, his hair and the tails of his tunic streaming in the high night air. The breeze made the boy's wounds ache and throb and his fingers tightened about the chair arms. It was worse than he had claimed and the likelihood of him passing out was a real possibility. He knew if that happened he would fall and that would be it. Taking deep breaths, he stared about him and tried to stop thinking about the pain. He had to remain conscious.

The stars were scintillating points of white, blue and silver, larger and clearer than any in the real world. Away to the right, over the far, eastern hills, a full milky moon was rising. Its light was strong enough to cast long shadows over the land. Beyond the forest, Lee could see the fields and pastures of the small, isolated farms that skirted the realm of Mooncaster. In the far distance, the majestic walls and turrets of the White Castle reared above the landscape. The effulgent moon made its stones shine like snow and turned the moat to tinsel. It was a ravishing spectacle, the most beautiful castle ever imagined. The sight of it inspired loyalty and belonging and a desire to be ruled by an absolute, but benevolent, monarch.

Lee hated every part of it and liked to imagine what a nuclear warhead from North Korea really would do: a vast smoking crater, scorched fields and charred forests, heaps of cinders where the Punchinellos had stood... This apocalyptic musing put a smile on his lips.

But nothing marred the serenity of the scene laid out before him. Silken banners flew above the towers of the four Royal Houses and the windows of the Great Hall were aglow with hundreds of candles blazing on the chandeliers and mirrored sconces. In one of the smaller towers coloured lights were flickering and fizzing and Lee guessed that was where the Court Magician, Old Ramptana, was tinkering with his experiments.

Eclipsed by those mighty walls, the village of Mooncot was engulfed in the cosy dark. Only a few points of light pricked that gloom, but threads of smoke climbed from every chimney. The Ismus's subjects were content and snug in their humble, ordered existence.

Lee couldn't begin to guess what *Fighting Pax* would mean for them, or the Jaxers in the real world.

The wooded slopes rolled beneath. Peering over the side of the chair, he saw bald areas where the gnomes of the mine had felled trees for their smelting furnace. That hill, called Rustridge because it was rich in iron ore, was a honeycombed warren and their excavations ran deep. It was rumoured that their tunnels extended far beyond their boundaries. In the remote farms, when the children were awoken by strange noises in the night, their mothers told them it was the "lowly men", deep under the ground, tapping on rocks with their little picks. Digging outside their border was forbidden and the Gnome King denied such slanderous accusations at the annual tribute-bringing. But the number of gnomes among Nimbelsewskin's gruesome servants suggested that the exit to at least one such illicit tunnel was located somewhere in Hunter's Chase.

Rustridge was quickly left behind and Lee turned his gaze to the next of the great thirteen hills that encircled Mooncaster.

He saw a dark, brooding presence on the horizon. This was Judgement Hill, where, according to the book, the Dawn Prince himself had once vanquished the army of ravaging beasts from the barren wastes of Missio. In that bloody battle, he slew all but one, Mauger, their great chieftain. Then the two fought a bitter, violent contest that endured for three days and nights. But finally, upon the lofty crag known ever after as Abjure Rock, the Dawn Prince was victorious. Mauger was defeated and the Dawn Prince dragged it back to the White Castle, subduing it and bringing it to heel like a wild dog broken.

In the years that passed, trees grew densely over the carcasses of the slain army. Thickets of thorn and tortured pines thrived up there on the high, wind scoured slopes. Ivy strangled every bough and was strung between the trees like a choking web. No animal would live up there and birds would not nest. Only large bats flew over Battle Wood, but they didn't make their home in it. They roosted in the crumbling walls around the base of the Black Keep, this ancient fortress built into the highest peak.

When Lee beheld it, he forgot the pain of his wounds. The fortress was a solitary,

The BLACK KEEP

octagonal tower, spiking up into the starry heavens. Its sides were sheer and smooth, tapering towards the summit. It was taller than the Keep of the White Castle and far, far older. The Dawn Prince's battle against Mauger's army had been waged around it. Blood had been spilled against its stones, and claws and steel had left their marks, but it endured.

There were no windows and no entrance, but at the very top there was a dome, built upon eight pillars and open to the elements. Suspended within was a great lantern wrought from crystal. Its light did not spill over the surrounding countryside. It was directed down on to the flat roof and nowhere else. Not one night had ever passed without the flame burning steadily.

Lee's curiosity mounted. As the chair flew him closer, he could see that under the dome was a circular table made from the same stone as the tower itself and four figures clad in black hooded robes were seated round it.

The Ismus reached the tower before him. Lee saw the Holy Enchanter sail down and land behind the parapet. Then the boy was fascinated to watch him bow respectfully to the seated figures, who took no notice.

The sewing chair followed and was soon floating down beside the Ismus. The spinning wheel clicked to a stop and the treadle was stilled.

"This way," the Ismus muttered to Lee in an urgent voice as he circumnavigated the dome's pillars, and lifted a trapdoor set into the flagstones.

The boy hung back. He stared into the pool of lantern light, at the motionless, robed figures. They were playing cards, but the hands that held them were just yellowed and ancient bones.

The Ismus came hurrying back. "Do you want to see her or not?" he hissed impatiently.

"Who's the four dead dudes?" Lee asked.

"They are none of your concern – and they are not dead."

His words were proven when one of the figures placed a card on the table and another leaned forward to examine it.

"Poker night with the supermodels then, huh?" Lee commented.

"Miss Benedict is waiting," the Ismus reminded him irascibly.

The boy rose from the chair, cringing at the pain in his leg. To his annoyance and humiliation, he had to hold on to the Ismus's arm to keep from falling over.

Then something remarkable occurred. One of the card players diverted its attention away from the game and the shadow-filled hood turned towards them, watching their progress towards the trapdoor.

The Holy Enchanter's reaction was startling. He shielded his pale face with his hand and muttered words of protection under his breath.

Lee couldn't believe it. Here was the Ismus, the mighty Austerly Fellows, scared by something out of a heavy-metal video.

"Hey, how's it goin', bro'?" Lee called over to the table, just to wind him up further. "Be lucky, yeah – and stay sharp. Make sure them other guys cough up if you win. No welchin' on him, is you hearin' me?"

The hooded figure gazed at him a moment longer then returned to the game.

"Get down there!" the Ismus ordered when they reached the opening. "You chattering imbecile."

Lee looked down. A long flight of worn stone steps wound deep into the tower. This wasn't going to be easy, but poking fun at the Ismus would make it a whole lot better.

"Always tagged you for a gambler," he said, taking the first step. "What with the hearts and clubs crap in your book."

The Holy Enchanter waited until they were both out of sight of the card players before answering.

"You don't know what you're talking about," he said.

"Maybe you should've written *Dancing Bingo* instead?"

"That wasn't any game of chance you would understand," the man uttered gravely. "And it has been played for longer than you can begin to imagine. If you knew exactly what had taken an interest in you just now, the knowledge would sear your soul and unravel your mind."

Lee let out a derisive laugh. "I get it," he said. "That up there is one of the oh so many things you didn't put in your book. Them scraped-off skinnies were here already – way before you bust into this other dimension, or whatever the hell it is, and redecorated. You're not just a squatter, you're an illegal, ain't ya?"

The Ismus ignored him. Lee grinned despite the pain.

Their progress was slow, but the spiralling way down was lit by small silver lamps. Eventually they reached the next level. A tall archway stood beside the steps, and beyond was a huge chamber.

Lee took a moment to catch his breath. He let go of the Ismus's arm and leaned against the stonework. His head was aching and he felt weak. When he gazed into that great room, he thought the Ismus had tricked and betrayed him after all. Was he going to fly off and leave him stranded in this tower? Was this place really a prison? Had it been one huge con to shut him out of the way? He could feel his temper rising and that renewed his strength.

"What is this?" he snarled.

The room was stuffed to overflowing with playing cards. They were larger than the usual sort and had an antique look about them, with ragged edges and rumpled corners. The images on them were different to the designs he knew; there were no suits, no numbers, just pictograms of things like Famine, War, Death of a Ruler, Greed, Plague, The False Prophet, Madness, Flood, Birth of a King, Fire, Riches, Downfall of Empires, Rise of a Tyrant, Division, Blossoming Faith, Terror, Destroying Lust, Bountiful Harvest, Storm, Folly, Crossed Swords, Death of Innocents, Jealousy, The Unfettered Beast... The variety seemed endless. There were so many, they formed mountains that touched the ceiling. A channel had been created through them, leading from the archway, like a canyon through a rocky domain. Where one of the peaks had come slithering down, the pass was almost obliterated.

"There are nine levels in this fortress," the Ismus informed him. "And each is a chamber just like this. What you see here are spent cards, those that have already been played in the age-long game above. This is what happens to them when they are shed. Once they have been placed on the table, they cannot be used again. Nine levels, nine chambers; eight are repositories of spent cards, the other is stacked high with the as yet unplayed packs."

"Not so high as it was, Master Fellows," a new voice interrupted from below. "Not nearly so high as it was."

Lee turned and saw the broad head of a small, narrow-shouldered creature ascend the lower steps and enter the circle of lamplight.

It was the gloomiest face he had ever seen, with a frowning mouth that drooped at the corners, accentuated by the tufts of grizzled whiskers that sprouted there. The eyes were a dull, slate grey and heavy-lidded, and the long nose between sagged at the tip. Deep furrows ploughed across the forehead, and a flapped, cotton skullcap was tied beneath the receding chin.

The creature wasn't quite as high as Lee's knee. He wore a simple woollen tunic, belted with leather, and over that an apron. In his hands he carried a silver tray upon which was a fresh deck of cards, tied with a thin red ribbon and sealed with black wax.

"Never use the long ladder now," he said with a morose shrug. "I can reach the topmost decks with just the middler, and if that isn't tenebrous news I don't know what is."

"The game is far from over yet," the Ismus remarked.

"Much nearer the end than the beginning," the newcomer answered. "On the brink I'd say; it's getting mighty close to the brink and ready to totter."

He sucked in one cheek and chewed on it thoughtfully. Then his mirthless eyes flicked askance at Lee.

"I know you have your permissions and warrants and testaments, Master Fellows, but you shouldn't go fetching your squire to this place. It's nowhere to come gawping and goggling."

"Call me Ismus; that is my name here, you know that full well. I am the Holy Enchanter of Mooncaster."

"Yes, and my name may also be Dogsbody, or Stairtrotter, or Drudgegoat, or Fetchclod, or Workworm and any other menial honours Them Upstairs might bestow my way if ever they deigned to utter one word or several."

"Be grateful they do not. And this is not my squire. It is the Castle Creeper."

The grey eyes studied the boy inquisitively.

"Creeping, is it? Don't sound a solid reason for his face to be so dark. What's he got to be so desponding about? Let him trot up and down these stairs for half as long as I have, then he'd have cause."

"Cut the racism," Lee warned. "Or I'll dropkick your whiny Oompa Loompa ass right down them."

"And he's bleeding on my nice clean floor! I fail to see why you bring your Castle Creeper cove to this fortress to have him leak his messy blood on my scrubbed stones."

Holding the tray to one side, he scrutinised the floor and tutted loudly at the trail of scarlet spots leading from the trapdoor. It was only then Lee noticed that the legs that showed beneath the apron were hoofed like a goat.

"What is you?" the boy asked.

"A body with too much to do, day and night – and now you've brought me even more toil to keep me from my cot!"

"This, my dear Creeper," the Ismus declared, "is Grumbles, the Conservius of this tower. It is he who keeps the endless game above supplied with fresh cards and takes away the old ones."

"Would that were my only labour!" bemoaned the creature. "Who else is there to keep the lamps and the great lantern burning? Who else sweeps these three hundred stairs daily? Who else has to catch his own dinner with only an old hat on a stick and has tasted naught but bat and spider, glugged down only by rainwater, since the beginning? Who else has to brush snow off the dome and stop leaves landing on the table? Who else hasn't had a proper curl-up in his cot since before the ninth chamber was started on? Who else spent three months clearing a way through the old cards in there to make room for a bed and got buried more times than a goose has feathers? Not that I'd know what a goose looks like after all this time, for none fly over this benighted spot. Grumbles the put-upon, that's who!"

"Bed?" Lee asked, sick of his moaning. "What bed, where?"

"Why through yonder!" Grumbles exclaimed, nodding down the pathway he had made through the vast horde of used cards. "Behind that recent slippage, just go and see how hard Grumbles labours – as if Them Upstairs didn't keep him fully exerted."

Lee felt his heart beat faster and he lurched forward, unaided. The card cliffs loomed upon either side and soon he was wading through the drifts and dunes that grew higher and higher until they were up to his waist. Then he hauled and pushed his way across the surface, slithering and sliding to the top. It was exhausting work. The chains came loose from round his arms and raked the cards behind him, and his leg was agony, but he drove himself on until he could look down the other side. Then he choked back a cry.

Behind this musty scree, in the centre of a deep, cleared crater, was a gilded bed carved with intertwining leaves and flowers, overhung by a lilac awning of gossamer-like gauze. Under that, the figure of a beautiful girl lay upon a coverlet of fine ivory linen and, across the lacy bolster, her golden hair was arranged in lustrous whirls.

"Charm!" he yelled.

The boy threw himself down the slope, rolling and rattling against the carved bed base at the bottom. With cards stuck to the sticky patches of blood on his leg, he picked himself up and the silky gauze billowed before his breath.

"Hey," he murmured gently, as his eyes drank deep.

She had haunted and tantalised his dreams so often, he was half afraid this ethereal vision would melt like smoke. But there she was: Charm Benedict, more lovely than he had ever seen her. The sixteen-year-old model from Lancashire was actually lying there – for real. Even so, it was almost impossible for Lee to believe his own eyes.

There was a supernatural serenity about her. The face was pale as a winter dawn and her lips were a delicate rose. She was arrayed in a gown of creamy velvet and her arms were folded lightly across her chest. Through the tears that smudged his sight, Lee could see the subtle rising of her breast as she slept.

"Brazil nut in the room," he said softly. "I came to get you, babes. Dunno if you can hear what I'm sayin', but I want you to know there ain't nuthin' can keep us apart, you got that? Nuthin' and nobody. Not even this trashy bling I got hanging from these cuffs. We is connected, hun, and nuthin' can break it."

Raising his hand to his ear, he pulled out the diamanté stud, then lifted the gauze and leaned inside. His fingers looked coarse and brutish compared to her porcelain elegance and the links of his chains snagged the coverlet. Drawing close, he pressed the stud into one of her hands. The flesh was cool, but not cold.

"Kept it safe for you, Sweets," he whispered. "Soon we'll be together, proper and exclusive, yeah? I gotta do somethin' first. You'd prob'ly try an' stop me, but I'm gonna be real strong and sort it. Just trust me."

There was a patter of small hoofs behind and Grumbles came scampering expertly over the rustling cards, with the tray still in his hands. The Ismus floated down beside him.

"I told you I could keep my side of the bargain," he said.

"Had to be sure," Lee replied, not taking his eyes off the girl. "She likes pink though; she shoulda been dressed in pink. It all should be pink."

"Such a pretty lady," Grumbles observed. "Is she of royal lineage?"

"Only totally," Lee replied.

"Her subjects have good reason to be downcast then. They must be wretched and fraught with hair-pulling without her. Why, sometimes I steal in and gaze, just for the gladness of it. A most foreign sensation for me it is too."

"You can kiss her," the Ismus told Lee, "but it won't wake her like in old stories although, in the original Grimm version, the prince was so enamoured of the sleeping princess he did a lot more than that and she only awakened after giving birth to twins."

He gave a dirty little laugh, then added, "You could try, but even that wouldn't wake up this one. You need to fulfil your end of the contract first. That is why she is in this tower. She is not yet wholly in the Dawn Prince's Realm. That can only happen once the Bad Shepherd is dead."

Lee closed his eyes. He desperately wanted to hurt that repulsive man. He made everything sound sordid and vile. But he swallowed his temper and bit his tongue. His wounds were aching and he felt faint.

"I know what I gotta do," he said presently. "I do that one thing and she'll wake up, yeah?"

"That is the deal, yes. Once you have upheld your side, her eyelids will open."

"No tricks? She'll be my Charm? Not just something that looks like her? Not like them dead dolls of the psycho tailor? And she'll know me, yeah?"

"No tricks. She will be the same girl you knew back in the camp, with all her memories in place."

Lee held up a hand. "Not that last day," he objected. "I don't want her to know any of that – she don't need to know what they did to her."

"As you wish, so shall it be."

"And what about me? The coma version back home in that hospital room? I can only live here while I'm OK there. You gotta be sure to take care of that."

The Ismus gave his crooked smile. "Your unconscious self has already been airlifted out of North Korea," he informed him. "You will be kept in a secure intensive-care unit for as long as necessary. No harm will come to you there, you have my word."

"You know what's goin' down back there then, huh?"

"I straddle both worlds."

"So tell me."

The Ismus stared at him intently. "Your friends are all dead, I'm afraid," he said, barely concealing the relish in his voice. "They attempted some foolish escape and the North Koreans executed them without mercy. There are no survivors, not a one."

Lee could feel himself slipping into darkness. He tried to fight against it.

"Couldn't end no other way," he said with difficulty. "Told them they was dead meat walkin'."

"It might comfort you to know," the Ismus continued, "that *Dancing Jax* has now taken over the military base and is spreading into the rest of that country."

"So you finally got the whole world."

"And just in time for Christmas – I must have been an extra good boy this year."

"Must be a first for you."

"And what a Christmas it shall be... over there."

Lee turned his attention back to Charm and stroked her soft cheek with the back of his hand. He didn't want to leave. He wanted to climb on to the bed next to her, hold her in his arms and fall into a deep sleep too. But that couldn't happen. He had a task to perform. This talk of Christmas was to remind him of that – as if he needed to be.

"I had to come here," he said. "See what I was doing this for. Make sure it was real, so it'd be worth it, worth getting damned."

"You shall live as a king here," the Ismus promised. "And she will be your queen. If you wish, there will be children. Hardly damnation."

Lee planted a gentle kiss on Charm's brow.

"I gotta go now, babes," he told her. "But we'll be together real soon."

He withdrew from beneath the awning. There would be all the time in this world for kisses later, after he'd confronted the Bad Shepherd. Taking one last look at her through the misty gauze, he turned a determined face to the Ismus.

"Where is he then?" he asked. "Where is this shepherd guy and how many pieces do you want him in?"

The Holy Enchanter clapped his hands with delight. "I applaud your enthusiasm," he said. "And you have no qualms, knowing who it really is?"

"What's important to me is all I care about. You want me to waste Jesus Christ and wipe him out, making like he never existed back in the other place, just as I did to your Jangler? I says amen to that! Now tell me where he's at and gimme the biggest goddamn knife you got."

A grimace contorted his face and he felt giddy.

"First you must get that leg seen to by the Physician," the Ismus told him. "You're of no use to me in that state."

"The leg is fine. I can manage, just..."

Lee staggered. The faint he had been holding off would be refused no longer. Darkness came roaring in. He collapsed into the cards and they flew up around him like great rectangular butterflies.

"Sweet oblivion," Grumbles observed enviously. "Best escape from the travails that hound us. Would that I could swoon my cares away when the fancy took me. What luxury that is."

The Ismus stood over Lee's still form and rolled him over with his foot.

"A truly blessed Christmas for everyone," he said. "It shall be the most spectacular festive season for the entire world."

His eyes moved from Lee to the card mountains surrounding them.

"I shall need your help getting him upstairs," he told Grumbles.

Grumbles groaned. "Another burden," he complained. "Another trespass on my charity."

A brutal sneer darkened the Holy Enchanter's face and he rested his foot on the boy's neck.

"Back to the White Castle for you, Creeper," he said with scorn. "But know this: I shall never forgive you for Jangler – not ever."

12

"WELL, THAT'S JUST typical, isn't it? Look at the state of you, lounging around like some bedraggled roué. It's disgraceful and sadly pathetic at your time of life. Just what do you think you're doing? Wake up!"

"Leave me alone, Evelyn," the old man groaned.

"I shall not! See what happens when I'm absent. You slide into these slovenly ways..."

"Shut up, my head is killing me!"

"So it's drink, is it? I hope that hangover stays with you till suppertime. I always knew your weakness was the bottle, but even I never suspected you'd end up dossing down in corridors. It'll be the gutter next, mark my words. And don't you ever tell me to shut up – it's plain to me that you need my firm, guiding hand if this is what you get up to in my absence."

"Evelyn!" he shouted angrily.

His voice echoed back to him and his head throbbed even more.

"Alone and yet alive," he murmured, filling the aching silence with a quote from *The Mikado*. "Oh sepulchre! My soul is still my body's prisoner!"

Gerald Benning opened his eyes and sucked the air through his teeth.

He touched the side of his head and winced. There was a large lump where he had struck the floor.

Then he remembered.

He tried to stand, but felt so weak he had to sit down again and it was some minutes before he could manage another attempt. In that time he took in his surroundings and shook his aching head mournfully. It was bitterly cold and the base was strangely silent. The only noises were made by the wind travelling through the tunnels and banging doors. Gerald knew that could only mean the main entrance was fully open. Down the corridor, on the furthest jeep, a solitary headlight had remained intact. Hours had passed since it had been left on and the battery was almost flat. The bulb was dim, yet there was just enough light to make out the shadowy forms of corpses. The place was littered with them. So much killing, so much death. It smelled like a butcher's shop. But what about...

"Maggie!" he cried, lumbering to his feet and staring around wildly. "Maggie? You here? Hello? Anyone? Hello?"

He staggered to the refectory and looked inside. It was empty. Tables and chairs had been overturned. He tried not to imagine the struggle that had taken place here, but faces of terrified children flashed across his imagination. What had happened to them? Where were they? Crossing to the stove, he touched the metal. The fire had burned out long ago; the stove wasn't even warm.

Gerald blundered out. It was too dark to identify the dead. Slithering over congealed blood, he made his way to the nearest jeep. Because the generators on the base were so unreliable he knew every military vehicle was equipped with a kit in case of power failure and emergencies. Groping under the seats, he found what he was looking for and switched the torch on.

"Dear Lord," he breathed, when the beam revealed the gruesome horrors around him. "Please don't let Maggie and the others be here."

The next hour, as he shone the torch into those dead faces, was the grimmest of his life. The English children weren't among them, but he was too sickened to be relieved. When the beam disclosed the face of Doctor Choe Soo-jin, Gerald tried to forgive her for what she had intended to do in her zealous quest for a vaccine. But he couldn't. Instead he wondered what had happened to little Nabi and her sister. Were they somewhere here too?

Nauseated by the smell of blood, he couldn't go on with the search. He climbed the stone steps that led to the terrace and gulped down the fresh, freezing air. The fog had gone completely and the darkness of evening now covered the mountains. In the far distance, he could hear the horn of a truck honking playfully and automatic rifles firing at the sky. *Dancing Jax* had gone out into North Korea. It wouldn't take long for this isolated nation to fall, just as the rest of the world had done. Helicopters were probably already flying in from the neighbouring countries, with book drops and readings over loudspeakers. This country was finished.

Gerald leaned against the low wall. He had never felt his age weigh so heavily on him before. Steeling himself for any new grisly discoveries, he went back inside. First he investigated the small dorms, but they were empty. Then he went to Lee's room.

The lad from Peckham was not there, but his four guards were on the floor. They were dead. One of them had been shot, but the others...

their injuries were horrendous – worse than those decapitated soldiers near the jeeps. Gerald couldn't begin to guess what had inflicted these wounds, but he was more curious about the bed's new occupant. Lee was no longer here, but the body of General Chung Kang-dae was.

Gerald moved closer. There was a tender reverence to the careful way in which the General had been laid out. He looked like a deceased leader, lying in state. His arms were folded across his chest and, though his uniform was stained with blood, his face and hands had been washed clean. Only one person would have done this.

"Eun-mi?" Gerald called. "Are you here? Eun-mi?"

In the cramped space behind the large mirror, the seventeen-year-old North Korean girl uncurled from the foetal position in which she had spent the past few hours and gazed into the room beyond, where the white-haired Englishman was sweeping a torch beam over the walls. She had thought he was dead. Reaching for her gun, she rose to correct that error.

Gerald left the medical room and turned the corner into the prohibited area. The discarded mop and bucket were still there, but had been kicked to the wall. It was time to see what lay beyond those forbidden doors.

Spencer didn't know how long he had been strapped to the examination table. In spite of the enormous discomfort and constant fear, he had nodded in and out of sleep. But now his stomach was telling him, with rumbles of increasing volume, he had missed two meals and his mouth was parched. He had no idea what had occurred outside those soundproof doors, but the fact that no one had been back here couldn't be a good sign.

"Well, you wanted a bit of privacy," he reproached himself. "You got that right enough, you pillock."

He tried to persuade himself that the absolute darkness was a blessing, as it meant he couldn't see the Marshal's corpse lying on the next table. But not being able to see it was actually worse. If it moved, how would he know? Did that book have the power to resurrect? According to the Ismus it did; that's what he'd promised Lee. What if it turned dead bodies into zombies? The reanimated Marshal might slip silently off his table, or just reach across for him...

"You're such a wuss, Herr Spenzer," he scolded himself, using the nickname Marcus had given him back in the camp. "Things are bad enough without you inventing new horrors."

And then the doors opened and a light shone in. To Spencer's eyes it was blinding and he squinted as he wondered who had finally come into the lab and what their intent was.

"Spencer!" Gerald exclaimed in astonishment when the torch beam fell on the anxious boy's face. "What are... are you all right?"

"Get me off this ruddy table!" Spencer cried, overjoyed to hear that familiar voice. "I've been here like forever! What's been going on out there?"

Unfastening the buckles, Gerald told him everything he knew. Spencer uttered a horrified groan.

"It's all my fault," he confessed.

"Rubbish. How could it be? There, that's your feet done. You'll probably get nasty pins and needles so don't try and move too much straight away."

"It is my fault!" the boy insisted. "I turned Doctor Choe. I recited the beginning of DJ at her and the book... it sort of came alive. I didn't expect that. I just wanted to stop her. She was going to saw the top of my head off and take my brain out. Seriously – I know it sounds ridiculous now, but that's what she was going to do. She was round the twist, but I swear I never thought it'd lead to—"

"You've nothing to feel guilty about," Gerald assured him. "*Dancing Jax* was going to take over here anyway; you just speeded it up a little, that's all."

"Was it really a massacre out there?"

"Yes, and you'll need a strong stomach to walk through it."

"And our lot? Where's Maggie and Lee and the rest?"

"I don't know yet. I've not had a chance to search properly. They might be anywhere in the base by now, if they're here at all."

"You mean... they could be dead as well?"

"No, that's not what I mean. I've a feeling this facility has been evacuated, so don't think like that. We won't give up hope until there's no hope left. Now that's the last buckle; you're free."

Spencer flexed his fingers and stirred his stiff arms. Then he rubbed his throat and sat up gingerly.

"Can you see my glasses?" he asked. "The doctor took them and put them down someplace."

After some minutes, Gerald found the spectacles on the counter and the boy received them gladly. But the first thing he saw through their lenses was Eun-mi framed in the doorway.

Caught in the torchlight, the girl's face was a snapshot of heartbreak and hatred. Her eyes were raw and her usually neat, scraped-back raven hair was hanging loose and untidy where she had wrenched and torn at it. She looked so distressed and dishevelled that Spencer almost didn't notice the gun in her hand.

"You!" she blurted in a voice curdled with emotion. "Look what you do. This your fault!"

"Eun-mi," Gerald said gently. "I'm very sorry about your father."

"He great man!" she snapped, pointing the pistol at him. "He most brave. He... he die hero, trying to save Republic."

"What happened here?" Gerald asked softly.

The girl swallowed and took a deep breath, finding strength in her anger. "You foreigners, you happen," she said. "You soft, weak, degenerate. Think only of self and pleasure. You bad people, you breed sickness. Eternal President Kim Il-sung was wise to keep his people safe from your kind. You corrupt all you touch. You bring this disease to base, you dirty. I kill you."

"Wait!" Gerald said. "You know that isn't true now. You saw the skeleton earlier; that wasn't part of any sickness."

Eun-mi's arm drooped. "I... I do not believe in bones that walk," she said. "But... *kirin* was here. I saw what it did. I saw it kill good soldiers of Korean People's Army."

"Don't you think there's been enough killing here today? Put the gun down. Tell me, what about your sister? Where is Nabi?"

"She read book over speaker," the girl answered slowly, still feeling the shock of hearing that young voice blare from the tannoy. "Then everyone in base, they think they in fairy tale."

Gerald managed a faint smile. "But not you, eh?"

"She's one of us," Spencer murmured. "She's a reject!"

"I not like you!" she denied sternly. "My blood pure. I not weak, I not soft!"

"Er, you're not a Jaxer either," the boy said. "So we've got something in common."

A look of disgust appeared on her face.

"What else happened?" Gerald asked.

"Fat man come to take black-skin boy away."

"Where did they take Lee?" Spencer asked. "What about the others, the other refugees?"

"Out of base. I hear fat man tell soldiers take them to helicopter."

"This fat man," Gerald asked, "who was he?"

"Same as you."

"A Westerner?"

She nodded. "He look fool, in uniform of pale leather, too small for him."

"The Jockey," Spencer breathed. "The Jockey's been here – and he's got our friends."

"He's got Martin too," Gerald added. "That's why he was called away so abruptly earlier. What a mess."

"Also Nabi," the girl told them sorrowfully. "My sister, she go with them."

"Did they say where they were flying to? Which country? China, South Korea – Japan?"

Eun-mi thought back. When she had heard the Jockey's jeep arrive, she had hidden behind the mirror and witnessed everything from there.

"He say he was taking black boy to Ismus," she said. "To the new castle, for special jingle day."

"They're going to England," Gerald declared. "To that replica of Mooncaster they're building in Kent."

Eun-mi made a decision and returned her pistol to the holster. "I kill you later," she promised. "First I must find sister. Save her from fairy tale. You will help. We go to UK."

"Go back home?" Spencer cried. "That's crazy. You don't have a cat in hell's chance of finding her there and, even if you did, she wouldn't go with you now she's been turned. Besides, we won't get that far, we'll be stopped. We're aberrants – they shoot us on sight – and England's crawling with monsters from the book. Tell her, Gerald."

The old man didn't answer straight away. He was trying to think, but his head was still throbbing and he felt frail and in need of a long rest. Finally he said, "Eun-mi's right. We have to return to England. There's no point staying here or running away any longer. She wants to find Nabi and we should try to save Martin and Maggie and the others from whatever foulness the Ismus has in store for them, or at least be with them. Even if there was somewhere else to run to, there'd be no point. We're getting close to the end now, the last chapter of whatever he's got planned, and, if I'm correct, we've only got five days left."

"Why five days?" Spencer asked.

Gerald shone the torch beam on him. "Because that's the 'special jingle day' Eun-mi heard the Jockey talking about," he said gravely. "Christmas Day. Austerly Fellows isn't going to let that slip by unmarked; it'd be irresistible for someone as sick and twisted as that devil. He's going to give the world one huge and final evil gift."

"Like what?"

"I don't know, but it'll make *Dancing Jax* look like the 'Teddy Bears' Picnic' in comparison."

"We go now," Eun-mi instructed urgently.

Gerald helped Spencer off the table. The boy gave a yelp.

"You were right about those pins and needles!" he exclaimed, wincing as he walked. "Ow ow ow!"

"No waste time," Eun-mi scolded. "We hurry."

"Have you thought how we're going to get to England?" Gerald asked her. "Your country is going to be in turmoil whilst the book takes over. There'll be rioting and worse. No flights will be leaving. We don't want to get caught up in that."

"We not fly from my country," she told him. "First we use secret tunnel into China. We get plane from city nearest to border – Dandong."

"How far is that?"

"Two day in jeep if road good."

"...And if we don't get lost en route."

"Er... passports, ID, money?" Spencer put in. "We can't go anywhere without those."

Gerald dipped into the pockets of his overcoat and brought out a pack of playing cards and some safety pins. He had intended to distribute them to the other refugees earlier.

"This is the only ID we need," he said. "We'll bluff it out. China's been under DJ's influence long enough now. Nobody there is going to dare question Mooncaster royalty. Here, Spencer, you can be the Jack of Clubs; everyone loves him. Miss Chung, I reckon you're a Jill of Spades. People will be wary of you and that's even better. I'll be the King of Diamonds. We'll deal with our lack of funds when we have to."

"Now we go," the girl insisted as soon as the cards had been pinned in place.

"Wait a moment," Gerald replied. "I want to see what lies behind the other doors in this section. There might be someone else hiding or trapped."

"This area forbidden," she said crossly. "You not allowed – is place restricted."

Gerald almost laughed at her. "Please don't tell me you're being serious," he said. "It's all a bit too late for that, dear. Besides, we're going to need to take a few things with us."

To her annoyance he swept past with the torch and crossed the corridor to another set of double doors. Beyond them was a large medical ward, filled with empty beds stacked with pillows and rolled-up blankets. A wood-burning stove, much larger than the one in the refectory, stood in the centre.

"And we were freezing in those poky cells," Spencer muttered bitterly. "When there was all this."

"I knew the one medical room Lee had was never enough for a facility this size," Gerald said. "Those beds look a lot more comfortable than the mean wooden bunks we've been wrecking our backs on."

After collecting some rolled blankets, they moved on to the door next to the lab. This was usually kept locked, but not any more. Inside was a second door, made of thick steel with a combination lock, like that of an old-fashioned safe. It too was open.

Gerald directed the torch within, but didn't enter. He didn't trust Eun-mi. She might just close the door on him.

The interior of the vault showed signs of violence. The top-secret files and documents that had lined the shelves were strewn on the floor, ripped up and trampled upon as though by a wild beast. Lying open, on the ground, was the long metal box that had contained Malinda's wand.

Spencer let out a great shout and dashed forward, stooping to snatch something from a dark corner, and emerged with his beloved Stetson clasped to his chest.

Gerald smiled at him. "Welcome back, cowboy," he said gently.

Spencer was overwhelmed and practically in tears. The hat meant everything to him. It was like being reunited with his closest friend. Closing his eyes, he held his breath and placed the Stetson on his head. Eun-mi didn't disguise her distaste.

The other doors in the prohibited area led to equipment stores and finally Doctor Choe Soo-jin's own living quarters. These two rooms were clinical in their precise neatness and intimate items like toothbrush, toothpaste and soap were arranged on the small sink with an almost mathematical balance. The absence of anything that provided more than basic comfort was countered by the abundance of medical textbooks. There were row upon row of them on four long shelves that reached from the small single bed in one corner to the kitchen area in the other.

Spencer looked in the cupboard beneath the two-ring electric hob and was disappointed to find the doctor didn't keep a well-stocked larder. There was a jar of *kimchi*, another of soybean paste and a bottle of sesame oil. Although he had never been keen on the pickled, fermented vegetables, he was so ravenous he tucked into the *kimchi* immediately.

Neither Gerald nor Eun-mi wanted any; they couldn't face food and Gerald wondered if the boy would be able to keep it down when they made their way through the carnage of the corridor.

"We'll need to find grub for the journey," Spencer said as he ate noisily. "We'll have to see what's in the kitchens, if there's no one about. You sure this base is deserted?"

"Someone would have been to investigate this section by now if it wasn't," Gerald told him. "Or we'd have heard something. There's only us and the wind in this mountain now."

"Bit like here then," Spencer said, nodding at the practically bare room. "No photos, nothing. Didn't the loony doctor have any family? Bit weird."

Gerald reflected that he had never bothered to ask those questions of her. She had always seemed too much of a machine to warrant enquiries in that direction. It was strange that there was no hint of her private self here though, nothing to say who this person had been. No trace of a real human life.

A small desk stood by the bed. On it was a laptop, notepad and a leather-bound book, again set out with impeccable symmetry. While Spencer wolfed the last of the jar's contents, Gerald flicked through the book. It looked like it was her personal journal, half filled with her tidy Korean writing. He was tempted to ask Eun-mi to translate, to see if it revealed a different side to the doctor. Did she write poetry in her spare time or were these merely the dry reiterations of her daily routine? Suddenly he felt like he was prying too far and closed the book. A square of paper fluttered out.

It was a photograph, cut from a magazine, and, judging by the slight yellowing, some years ago. Gerald shone the torch down and studied it with interest. Why would the doctor keep this, but nothing of her own family? It was an old studio portrait from the beginning of the last century. The face of an unremarkable Western woman with greying, almost whiskery hair was staring over the photographer's shoulder. There was a sadness about her eyes, as though she had sacrificed a great deal. Gerald didn't recognise her. Turning the cutting over, he found that Doctor Choe had written the subject's name in faint pencil: 'Marie Curie'.

Chancing upon this almost teenage expression of hero worship and aspiration, Gerald finally felt sorry for her.

"There's nothing more here," he said quietly. "Where is this secret tunnel, Miss Chung?"

The entrance to the tunnel was over on the far side of the base, in the munitions section. It had been constructed so that the Chinese leaders could enter North Korea in secret, back in the days when they were close allies. But Kim Il-sung had ensured it was wide enough to allow for an invasion force to pass through swiftly, should that special relationship ever deteriorate.

Transport was of prime importance, so Gerald set about finding which of the four jeeps in the corridor would start, while Spencer retrieved the three torches from the other emergency kits. The boy tried not to look at the bodies around them and he wished he hadn't been so greedy with the *kimchi*.

Eun-mi desired some minutes alone with her father, for a final farewell. Bowing before the figure on Lee's bed, she begged his forgiveness and swore she would bring Nabi home.

"Do we have to bring her along?" Spencer muttered to Gerald as they pushed the hindmost jeep out of the way so they could drive past. "I mean the dislike is mutual and she's ruddy scary."

Gerald started the next vehicle in line and reversed it out of the corridor, into the main passage.

"I know; she's never going to win a Miss Congeniality contest," he said. "And she could make a bag of lemons seem like the sweeter option, but cut her some slack. She's just lost her only parent and is upset and anxious about little Nabi. For the time being we've been thrown together so let's try and make the best of it. What's that film with John Wayne where the Red Indians have kidnapped his children and he has to go find them?"

"Er, *The Searchers*, and they were his nieces, and you absolutely can't call them Red Indians. They were Comanches – brilliant movie."

"Well, this will be our version of that."

"I hope not. Don't you remember what happened? It's mega bleak, which is great for a movie, but not real life."

Gerald shrugged. "The only cowboy film I remember the plot of is *Calamity Jane*."

"It's so awesome you worked with the Duke. It really is the most mega thing ever. What was he like?"

Gerald shook his head. "So long ago now. I only recall him making a fuss about his toupee not staying on. It kept sliding to one side. He was grateful to me because I had better wig tape than the make-up girl."

That wasn't the type of anecdote Spencer had been expecting.

"His hairpiece went up for auction a few years ago," Gerald continued. "I almost bid for it, but Evelyn wouldn't give it house room."

Irritated he had mentioned Evelyn again, the old man went to collect some rifles.

"In any case," he said on his return, "we need Eun-mi because she speaks Mandarin and we don't. We'll never find our way to Dandong and get a flight to England without her."

"And she won't find her way to Kent without us when we get there."

"I'm not going to Kent," Gerald said quietly. "Not straight away at any rate. There's somewhere else I need to be first."

"But Maggie and Lee!"

"Where I'm going might help them a whole lot more. Shh – don't tell Miss Laffalot I said that. Here she is."

Eun-mi emerged from the gloom of the corridor. The girl did not look at them. Her stony mask was back in place. She had composed herself, scraped her hair back into its usual tight bun, smoothed and straightened her tie, and the jacket of her uniform was buttoned up fully. A Kalashnikov was slung over her shoulder and under her arm she carried extra blankets. Putting them in the jeep, she climbed on board.

"We go," she said curtly, annoyed that the old man had taken it upon himself to get behind the wheel.

"Whip crack away, whip crack away, whip crack away," Gerald sang, driving off. Eun-mi glowered at him.

Sitting in the front, Spencer had to hold one of the torches to show the way because the headlights were smashed. That small circle of trembling light pushed a meagre path through the pitch-darkness before them as the jeep crawled along.

Spencer shuddered. The weight of the mountain pressed close on every side. He could almost feel it as an aggressive force, bearing down. In spite of the cold, his palms began to sweat. He was never gladder to be wearing his Stetson once again and he concentrated his mind on the bright memories of the Western movies he used to live for.

The usually bustling thoroughfares of the military base were deathly quiet and empty. On the way to the main concourse, they stopped at the kitchens. The midday meals had been prepared, but were never distributed. They took as many as would fit in the jeep, in case the journey to Dandong took longer than anticipated.

A winter gale was blasting in through the great doors of the main entrance and a wedge of bright moonlight reached deep inside. Loose papers were whirling around the cavern where the trucks, jeeps and bicycles were normally parked. The base personnel had piled into, and on to, every available vehicle and abandoned the mountain en masse, to go and spread the blessed words of Austerly Fellows to the rest of the country.

But not quite everyone had managed to catch a lift. As Gerald drove on to the vast mosaic floor and the seven-metre-high statue of Kim Il-sung loomed into the moonlight, they saw five figures beneath it.

They were soldiers of various ranks. Empty bottles of *insamju*, ginseng-infused vodka, were rolling along the ground propelled by the wind, and the men were loud and boisterous. They were laughing and singing a coarse Mooncaster May-ing song, in perfect English.

"Bottom – oh, bottom, let's drink to the bottom.
And fill up our tankards once more.
Then we'll plait sweet Dulcie's hair.

And twine some bright daisies there.
Was there ever a cherry so ripesome or merry?
Kiss her once and thrice, then kiss her bare.
Bottom – oh, bottom, let's drink to the bottom.
And fill up our tankards once more."

Eun-mi was incensed. The men were not only singing, they were lurching around in a drunken circle, using the revered statue as a maypole. They had torn down one of the huge flags hanging above the tunnel entrances, ripped it into long, ragged ribbons and tied them round the bronze wrist of Kim Il-sung's outstretched hand. This insult to the Eternal President was monstrous and unpardonable.

The girl yelled at the men in Korean and they staggered to a swaying halt as the jeep approached.

"Who's this?" one cried in surprised amusement.

"More merry folk, come to join the revels!" another giggled. "Come ye, come ye – 'tis a joy to greet friends and neighbours this blessed morn."

"Stop jeep!" Eun-mi snapped at Gerald.

"We don't have time for this," he warned her. "We shouldn't get involved."

Grunting in anger, she jumped from the moving vehicle and stormed over to the men. Glancing at their insignia, she saw that the highest rank was a *sojwa*, or major. The rest consisted of a *jungwi*, or first lieutenant, and three grunts.

"You are disgusting!" she raged at them. "Evil and weak!"

"'Tis the Jill of Spades!" another declared, seeing the playing card

199

pinned to her uniform.

"I am the daughter of General Chung!" she announced proudly. "You dishonour the memory of our Supreme Leader's grandfather."

The men pulled faces and tittered.

"We don't want to play them games in this dream no more," the Major said.

"And we're not speaking that funny sleep chatter neither. The grand old tongue of the Dawn Prince is good enough for us."

"Stop pretending, princess. Come dance and drink with us. We'll be waking up in Mooncot soon, with a hard day of toil in the fields ahead, so none of this matters. What's it all about here anyway, eh? Why are our dream families starving and eating grass when them at the top are fatter than Old Edwin's pig?"

"Do royal lips taste different, do you reckon?" another wondered aloud.

"I wouldn't know. I've only ever kissed village maids, when the missus wasn't looking."

"How's about it, princess? Give us a go, just this once."

"Be real charity to the poor that would."

"The deserving poor."

"I'll wager you're keen to know if we taste sweet as honey-speeched princes, or savoury like a steak pie."

"There's plenty of meat in my pastry!"

"She can practise her charms on us. We don't mind, do we, boys? We won't tell nobody."

"I've got a hatful of kisses going begging. The missus prefers her chickens to me."

"Ah, you wouldn't want his kisses to spoil now, like uncollected eggies, would you, Your Highness?"

Two men blundered forward and made a grab for her.

Gerald had stopped the jeep. Seeing her in danger, he took up a rifle. But Eun-mi could take care of herself.

She gave a controlled shout. Then, in one graceful movement, she spun round and her left foot cracked the nearest head. Her arm followed swiftly, delivering a sharp blow to the other man's neck. Both of them tumbled over, gasping.

Without hesitation, the girl launched herself at the others. She dived among them and her limbs lashed out. The flat of her hands flew into astonished faces. Her heel felled one of them behind her, like a tree. A chop with her hand dropped another. Grabbing an empty bottle, the Major smashed the end and rushed at her. She ducked and flipped herself about, catching hold of his arm. Using his own momentum, she threw him forward. Then she jumped up and landed her foot in his stomach.

The man yelped and struggled for breath.

"You bring shame to that uniform!" she shouted in Korean. "You are a disgrace to the People's Army!"

Angrily, she reached down and tore the star of rank from his shoulder.

"Get out! All of you!" she commanded. "Go run on the cold mountainside, like the rabbits you are."

The men wavered and looked at one another. She could see they were preparing for a second attack. Their eyes exchanged their intent and they nodded to one another. The First Lieutenant had barely risen to his feet when Eun-mi slammed into him. The man was battered backwards. Each blow, each kick was punctuated by a sharp yell from her. She gave him no opportunity to retaliate, no window to strike out. She rained blow after blow on him and, when she finally stopped and struck a taut, poised stance, he fled through the main entrance.

Eun-mi turned to face the remaining four. The steely glint in her eyes was enough. Cowed, they knew they were beaten and they ran after him, into the bitter, wintry night.

Still seated in the jeep, Spencer's mouth was hanging open.

"Er... like, woah," he said. "That was so cool."

The girl made no answer. Emitting a sharp blast of breath, she expelled the pent-up tension and her body relaxed. That had felt good. Then she gazed up at the long ragged strips tied about the statue's wrist and her jaw tightened again. Moments later, Gerald and Spencer were watching her climb the bronze figure with the utmost care and respect.

"You weren't wrong when you said she was scary," Gerald muttered, getting back into the vehicle.

"Was that kung fu? It was awesome. I should have had some martial arts and Westerns crossover stuff in my DVD collection. I did have *The Magnificent Seven* – that's a remake of a samurai thing. I love that movie, best theme tune ever. Even thought about shaving my head once, like Yul Brynner. After coming so close to it today with Doctor Choe, I don't think I'll bother."

"It wasn't kung fu," Gerald told him. "I think we've just been treated to a glimpse of Juche Kyuksul, the martial art of the army here. I had no idea our Miss Chung was so skilled. She really is driven, isn't she? Look at her shin up that statue. One minute she's battering the living daylights out of five hefty blokes and the next she's humble as a kitten – she's apologising to that thing for clambering over it."

They waited while the girl inched herself along the extended arm of Kim Il-sung to dutifully untie the torn strips of cloth. Once free, the wind claimed them and they whipped around the cavernous space, writhing and snaking in the air – like gymnasts' streamers. Staring at the large bronze hand, Eun-mi caught her breath and stretched out her own to touch it, then drew back and rapidly returned to the ground.

Before rejoining the others, she laid the Major's star at the statue's feet as a token and sank to her knees, bowing her head till it touched the mosaic floor.

"Most beloved Eternal President of the Republic," she murmured reverently. "This darkest day, the purity of the blood has been soiled. I, Chung Eun-mi, daughter of the People's Army, pledge to do all in my power to restore the true order. I shall be a human rifle, a human bomb in your service, a dagger of your hand – to strike at the diseased heart of the Western enemy who has done this most terrible thing. This I swear, on my honour, on my life, on the memory of my noble father, General Chung Kang-dae."

She stayed in that position for several minutes, then stood, bowed once more and returned to the jeep.

"Go," she instructed.

"Anything you say," Gerald replied.

"That was amazing what you did back there," Spencer enthused. "Can you break bricks with your fist as well?"

"You want me to demonstrate with your head?" she asked.

"Bye-bye, Titipu!" Gerald called as they left the moonlit cavern, where the strips of red and blue cloth continued their serpentine waltz about the bronze statue.

"Dandong merrily on high," his voice sang out as the jeep passed into the tunnel leading to the munitions section.

Eun-mi glanced uneasily over her shoulder. The base was wide open and unguarded, its secrets and military might vulnerable to anyone. Her young features set hard and stern. Her duty was clear: it must not fall into the hands of an enemy nation. It was as if the voice of the Eternal President was speaking to her directly, making his will known.

The jeep bore deeper into the mountain. Deep black mouths of chambers and smaller passages sped by until the tunnel opened out around them and they were in a vast munitions store. Drums of fuel were stacked in high, orderly rows that formed wide avenues through pallets loaded with ordnance and rocket launchers. There were crates of grenades and explosives, shells of all sizes, and Spencer counted the outlines of over twenty tanks. There may have been more, but a regiment of towering missiles obscured the view. Neither he nor Gerald could guess at the size of this lethal stockpile. The torch's beam didn't reach to the furthest corners of this massive place and it took them almost fifteen minutes to drive from one side to the other. Gerald shook his head. There was enough here to mount a devastating attack on China. At least that was one war that had never happened, and now never would.

"Stop!" Eun-mi commanded sharply.

Gerald braked and the girl leaped out. She hurried back to where an abandoned guard hut stood against the rocky wall, and where an enormous metal screen covered a huge entrance.

The rusting barrier was held in place by two iron rails so that it could be slid aside. Eun-mi gave it an experimental shove. A boom and squeak of metal resounded through the vast arsenal. The barrier hardly budged.

She called the others over and together they heaved and pushed the screen over the rails. Thunderous clangs and grating squeals echoed in the darkness around them. When there was enough clearance to get the jeep through, even though the barrier was still not even halfway across the opening, they stopped and caught their breath.

"That's the secret way into China?" Gerald asked. "How far does it go?"

Eun-mi didn't bother to reply. She returned to the jeep and took out another torch.

"You stay," she ordered. "You wait."

"Where are you going?" the old man demanded as she ran back the way they had come, down the avenue of oil drums.

"What's she up to?" Spencer asked.

"I've no idea. But I don't trust that girl one bit. Let's get back in the car and be ready."

Gerald reversed the jeep and turned it towards the secret way. Then they waited. After several minutes, he switched off the engine. What was that girl doing? They stared into the immense dark space. Every now and then they could see a faint glimmer of torchlight in the distance, when it caught the curves of a standing missile, or when its feeble beam angled upwards.

"Must be half an hour now," Spencer grumbled.

"More than that," Gerald reckoned.

"You sure we need her?"

"Unfortunately, yes."

"But won't everyone in China speak English now because of DJ?"

"We can't bank on that. What the hell is she up to?"

Ten minutes later, they saw the torchlight bounce frantically into view as Eun-mi came racing back.

"About time!" Gerald called.

"Start jeep!" she shouted as she ran towards them. "Start jeep!"

Gerald didn't like the fearful urgency in her voice. He obeyed hurriedly.

The girl rushed up and threw a canvas satchel on to the heap of supplies on the back seat next to Spencer. One of the straps wasn't buckled properly and a grenade rolled out.

"Ruddy hell!" the boy cried in alarm.

"Get out of driving seat!" Eun-mi was yelling at Gerald. "I drive now."

"What?" Gerald asked in annoyance. "Just get in."

"You drive like old woman!"

"Oh, you have no idea!" he replied with an ironic laugh.

Eun-mi pulled out her gun. "I drive!" she insisted.

Gerald slid across to the other seat.

"A gun really isn't a substitute for the word 'please', young lady," he admonished her.

The girl wasn't listening. She looked quickly, and anxiously, over her shoulder then pressed her foot down. Spencer almost lost his Stetson. The jeep went screeching into the secret way and Gerald realised what she had done.

"No!" he exclaimed in horrified disbelief. "Even you're not that mad!"

Eun-mi was too busy concentrating on the way ahead to answer. The jeep hurtled through the deep dark at breakneck speed. She put her faith in the protection of the Eternal President that it would be fast enough.

In the back seat, Spencer had his work cut out, keeping hold of his hat while trying to stop more grenades bumping out of the satchel as the jeep careered recklessly along.

"Slow down!" he yelled.

And then he felt and heard the first explosion. It was immediately followed by another and another – then an even greater rumble that shook the very air. Spencer tried to cover his ears, but the blasts thumped inside his chest and there was no escape from them.

Suddenly the darkness lifted and an angry glare banished the shadows, followed by a wave of heat. Spencer turned and his glasses became mirrors for an inferno. The munitions store was in violent eruption.

"Faster! Go faster!" he screamed at Eun-mi.

The girl couldn't make the jeep go any faster. It was already difficult to control and, up ahead, she saw the underground road turned a tight corner. There was no chance they'd negotiate that bend at this speed. She would have to slow right down or crash into the curving wall.

Behind them, the firestorm roared through the half-open barrier and came raging down the tunnel.

"We're not going to make it!" Spencer wailed.

Gerald closed his eyes and, in the midst of that deafening tumult, heard Evelyn's voice berating him.

Above them, the entire mountain shook. The helipads buckled then collapsed as the labyrinth of excavated tunnels were destroyed in a chain reaction that engulfed the intercontinental missiles in their silos. Terraces went crashing down the crumbling slopes and fissures were torn open. Jets of white flame pierced the winter night. Missiles launched and sliced the sky with searing trails, only to detonate high in the atmosphere, go spiralling into the sea or set the surrounding forests aflame. The fulminating fury turned the night into day. It could be seen as far away as Russia and Japan and the tremors were felt deep into China.

13

7.30am, 20th December, Toronto

THE WINDS BLUSTERING around the top of the CN Tower tore at the velvet tails of the Ismus's short jacket and his mane of black hair streamed about his pale face. He was standing over the roof of the revolving 360 Restaurant, 356 metres above the ground – a sickening height with, quite literally, breathtaking views across the city and Lake Ontario. The tops of skyscrapers were far below and the sun was rising dim and watery and insignificant on the horizon. He appeared to be striding out of the dawn sky.

The tower's EdgeWalk attraction, the highest full-circle, hands-free walk round a building, was a striking way to create an immediate impression when the satellites beamed these images to the watching world. Even with the safety harness tethering him to an overhead rail, it was still a feat of great daring at this time of year in those gusting winds, and a brilliant way for the broadcast to commence. The cameraman wouldn't venture out on to the metal grating that was no wider than an average pavement. There was no safety barrier, just a sheer drop, so he leaned out of the main pod as far as he could stomach and, even though he too was attached to the rail and believed this to be only a dream, it was still terrifying.

"Your Royal Highnesses," the Ismus began, shouting above the gale, "Under Kings and Under Queens, Jacks and Jills, lords and ladies, knights and pages, kitchen maids and cooks, honest salts of Mooncot, not forgetting the little boys and girls. Each one of my dear, devoted, loving and, dare I say, lickable subjects around this nonsensical dream world, congregate before your goggle-boxes and bend your ears my way, for I bring you gladsome tidings."

The cameraman backed further inside and the Ismus followed, the familiar crooked smile broader than ever as he unclipped the harness.

This important broadcast had been trailed across every media format since the beginning of November. Social networks had gone into meltdown with frenzied speculation over what it might concern and the international press clamoured for interviews from the Holy Enchanter and hounded every prime member of his Court. But not even the sly Jill of Spades would reveal any details, although that was only because she didn't know any. The Ismus had smirked at the frantic journalists and bid them a good day for when they next awakened back in Mooncaster. It was maddening. They were gasping for news.

The widespread rumour was that the announcement would pertain to the book he was writing. Just what was *Fighting Pax*?

The world was desperate for the smallest scrap of information. Even those politicians who still played out their pointless dream lives in government had abandoned the pretence of attending to state business. Instead they indulged in fanciful guesswork inside their parliaments and senate houses. Such was the level of hype about this mysterious broadcast. As the weeks dragged on, the anticipation became excruciatingly intense. Everyone on the planet who had access to a television or the Internet was guaranteed to be glued to this live transmission.

At last the long-awaited hour arrived. Factories and offices ceased production and workers crowded before the large TVs hired specifically for this one event. The thousands who had abandoned the cities to live a simpler, medieval sort of existence scrambled hastily to find their way back to technology. In other parts of the world, populations roused themselves from sleep and tuned in. Huge outdoor screens had been set up in the more remote regions of the planet, and whole villages and tribes traversed desert, jungle, forest, savannah and Siberian tundra to view this vital address from their revered leader. Clutching their copies of *Dancing Jax*, they congregated in their multitudes, falling to their knees when the broadcast began.

And there he was, leering at them down the lens, seemingly greeting each one – and they drank in his words.

"Do forgive me for interrupting your funny old dreams here," he said, now inside the tower's revolving restaurant where members of his Court were gathered in their finest robes and gowns, for they too were on tenterhooks to hear his news.

"I have the tastiest revelation I must share with you all," he continued. "One that will feed and nourish your hungry souls forever more. But, before we get to that juicy feast, have a gander at this."

The picture cut away to previously filmed footage of sickly brown smog hanging over a heavily industrialised town, where tall chimneys pumped out plumes of filthy smoke and gases.

"What you're seeing here," the Ismus's voice-over informed his audience, "is just one of the many manufacturing plants where they make components for hand-held gadgets like tablets and smartphones. I think this charming spot is in China somewhere, but there are lots of them just like this. Look at it: they make touchscreens for your fun little gizmos in there and it's working full steam ahead at the moment, isn't it? Although that isn't steam; it's a wonderfully noxious fume that Haxxentrot herself would be proud of. Now, because health-and-safety regulations are a tiny bit mythological out there, about fifty workers a year drop dead in those places, and many more collapse with long-term illnesses. Just lately they've been keeling over like skittles, but that's OK, as they're churning out more devices than ever before. The old sixteen-hour days are luxuries of the past for them. Those gorgeous employees are eschewing their rest periods and producing more gimcrack toys for you than ever before. No more mass, stress-induced suicides now – they don't have time. They're slaving till they drop, bless their poisoned ickle hearts, corroded lungs and blood so full of lead the Limner could sketch with it."

The factories disappeared and were replaced by another filmed insert. This time it was the interior of a vast warehouse, the size of an aircraft hangar, crammed from floor to lofty ceiling with crates and boxes. Forklift trucks were gliding down the aisles between them, to the strains of 'The Blue Danube', and filling lorries at the loading bay. One of the forklifts came zooming towards the camera. It turned sharply and there was the Ismus behind the wheel, a hard hat perched rakishly upon his head.

"And here are some of those very gadgets," he said, waving grandly at the packed warehouse. "All parcelled up and ready to go forth into the world. Normally they'd be played and posed with, but every single device here and every other device being made elsewhere have a far more important destiny ahead. These aren't going to sit in shops to await purchase by cool kids and people who won't shift out of Starbucks three hours after they've swigged back their one measly mocha, oh, no – because I am giving them away!"

The picture switched back to the 360 Restaurant where the Ismus was now reclining on an overstuffed sofa of crimson velvet, arms outstretched and laughing.

"Yes!" he declared. "You heard right. I am giving those tablets away for free. Not hundreds, not thousands, not even hundreds of thousands – but millions of them! Special shipments are already on their way to the most extremely poor, shabby and squalid areas of the globe. Those impoverished people might have to walk six hours to the nearest clean water supply and wear flies as face fashion, but, within the next few days, they'll have their very own Kindle or Nexus or Samsung to amuse themselves with and take their minds off famine or disease or whatever 'want' is trending with them at the moment.

"Generous, you say? Foolishly extravagant? Well, perhaps just a smidgen, but even here in this turgid dreamscape I am not free of the compassion I feel for my subjects. It is my ambition to provide the underprivileged masses, in their slums and shanties, mud huts and tin shacks, with their own personal link to the Internet. I know they're watching me right now on big screens, but that isn't good enough – and it simply won't do for what I have planned. Every communication satellite is going to be dedicated to providing free Internet access. There won't be a cranny on this planet that won't have coverage."

Assuming a righteous pose, he brandished a forefinger in the air and declared, "I have a dream that one day every valley shall be connected and every hill and mountain shall be emailable."

Snickering, he gazed lovingly down the camera again. "And why do I do this?" he asked. "Because those whispers you may have heard are right: your Holy Enchanter has been a very busy boy lately – very busy indeed."

He reached out a hand and one of the two Harlequin Priests who stood behind him passed over a sleek black laptop. The Ismus received it with great solemnity and turned it towards the camera.

"This is no ordinary computer," he said gravely. "It is now the single most valuable object in this existence."

He paused to let the drama of his words sink in. The courtiers around him held their breath and every eye was fixed upon the laptop.

"These many months now," he resumed, "I have been toiling ceaselessly to deliver unto you all a most wondrous gift. Our true lives in Mooncaster are spoiled only by the monotonous interludes of these lustreless dreams, where we are compelled to partake in drab charades. But not for much longer, you dear, darling, rosy-red apples of my eye. The secret work contained herein shall make an end of that. No more will you goodly swains nod at your hearths after tilling the fertile loam, only to find yourselves drudging in a dead-end job here, unfulfilled, with a carping spouse and grasping, ungrateful offspring. No longer will you carefree youngsters curl up on your cots after playing in the woods and fields or splashing in the millpond, only to discover your dream self has exams, can't afford the latest must-have, overhyped piece of crap, or is being victimised by bullies or worse.

"No, my dearest loves, these colourless, arduous night-times will be no more. I have engineered a final solution – an ultimate escape. Just as the sacred text of *Dancing Jax* first showed you the way to your true, waking selves, this new book will enrich it a hundredfold and dispense with the need to inhabit this banal abstract whilst you sleep. Think of it: your dreams will be as joyous as your days. These fresh words will guide you and make your bliss complete. It is the furtherance we have waited and ached for. My adoring, patient assemblage, I give you the one and only, the unparalleled and supreme – *Fighting Pax*."

In the restaurant, the members of the Court applauded and the privileged, invited press joined them. Toronto echoed with cheers and car horns blared. Around the world there was a roar of ecstasy.

Presently the Ismus held up his hand for silence and the planet obeyed.

"Indulge me a few moments more," he asked. "I must elaborate. There shall be no printed copies of *Fighting Pax*, no hardbacks, no paperbacks, no serialisations in newspapers, no audiobooks. It will be available solely as an e-book, for download only. That is why I am giving away so many e-readers. Distribution has already commenced, on a scale hitherto... ahem, 'undreamed' of. A veritable army of volunteers has been, and still is, working round the clock to deliver them to each village and every isolated outpost of humanity. And yes – Amazon does deliver to the Amazon. This will take several more days, but I am confident it will be accomplished in due time. When the file goes live on the Mooncaster website, my wish is for everyone to read it simultaneously."

His face assumed a wounded sincerity and his eyebrows lifted in the middle. "There is only one circumstance that could possibly ruin my glorious plan..." Suddenly the picture cut away to a specially prepared featurette that had taken a team of stop-motion animators three months to create.

There was a model of the Ismus, executed in the cartoon gothic style of Edward Gorey, with exaggerated long limbs and large eyes. It was foam latex over an articulated armature, clothed in a detailed, miniature version of the same costume he had just been wearing. The setting was the fireside in a Victorian mansion, with panelled walls and a stone fireplace carved with humorous, gargoyle-like faces. A comical stuffed owl, under a glass dome, blinked its oversized eyes. The head of a lion, mounted as a trophy on the wall, twitched its nose haughtily, while a Punchinello Guard, which was even uglier than its real-life counterpart, came scampering in, dressed as a butler, carrying a letter upon a silver salver.

The colour palette of the scene was rich browns and reds, highlighted by the flickering golden glow of cellophane flames crackling in the hearth.

The Ismus puppet was seated cross-legged in

an ornate, high-backed chair, topped by two wooden finials shaped like goofy bats.

"Urgent missive, Your Lordy Lordship!" the Punchinello announced, bowing so low his nose and chin bent sideways against the floor. A rascally-looking mouse darted from a doorway in the skirting to give the butler's nose a tremendous kick, and was safely home before the Punchinello could catch it.

The Ismus character looked up from the e-reader he was engrossed in and took the letter in his spindly fingers.

"At this hour of night?" he asked in astonishment, glancing at the ormolu clock, which was snoring noisily on the mantle. "Whatever can it mean, Swazzle?"

He scanned it quickly then gave a cry of woe that made the stuffed owl fall off its perch in the dome and the butler's starched shirt front flip up and smack his chin.

"Calamity!" the Ismus wailed. "What are we to do?"

"My Lord?" the butler enquired, wrestling with his shirt front and glowering at the mouse hole.

The Ismus waved the letter then wilted in the chair and began to sing.

"The Chinese factories are telling me,
a most horrid probability.
'Tis an outcome I did not foresee.
Oh, what am I to do?"

The Swazzle butler fanned him with the salver and, in a squawky voice, sang back:

"What do they say that is so awful?
Shall I sort them in ways unlawful?
Chop some heads till we have a drawer full?
Anything I can do?"

The Ismus passed him the letter and answered:

"Although they're working day and nightly,
here's the news that does a-fright me
and makes me clench my buttocks tightly.
Oh, what am I to do?"

The butler read the letter and threw it angrily into the fire as he replied.

"They can't fulfil your expectation!
A very vexing situation!
I understand your lamentation.
I would flush them down the loo."

The Ismus rose from the chair and brandished his e-reader, twirling it around on his fingertip.

> "*I wanted these for everybody.*
> *The factories have been quite shoddy.*
> *Far too few and way too tardy.*
> *Oh, what am I to do?*"

Around him, the owl, the lion's head, the stone faces on the fireplace – even the wooden bat finials – joined in with the song. The mouse too popped its head out and squeaked in tune.

> "*Oh, what is he to do?*
> *His plans have fallen through.*
> *For his book's grand debut.*
> *It makes us want to spew.*"

The Ismus dragged his feet to a large, floor-standing globe and spun it sadly.

> "*Were there ever such dismal facts?*
> *Half the world can't read* Fighting Pax.
> *Not enough tablets – PCs or Macs.*
> *I'm feeling very blue.*"

He heaved a great sigh and hung his head while the surrounding faces continued in a glum chant.

"He's feeling very blue.
There'll be a massive queue.
It's a problem he can't chew.
He's well and truly screwed."

With that, the Punchinello butler came bounding forward, a tablet in both hands, as he sang joyously.

"Here's an answer given gladly.
All because you were treated badly,
you can have my old iPad 3.
That is what I can do.
I really don't need two!"

The Ismus puppet gave a delighted shout, which woke up the ormolu clock. Then he clapped his hands and danced around.

"That's the solution neat and tidy.
Thanks to you, my good Man Friday.
Now the world will not deride me.
This is what they can do!"

He turned to face the camera and fell to his knees, wringing his hands imploringly.

"All of you who love me dearly,
hear me now and listen clearly.

If you've some you don't need really,
you can be generous too!

Give your spares, your old e-readers,
to the poorest, direst needers.
Time to be charity cheerleaders.
Doesn't matter they're not new!

Fighting Pax *will be a sensation,*
thanks to your very kind donation,
to all of those who know privation.
Blessed be to you!
Most blessed be to you!"

The last verse was sung by every character. On the final sustained note, the fire roared up the chimney, the bats spun round, the owl's dome shattered, the lion's head fell from the wall and flattened the mouse, the butler's braces snapped, his trousers dropped down and the clock's face popped out on a spring. The Ismus puppet beamed and blew the audience a kiss.

The picture faded to black and the real Ismus reappeared in the revolving restaurant, leaning against one of the large windows.

"Whimsy always sells a message best," he observed. "So there you have it. Even the frenzied activity of those factories in the Far East won't quite manage to produce the amount of devices needed in time. This then is my appeal. There are countless of you out there who possess more than one of these gadgets. Either they're ever so slightly out of date and you've upgraded, because you just have to own the very latest model, or you like to keep one in the lavatory, or the manufacturer's built-in obsolescence has slightly impaired its functionality – whatever the reason, you'll have a stash of disregarded hardware with nothing to display but dust. What a criminal waste, when there are so many in desperate need. I have set up donation centres in the major cities and special collection vans will be touring your country. Give generously so that we may all leave this gruelling greyness together and enjoy our lives in the Realm of the Dawn Prince as never before. Forget about humanitarian aid; what those poor people really need is gadget aid. That is all that matters now. Those people need your old stuff."

The risen sun formed a halo round his head, as he intended it to. He pressed his fingertips together as if in prayer, but his dark eyes continued to glint into the lens.

"Some of you out there will be aware of a quaint festival soon to be celebrated," he said. "We of Mooncaster have our Feast of the Deep Frost; certain places here have a muddled holiday called Christmas. I have decided to coincide the grand release of *Fighting Pax* with that. Together, we shall 'e' the world, let them know it's Christmas time."

He turned to the panoramic views of Lake Ontario outside the window.

"Beyond that gleaming water," he said, "beyond the land behind it and the ocean beyond that is the country called Britain. That is where the replica of the White Castle is being built – exact to the last stone. From that place, just a few days hence, on the twenty-fourth of this month, at the stroke of midnight, Greenwich Mean Time, I shall unleash

Fighting Pax unto you all. In the lead-up to that glorious event, there will be the most incredible entertainment. I have devised the most splendid night, replete with diversions: games, jollity, uproarious carousing, unrivalled even in the Realm of the Dawn Prince. We shall blow one final trumpet blast, loud enough to shake the stars from the sky. And finally we will play the newest and best party game of all: 'Flee the Beast'."

He beckoned the camera closer. "As that will mark the end of our grey penances here," he said, "I'm determined to make it the wildest, most memorable dreaming you've ever had. So why not join me as my guests? I, the Holy Enchanter of Mooncaster, am inviting each and every one of you, wherever you are, to fly to Britain. Make your way to Kent, the garden of England. Don't just watch it on your TVs, get on a plane; make it one hell of a Christmas Eve. All shall be welcome and the flights won't cost you a penny. This year, *Fighting Pax* is going to ensure it will be the merriest Christmas ever. Blessed be."

Chuckling, he stepped out of shot and the wintry sun dazzled the picture. The broadcast was over. Across the planet the channels reverted to their usual programming schedules.

The Ismus thanked the cameraman and bade him go enjoy the large breakfast buffet laid on in the restaurant. Then he strode into the midst of his courtiers and journalists and they swarmed about him like gnats.

"A night of revels, my Lord?" asked the plump Queen of Hearts. "How shall I obtain a new gown in time? I should scold you for keeping that secret from us ladies, but tell me, *Fighting Pax* – is the bluest blood of the four houses not to have first taste of it?"

"No sampling, no previews, no exceptions," he replied sternly. "Everyone will read it together."

"But surely…"

"That is my final word," he said sharply.

The Queen of Hearts curtsied and kept her head lowered until he and his black-faced bodyguards had passed. Then she looked about for the Queen of Spades, to cluck and debate with, but she was nowhere to be found. Instead she heard her daughter's voice laughing and cooing somewhere, flirting with somebody new, as usual, and through the chattering throng saw it was the cameraman. The Queen of Hearts bristled. He was but a lowly Three of Clubs castle carpenter in the true world. She would have to stop that unsuitable dalliance immediately.

The usual petty squabbles and rivalries of the Court were taking place as normal, but today they were coloured by the impending thrill of *Fighting Pax*. With her infant son in her arms, the Lady Labella gazed out of the window, at the city far below. The larger creatures had retreated from the sunrise and were now hiding in underground car parks and subways. Only the slime trails they left behind glistened in the morning light and scavenging beasts tore apart what morsels of prey had been discarded.

"To never visit this unhappy land again," she murmured. "How well that wouldst be. To spend the entire night rooted in the White Castle. What perfect peace. No more of this processing from country to country."

Nearby, the Jill of Spades had managed to corner the Jack of Clubs as he was ladling out a dollop of steaming porridge from an immense cauldron, and was demanding they go hunting together when they woke up in Mooncaster.

"I must decline, Lady," he said flatly. "Your hands are too bloody for my liking. You dispatch both quarry and hawk if they displease you, and I have seen the scarlet stripes on thine horse's flank. I have no wish to observe yet more of your hard-hearted cruelty."

The dark-haired girl pressed her lips together crossly. "You nurse your grudges overlong," she told him as he drizzled honey into his bowl. "I have a new hawk I wouldst try, better than the other."

"Then pray gallop out with the Jack of Diamonds or the Jill of Hearts. Let them be your playfellows, for I shall not."

"And where will you be?" she asked sourly. "Away in the hills with your proud horse? Again? The beast that will suffer no stable lad to approach it and bites the other mounts if they dare look in its direction? Have you heard what the common tongues are wagging?"

"I think I am about to."

Ignoring the insult, she said, "They say that your thoughts and your heart are ever upon Ironheart, your thunderous steed, and that it is in truth a maiden under some enchantment. You spend so much time alone with her, she must be beautiful and diverting indeed. At what distance from the White Castle does the bewitchment fail and her appetite turns from hay to princes? Or does she receive her oats as gladly in whatever form?"

The Jack of Clubs made no reply, but brushed past her, licking his spoon. The girl's eyes blazed at him angrily.

Creeping away from the main group, the Jack of Diamonds ducked behind a table and crawled along the floor, unnoticed. His palms were itching like never before. To be in the same room as the most valuable object in this existence was unbearable for Magpie Jack, the light-fingered knave of Mooncaster. Throughout the broadcast his eyes had been locked on the Ismus's laptop. Then, to his astonishment and unbounded glee, he watched the Holy Enchanter leave it unattended on the crimson sofa. There it was, momentarily forgotten, the one and only copy of *Fighting Pax*. It made the boy almost sick with trepidation as he crept closer. If he could steal it away and be the first to read it, that would be the pinnacle of his pilfering so far.

Stealthily, he made his way nearer, using the tables as cover and shooting sly, backward glances at the breakfasting Court and the hungry press. His knees shuffled over the carpet. Almost there now, almost there. The velvet sofa was right before him. He reached up a greedy hand and touched the cool black metal of the laptop.

Suddenly another hand flashed out and slapped his knuckles hard. Before he could reach for the dagger at his belt, his head was torn back by his hair and he found himself staring up into the face of the Queen of Spades.

The sharp-featured Under Queen had been observing him the entire time. The pupils of her eyes were enlarged and empty and her lips curled into a snarl.

"I should inform the Holy Enchanter of this," she hissed at him. "How long would you languish in gaol this time, Magpie Jack? Leg irons and a sojourn in the knee-crackers would put an end to your creeping crawls."

"Pray don't!" he entreated. "I meant no harm – upon my honour. I swear it."

The Queen of Spades gave a disdainful snort that made her raven ringlets jiggle about her ears. "What honour is there in you?" she asked. "You are a thief, boy. A dirty, sneaking cutpurse who would pull the jewels from the crown on your own father's head and twist the rings off your poor mother's fingers. 'Tis high time you rekindled your acquaintance with the devices of the dungeon."

Digging her fingernails deep into his wrist, she enjoyed watching his panic and dread increase.

"I am blameless!" he pleaded. "You know full well Haxxentrot placed this curse when she caught me in her tower – and I only ventured there by the earnest bidding of your daughter."

The Queen of Spades pretended to take pity on him. "Then grant me the pleasure of curing your palms of that oh so wicked spell," she said.

"There is no remedy!" Jack answered. "Malinda herself told me. It is to be my life-long torment."

The Under Queen chuckled softly. "Surely only whilst your hands remain jointed to your arms?" she said. "One deft blow with a blade would sever the witch's curse completely. There are many knights who would be more than willing to aid you in this. Why, Sir Darksilver, whose brace of emerald daggers you abstracted last summer, would be beyond glad to assist you. Shall I summon him hither?"

The Jack of Diamonds gasped in horror and shook his head.

"Clemency!" he begged.

"You do not wish to be rid of this affliction?"

"Not at the price of my hands!"

"They would make a tasty morsel for Mauger, the Growly Guardian of the Gate. I'm sure the beast would enjoy some finger food."

The Queen of Spades allowed the horror of that to sink in, toying with his fear, then let go of his wrist and wrinkled her face in disgust.

"Begone, you lukewarm puke curd," she commanded. "We will say no more on this."

The boy didn't need to be told twice and made a hasty retreat back beneath the tables.

A playful smile lifted the corners of the woman's mouth and she turned her keen attention to the velvet sofa and the unattended laptop.

Moments later, she was sidling behind the restaurant bar, with as casual an air as she could manage, even though her pulse was racing. When she was certain no one was watching, the Queen of Spades dipped out of sight and placed the laptop reverently on the floor. With trembling fingers, she opened it and switched it on.

The Ismus's desktop wallpaper displayed an image of some old-fashioned Bakelite device with an illuminated dial showing strange symbols and the letter forms of an archaic language. This held no interest for the Queen of Spades; she was too overjoyed with the discovery that there was no password protection. The Holy Enchanter really was exceedingly careless.

There was only one folder on the desktop and it contained just one document: *Fighting Pax*.

Holding her breath in her excitement, the Queen of Spades clicked on it and began to read.

The rays of the morning sun diminished and the lights in the restaurant dwindled until darkness surrounded her. She felt an icy breath on the back of her neck that caused her to shiver and she began to rock backwards and forwards...

14

THE JILL OF HEARTS tossed her head back and laughed at her mother's plump, scolding face. The Queen of Hearts had just sent the cameraman away with a haughty warning ringing in his ears and was trying to instil some decorum into her flighty daughter, in between taking sparrow-sized bites from a thick slice of bacon, impaled on a daintily held skewer.

"You should be ducked in the millpond every sunrise and sunset!" the Under Queen chastised. "The blood's too hot in your veins, that's the trouble. Menfolk are not safe near your siren flame. Must you beguile and singe every one? You cause naught but strife and disharmony 'twixt spouses and the betrothed, then you sow discord and rivalry amongst the poor 'prentices and kitchen boys."

"I would be a very pale flame if moths were all I enticed," Jill answered with a smirk. "There are other creatures, with brighter wings."

"Enough I say! I must needs consult my book of physic and gather some simples from the Gentle Garden to douse your appetite, my graceless girl."

The Jill of Hearts stopped listening to her. She called to mind that, on market day, there was a merchant who dealt in the most marvellous mechanical wonders. One of them was a golden cage in which a delightful silver bird, composed of the daintiest cogs and wheels and fine chains, could be made to sing, spread its wings and bob its head by means of a winding key. It had but one song and, though she had heard it on many occasions, she never grew as tired of it as the sound of her mother's monotonous reproofs and she wished the Under Queen also had a key that she could remove so that she could fling it into the moat.

Glancing across the long table, she saw the handsome cameraman disappear into the crowd and she cast about for a fresh victim to practise her bewitching smile upon. But here, in the revolving restaurant, none of the other new faces caught her interest. Her lovely eyes fell upon the Jack of Clubs. The dawn sunlight was shining in the gold of his hair, and the velvet of his tunic was stretched taut across his shoulders. The old familiar hurt ached in the girl's heart as she remembered the curse of the Mistletoe King.

She was the daughter of the House of Hearts and could gather suitors as plentifully as children pluck daisies, except for the one she truly desired – that would always be denied her. She took little comfort from the knowledge that the Jill of Spades had even less success at capturing his attention. It was well known how much he disliked that cold-hearted princess. If only he would spend less time riding and tending to his horse and hawk. If only she could be the quarry when he went hunting. She would give him the best sport of his life and would let him carry her back to the White Castle as a trophy.

"Perhaps 'twould be best for all to keep you in a tower," her mother was prattling on, "behind locked doors! That might quell the disputes and give bruised affections time to heal."

The girl continued to feast her eyes on Jack. He was conversing politely with three ladies-in-waiting from the House of Diamonds, oblivious to the effect his good looks and athletic appeal had on them. For a while, they tittered behind their hands and tried their best to hold his gaze for longer than courtly manners might expect. Presently Jill became aware that the ladies, and Jack too, were distracted by something across the restaurant and then she realised that everyone, except her mother, had stopped talking and was staring in one direction.

The Jill of Hearts followed the collective gaze.

"Will she never halt that flabby tongue?" a bitter voice suddenly cut through the shared silence, "She makes more noise but less sense than a frighted goose. Is the only way to silence her honking to follow the example set by the Bad Shepherd? Is that the answer? Is it?"

The courtiers had parted and the Queen of Spades came staggering through from the bar area. Jill's eyes widened. She had never seen the Under Queen so haggard and ghastly. What could have happened? She looked like an apparition conjured from the grave on the Night of All Dark.

At last the Queen of Hearts became aware that something was happening behind her and she spun about quickly so as not to miss a moment of any new Court sensation, not realising she was about to be the focus of it. At the edge of the crowd, the Ismus folded his arms and the famous crooked smile played across his lips. He was mildly surprised to learn it was not Magpie Jack who had taken the bait of the unguarded laptop.

"Behold!" the Queen of Spades spat as she stumbled forward. "See how we robe the kine of Mooncaster in velvet and jewels."

The Queen of Hearts blinked at her in astonishment.

"Mark how she bats her bovine lashes!" the other announced bitterly. "As though the butter from her hanging udders would not melt in her venomous mouth. Yea, in truth, beneath those heaving rolls of grease and lard she is, at the core, a twisting viper. At last it is made plain to me, Madam. Now your perfidy is laid bare!"

"Dearest Lady!" the Queen of Hearts exclaimed. "What strange affliction is this? Are you in need of a purgative? I could prepare..."

The Queen of Spades let out a shrill scream and rushed at her like a mad dog. Her demented fury was horrible to see. Seizing the other woman's chestnut hair with her right hand, she wrapped it tightly round her fist and gouged deep scratches across the shocked face with the fingernails of the left.

The Queen of Hearts was so startled, she could only shriek helplessly and the skewer fell from her grasp. Her old friend was screeching vile oaths of vengeance right into her face, but she did not understand what she was supposed to have done. Before she could protest or retaliate, she felt the hair being torn from her scalp and she was dragged roughly along the side of the table.

Plates and goblets went flying as the Queen of Spades dashed them out of the way. She snatched at knives, but discarded them as being too efficient and painless. Then her wild, glaring stare alighted upon the perfect punishment and her frenzied fingers closed round the heavy iron porridge ladle. She raised it high above her head as the Queen of Hearts flailed her dumpy arms and squealed for her life.

The surrounding courtiers looked on in puzzlement, unsure how to react. What were the Under Queens doing? What unknown quarrel had prompted this unseemly display? They glanced over at the Ismus to read his expression, so that they might follow his lead, and were reassured to find him enjoying the unruly spectacle. Encouraged and comforted, they resumed viewing the violent entertainment with indulgent smiles. The two Jills, however, were simply annoyed. Their royal mothers were brawling like a couple of ale-sodden slatterns in The Silver Penny. When this shameful dream was over, they would remind them of this back in Mooncaster.

"It was you!" the Queen of Spades screamed in rage as she battered the other woman's head with the iron ladle. "You did it! You did it!"

Bellowing, she hauled her up by the hair and rammed her face into the cauldron of steaming porridge, shoving it under and pressing down with all her strength.

"Collect the fee owed to you!" she thundered. "In the coin of your own minting. You who put death in your potion pot, collect it now from this one. A fitting retribution!"

The Queen of Hearts' floundering struggles were brief and the urgent gurgling soon stopped.

When the final bubble broke the surface of the porridge, the only sound to be heard was the heaving breath of the Queen of Spades as she tottered backwards, swaying unsteadily. Her eyes rolled up, showing only a bloodshot wedge of white, and a violent jolt snapped through her body. Then she wilted and collapsed in a faint.

The strong arms of a Harlequin Priest were there to catch her.

Around them the courtiers began to murmur. They were still

confused. Then the Queen of Spades' eyelids fluttered open. Her pupils were shrunken and she squinted up at the Harlequin's face in a daze. Her mind and vision were blurred.

"Miller?" she whispered uncertainly. "Is that you? I feel dog rough. Have... have you got a smoke?"

The Harlequin said nothing.

Dragging a trembling hand over her eyes, she extricated herself from his arms and peered at the coloured diamonds tattooed on his face.

"What the bloody hell have you gone and done? Just how much did we knock back last night? Howie's made a right mess of you. He shouldn't have..."

Queenie stopped. She had reached up to touch the man's inked cheek and in that moment saw the bright red blood on her fingers.

"Miller?" she uttered in alarm. "What's this?"

Then, suddenly, she was aware of her surroundings. Forty-six-year-old Queenie, whose holiday destinations had only ever included sun, sand and sangria, found herself at the top of the CN Tower, hemmed in by an audience of strangers wearing fancy dress. Miller was also in a weird get-up and, with a start, she realised that she too was tightly laced into some bizarre, old-fashioned gown of black silk and taffeta, heavy with embroidered jet beads.

Queenie's head reeled. She stared at the unknown faces and began to feel afraid. There was something uncanny about their eyes; they were dark and glassy and they were studying her with doubt and suspicion.

"That is not the Queen of Spades," one of them declared.

"Who is that uncouth person?" asked another. "Where did the Queen of Spades vanish to? What magick is this?"

The faces began to look stern and the voices sounded hostile.

"What's happening?" Queenie cried, holding out her blood-soaked hands. "Miller – for God's sake, tell me! Please!"

The Harlequin Priest opened his mouth, but made no answer and Queenie wailed in revulsion when she saw the stump of his severed tongue waggling inside. The Harlequin frowned at her and pointed to a black patch on his robe to indicate his displeasure.

Stumbling from him, she blundered into the intimidating crowd, pushing them out of the way. For an instant, she thought she caught sight of another familiar face. Was that Tommo? He and Miller were inseparable; they were practically a double act. When she saw he was wearing the same diamond-patterned costume, her panic escalated and she lurched the other way. Then she saw a face that she definitely recognised. It was thin and clever and framed with shoulder-length black hair.

"Jezza!" she called. "Jezza!"

The leader of the old gang back in Felixstowe gave a soft chuckle and strode forward to greet her.

"I am the Ismus," he corrected with some amusement. "Have you forgotten already?"

Queenie looked intently at him, confusion scoring her brow. Of course it was Jezza; there was no question about that. But she had never seen him so groomed and elegant. Where was the shabby leather jacket that was never off his back?

"Stop mucking about," she pleaded. "I don't like it here. Help me, Jezza."

"There is no Jezza."

Before she could argue, something heavy and wet fell to the floor behind her. A hideous sense of dread closed round Queenie's soul and she turned, stiff and slow.

The body of the woman she had just murdered had slumped from the table. The cauldron was lying on its side, dripping gobbets of blood-streaked porridge down on to her upturned face.

In spite of the preposterous medieval costume and the tangled mess of the corpse's hair, Queenie recognised her. Taking a hesitant step closer, she gazed at the dead woman in disbelief and sank to her knees next to her.

"M... Manda?" she uttered hoarsely. "Oh my God! Manda!"

Reaching out, she took hold of her old friend's hand and pressed her lips into the palm.

"Who did this?" she wept, tenderly wiping porridge from the dead face with the hem of her own gown. "What swine did this to my Manda? Call the police, Jezza. They've got to get the animal who did this. Hurry!"

"But you did it," the Ismus told her brightly. "You bludgeoned her, walloped her good and proper. Then you drowned her – and relished every brutal moment."

Shaking, Queenie lowered the plump hand. Tears were streaking down her ashen face. The man's words pounded in her head. Abruptly, and with an agonising spasm, the memories came swarming back and she knew what she had done.

Screaming at the top of her voice, Queenie recoiled. Doubled over, clutching her stomach, she fled through the assembled courtiers, her anguished, desolate cries never stopping.

The Ismus watched her lurch away and listened with satisfaction to the music of her despair. He turned to the Harlequin Priest that Queenie had known as Miller, before the power of *Dancing Jax* had mastered him.

"Consult the reserve list," he instructed, gazing down at the dead figure on the carpet. "We require a new prime Queen of Hearts. Attend to that as soon as possible. I would have the four Royal Houses represented fully at the great revel on Christmas Eve. The viewing public will expect nothing less. We must give our audience what it wants. Everything must be perfect for the global download."

The priest bowed and pointed to a green patch on his robes to signify his agreement.

Queenie staggered on blindly. She didn't know where she was – or where she was going. She just had to escape this nightmare if she could. The sinister crowd back there: Jezza, Tommo and Miller and Manda's body – she couldn't get them out of her head. It couldn't be real. It was impossible. But her own scalding guilt told her otherwise. Hot tears of grief and horror blurred her sight and she blundered into walls and against doors. Then she tripped and hit her chin on a metal step. A biting draught of winter air was blasting from above and she picked herself up to scramble higher and meet it.

Soon a cold gale was tearing at the voluminous gown and the absurd ringlets were thrashing behind her ears. Queenie drew a sleeve across her eyes and gazed out at the endless sky.

The exit to the EdgeWalk was before her. The 360 restaurant, and the torments it contained, were now directly below. Queenie's screams had ceased. She felt utterly annihilated. She was a vessel that had been totally drained and she knew she would never find any peace or solace again. She would never be able to live with what she had seen and what she had done since the book had taken her over. It was more than any conscience could endure.

As she stared out at the vast panorama, high above Toronto, searching the bleak December sky for answers or the hope of absolution, her lips moved hesitantly.

"Is there anything out there?" her cracked voice rasped in hollow desperation. "Is there? Anything? Anyone? Up there?"

She hadn't prayed or thought about such things since she was a little girl. Now, in her darkest moment, she fumbled for words and begged for help – for strength.

The bitter wind that howled about the lofty tower was the only response.

"No one to forgive me?" she whispered, shambling forward. "Nothing."

The crushed woman passed through the exit and stepped mechanically out on to the narrow platform on top of the tower's main pod, 356 metres above the ground. There was no safety rail, no barrier, just a perilous drop. Alone, high up on that concrete needle that dominated the cityscape, she was a tiny, forsaken speck.

With the taffeta lashing fiercely around her, like the sputtering of a great black flame, she approached the brink.

"No one," she mouthed in meek acceptance and the high winds ripped her devastated voice away.

In the restaurant beneath, the Ismus had retrieved his laptop from behind the bar and was just closing the precious document when

Queenie plummeted silently past the windows.

"Naughty girls who open their Christmas presents too early," the Ismus told himself with a gratified smirk, "spoil the surprise and have only themselves to blame."

The startling sight went without comment by those who had witnessed it. The everyday trivialities and intrigues of the Court of *Dancing Jax* were more engaging topics. Even the Jill of Spades had her thoughts on other matters and the Jill of Hearts was gazing longingly at the Jack of Clubs once more. In the arms of the Lady Labella, the infant began to cry.

Turning to the Harlequin Priest, the Ismus said. "Choose a new Queen of Spades from the reserves also. Now get my jet ready. We've got to get back to England. There's so much to do, so much to prepare for the big night. I want to leave in an hour. I've got a Korean takeaway waiting for me back home – I don't want it to spoil."

15

Spencer was drifting in and out of an uncomfortable sleep. His head, half buried in his Stetson, vibrated against the car window. His nerves were a strung-out mess. It had been an absolutely exhausting few days, and he tried to snatch back the rags of slumber and smother himself in them before they evaporated completely.

When the munitions store in the mountain had erupted, they had barely made it out with their lives. It was only the collapse of the tunnel roof behind that saved them from being caught in the pursuing inferno, but the dangers were far from over.

As Eun-mi raced the jeep through the shuddering darkness, a jagged crack ripped the underground road apart beneath them. For several desperate minutes they'd driven along an ever-widening chasm, until one side lifted sharply. The girl wrenched at the steering wheel. There was a scream and a scrape of metal on the lifting ledge of rock. Then the jeep vaulted across the yawning ravine and screeched on to the lower level, roaring down the quaking tunnel ahead. Grit and stones poured on top of them and great chunks of the mountain slammed or slid on to the road behind. When the wall split open, right in front, and a vast boulder came grinding into view, Eun-mi pressed her foot down and skidded round it. The massive stone caught the back of the jeep and Spencer nearly fell out as the glancing blow crumpled the rear corner like foil.

He wasn't sure how they survived that. The rest of the journey beneath the exploding mountain base was a hideous blur of feverish terror, and the fear of violent, crushing death was a constant passenger. When they finally emerged, crashing through the bushes and undergrowth on the Chinese side of the Baekdudaegan Mountains, he discovered that the fingers of his right hand had dug deep into the seat, puncturing the leather, and had twisted the steel springs beneath. Khaki paint was impacted under the nails of his left, where he had clawed the vehicle's side, clean down to the metal.

He had never expected to breathe in the open air again and he praised the North Korean girl for getting them out of that collapsing tomb alive. Eun-mi made no response. The hazards were not done with. The ground was still juddering and shifting under them and wildfires were blazing far and wide.

When Spencer glanced behind them, the mountain was belching flame, and oily smoke poured from every fissure. Looking at Gerald, he was shocked to see how aged and frail the old man appeared. But there was no opportunity to shout to him to see if he was OK; the jeep was bouncing over rugged terrain and Spencer was clinging to the seat for dear life again.

Through thickets of flame and swerving round the debris of the ruptured mountain, they passed into the night and the rumbling booms eventually receded in the distance. Soon they were wrapping blankets round themselves as protection from the biting Chinese winter. The cutting wind that numbed their faces saved their lives, for it battered back the clouds of chlorine, sarin and phosgene that spewed from the stockpiled chemical weapons, blowing the lethal gases back into North Korea.

And so the long journey to Dandong began.

Eun-mi drove for six hours without a break before her head began to nod at the wheel and Gerald demanded she stop. Once he had made certain she ate something, the old man took over and she slept fitfully. After that, they rotated every four hours. Spencer could only sit in the back, watching the frost-ringed stars overhead.

The mountain track was deserted and the surrounding country was desolate and shrouded in darkness. At some point he dozed. When he awoke, the world was cold and grey. The ridged landscape seemed to go on forever. Stony hills and gullies, dotted with bare trees, surrounded them. There was no sign of another living creature. It was some time before they left the winding way out of those blank and empty hills. In the afternoon, they saw the first remote building in the distance, then ploughed fields began to break up the wilderness. Gradually the rough track that their beaten-up jeep rattled along evolved into a road and, for many kilometres, ran parallel with a raised pipeline. Then a march of electric pylons could be seen and the hum of the wires gave a new soundtrack to their journey.

Spencer must have fallen asleep again for he jolted awake when Gerald braked.

The boy blinked and rubbed his eyes. They were still in the middle of nowhere and he thought they'd halted for another toilet stop when he realised Gerald and Eun-mi were staring across the scrubland at one of the pylons. At the top of that latticed tower, where the power lines ran through the triangular arms, were clusters of dark, glistening eggs, each one over a metre in diameter and round, like massive black pearls. Suspended beneath them, trussed in sticky strands, was the carcass of a cow, its four legs dangling in mid-air. It was to be the first meal of whatever was going to hatch from the eggs and the first reminder that the world was now full of unnatural horrors.

Gerald drove on in thoughtful silence. Eun-mi began to keep an even more watchful eye on the road and held one of the rifles in readiness. Spencer didn't like to try and guess what had laid those eggs and where it might be now, or just how many of them there were.

Day passed into night. Eun-mi was at the wheel again when the first noises were heard overhead. Up there, in the dark, large creatures were croaking and screeching. Spencer could hear the leathery slap of wings in flight and he cowered in his seat. Suddenly they all felt a rush of fetid air as something came swooping down. Gerald raised the AK-47 and fired blindly into the night.

For the briefest, stuttering instants, Spencer saw a hideous horned head, with eyes like headlamps, illuminated by the automatic rifle fire. Jaws packed with razor teeth were wide open, ready to rend and tear, and the span of the bat-like wings was twice the length of the jeep.

There was a horrendous shriek and the stench lifted. They heard the creature veer off, screaming in pain. Then, up there in the teeming darkness, the rest of an unseen host attacked it. There was a clamouring din of violent death and Eun-mi drove as fast as she could.

Nothing else came near them that night, but they continued to hear harrowing cries in the distance, on every side.

Only when the dawn approached did the fearful noises cease.

The barren countryside was behind them. Farms and villages became more numerous and the River Yalu could be glimpsed far off to the left. Rustic dwellings gave way to drab concrete buildings and, before midday, they were in the prosperous city of Dandong.

The streets were quiet. They saw no traffic and they drove through the hushed cityscape wondering what had happened – even Jaxers went about their normal business when they weren't lost in the book. Following the road signs, Eun-mi headed for the airport. This was on the other side of the city and it wasn't long before they understood. The approaches were clogged with vehicles and people tramping on foot, wheeling barrows of belongings. Most of them were dressed as their characters in *Dancing Jax*, rocking backwards and forwards as they shuffled along, with their heads bent over those evil pages.

It was an exodus and looked as if the entire population was headed there, but these were the stragglers. The rest had gone to the train station or travelled by bus to Beijing because the airport here was so small, with only a few scheduled flights per day.

There was no way the jeep could get through the snarled gridlock; the vehicles weren't moving. Eun-mi decided they would have to walk the rest of the way and Gerald agreed. The girl passed rifles to him and Spencer, and took up the satchel of grenades and a blanket roll.

"Don't be absurd!" Gerald protested. "Even if we get anywhere near the airport, they're never going to let us in with these. Just leave them."

Eun-mi wouldn't listen and Gerald and Spencer exchanged weary glances. She was maddeningly headstrong and seemed determined to get them arrested or worse.

Spencer eyed the pushing and shoving of the mob and couldn't see the point. It was impossible and impassable.

"Might as well give up now," he groaned. "Isn't there another way? Somewhere else to try?"

"No other way!" Eun-mi snapped. "This only chance. You follow."

"Then remember," Gerald warned, "we're supposed to be part of this. Don't say or do anything that will give us away as different. If someone praises that book, you bloody well join in – and make it convincing."

The girl made no answer and started barging into the crowd. Angry shouts ensued, but, as soon as the Chinese saw the playing card pinned to her uniform, the indignation vanished and they chattered excitedly. The Jill of Spades was here, and behind her were the Jack of Clubs and the King of Diamonds! They cheered and applauded, bowing down before the royal latecomers.

The news rippled swiftly up through the jostling river of cars and people. To Eun-mi's surprise, the inhabitants of Dandong squeezed together more tightly than ever and cleared a route through the centre to let them pass.

The girl turned back to Gerald and Spencer.

"Hurry," she ordered.

Spencer pulled the Stetson down over his eyes.

Just over an hour later, they found themselves in the main airport building. The place was heaving, but there was no sign of any security. The noise and the jostling of thousands of people clamouring to get a seat on the next plane out was unbearable. There were so many jammed inside that, even with the deference shown them due to their pretend royal status, they found it difficult to make their way through.

"What on earth is going on?" Gerald shouted above the din.

Eun-mi glanced up and saw the answer on every large display screen.

"Yes, it's only two more days till the eve of Christmas and the publication of *Fighting Pax*!" chirped a bright, friendly voice, over images of snow and artificial trees festooned with lights, with tinkling music in the background.

"If any of you are still undecided, what in Mooncaster is wrong with you? Are you aberrants? It's your last chance to come on over and join us for the biggest celebration this grey dreamscape has ever known. Don't sit back and watch it on TV – come to England and watch it for real! Get the full experience. See the replica of the White Castle! See the Court of the Holy Enchanter. Browse the wares in the marketplace. Dance to the music of the minstrels. Eat in the reconstructed tavern of The Silver Penny and thrill to the biggest night of your lives. So what are you waiting for? Jump on a plane and fly over. Everyone is welcome. Have the trip of a lifetime. This is a must-not-miss opportunity. One final revel to end all revels before the grand publication of *Fighting Pax*."

The picture changed to footage from airports around the world where panicking hordes were clambering over security barriers, scaling baggage conveyors to get into the holds of aircraft and charging on to runways. It was grotesque and insane.

"Airports everywhere are crammed to capacity and every plane is standing room only – budge up there, Granddad! Watch out for those overhead lockers – that's where they put the baby! Don't let long queues put you off; get here any way you can: by ship, rail – remember it's all totally free, courtesy of our Holy Enchanter, the Ismus. Why just sit there? Come to England by any means possible, even hang-glider or hot-air balloon. What's this? That's right, girls, keep pedalling – we'll see you in Kent!"

The final pictures had been of two elderly ladies in a lemon-sherbet-coloured pedalo, three miles out from Miami Beach, grinning and waving, with copies of *Dancing Jax* in their aged hands as they cheerfully headed further out into the Atlantic.

Then bright, chunky letters filled the screen and the voice announced, "Just two more days left, just two – until..."

The letters flashed a festive green and red.

And the whole thing looped back to the beginning.

"We've got less time than I thought," Gerald said. "Whatever Austerly Fellows has planned, he's going to do it on Christmas Eve."

"Have we got time to get there?" Spencer asked. "Can we even get there?"

Gerald gazed around at the sea of impatient, agitated Jaxers that filled the terminal building. "We're going to damn well try!" he said.

"This way!" Eun-mi urged, as she forged ahead to the departure gate. "You too old, too slow!"

"That's hardly breaking news, dear. I'm fully aware of both

headlines – have been for some time."

It was only because they were the last remaining Mooncaster royalty in Dandong that they managed to get on board the next plane out. To Gerald's amazement, not one person questioned or challenged them about the weapons they carried so openly. There were no security checks, no passport control, nothing. The world had nudged a little closer to a final madness.

Once on board, they discovered that the video hadn't exaggerated: it really was standing room only, like the London Underground during rush hour. All weight and safety regulations were cheerfully disregarded with people wedged into every space and filling the aisle. They were all high number cards, tens or nines, being knights or ladies-in-waiting, and, when they realised there was royalty among them, those with seats were quick to offer their places.

Gerald assumed a haughty, kingly manner and accepted the nearest three. Spencer found himself next to a window overlooking the wing. The boy stared round at the packed aircraft with increasing dismay and he clutched his Stetson fretfully.

"There's too many," he hissed at Gerald. "There's no way this can take off, or if it does it won't stay in the air long. This is worse than getting out of the mountain. At least death would have been instantaneous in there. This is crazy. I want to get off! Seriously, I have to get off!"

He tried to rise from the seat, but Gerald pushed him back.

"Sit still and be quiet," the old man told him. "If you make a scene, the game's up for us."

"You are baby," Eun-mi said with disgust as she stowed the rifles, grenades and her blanket roll in the overhead locker.

"Er... I'm just ruddy sensible," the boy replied anxiously. "This is mental. We're all going to get killed on this death trap. Plummeting out of the sky is, like, near the top of the ways I do not want to die."

"Spencer," Gerald said with an edge in his voice. "There simply isn't an alternative. This is our only possible chance of getting back home and it's a miracle we managed to get on board. If you try to get off this aircraft, every single one of these passengers will know you're an aberrant and rip you to pieces. Where does that rank on your scale of doom?"

"About the same actually! If I believed in something I could pray to, I'd be doing it like crazy right now."

Gerald smiled reassuringly at him. "Of course there's a something," he said. "I don't mean the twisted God-squad stuff, spouted by bigots and hypocrites in black frocks. I've spent my entire life and career being hated by that lot. No, there's something bigger than that, but it's too huge and too wonderful to be put in a book for people to hit one another with."

"How can you think like that? I mean, after everything?"

The old man gave a small laugh. "That's why I'm surer than ever. We're up to our necks in shadows, Spence, but you can't have them without there being a bloody big light on somewhere. Evelyn always says—" He stopped himself abruptly and rubbed his eyes. Would she never leave him alone?

"More fairy tales," Eun-mi said sourly. "You should not tell him such lies. That is why the West brought this sickness on itself and infected my country. Why must we always suffer because of you?"

"Breathe deeply and try to relax and blot it out," Gerald resumed, ignoring her. "Don't work yourself into a state."

Spencer crumpled the hat to his chest and looked out of the window. What he saw there made it even worse. People had clambered on to the wing and were waiting for take-off. He turned back to Gerald, who was humming 'I've Got a Little List' to himself.

"Have you seen...?"

The old man nodded, but there was absolutely nothing they could do. "There's probably more crouched up in the spaces for the landing gear," he said. "And in the hold – and hanging on to the tail."

"Will make plane lighter when they fall," Eun-mi commented with cold practicality. "That is good."

Gerald bit his tongue to avoid an argument and Spencer covered the window with his Stetson.

The plane began to taxi to the runway. Presently it picked up speed and took off. The people in the aisle fell into one another and across the seats. Spencer gritted his teeth as the aircraft climbed higher. This was it.

After half an hour in the air, when the passengers had settled once more and were absorbed in reading the book, the boy dared to peel back the brim of his hat and look out.

The wing was empty, except for one solitary figure who had somehow managed to survive the sub-zero temperatures and remain clinging on. Spencer saw the frost on the man's hands and the ice in his hair and realised that, if he wasn't dead already, he soon would be. Then, as he watched, the man's frozen fingers came loose and he slid away – disappearing into the clouds. Spencer re-covered the window hastily.

"Try and get some sleep," Gerald suggested softly. "You'll need all your strength when we get home. The worst is yet to come."

A little after 5pm GMT, over twelve hours later, the plane touched down at Stansted. The dark December sky was full of aircraft coming from every part of the globe. As soon as one landed, another came in straight after. The smoking remains of a crash burned across seven of the surrounding fields. So far, Stansted had got off lightly. Every other UK airport and airstrip had experienced catastrophic disasters. At Heathrow, two runways were submerged beneath a blazing holocaust of tangled, white-hot metal. And still the planes came in to land, flying down through the black, blinding smoke. Explosion after explosion thundered across the night and hungry creatures gathered round the flaming wreckage, waiting for fires to die.

Spencer could not believe they had made it and when they stepped on to the tarmac he almost fell on his knees to kiss the ground. But Eun-mi was already striding on, pushing through the other passengers, satchel of grenades over one shoulder, automatic rifle slung across the other, blanket roll tucked under her arm. They soon discovered there was no security or Customs here either. Every gate was open and the influx of *Dancing Jax* pilgrims came flooding through.

"How far is new castle?" Eun-mi demanded. "Where is Kent place?"

"A couple of hours' drive," Gerald informed her.

"So we need vehicle."

This was less of a problem than any of them expected. Leaving the main concourse, they stepped out on to the long, straight road, and found that special coaches had been laid on. At least seventy of them were lined up and thousands of people were trying to board. English Jaxers dressed as pages and serfs were attempting to keep some semblance of order and usher them into queues, but the eager excitement of the new arrivals made this a difficult task.

Eun-mi was about to join the nearest queue when she saw Gerald hang back and lead Spencer away.

"We go!" she shouted to them in annoyance. "Get on bus."

The old man shook his head. "We're not going that way," he told her. "Not on a coach."

"You come!" she commanded, moving her hand to the holster on her hip, threateningly.

"Oh, give it a rest," Gerald said. "You're not going to shoot us now. Get on your coach and I wish you the best of British, whatever that means nowadays. I really do."

Eun-mi scowled at him, but she didn't take out the pistol.

"You – old fool," she snapped angrily as she turned away and followed the shuffling queue.

"She's full of stale news today," Gerald observed.

"I'm glad she's gone," Spencer declared. "She never lets up, does she?"

"She's a maiden, cold and stately," Gerald sang.

"Do you think she'll find her sister?"

"Not a hope. Little Nabi will be right in the thick of it by now. Eun-mi won't get anywhere near Austerly Fellows and his entourage. She might be determined, but that won't be enough. I don't think she'll even get within several miles of the place. The traffic on the roads to

Kent will be the worst jam there's ever been. Half the world is making its way there. She'll be stuck on a bus for days, not that there'll be any days after tomorrow."

"But you think we can get through?"

Gerald shrugged. "I've got a very silly idea, that's all, but sometimes they work best."

"I hope Maggie and the others are still OK."

"You and me both, Spence."

"We won't be able to help them, will we? I mean this is it now, isn't it? The end of everything. We're just going to be with them, aren't we?"

"If we can be," Gerald said. "If we can. There's nothing else we can do."

Crossing the bustling road, they went in search of another mode of transport. The car park was nearby, but they didn't even need to go that far. Dozens of airport taxis were pulled up, abandoned. The drivers had boarded the coaches days ago. None of the cabs were locked and they all had keys in the ignition.

"No crime," Spencer explained when he saw Gerald's puzzlement. "No theft to worry about, no muggings, no murders, no drugs."

"No humanity."

Putting their rifles on the back seat, they got in and Spencer turned on the radio.

Every station was broadcasting the same repeated message, in between the usual jaunty Christmas songs, which seemed hideously inappropriate this year.

"Can you believe it? Only one more day till the night before Christmas and the awesome publication of *Fighting Pax*! Our tinsel and baubles are moist just thinking about it. The county of Kent is bursting at the seams, but there's always room for more. If you're not here then why not? Don't miss out! Come join the spectacle. The fun is just beginning and soon it'll be time to play Flee the Beast. What are you waiting for?"

And then Boney M began singing about Mary's boy child. Gerald grimaced and turned them off. Adjusting the rear-view mirror, he prepared to drive away.

"What's wrong?" Spencer asked when the car didn't move and he saw the man's face register surprise.

Gerald turned in his seat and Spencer noticed a figure come walking round the cab to stand outside the driver's door.

"I drive!" a familiar voice barked.

And there was Eun-mi, stiff and belligerent, still wearing the same scowl.

"Missing us already?" the old man teased when he rolled the window down.

"Too many crowd, not enough bus," she retorted. "Take too long. This better way."

Gerald almost laughed. That was such a blatant lie. She was alone in a foreign country and, for all her bravado, was still very young. But she would never admit to being afraid, so he didn't press her.

"Yes, you're right," he said generously. "Get in, but I'm driving. You have no idea how to get there."

The girl accepted the logic of this, but refused to sit in the back. With a roll of the eyes and plenty of grumbling, Spencer got out and assumed his by now familiar position.

"To new castle," Eun-mi directed as Gerald drove off.

The old man said nothing. There was somewhere else he had to go first.

And so Spencer dozed, with his head against the window, and the amber glare of the street lamps skimmed across his face. He didn't stir when they pulled into a deserted garage for petrol and Gerald stocked up on supplies, and not even at the sound of unearthly cries in the distance. Such noises were no longer extraordinary. The only thing that registered vaguely was the fact they weren't nearby.

Almost an hour later, when he was waking and it was no use trying to chase after the last elusive, comforting dregs of sleep, he sat up and scratched his head.

There were no more street lights. They had left the main roads behind and were travelling down a country lane, margined by high hedges. It was pitch-black out there, but Spencer didn't have time to wonder where they were. Eun-mi was arguing with Gerald.

Throughout the journey, they'd passed a lot of traffic going in the opposite direction, but their lane had always remained totally deserted. No other vehicle was going this way. The North Korean girl's suspicions increased steadily until, at last, she challenged Gerald.

"This not the way!" she snapped. "Where we go? Take me to castle!"

It was no use pretending any longer – Gerald had been rumbled.

"No, this isn't the way to Kent," he confessed. "I have something more important to do first."

The girl could not believe it. What could possibly be more important?

"You stop car!" she commanded in outrage, slamming her fist on the dash. "Turn round. I must get to castle! You stop!"

"We're just about there," Gerald said. "We've still got plenty of time to—"

His voice broke off. Eun-mi had pulled her gun on him and pressed the muzzle against his head. With steel in her voice, she said, "You bad old man. You do what I say or I shoot."

Gerald put his foot on the accelerator and the taxi sped faster down the darkened country lanes.

"You do that, dear," he warned defiantly, "and the only place we'll end up is in a ditch – dead or dying."

"I shoot!" she promised.

"If you want to see little Nabi again, you'll put that silly thing away. Trust me, where we're headed might actually help us."

"Stop car!"

"Not until we get where I'm going."

"Stop! I will shoot!"

"Don't be ruddy stupid!" Spencer shouted.

"Almost there," Gerald said.

Eun-mi glanced out at the empty road streaking by beneath the headlights. Every moment was taking her further from where she wanted to be. It was not to be tolerated.

"Stop car!" she demanded one final time.

The girl's face set hard as stone. Why was he ignoring her? She didn't make empty threats; he should know that by now. He had brought this on himself; she had given him enough chances. More than she should.

Bracing herself for the imminent crash, Eun-mi pulled the trigger.

"No!" Spencer yelled.

But there was no deafening shot, just a click.

Gerald raised his eyebrows. "I wondered if you'd actually do it," he said with measured disappointment. "I'd hoped we'd progressed beyond that stage – obviously not. I took the liberty of removing the bullets when you nodded off on the plane."

"You really would have shot him!" Spencer cried in shock. "You'd have killed him! You're off your head you are! Your whole lousy country is off its head! Why didn't you shoot your maniac leader and your crazy Generals and do yourselves a favour?"

His words cut deep into the grief and guilt the girl had stifled and bottled up regarding her father. Now they came raging to the surface and she finally lost control. Shrieking, she spun round in the seat, grabbed hold of Spencer's shirt and dragged him forward. Then she drew her other arm back to deliver a hideous blow to his face.

Gerald slammed on the brakes. The car skidded in a sharp curve across the road and Eun-mi was flung off balance, hitting her head on the windscreen.

"You all right, Spence?" he called out.

Spencer had slithered off the back seat. "Just dump her here," he said, fuming as he reappeared. "We don't need her any more. Get rid of her, she's a ruddy liability, she's going to get us killed, she's off her rocker."

Gerald pulled off the lane and into a gap in the trees and hedgerow, where an unlit track receded into darkness beyond the reach of the headlights. He killed the engine and got out, taking one of the rifles and the bag of grenades.

Breathing hard, furious with herself for failing and determined not to show how much her head hurt where she'd struck the windscreen, Eun-mi folded her arms. Her eyes followed Gerald as he walked round the cab to open the passenger door.

"I not move," she said proudly. "I am the daughter of General Chung Kang-dae – I will not kneel on ground and be shot. Shoot me where I sit, old man, if you have the stomach."

"Oh, if only you were aware how funny that sounds," Gerald answered. "Now don't be such a melodramatic diva. We don't go in for murder like that here, but I don't trust you as far as I could throw you, which really isn't very far, so I'm not leaving poor Spence on his own with you. You'd better get out so he can lock himself in."

"Er... what?" the boy asked. "What's going on?"

"We're here, Spence," Gerald explained. "This is it. I'm just going to walk up ahead for a short while. I want you to stop in the cab and be safe. If I'm not back in an hour then get out of here – fast."

Spencer spluttered and shook his head in protest. Before Gerald could stop him, he jumped out of the taxi.

"There's no way you're going anywhere on your own!" the boy declared hotly. "We've been through too much to split up now. We're like Butch and Sundance."

Gerald almost laughed. "Thank you for the 'Butch'," he said. "But you don't understand. This place – it's too dangerous."

"What? More dangerous than almost getting my brain scooped out? Than escaping through an exploding mountain? Driving through the dark with those winged nightmares overhead? Flying in an overcrowded death trap? More dangerous than being a prisoner in that camp with Jangler and those filthy guards? How could anything be more dangerous than any of that? Where is this place? Where the hell are we?"

"Suffolk," Gerald told him. "Just a few miles out of Felixstowe. At the end of this track is the old family home of Austerly Fellows, where all of this evil and horror first started."

16

Spencer was speechless. The bare twigs and branches of the winter trees stirred, although there was no breeze.

"So, please," Gerald advised softly, "get back in the car and wait."

The boy looked around nervously.

"No chance," he refused again. "I'm sticking with you. That's what friends do."

"You've got no idea what might be in there!"

"Er... have you? See! This is just like when Butch and the Kid leap off the cliff in the movie. We've been jumping into the unknown for days. Why stop now? Besides, I'll go absolutely crazy sat here waiting, imagining all sorts. It'd be a hundred times worse."

Gerald was about to argue when Eun-mi emerged from the cab.

"Ismus live where?" she demanded, staring around and behaving as if she hadn't just tried to kill them both.

"There's a house further on," Gerald repeated, pointing up the track. "He doesn't live there any more. But it's where he grew up."

"Why you come here?"

Gerald glanced around and lowered his voice to a whisper. "Because the inside of that house might just hold some clue, some secret that could help us. We need every tiny bit we can get."

"Help us do what?" Spencer asked doubtfully.

"Defeat our enemy," Eun-mi declared.

"Don't get too excited," Gerald cautioned. "Austerly Fellows is unassailable now. The best we can hope for is a way to help find our friends, and your sister. There has to be something in there."

Eun-mi considered for a moment then nodded. "I get rifle," she agreed.

"No way!" Spencer blurted. "You're not getting your hands on a loaded weapon again! After what you just did – you should be tied up."

The girl sneered at him. "Do it," she invited, holding her hands out for him to dare tie together. "It only take two moves to twist and break your neck. Then I have rifle."

Spencer jumped back in alarm. "See!" he cried. "She's rabid! Lock her in the car! Put her in the boot or something!"

"Miss Chung!" Gerald snapped sternly. "If you want to be treated civilly, you'll have to behave yourself. Stop trying to scare Spencer. There's enough of that still to come without you adding to it. Now I'm probably a stupid geriatric for doing this, but... here."

To Spencer's dismay, he handed her one of the AK-47s. "Just remember," the old man told her, "you need us more than we need you now. I'm trusting you with this, so stop mucking about. If we're all going up to the house, which I still think is a bad idea, we have to keep calm and alert. Your military training will be useful."

"How many guards?" she asked. "We must form strategy."

Gerald shrugged. "If there were any," he began, "I'm hoping they've gone down south like everyone else. But it's not human guards we need to worry about anyway. There might be other things in that place."

"Nice," Spencer commented.

"I wish you'd stay here in the cab," Gerald said.

"Not on your life. Butch and Sundance, remember?"

"We go!" Eun-mi ordered, prowling forward. "You follow. I lead!"

Gerald sighed. "And there goes Calamity Juche."

"Or Eun-mi Oakley," Spencer said.

Gerald managed a weak smile and they crept cautiously along the overgrown track. When the girl in front gave a shudder, they thought it was only because of the chill December air. Spencer ran a finger round his collar. For some reason it had become uncomfortably tight.

"Never thought I'd ever find myself here again," the old man muttered, glancing into the darkness of the surrounding trees. "As kids, we were all absolutely terrified of this place. It was much more than the local spooky house. This was the real deal and it was what parents threatened you with if you misbehaved. Never mind the slipper and no presents from Father Christmas: they used to tell us we'd be brought here and left. Talk about mental cruelty; no wonder we all wet the bed till we were teenagers."

"Why, what happened here?"

"Back in the 1920s and 30s, this was where Austerly Fellows practised all manner of hideous rites. He founded occult societies and called himself the Abbot of the Angles, amongst other titles. Stories of his depraved gatherings were known throughout the country, but he had so many powerful people under his control, he couldn't be stopped. The nearby villagers used to bolt their doors and wear their knees out in prayer when he was in residence. They said he was a devil and they weren't being fanciful or overly superstitious."

He paused. Was that a girl's mocking laughter? Eun-mi was several paces ahead and did not turn round. Her head was low and her shoulders tense; she appeared to be completely focused on her reconnaissance. So why had she laughed? She was such an odd person. He would never understand her. The North Koreans were a strange people and she more than most.

"Yes," he continued quietly, "a place of horror to be avoided and shunned. Not even the prospect of hidden treasure could tempt us into the grounds. It was the Chernobyl of its day, in a supernatural sense."

"Treasure?" Spencer asked, wrestling with his collar again – why was it so tight?

"Oh, yes. That last great party he gave, the night he disappeared, was filled with society's A-list. Rumour was that they came charging out of there in such a blind panic, they fled into the trees and lost their diamonds when they stumbled. There's some around here who still call it Sparklers Wood – or rather there were, before DJ claimed them."

The old man took a breath and recalled his youthful fascination for that story. He had imagined necklaces, earrings and tiaras hanging from branches like tinsel and roots growing through discarded bracelets. He had never dared come and look for himself though; even passing the entrance on the lane required a stout heart. Only the bravest kids would risk a few wobbly steps up the track and thus win the respect of their peers.

"Diamonds and sapphires!" Eun-mi cooed unexpectedly.

Oh, she really is a weird fish, Gerald thought. *Who'd have guessed*

263

the bright shiny beads of Western capitalism would hold any fascination
for her? Or maybe she's still laughing at us?

Suddenly Spencer coughed and the rifle dropped from his grasp. He staggered backwards, pulled to the ground by an unseen force. The Stetson fell from his head and he clawed at his throat. His collar was choking him. Gasping, he tried to cry out, but his voice was crushed. It was worse than when he was strapped to Doctor Choe's operating table. He tore at the neck of his shirt. He could feel it constricting and squeezing. Then a violent, heaving wrench had him slithering down the track and he couldn't stop.

Gerald rushed to help. Spencer flailed desperately and reached out for the old man's hands.

"Let him go!" Gerald shouted at nothing, swiping the empty air behind the boy's head. "Let him…"

His words faltered when he saw a grey, smoky shape come floating down from the darkness above, descending through the twigs and branches. It was blurred and indistinct, but he could see it was the figure of a young woman. Her head was tilted at a horrible angle and her dead eyes bulged hideously. A black, swollen tongue protruded from her gaping mouth and the rope that formed a noose round her neck disappeared up into the night. As it drew closer, the apparition stretched its hands towards them.

"Get back!" Gerald yelled, his breath forming clouds of vapour as the temperature plummeted. "In the name of God, leave us!"

Then he heard that same laughter and Eun-mi was beside them. She aimed the rifle upwards and the effect was startling. The ghastly spectre covered its gruesome face and retreated swiftly, rushing like wind-shredded mist, high into the tops of the trees.

Spencer hacked and retched, gasping to catch his breath and clinging to Gerald's arm.

"Thank you," the boy said when he could speak again.

"It wasn't me," Gerald told him. "It was our Miss Chung. Seems one look from her is enough to drive evil spirits away."

"That's what it was? There's ghosts now as well?"

"After what Austerly Fellows did here, as the old song says, 'Anything Goes'. You bet there'll be ghosts – as well as everything else you can think of, and more besides."

Spencer's skin crawled. But there was no going back now. He turned to Eun-mi, but she was already striding back up the track.

"Get a wiggle on, boys!" she called to them. "We don't have all night."

"I don't get it," Spencer said. "What did she do? How did she chase that horror away?"

"No idea," Gerald murmured, helping him to his feet and glancing warily up at the treetops before gazing suspiciously at Eun-mi's receding figure. "But since when does she call us 'boys'? And 'get a wiggle on'?"

They watched as she stooped to pick up Spencer's hat. She placed it on her head and twirled about, brandishing the assault rifle as she struck poses.

"What's going on?" the boy hissed.

Before Gerald could answer, they heard her giggle.

"Pure Tom Mix!" she exclaimed. "What a perfect hoot!"

Spencer gripped Gerald's arm.

"That's not Eun-mi," he hissed.

The girl spun round slowly and tipped the brim of the hat back with a playful wink as she pouted. The face, the clothes belonged to the daughter of General Chung Kang-dae, but the personality that animated those familiar features was completely different.

"Of course it isn't her, darlings," she said, grinning wider than the girl's face was accustomed to. "I'm bags more fun. I was going to keep you in the dark for simply ages, but I never could keep a secret. What a bluenose pill she is. I saw that the moment you motored up. Couldn't resist slipping in to try her for size. It's a whizz of a fit, don't you agree? I thought the arms might be a teeny bit short to begin with, but they're not at all; they're rather spiff, aren't they? And she's got excellent pins!"

Hitching up the skirt of the North Korean uniform, she stood on tiptoe and craned her head back to inspect her calves.

"They really are the berries!" she declared, nimbly executing some old-fashioned dance steps. "I could cut a rug for hours on these."

"Who are you?" Gerald asked sternly. "What are you?"

"Now don't be boring, darling," the girl said with a tut. "The wardrobe will have to be tipped though, it's drabber than the Salvation Army, and these shoes – ugh. At first I thought she had club feet. Ghastlygaskins!"

"Where's Eun-mi? What have you done with her?"

"Such a silly name," the girl groaned in exasperation. "How about Anna May Wong or Shanghai Lil instead? I like that buckets better. Exotic lotus blossom of the mystic Orient."

"She's from North Korea. Her name is Chung Eun-mi."

"Details, darling, petty details."

"Let her go."

"Don't be tiresome – I'm only borrowing, it's not for keepsies. She's still in here. I haven't hurt her, although it feels as if this face might crack. Does she never smile? How do you put up with it? There's a rotten bump on her head – what happened there? Which of you two naughty boys clonked her one? I wouldn't blame you, she's frightful. I'd have pushed her off a balcony if I'd known her. Of course, one didn't socialise with people of her sort – might have been a hoot though."

Chuckling, she approached them, arms outstretched.

"Divino to meet you," she greeted them enthusiastically. "Estelle Winyard, dead spinster of no particular parish since 1936 – oh, corks, that makes me sound positively ancient and fossilised. I'm not at all really, honest injun. Have you heard of me? Daddy is quite a big noise – or was, I should say. It's been a while since that Fellows beast fried the life out of me."

Embracing Spencer warmly, she planted a flamboyant kiss on both his cheeks. The boy recoiled. It was more than disconcerting to be squeezed by the usually stony-faced and emotionless Eun-mi. Even if it wasn't her actually doing it, they were still her arms, still her lips.

"Now I know your names," she gushed, tapping her temple. "There's a bit of osmosis going on in here. You're Spencer, the Wild West aficionado, aren't you? I used to have a pash for Gary Cooper, though I preferred parties and sin to movies. I only sneaked in to see what the servants were gassing about the whole time and a strange man touched my knee in the dark. I stuck a hatpin in him where it would hurt most and he screamed all the way through Donald Duck. Would you believe I was the one the usherette threw out? Outrageous! Oh, please let me keep this hat a ickle while longer; you will, won't you? I always looked stunning in chapeaux. I got banned from Ascot in my last summer, lost a bundle on Alcazar in the Gold Cup, so I scandalised the Jockey Club and gave three gee-gees the shock of their lives – such larks! You are a pet!"

Turning to Gerald, she lifted one foot off the ground as she hugged him tightly. "She's got such jumbled thoughts about you," she announced. "You think Shanghai Lil's a puzzler? You're the jolly old Times crossword to her. First she hates you, then she respects you. It's all very mixed up in here, and then there's the big barred and bolted door, holding back the memories she's shut away, but now they're starting to seep out. There's one of a cherished grandfather being hauled off to a labour camp, which is frightfully grim. Sometimes she confuses you with him. She's a heck of a mess, to be frank, and that door is creaking and buckling under the strain. When it finally bursts open, heaven knows what will happen to her, or what she'll do. And on top of all that, of course, there's the hold-the-front-page business about her father – not to mention that gruesome red piano when she was a girl—"

"I don't want to know," Gerald interrupted. "Thoughts like that should be private."

"Not according to Pater; he was a newspaperman – tycoon really. His motto was print the personal peculiar."

"Sounds like a muckraking hack. I've met plenty of them. Now have you had your fun? Give us back Eun-mi."

"Er... do we have to have her back?" Spencer spoke up. "This one's much nicer."

"There!" Estelle gurgled. "Didn't I say so? What would you want misery guts back for? She'll turn on you the first chance she gets, you know. She's already planning her next double cross."

"She's a rattlesnake," Spencer agreed.

"Anyway, you want to poke about in the house, don't you? Well, you'll never get through the front door of that doomy old mausoleum without my help. I can be your tour guide!"

"Makes sense," the boy said to Gerald.

"None of this makes any sense," Gerald countered. "Why should this disembodied... thing help us?"

"'Thing'? How ungallant and dreary of you. Listen, darling, if I can get back at AF in any way I can then that's good gravy. Don't look a gift gee-gee in the mouth, specially one with bows on. Consider yourself bally lucky I took a shine to Shanghai Lil, otherwise something very nasty would have pounced by now and you'd be so much party food – devilled ham, most probably."

"She has just saved me from getting strangled," Spencer reminded him.

"We don't really have much choice, do we?" Gerald muttered flatly.

"Settled then!" Estelle cried. "Now stick with me and don't wander off the path, as my dear old nanny used to say, not that I ever listened. You wouldn't believe what lurks in those woods and it's got far worse lately. Things that used to be no more than noises in the shadows have grown shapes – give me the absolute heebies."

She led them up the track and Spencer shot fearful glances at the darkness under the nearby trees. He caught the glint of many eyes watching them and saw curls of grey mist move slowly over the ground. The undergrowth rustled, as unseen creatures shadowed them. But nothing leaped out or came close enough for him to see clearly and he wondered if that was because of Estelle. But why should she exert such an influence over those skulking watchers?

Then the track left the woods and Spencer beheld, for the first time, Fellows End.

The gables of Austerly Fellows' country home reared into the winter night. It was an ugly, heavy-looking building, with an octagonal tower at one end. There was a brooding tension and hostility about it. Spencer wanted to turn and run away. Gaps in the imperfectly boarded-up windows were slits for whatever dwelt in there to stare out at them. The boy shivered.

Gerald gripped his rifle tightly, although he had no idea what use it might be in there.

Eun-mi's face chuckled at them.

"Revolting, isn't it?" Estelle declared. "You both look like you could use a stiff slug of gin. Come to think of it, that's not a bad idea. I could murder a Singapore Sling right now – it's been a lifetime! I don't suppose you came prepared? No... it was too much to hope for. Bet you don't have any ciggies either. What a pair of duds! My first time back in the flesh and I'm landed with a couple of Shirley Temples."

Huffing with disappointment, she turned her attention back to the building. "Was there ever such an ungainly stack of unlovely bricks?" she commented. "First time I saw it, I wanted to get as far away as possible – if only I had. You quite sure you want to go inside?"

"Not remotely," Gerald answered. "But we have to."

"Come on then, boys – let's drop in and see what's cooking."

"Wait, is it empty?"

"It's never been empty," she told him darkly. "Even before AF came here as a young monster, there was always something. Maybe it was waiting for him; maybe that's why he came here. I don't know. I don't ask those sorts of questions. I don't want to know those answers."

The driveway had benefited from recent attention. Trees that had grown up in the centre had been uprooted and the holes filled in. Fresh gravel had been strewn down and deep tyre tracks showed that a truck had been a recent visitor.

The possessed girl went crunching across and approached the front door that was wide open. Spencer had the feeling it had opened specially for them and he wished he'd stayed in the car after all.

Skipping up the steps, Estelle turned round and beckoned playfully.

"Don't bother to wipe your feet," she said. "It's what you may have to scrape off the rest of you when you leave you should be worried about – if it lets you leave."

Gerald turned to Spencer. "Off the cliff?" he asked.

The boy hesitated then steeled himself and nodded. "Off the cliff," he affirmed. "For Maggie and Lee and the others."

Together they ascended the few steps and went inside Fellows End.

It was darker inside that house than beneath the mountain in North Korea. The reek of damp and rottenness assaulted their nostrils and they closed their mouths against it. Gerald took a torch from his coat pocket and snapped it on.

There was a sense of the darkness as a tangible force being thrust back by the sudden light and the atmosphere almost crackled. Overhead timbers creaked and door after door slammed. The house was angry.

Eun-mi's face was caught in the beam, but, for an instant, her nose looked different, pert and upturned, the eyes appeared rounder, the lips fuller and the skin pale. It was only the briefest moment, but Gerald could have sworn he was looking at a young European girl: beautiful, but spoilt.

Spencer's gaze was elsewhere. He thought he'd heard something scuttling over the warped parquet floor.

"Welcome to blazes," Estelle said with a nervous laugh as she moved out of the torchlight. "This is where AF waited out the decades, after that terrible night of dedication. This wretched tomb absorbed him like a sponge and his essence occupied every room, every corner. I can't begin to tell you what it was like for... we who are bound to this place, how he tormented and toyed with us. There were no havens here, nowhere safe to hide, no escaping. Just the dark and him, the dark and him – always."

She fell silent and a spasm of pain passed across Eun-mi's face.

"He's gone from here now," Gerald said. "He can't torture you any more."

"Yes, he's gone, but the walls, the floor, even the paint and the peeling varnish, they remember him. And then there's us, the ones left behind; we can't escape, we're still lodged here, with the... newcomers."

Stepping into the middle of the large, panelled hall, she revolved slowly.

"Where would you like the tour to begin?" she asked, shaking off the grim mood. "The scullery? AF's bizarre boudoir? How about the cellars? That's where he kept those nasty little books you know. All those years sealed up in crates, waiting patiently for eager eyes to drink in their words."

Gerald swept the beam around. He wasn't sure where to begin. Martin had told him all about his one visit here, when he'd encountered the Ismus and his bodyguards in the conservatory. From that account, there didn't seem to have been anything to discover on this floor.

"Is the cellar where they held their rituals?" he asked.

"I was only ever present at one, darling," she replied. "But no, that wasn't down there. It was upstairs, in the special room. I don't want to go there."

"We'd best take a look at it."

The girl pretended not to hear and reached for Spencer's hand.

"You must see the ballroom!" she enthused, pulling him further down the hall towards one of the doorways. "We could do the Lindy Hop. But don't scold me if I make a frightful hash of it – it's been an age!"

Spencer snatched his hand back.

"I don't dance!" he spluttered. "And there's no way I'm going to start now."

Estelle threw Eun-mi's arms round his neck and looked at him imploringly. "Don't be beastly," she pleaded. "I'm sure you'd be the most marvellous hoofer if you'd loosen up."

Before he could stop her, she whisked his spectacles away.

"Why, Spencer!" she exclaimed, studying his face appreciatively. "You're turning into quite the elephant's eyebrows. In a few years you'll be the gigolo who breaks all the girls' hearts."

"Except for the acne, you mean."

"Poppet!" she cooed. "That will fade, and then just think how splendiferously rugged and tough you'll look. They'll be swooning at your feet."

"Leave him alone," Gerald warned her.

The boy grabbed his glasses back. "None of us will be here in a few years," he said.

"Oh, poor bunny!" Estelle cried, cradling his face. "And here you are, never so much as kissed a girl, have you? How perfectly dismal and bleak. Would you like to do it now? There's a little room over there; we could creep in, just the two of us, and have a powwow, with the emphasis on the wow. I could show you a heap of things better than cowboy films. Shanghai Lil has never kissed anyone either; what a locked-up little icebox she is. Oh, come on, do – it would be too precious. I'd feel like a referee at the all-in wrestling. I'll give you both a fantastic time! I was top of the class at the old fornication. I'm sure I haven't got rusty at that and she's hardly a Bonzo, is she?"

"Stop this!" Gerald shouted angrily.

"Yes," Spencer cried, flushed in the face. "Get off!"

Estelle untangled herself from him, amused. "Just teasing," she said, before turning to Gerald. "I shan't ask you to come into that little room. I know a daisy when I see one."

"Don't even," the old man growled. "I've been harassed and hated by experts; you don't come close, love."

"Teasing, darling. That sort of thing never bothered me. The debauchery I've seen at orgies in Fitzrovia would wave Caligula's hair. When did everyone become so dour and cranky?"

"Since that book was brought up from the cellars," Gerald told her.

Spencer gazed at the stairs. "We going up then?" he asked.

The old man nodded.

"You really shouldn't, you know," Estelle said quickly. "It's the most dangerous part of the house. There's no protection. It will get you."

"There's no protection anywhere, is there?" Gerald asked. "If it's going to get us, I can't see what difference it makes where that happens."

Placing a hand on the banister, he shone the torch upwards and started when he saw hundreds of pale eyes gleaming back at him. They scattered swiftly, vanishing into the shadows or rushing up the walls.

"Er... looks a bit crowded," Spencer said.

"Those are large spider-type beasties," Estelle told him with a grimace. "Horrid articles, as big as terriers with stalky legs. A horde of them came through a few months ago. Most of them dashed out into the woods, but lots stayed behind and now they infest one of the bedrooms at the end of the landing. You can hear them growling at each other."

"Doggy-Long-Legs," Spencer put in. "I've seen them before."

"Is that what they're called? Fancy! They crawl along the cornices and lie in wait, dropping on whatever passes underneath."

Spencer backed away. "They're dead vicious," he told Gerald. "I mean really... really bad."

"You'll be wearing one as a titfer in no time if you go up there," Estelle added. "And it'll yomp through your head as if it were a toffee apple."

Gerald passed the torch to Spencer. "Keep it steady, Spence," he said. "I'll just see how far I can get."

"Stubborn old duck, isn't he?" Estelle commented as Gerald began to climb.

"He's ruddy epic is what he is," Spencer informed her.

Keeping his eyes on the way ahead, Gerald crept up to the half-landing where the staircase turned left. The panelling was scored and broken and slime trails, wider than the span of his hand, glistened in the trembling circle of light. He could hear the furtive sounds of clawed legs scraping over wood and plaster, but, when he stared up at the main landing, there was no sign of those creatures.

"Seems clear so far," he said.

"Not like those things to be shy," Spencer answered. "Just be..."

The sentence went unsaid. Beyond the torchlight, in the dim gloom above, he had seen shapes scurrying across the ceiling. Then a fleck of falling spittle passed through the beam. Angling the torch upwards, he saw that the ceiling over the staircase was now carpeted with furred bodies and round, gleaming eyes glared down. All at once, the Doggy-Long-Legs dropped, en masse.

"Watch out!" Spencer yelled, while Estelle shrieked.

Gerald's rifle swung up and roared fiery blasts. Plaster exploded across the ceiling and every Doggy-Long-Legs that was about to fall directly on to his head splattered into lifeless tatters. The rest landed on the stairs around him. Snapping their jaws, they hopped about to leap up at his face. But they burst and jerked as the bullets tore through them. Dark blood, spent casings and splinters of wood, bone and plaster filled the air, and the din of the automatic rifle was matched by squeals and screeches as the attack became a frenzied effort to escape.

Fleeing Doggy-Long-Legs hurtled down the stairs, racing over Spencer's feet, but giving Estelle a wide berth, then through the hall to reach the front door. Parquet tiles shattered around them as the bullets followed. Gerald was determined to drive them out and kept his finger on the trigger, even after the last had sped into the night. When he stopped, his shoulders sagged and he lowered the rifle slowly.

The staircase was a slope of carnage. Stick-like legs poked up from furry carcasses and fang-filled mouths gaped wide. Bulging black eyes stared out lifelessly, their fury spent, growing dim and dull as the floating plaster dust settled.

"Ugh!" Gerald uttered with a shiver. "Never did like creepy-crawlies."

"You were brilliant!" Spencer said. "They won't be back any time soon."

"Won't they? I don't know. Let's hope not; but I'm an idiot – that was the last of my ammunition. I should have brought another clip with us from the cab."

"We've still got ours," Spencer reassured him. "We'll be OK."

Estelle gave a little cough. "Those spider beasties are the least of your problems," she told them.

"Give me your rifle, Spence," Gerald said. "I'm going on alone. You stop down here."

The boy kept hold of the AK-47 and shook his head.

"Let's not do this again," he said. "We're already off that cliff. I'm coming with you."

"Then mind where you tread."

The boy began to pick his way through the dead Doggy-Long-Legs. The bare wood was sticky and wet and he reached for the banister in case he slipped.

"You really are a pair of brutes!" Estelle exclaimed, arms folded at the bottom of the stairs. "Abandoning a poor defenceless girl alone down here. What despicable rats you are!"

"Somehow, my dear," Gerald said, without turning round, "I don't think you're as defenceless as you make out. You are dead after all."

"I wasn't talking about me," Estelle answered. "I can skedaddle any time I please. I was talking about Shanghai Lil. Anything could happen to her down here. She's only human."

"That's debatable," Spencer mumbled.

"Then bring her up here with us," Gerald said.

"I told you, I don't want to go up there."

Gerald halted and looked down at her. "So why don't you get out of Eun-mi's body and let her follow us up without you?" he suggested.

Estelle twisted the Korean girl's mouth to one side, then gave a surly toss of her head.

"I'll come up," she submitted grudgingly. "But you're both unspeakable cads making me do this."

"Thought you would," Gerald murmured under his breath.

Crunching and squelching up the staircase, the three of them made their way to the first floor where they paused and shone the torch up and down the long landing. Every door was firmly shut and, at the far end of each wing, the two sets of stairs that climbed to the next floor were engulfed in shadows that the beam couldn't reach.

The dirty, tattered webs of Doggy-Long-Legs, hanging from the ceiling and draping the walls, stirred faintly. Blank expanses, where portraits of the Fellows family once hung, were covered in old slime trails and the floorboards were crusted with the same.

"Big snails?" Spencer ventured in a low voice.

Estelle shook her head. "Nothing so charming," she told him.

"Now give me your rifle, Spence," Gerald said, and the boy swapped without argument.

"That won't be much use this time," Estelle said dryly. "You should have brought a cannon."

"What made these trails?" Spencer asked.

"Don't expect me to know what it's called. I never saw any of them in the zoo with Nanny. I only know it's very big. You can hear it squirming about up here and dragging itself across the floors above. Since it arrived, it's never ventured down to ground level though – I don't know why."

"Er... where is it now?"

"Not here," she said thankfully. "Those spider beasties learned to avoid it, so it's probably squelching about on the second floor or the attics. What luck for us! Of course, there are other things..."

Spencer's skin tingled and he could feel the hairs rising on his neck. Gerald felt it too. The atmosphere on this level was crackling with static and an unpleasant metallic taste formed in their mouths.

Estelle regarded them keenly. Any sense of playfulness had gone from her.

"AF's machines were never switched off," she explained. "They've been tuned to the same signal since 1936. It's stronger up here."

"What machines?" Gerald asked.

"He called them his superheterodyne henge," she said solemnly. "He used them in his ceremonies. Listen, can't you hear them?"

Spencer and Gerald suddenly became aware of the low electronic hum that had surrounded them since they'd entered the house. It had been droning so softly in the background they hadn't even noticed.

"Machines, in ceremonies? How does that work?"

"With the greatest efficiency," Estelle said. "Sometimes there's music too, brief snatches of dance bands that sound like they're playing underwater. I think that's the doing of AF's sister."

"Augusta," Gerald said. "And she wasn't really his sister at all."

"You're remarkably well informed about his family. I suppose he's hugely famous out there in the world?"

"My grandmother was in service here. I learned it from her."

"Did your granny tell you how deranged AF's limp, not-at-all-sister was? Not quite the full shilling, as they say. *Quelle surprise* – growing up with him, I imagine. Apparently though she was a bit of a boffin – she could certainly bore for the Empire on all things Marconi. She told me she helped AF in his work. I rather think that meant more than just being a hostess at the gatherings of his Inner Circle and hogging the gramophone. She may actually have had a hand in the design of those oversized wirelesses, or whatever they are, in that hateful room. That would account for the garbled scraps of Al Bowlly that waft through this place like so many miasmas. She was fixated on him, an absolute monomania. I couldn't bear the sound of his dirgey voice back when I was flesh and blood, but after being tortured by it all these years, well... it's the proverbial red rag."

"Never heard of him," Spencer said.

"Don't let Augusta hear you say that," she hushed quickly. "She'll want to educate you. Not that I've ever seen or even felt her wet-lettuce presence here. Do you know what happened to her that night? There's not a whisper of her in the house – or out in the grounds. That's always been a mystery to me. Maybe she was guzzled by the machinery; that would explain a lot."

"Augusta wouldn't be here," Gerald said. "She survived that dreadful night in thirty-six. But it broke her mind and she spent the rest of her life in an asylum. That's where she died – a long way from here."

"Lucky bitch," Estelle said with bitter envy. "Even that was better than what I had to endure."

Spencer held up his hand. "Shh," he hissed, turning his head and listening intently. "There..."

Mingled with the constant electric hum was a new sound – a wet sucking and squelching.

"It's on its way," Estelle breathed, edging away. "It'll be coming down to this landing soon. I'm not staying for that!"

Before she could leave, Gerald caught her arm and pulled her back.

"Show us this special room," he urged quickly.

"There isn't time!" she insisted, trying to break free. "If that horror catches us..."

"So make it quick!"

Estelle glanced at the darkness at the end of the landing. The repulsive slithering sounds were louder now.

"I can't!" she cried.

"You're wasting time!"

"I shan't do it!"

"Then you, Winnie the Wisp, can clear off, back into the ether, or wherever you're from, and let go of Eun-mi because Miss Chung isn't going anywhere without us and we are going to look in that room!"

"All right – all right! I'll show you. But hurry! This way."

Gerald pushed her in front and she ran to the far end of the west wing, where the main building joined the tower. Gerald and Spencer raced after her. The girl stopped at a large door that was unlike any of the others they had seen. It didn't match the heavy Victorian panelling of the rest of the house. This was smooth and covered in sleek veneers, with a long chrome handle.

Estelle hesitated before touching it. A bright blue filament of energy sparked across with a loud SNAP, which made Spencer jump.

They could actually feel the hum now. It resonated against their eardrums, buzzed in their chests and set their teeth on edge.

"Are you absolutely sure?" she asked one last time. "You won't find any answers in here."

"Open it," Gerald said resolutely.

The girl clasped the handle and Spencer let out a startled, "Woah!"

Eun-mi's hand was shifting in and out of X-ray. He could see the bones inside her flesh. For an instant, there was only a skeleton standing there, wearing the uniform of the People's Army of North Korea, a Kalashnikov slung over one shoulder and his Stetson perched on the skull. Then she was back again, but the ends of her hair were lifting.

"Not my doing," Estelle assured them. "It's what's in this room. You still think you want to go inside?"

She saw by their faces that they were determined.

"Just a moment," Gerald said quickly and he set the bag of grenades on the floor. "Best to be safe than sorry. We don't want whatever forces are fizzing in there to detonate these."

Estelle said nothing and pushed the door open. Spencer chewed his bottom lip and followed Gerald inside.

At once the metallic tang in his mouth became unbearable and he had to spit out the saliva that had turned to a weak acid around his tongue. Then he saw that all three of them were jumping in and out of X-ray. Intense pulses of UV came after, which caused the old man's snowy hair to fluoresce like a halo and Eun-mi's white shirt to zing out.

"Er... like, amazing," Spencer gasped. Holding a hand up before his face, he waggled his fingers and saw the fine network of nerves and arteries branching across the muscles and tendons. His marvelling, flesh-framed smile grew even broader when his gums disappeared, exposing the grinning skull beneath.

"I really don't think we should stick around here long," his skull said before the rest of him reappeared once more. "No way this is healthy."

"It's nowhere near as violent or toxic as it was that night," Estelle commented. "This is just the thingamabobs ticking over with gaudy party tricks thrown in. When it gets really lively, that's the time to dive for cover."

"Even if it is harmful," Gerald said grimly, "we only need to make it through another twenty-four hours. That's when it's all going to end, when whatever Austerly Fellows has got planned is due to happen. See if you can find anything that could help us reach Maggie and the others. There might be a file, notes – anything."

Spencer didn't need reminding. He turned his attention to the room and marvelled at it. He had never expected to find anything like this in a dingy old house. The room was octagonal and the only one in the building to be illuminated. Since the destructive night of dedication in 1936, it had been restored to its stylish glory. Within frosted sconces of Lalique glass, electric lights dipped and dimmed as the current fluctuated through the ancient wiring. More sleek veneer was in abundance over the walls and a radiating star motif, with lightning flashes, was set into the domed ceiling, reflecting the same design done in copper on the floor. Around that, twelve large Bakelite consoles were arranged in a wide circle and Gerald was studying their glowing dials. It had all been meticulously maintained.

"Martin would get a real kick out of this place," the boy said. "It's just his thing, isn't it? Sort of old-fashioned sci-fi."

"Flash Gordon meets the Ovaltineys," Gerald agreed with a sad half-smile. "He'd be humming Freddie Mercury if he was here – and then Maggie would join in, off key as usual."

"Only time I ever talked to him about anything other than DJ was about his love of genre stuff. We had a really good geek-out once. He promised that, if by some miracle everything got back to normal one day, he'd show me a Sean Connery movie set in space that was a retelling of *High Noon*. Er... some hope."

"This is like some movie set," Gerald observed.

"AF was a showman," Estelle said. "He adored his theatrics, dressing it all up and making it even more imposing and intimidating – as if it needed any help there."

Spencer couldn't see anything that might help them. It was useless. "Do you think they're still alive?" he asked.

"They are, until we know different," Gerald stated strongly.

Spencer ran a hand across one of the consoles.

"These are crazy, like radio tombstones."

"One of them is missing!" Estelle declared abruptly, with some surprise. "There should be thirteen. One for each member of AF's foul coven, and then his own bigger box of tricks. But that isn't here.

They've taken it away."

Gerald knelt to examine the floor where the master console had been. There was an indented impression and evidence of scorching, showing the device's large footprint, not much to indicate what had stood here for almost a hundred years.

"What did it look like?" he asked.

"I didn't have time to draw a picture," she answered. "I was rather preoccupied... it had more bells and whistles on it than the rest though."

"So what are these?" Spencer asked. "They're not just old-fashioned radios, are they? They're more than that."

"Receivers of some sort," the old man answered. "But receiving what? Each of these dials is different."

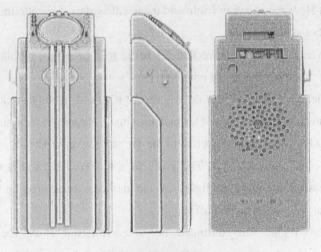

"We had something like them in the camp – smaller, but the same sort of thing. Jangler called them bridges."

"Bridges?"

"Yes, I think... I think it's how the Punchinellos came through – them and the other things: the Doggy-Long-Legs and the nightmare that got Marcus. I think these radios open the way."

"Demon souls, come here in shoals," Gerald muttered, reciting from *The Sorcerer*, another Gilbert and Sullivan opera. "Appear, appear, appear."

Approaching the nearest console, Spencer looked at its glowing dial, where the needle was trembling over numbers and mysterious symbols. He reached to touch one of the switches, but thought better of it and left well alone. A spark leaped from the dial's metal bezel and struck his palm. He leaped back in fright and the needle gave a twitch to the left. Another symbol lit up.

"What... what do you reckon it's tuned to?" he asked, rubbing his hand. "Where's the signal coming from?"

Estelle snorted. "Where do you think? It's not Luxembourg, that's for sure. These nasty toys of his pick up a much longer wavelength than that. AF opened up a direct line to the deepest region of Hell."

Spencer turned to her. The girl's face flickered through a rapid succession of coloured lights as the devices thrummed and the indicators blinked on and off.

"That night," she continued, her voice faltering as she recalled being trapped on the oversized iron chair that had dominated the room back then, with the cruel eyes of the Abbot of the Angles leering up at her. "AF told me, taunted me... he said these sets worked on a very particular frequency. The more afraid I became, the louder those things grew; they were feeding on it and the signal got stronger."

"Wait," Gerald interrupted. "You're saying they're powered, or boosted, by fear?"

"Fear, despair, pain... yes. But what else would you expect from such a fiend as him?"

Gerald moved to one of the twelve lesser consoles. Its original headset was still plugged in and hanging by the cord. Picking it up, he listened at an earpiece.

At first all he could hear was a cacophony of crackles, shrill whines and whistles. Then, beneath that, he heard the intoning of a deep, echoing voice, chanting strange words in a harsh-sounding tongue. Gerald pulled back hastily. He yanked the headset from the socket and flung it across the room.

"Dear God!" he shouted in revulsion.

Spencer blinked in astonishment at his strong reaction. Estelle hardly seemed to notice. She was staring intently at the centre, where a brass grill covered an opening in the floor and jagged forks of naked electricity had started to flick in and out of the mesh. Tensing, she backed away and pressed against the wall.

"This room is where I died," she announced starkly. "Right there. That's where the vile devil electrocuted me – on an enormous iron chair."

Spencer still couldn't get his head round the fact that Eun-mi's body had been hijacked and taken over by someone who had been killed so long ago – and in this very room. He couldn't begin to understand what that must be like for either of them. But her words made his forehead wrinkle.

"Yet inside his White Castle, the throne stands empty," he said, quoting *Dancing Jax*. "That's described as a huge iron chair."

"It wasn't empty that night!" Estelle said sharply.

"It's empty in the book because it's waiting for the return of the Dawn Prince."

"I don't care about that stupid book! I'm talking about something real – something that was in this room."

"I've seen that chair," Gerald said quietly, recalling the day he'd left Felixstowe, driving a distraught Martin from the town to try and warn the world about *Dancing Jax*. "It was set up on an old war bunker, down by the golf course. They were burning an effigy on it."

"Oh, I can vouch that it's an extremely efficient brazier," Estelle said bleakly.

Gerald stepped from the consoles. "Then that's what he's doing," he murmured, hardly believing what he was saying. "That's what all this has been about, the real purpose behind the book. Austerly Fellows planned all of this from the very start."

"What?" Spencer asked. The old man was scaring him. On the dial another symbol was illuminated as the needle quivered a fraction further.

"That throne won't be empty for much longer," Gerald said. "Tomorrow night, on Christmas Eve – the global broadcast..."

"The flee the beast thing?"

The old man nodded, waiting for the boy to catch up.

"And the worldwide release of *Fighting Pax*. Whatever Austerly Fellows has got in mind, it's going to provide enough power, enough fear and despair for one colossal bridging – one last enormous terror to cross over."

Spencer finally understood, but he didn't want to believe it.

"No," he spluttered.

"What does it say in the book?" the old man asked. "Something about 'drawing nigh'. That's what all this has been for."

In a stunned and fearful voice, Spencer recited the words from *Dancing Jax*, the very same lines that had turned Doctor Choe.

"The Lord of Rising Dawn is drawing nigh. He is returning to the land that was his. His light shall crown the hills with crimson flame and we shall bow before his unmatched majesty."

They stared at each other in horror and Estelle gazed wretchedly at the central grill where the jags of energy spat and danced. The needles on every dial swung round and another diabolic symbol illuminated. And then, with a hiss and roar of static, a slow melody came pouring into the room and a mournful, crooning voice began to sing.

*

"*In the shadows, let me come and sing to you.*"

Estelle shrieked and kicked the wall behind her in anguish.

"Bowlly!" she screamed.

The song continued. It was as if the machines were mocking them.

"*Let me dream a song that I can bring to you.*
Take me in your arms and let me cling to you."

"Make it stop!" she shouted. "Shut it off!"

"*Let me linger long; let me live my song.*"

Lunging forward, she wrenched at the switches and twisted the tuners violently. The indicators flashed, the dials on each of the twelve consoles grew brighter and the music grew louder.

"Stop it!" Gerald shouted. "Don't touch them. You don't know what you're doing!"

"In the shadows, when I come and sing to you
In the shadows, when
I come and sing to you."

Gerald and Spencer dragged her clear. The girl resisted and fought for several moments, then went limp and sobbed into Gerald's shoulder.

A surge of sulphurous smoke came billowing up from the grill and a sudden squall rampaged round the room.

"In the shadows,
In the shadows,
In the shadows..."

The song continued to blare, distorting as the volume swelled.

"I can't bear it," Estelle wept as the unnatural gale whipped Eunmi's raven hair about her head. "You have no idea of the torment. Years and years and years of it – and him always there."

Spencer wasn't sure if she meant Austerly Fellows or Al Bowlly's singing. The X-rays flared again and Gerald's skeleton pulled away from her. There was nothing more to discover here and what they had learned made him feel sick.

Then, above the grille, where the electric sparks crackled more fiercely than ever, they saw a shape forming in the thick, twisting funnel of smoke. At first it was just a vague swirl of curdling vapour and shadow, shot with flames from below, but every passing instant refined and defined it. Something was coming through.

Aghast, they watched as the floating figure took on solid form and a pair of bowed legs and long, muscular arms stretched and flexed from the fumes. The deformed ridge of a humped back reared above a large, hideous head and the yellow smoke blew round a curved chin and hooked nose.

"A Punchinello!" Spencer cried.

"Time to go!" Gerald yelled.

Running on to the landing, Spencer made to slam the door shut behind them, but Gerald stopped him.

"Not yet," he instructed. "You two, head back downstairs and get out of here."

"What are you going to do? That thing in there will kill you on sight. You don't know what they're like!"

A loud, gargling squawk told them the Punchinello was almost fully corporeal and was now breathing the atmosphere of this world.

"Shoot it!" Spencer urged.

"I'll do better than that," Gerald answered, stooping to pick up the satchel of grenades. "Don't worry, I'll be right behind you."

"I'm not leaving you, even for a minute!" Spencer swore. "We get out of here together or not at all."

Gerald wouldn't listen this time. He pushed the loaded rifle into the boy's hands and ordered him to go.

"Come on!" Estelle pleaded, pulling on Spencer's arm. "Hurry!"

"Don't you do anything stupid and be a hero," Spencer warned him. "You come right after us, OK?"

"I'll head you off at the pass!" Gerald promised. "Now hightail it out of here, Sundance!"

Spencer managed a feeble smile. Then he and Estelle raced along the landing.

Gerald Benning looked back into the octagonal room, where the consoles were flashing and the hum had ramped up to a piercing electronic squeal. The thermionic valves in each unit were glowing fiercely and the song was thundering too loudly to be recognisable as music any more. It was a screeching, deafening din and the Lalique sconces rattled in their fittings.

Snarling, and baring its mottled teeth, the grotesque and naked Punchinello stepped out from the smoke. The red-rimmed eyes swivelled in their sockets and glared over at the doorway where the old man stood. Licking its scabrous lips, it came swaggering between the consoles.

Taking a deep, steadying breath, Gerald's trembling fingers closed round one of the grenades. Like most North Korean weapons, they were out-of-date leftovers from a lost or abandoned war. These were originally American M26 fragmentation devices, called 'lemons' because of their shape. Gerald only hoped they still worked. Pulling out the pin, he called to the advancing Punchinello.

"Honk-honk, nosy! Catch!" And he lobbed the grenade inside.

The Punchinello caught it and gave the object a suspicious sniff.

Gerald bowled another in after. "And one for the pot!" he yelled as he turned and ran.

On the landing, Spencer and Estelle slithered to a halt. They couldn't reach the stairs.

The boy's face fell and he blurted a shout of dismay. The way was blocked. The thing that had smeared the walls and floor with slime had descended from the level above and its glistening bulk filled the landing.

He didn't know what it was and couldn't see how far back its bloated body stretched. It was all he could do to keep from fainting or puking violently. The stench of corruption that beat from it was beyond anything he had ever experienced.

It was like a gigantic grey leech, and its pallid, quivering flesh gave off its own putrescent light. There was no head, no eyes, just a blunt end to the translucent, sweating skin that framed a cavernous mouth filled with circles of hooked teeth that continued into the pulsating body. It was like staring down a tunnel of jagged knives.

With disgusting squelching sounds, the gaping mouth quested the air. Concentric circles of trembling papillae dripped with rancid juices and Spencer knew it could sense them. A shuddering ripple travelled down its monstrous shape and it made a repulsive bubbling sound. Rearing up, it shivered and constricted, preparing to lunge forward and strike.

Spencer raised the rifle and wasted no time firing bullets into that stinking, gelatinous flesh.

"You can't kill it like that!" Estelle shouted. "It's useless!"

The boy ignored her, but, was he imagining it, or had the sound of her voice caused the reeking horror to convulse? The mouth squeezed together and it began to squirm and shrink back along the landing.

It was then the first grenade exploded. The Bakelite consoles split apart, dials smashed and the valves burst, releasing a violent pulse of kinetic force that punched through the entire building. A moment later, the second grenade blew up and a torrent of unnatural red flame engulfed the room and belched out of the doorway. The deafening music was stilled and the last indicator light blinked and went out as the shattered Bakelite cases melted. The shockwave juddered through the house and the doors slammed wildly. Windows ruptured into glittering shrapnel and slates were catapulted from the roof. Spencer was almost thrown to the floor. Behind them, the blazing octagonal room went crashing to the level beneath.

A noise like a pistol shot tore through the quaking structure, as a wide fracture ripped up the length of the tower.

Spencer felt the landing buckle and the entire balustrade fell into the hall below. The air bristled with static and oily black smoke was already flooding the passage. In front of him, arcs of electricity surrounded the huge, stinking, leech-like creature. The great mouth contorted and a crack of blinding energy caused it to spasm. A horrendous, frothing bellow issued from the immense, barbed throat and then, in an instant, the beast was gone. The landing was empty. Only a sheen of slime was left behind.

"W–what?" the boy stammered.

"What are you doing?" Gerald cried urgently as he charged out of the smoke and propelled them to the staircase. "Don't stop! Get out of here!"

Outside, the end tower was leaking blood-red flames and swaying ominously. The conical spire tipped and broke free, lurching through the air, bouncing and rolling over exposed attics, before plunging on to the great conservatory with a cataclysmic destruction of Victorian glass and iron girders. Then, in an avalanche of bricks and rubble, and an eruption of crimson fire, the tower came toppling down – demolishing the chimneys, snapping beams and rafters like matchwood. The roofs crumpled and collapsed. Gables caved, slamming on to the drive. Choking clouds of smoke and dust discharged into the surrounding woods. Fierce, cherry-coloured embers spat from the broken tower and illuminated the dark sky as they coiled upwards. Fellows End was in ruins.

Spencer staggered sideways across the gravel, spluttering through the blinding fumes. They had only just managed to outrun the pursuing debris and were caked in dirt.

Frantically they sought the track that led to the car. Then Gerald stumbled to his knees and spent a long time coughing and gasping for breath.

Spencer crouched beside him and put a hand on his shoulder. "We made it," he said, rasping because his mouth was so dry. "We got out of that ruddy awful place alive. Another cliff successfully jumped. Unbelievable!"

Estelle stood stiffly nearby, staring at the burning ruins through the strata of settling dust and curling smoke.

"At long last," she whispered, the infernal fires reflected in her eyes.

"It's finally gone," Gerald wheezed. "That's a sight gladder to me than all the ovations, all the awards I ever received. The biggest achievement of my life. The place of so many nightmares... and I brought it down. Not too shabby for a pensioner."

"But how?" Spencer asked, bewildered. "Grenades couldn't do all that, could they?"

"Not just them on their own, no. I think they let loose something far more destructive. It's gone anyway."

He flicked some of the dirt from his sleeves and a twinkle gleamed in his eye. "You know," he said, "if we keep destroying every place we go to, no one will ever invite us anywhere again."

Spencer's pent-up fear and anxiety finally burst out and, moments later, he found himself crying with laughter.

"We're so the worst guests!" he hooted, tears streaking through the dirt on his cheeks. "We'll get such a reputation."

Gerald joined in and, for a while, neither could say anything more. When they tried, they kept setting each other off. They could not believe they'd cheated the inevitable one more time and fell about on the ground, giggling like infants.

Eventually Gerald let out a great sobering sigh.

"I'm too old for this," he said with a shake of his head that loosed a blizzard of chalky dust. "I'm just about done in right now."

"Oh!" Spencer told him feverishly. "You haven't heard the best bit. When you blew up that room, those old radio things, the monster on the landing fizzled and vanished."

"Monster?"

"You didn't see it. It was huge and disgusting, a slug the size of a wagon train. It's what was squelching about upstairs. I thought we'd had it!"

He turned to Estelle. While they'd been wrapped up in their laughter, the girl had been standing apart, deep in thought. Rousing, she nodded in confirmation.

"It was there," she agreed. "Then, suddenly, it wasn't."

"And I remembered something else," Spencer gushed excitedly. "Back in the camp, when Marcus was killed by the giant worms, Jangler destroyed one of the radios there and they disappeared the same way."

Gerald's eyes widened. "Spence," he murmured. "Are you sure?"

"Absolutely! I bet there's not a Doggy-Long-Legs or anything else for miles around here now. They've been chucked back to where they came from."

Gerald rocked backwards. "That's incredible."

"You know what this means!"

"If we could smash them all? Every device like that? We'd rid the world of those hellish creatures completely. But Spence, that's crazy, there's no way we can. Those receivers will be in every country, in every aberrant camp – secret places we don't know about. How on earth? And what about the things that have hatched here since? Would they be thrown back?"

"That doesn't matter and we don't need to smash them all," the boy enthused. "Not right away anyway. Why wasn't the main console in that room just now? Because the Ismus has had it moved to Kent, for the broadcast. If we can destroy that one... his Punchinello Guards will disappear, that demon, Mauger..."

Gerald stared at him. "What are you getting at?" he asked.

"We might, just might, be able to put a spanner in the Ismus's grand plan. What if we could actually stop the Dawn Prince himself crossing over? Everything he's worked for, with DJ, would be ruined."

"Spencer..." Gerald breathed, hardly daring to believe what he was hearing. "If anyone lives through this, they're going to write songs and make movies about you. You're bloody incredible."

"As long as whoever plays me gets to ride off into the sunset, with *The Magnificent Seven* theme playing, that's fine by me. But seriously, you think we can do it? We stand a chance?"

"Don't ask me. I didn't think we could get out of Titipu alive – now look where we are."

"But getting to Kent, the castle replica. How do we even do that? The roads will be jammed. You said so yourself."

Gerald gave him a mysterious look. "I also told you I had a silly idea about that," he said. "It's so barking, it might just get us all the way in."

"Through that traffic? How?"

The old man tried to stand, but couldn't. He held out a hand and Spencer helped him to his feet.

"What I learned from those interminable coffee mornings with the big hats in North Korea is that the copy of Mooncaster they're building here is the biggest construction project in history. And what do massive works like that need?"

"Er... hard hats?"

"Service roads, Spence. Even if I hadn't seen them on plenty of satellite photos, I'd know they were there. Quarried stone and tonnes of excavated earth don't move themselves. They had to build umpteen new roads to cope with it. You should see how many cranes they've got down there. Those roads will be kept clear – no ordinary traffic will be allowed anywhere near them – and they go right to the heart of the site."

"Brilliant! But won't it be guarded? They won't let us use those roads either. Pretending to be Mooncaster royalty won't cut any ice this time. There'll be millions of Jacks and Jills and Under Kings and Queens there already."

Gerald smiled. "That's my silly idea," he said. "What we need is the help of someone no Jaxer would dare stop or question. Someone nobody ever dresses up as. We need one of the Aces."

"Like who? The Jockey? The Harlequin Priests? Could we get away with it?"

"Just a minute, Spence. There's something we need to sort before we go any further."

They'd been walking down the track, towards the taxi. Gerald stopped and turned back to Estelle who was trailing quietly behind.

"I think it's time now, don't you?" he said to her.

The girl shook her head unhappily.

"No," she said.

"You can't stay in there indefinitely. You have to give it up. Let Eun-mi go."

"I was only nineteen years old," she told him. "It isn't fair. I didn't ask to be murdered. I just want to be alive again. Even just for the day that's left."

"How fair are you being to Eun-mi?"

"You don't want her back! Spencer certainly doesn't. He called her a rattlesnake – and she is!"

"That's not the point. It's her body, her life. You don't have any claim to it."

"Let me come with you!" she implored. "I can help."

"It's over. Leave Eun-mi and be at peace, if you can."

The girl narrowed her eyes. "I know how you can defeat AF," she announced. "I mean actually kill him, stone dead."

"Kill the Ismus?" Spencer cried. "That's not possible."

She gave a grim laugh. "There is a way – I know it."

"What way?" Gerald demanded.

"Fair dos," she said, wagging a finger. "I'll tell you, but only if you let me keep this body; that's my price. It can't be too much to ask, surely? Not when the doom of absolutely everything is in the balance?"

"You're bluffing," Gerald said. "Austerly Fellows is untouchable."

Estelle laughed. "Oh, is he? I didn't spend all those decades cowering from him, being tormented by him, in that hideous mausoleum without learning something. AF has a weakness, which you could exploit to destroy him forever."

"What weakness?"

"I'm not going to blab it out like that," she said. "Not till you swear I can stay and we're miles from here."

"No deals."

"Wait!" Spencer interrupted. "If she really does know how to kill him... I mean that would be the best result ever. Wouldn't it? It'd be fantastic! Why are we even talking about it? If there's the remote possibility of getting rid of him completely..."

"See!" Estelle said. "Spencer knows what's more important. The treacherous Shanghai Lil – for the life of the most evil man who ever lived. How difficult a choice is that?"

"Even if I believed you," Gerald replied flatly, "the answer would still be the same."

"But Gerald!" Spencer protested.

"No, Spence. What she wants is just wrong. It's as black and white as that. This is exactly what we're fighting for, to give people the freedom to be themselves. That's what it comes down to. Could you really live with yourself if you agreed to let Eun-mi be taken over permanently?"

"I'd have a ruddy good go!"

Estelle tossed her head. "Nobody is going to live beyond tomorrow night anyway!" she snorted. "What would a day of guilt matter? Believe me, Shanghai Lil won't be any loss. Her father barely tolerated her, her own sister would sell her out to AF in a heartbeat, she's got nowhere to go. Why should you care?"

"That's enough!" Gerald snapped. "Party time is over – get out now."

The girl appealed to Spencer. "Make him see sense," she implored. "You don't want the awful Oriental back, do you?"

Spencer didn't know what to say. He trusted Gerald's judgement completely, but how could he not understand what a miraculous opportunity this was?

"She's keeping something from you, you know," Estelle pressed, seeing his hesitation. "Something vital, something you really should know about. You can't trust her, not a bit."

And then Spencer remembered what had happened in the moments before that monster had vanished on the landing. It had heard her voice and was afraid. He hadn't imagined it. Other things started to slot into place.

"Just who can we trust?" he asked. "Cos I don't think it's you."

"Darling boy!" she cried in an injured tone. "Whatever can you mean?"

"The things – the creatures that were out here earlier – they were scared of you."

"What? Oh, that is such rot!"

"Er... no, it isn't. They've all been terrified of you and didn't come near. Why's that?"

"You're talking gibberish, poppet."

"I'll have my hat back now. Eun-mi won't appreciate it on her head."

He reached out and took it, then Estelle pulled away sharply and raised her rifle.

"I really don't know why I tried to do it the painless way," she snarled and now her voice was filled with contempt and anger. The girl's face contorted: deep creases slashed her brows, cut down from her nose and veins tightened in her neck. The lips curled back and the eyes shone with a savage, bestial light. The transformation was sudden and hideous.

"I should have turned round and shot the pair of you at the start. I thought it would be more amusing not to, but the game wasn't worth playing. You two are ridiculous, you know that? A faded old pansy and a spotty weed. I only wanted a ride out of this cesspit, to take me beyond the boundary. Almost eighty years I've been stuck here, and yes, when he wasn't torturing me, I tortured everything else – and loved every malicious moment of the agonies I inflicted. He was an excellent and oh so very thorough mentor. When the foolhardy came to this place, it was me who drove them insane, me who caused them to shred their vocal cords with their screams, me who whispered darkness into the heads of silly young boys who broke in for a dare. Austerly Fellows got out of here inside a bragging layabout. This sour-faced rice maiden is my first-class ticket. Neither of you pair of inadequates will get in my way."

Her laughter was cold and cruel. Pointing the rifle at Gerald, she grinned and said, with an ugly sneer, "So let's begin with you, shall we? The inverted really should go first."

Sniggering, she squeezed the trigger. Then she stared down blankly when nothing happened.

"You should have asked Eun-mi where the safety catch is on those things," Gerald said, jumping forward and tearing the Kalashnikov from her grasp.

Spencer leaped in and grabbed hold of her clawing hands, twisting them round her back.

"Let me go!" she raged.

"You let Eun-mi go!"

"I'll kill her. I can stop her heart or make her brain bleed. What are you going to do? You can't hurt me without damaging her."

Gerald stared at her in disgust. She was right, what could they do? It was hopeless.

Suddenly Spencer started yelling in her ear. "Eun-mi! Wake up! Your leader wants you. Kim Il-sung the Eternal President commands you to obey. Wake up! Wake up!"

Estelle shrieked with derision. He really was feeble. Then her face twisted and she shuddered uncontrollably.

"I'll destroy you!" she threatened, but she wasn't speaking to Spencer or Gerald.

"Wake up!" the boy continued. "Kim Jong-un orders you! His father, Kim Jong-il, orders it. The People's Army commands it."

Estelle writhed and jolted. She screeched and vowed to butcher them all, but she was fighting an internal battle. Eun-mi was struggling to regain control.

Gerald nodded encouragingly at Spencer to keep it up and he wracked his memory to recall some of the North Korean words he had learned from little Nabi.

"Chung Eun-mi!" he roared, mimicking her father's voice. "Salute your General. Obey him. Salute your father!"

Estelle screamed. The girl's body arched and became rigid. Her eyes rolled back and her face froze. Her mouth locked horribly wide. Spencer almost let go of her hands in alarm when he saw streaks of white spreading among her long black hair. The contest within was taking a terrible toll.

"Never!" Estelle's ferocious voice howled up from Eun-mi's gaping mouth. "If I get driven out then I'm taking her soul with me. She'll be mine to torment – like I was to him."

"Chung Eun-mi!" Gerald commanded.

"No!" Estelle yelled.

The blank eyes clamped shut and she was shaking so violently, Spencer could barely maintain a grip on her hands. The last traces of black disappeared from her hair. It was now bleached totally white and her lips were turning a deathly grey.

Gerald stared at her anxiously. There was nothing more they could do. They were losing her.

At that moment Spencer saw something moving in the branches overhead. It was the hazy spectre of the hanged woman that had attacked him when they first arrived. The foggy shape came swooping through the trees and long, shadowy arms reached down.

Spencer let go of the girl's hands and darted out of the way, covering his throat.

"No, wait!" Gerald shouted. "It isn't after you, Spence – look."

The boy turned to see the apparition bear swiftly down upon Eun-mi's body and heard a strident female voice sing out, as if from a great distance:

"Let the high praises of God be in their mouth, and a two-edged sword in their hand..."

The ghostly rope round the spectre's neck unwrapped itself and the wraith's hands reached deep into Eun-mi's mouth.

There was a scream of terror and the girl shook more wildly than ever, like a rag doll worried by a dog.

The echoing voice continued.

"To execute vengeance upon the heathen, and punishments upon the people..."

Then the malignant spirit of Estelle Winyard was hauled out. It was a tangled mass of shrieking darkness, and the noose was now tight about it.

"To bind their kings with chains, and their nobles with fetters of iron..."

305

Still screeching and wailing, the girl's spirit was hoisted high into the air and dragged into the surrounding woods. The declaiming voice rang out in the night:

"To execute upon them the judgement written: this honour have all his saints. Praise ye the LORD."

And then there was silence. The agonised shrieks and the righteous condemnation faded. Spencer hardly dared to move. He stared through the trees in disbelief. Suddenly a familiar voice cried out and he spun round.

"FATHER!" Eun-mi had howled desolately. Then she collapsed.

Gerald and Spencer rushed to her. She was cold and still.

"Is she dead?" Spencer ventured.

Gerald searched for a pulse. It was very faint.

"She's extremely weak. That fight must have taken every ounce of strength she had. She needs complete rest."

"No hospital is going to take her! They'll know she's an aberrant."

"I know a place where she'll be safe. Help me lift her up. I'll carry her to the car."

Spencer wavered. Gazing at her, he was struck by how beautiful she was. The unnatural white hair framing her face and radiating over the ground heightened it, making her appear almost divine.

"She looks like an angel," he breathed.

"She'd punch you if she heard that," Gerald said, smiling.

"But what just happened?" Spencer asked when they eased her on to the back seat of the taxi. "What was that?"

"Going by the psalm reading," Gerald reflected, "I think it was the governess who committed suicide here, Grace Staplethorpe. Austerly tormented her into hanging herself. He was only six years old at the time."

"*Six? So young?*"

"He wasn't a normal child. I honestly don't think he was human at all."

"So why did she pick on me earlier?"

"You know, I wonder if we got it wrong. Maybe she wasn't attacking you."

"Er... hello – she was strangling me."

"Was she? Or was she trying to stop you from going to the house, and keeping you away from Estelle in the most direct way she could? Possibly the only way."

"Why didn't she attack her instead then?"

Gerald shrugged. "I'm only guessing, but you heard Estelle; she tortured everything around here. Her spirit was too strong, too angry. The fight with Eun-mi must have weakened her enough for Grace to finally turn the tables. But I'm no expert."

Closing the cab's rear door as gently as he could, he gazed back at the flickering glare of the fires crackling in the broken shell of Fellows End.

Spencer leaned against the bonnet.

"You think there was any truth to what she said?" he asked thoughtfully. "About there being a way to kill Austerly Fellows for good?"

"I doubt it, but we'll never know for certain. Now get in. Before we make that final journey to Kent, we desperately need to recharge. We've been doing far too much cliff jumping. I feel more like a clapped-out lemming than Butch Cassidy. I really am feeling my age. I'm just about spent, Spence. Eun-mi needs a long, healing sleep and I need the therapeutic cheer of a really strong black coffee. Luckily the place I've got in mind caters for both and is the only establishment in the whole of Felixstowe where you can get a decent espresso."

They got into the car and Gerald reversed on to the lane.

"Besides," he said, casting one last look in the mirror at the snaking column of glowing embers, rising like a swarm of fiery wasps above the trees, "going to that house wasn't the only reason why I had to come back here."

Spencer waited for him to supply the other, but, as they drove on, and Gerald fell quiet, he had to prompt him.

"Because," Gerald explained a little reluctantly, "when Martin and I had to leave in such a hurry, over a year ago... I left someone behind."

17

"GET YOU HENCE!" the Queen of Hearts commanded sternly. "This is no menagerie for you to be gawking. This young fellow is sore afflicted. He must have peace and rest."

"Quite so, quite so," agreed the Court Physician who had bumbled in after her, carrying his wooden chests and leather pouches.

The maids and ladies-in-waiting who had thronged about the bed drew back reluctantly. The mysterious stranger that the Holy Enchanter had brought back to the castle was the sole topic of conversation and they were hungry for news of him. Even the village was agog, for the blacksmith had been summoned in the middle of the night to free the boy from strange fetters.

Their curious stares were glued to the occupant of the bed and they didn't want to leave.

"Bless me!" gasped one of them. "What fiendish creature spits poison that can turn flesh so black? Were it one of Haxxentrot's evil crew? Is it still abroad? Are we as like to get bit by this monster?"

"Foolish talk and nonsense," the Queen of Hearts said sternly. "This fellow is as he was ever intended. The hue of his skin is no malady. He is from a different realm, that is all. He is the Castle Creeper; you must have heard rumour of him. Now begone and let the Physician minister to his hurts."

"For all his blackness," another of the girls said with a lascivious wink as she shooed them out of the door, "he's a fair-faced fellow."

The Queen of Hearts scowled at her and chased her out with a waggle of her plump hands.

"Save us from lusting wenches," she sighed. "'Tis task enough to keep my eyes upon my own wayward daughter. 'Tis a wonder we are not overrun with infants in Mooncaster."

The Physician mumbled as he nodded and busied himself with changing the bandage round the patient's leg.

"And everyone at such odds with one another lately," he said. "There has been a bumper harvest of quarrels and bruises this summer."

The Queen of Hearts agreed. Fights and squabbles erupted hourly nowadays. Only yesterday her husband had rowed with the King of Diamonds over some trifling matter and the King of Diamonds had determined to go hunting today so as not to have to sit with them at the tournament.

"And he hates the hunt, that one," she muttered to herself. "How like boys all men are."

She returned her attention to the Castle Creeper.

"The poor young princeling," she clucked with a pitying shake of the head. "I shall cull fresh herbs this very day from my garden and supply you with salves and unguents of healing virtue."

"Thank you, Your Majesty," the Physician replied with a grateful bow as he opened one of his chests and took out a glass jar. "That will be most beneficial I am sure. But first we must let out the badness that has entered in through these vicious bites. I shall put the leeches on him and restore the balance of his humours. There can be no remedy without the leeches. They are a patient's most bosom friend and our infantry against all galloping ailments. Then I must away to the tournament and make ready for the steady stream of the battered and the broken."

Using a pair of silver tongs worn on a long chain about his neck, he dipped into the jar and removed a glistening leech.

Suddenly his wrist was caught in a tight grip.

"If you is thinkin' 'bout puttin' that vampire snot on me, anyplace," Lee growled, "you is gonna get this here thing rammed right up where there ain't no weather."

The Physician saw that the boy's other hand was clutching a candlestick. He winced and wriggled uncomfortably.

"What a glory it is to see you awake and so robust of temper," he declared, returning the leech to the jar with quivering fingers.

"And such a fine morning to greet you, Master Creeper!" greeted the Queen of Hearts as she bobbed a dumpy curtsy.

Lee put the iron candlestick back on the table beside the bed and took in his surroundings.

It was a large, comfortable room, with panelled wood on the walls, carved with the crest of the Royal House of Hearts, which also featured in a stone shield surmounting the fireplace, where cheerful flames crackled in the hearth. Rays of sunlight streamed in through a large window and a pair of song thrushes were warbling on the sill. His bed was hung with tapestries and covered with luxurious furs and velvet cushions fringed with golden tassels.

Lee rolled his eyes. It was always too much here. Then he noticed what he was wearing. His North Korean clothes had been replaced by a voluminous cotton nightshirt with baggy sleeves and ruffles at the neck.

"Say what?" he groaned in disgust. "Aw, man, this is so not cool – and who the hell took off my pants?"

He looked at the man in the sober black gown with matching hat, then at the woman in dark red taffeta, wearing a coronet studded with small rubies. He thought he knew what all the prime characters looked like here, but he'd never seen her face before.

"My good husband's own personal valet attended you when you were brought in," she said. "There was no impropriety."

"Who's you?" he asked bluntly.

"This is Her Majesty, the Queen of Hearts," the Physician told him. "A most tender-hearted lady, and exceeding accomplished in the ways of physic and herb lore."

Lee studied her keenly. "You had Botox or a lift or what?" he asked her. "Cos there ain't no way you got the same head as before. Guess somethin' musta happened to the main player back home. Now that is interestin'."

The Under Queen did not understand him. "Riddles on an empty stomach cannot be good for your recovery," she said, bustling out of the room. "I shall inform the Lord Ismus you are awake at last."

"Breakfast, yeah – that's a great idea. My guts is roaring. Don't you bring me no soup or broth or no thin gruel though. I'll throw it right back at ya. I'm sick of warm slop. And get me my clothes!"

"The maid will bring you breakfast," the Physician told him. "And we shall see about your vestments. Alas, it was necessary to cut off your breeches, but the other garments were sent to the washhouse. No doubt they will be returned soon. Now may I continue with my examination?"

"You ain't no proper doctor," Lee said, waving him away. "I wouldn't trust you to squeeze a zit. There ain't no real medicines in this place, it's all pins and sucky slugs, magic plasters and letting out bile."

"I assure you," the Physician began, greatly affronted, "I have studied and practised these many years..."

"Bull!" Lee interrupted. "You studied squat, you is just a made-up character in a book who I ain't lettin' anywhere near me. My old gran'ma was more of a doctor than you. Leastways her bathroom cupboard was full of better drugs than you'll ever get your medieval hands on."

The Physician slammed the lid of the leech chest sharply and drew himself up.

"No one has ever had cause to question my skill before," he said indignantly.

"Maybe they didn't live long enough," the boy remarked.

"I shall bid you good morrow, Master Creeper. Courtly manners are certainly in short supply in the realm from whence you hail. Yet I shall be charitable and ascribe it to your injury and the overlong slumber. Now I go to where my expertise will not be derided. The lists make much work for me."

"Wait!" Lee called as the man strode huffily towards the door. "How'd you mean 'overlong'? How long I been out cold?"

"It is two nights since they brought you in," the Physician told him brusquely. "And I have tended your wounds and bound your leg afresh ever since. What you need most is to stay abed and you should move about as little as possible. You will find the abrasions at your wrists well on the way to mending, but of course that is in no part down to my skill – it must be the autumn breeze and the jocund song of the throstle."

With that final sarcastic comment, he departed, taking his paraphernalia with him.

Lee sucked his teeth and inspected the bandages around his leg. At least they were clean and it wasn't throbbing. Maybe the doctor guy knew a thing or two after all. He wondered what Doctor Choe back in North Korea would have made of this medieval medicine.

"She took more blood outta me than a hundred of them leeches ever could," he muttered, swinging his legs off the bed and leaning on the stout wooden bedpost as he put his weight on the floor.

"Not too bad," he said. "They won't be carving me no stump just yet."

Taking it slowly, he crossed to the window. The thrushes hopped about and welcomed him with their song.

"Take it and shove it," he growled. The birds flew off.

Lee leaned on the sill and gazed out across the battlements of the White Castle. It was a glorious day in Mooncaster. The morning sun was burning away the early mist that had risen off the moat. Horses were stamping on cobbles as they were led out of the stables by whistling grooms, the hounds were barking for young Bertolf to bring their breakfast, a maid was singing as she hurried about her duties. The tramp of heavy boots signalled the changing of the Punchinello warders and generous sprinkles of carefree laughter abounded.

Outside the walls, the peasants of the village had been about their chores for many hours. From his high window in the West Tower, Lee could see the main street winding between the quaint thatched cottages of Mooncot. From there it stretched beyond the mill, across the green countryside – towards the woods and forests that covered the slopes of the encircling hills.

"Who wouldn't want to believe this was real?" he murmured to himself. "Every day a new slice of perfect."

His wandering gaze continued to rove. Banners and pennants were being hoisted over the tilt yard that had been constructed outside the castle. There was to be a day of jousting and, in the meadow, livestock was being herded into pens and produce was being arranged on stalls.

"Must be some big day," he said.

"'Tis the harvest fayre!" a voice declared behind him.

Lee turned. A girl had entered without him realising. She placed a tray bearing a delicious-looking breakfast on a low table near the fire. Lee's stomach made a noise like a sea monster locked in a cupboard. He really was ravenous and hadn't seen proper food like that since the first days of the camp. There was bacon, ham, cold chicken, eggs, mushrooms, fresh crusty bread and a jug of watered wine. He was relieved to see there were no sausages.

Then he realised who the girl was. It was the Jill of Hearts. She had met the maid on the stairs and had insisted, in the strongest terms, on taking the tray from her. The maid had been sent away with her ears boxed.

Tossing her auburn hair over her shoulders, Jill turned her most winning smile on him.

"This day the simple peasant folk celebrate the turning of the seasons and hold an outdoor feast. It does not match our harvest revel here in the Great Hall, but it gives them much pleasure and the merrymaking can continue till after cockcrow. Much coupling occurs in the fields, to ensure next year's crops are plentiful."

"Nice for them thar poor folks, huh?" Lee said, limping to the table.

"Here, let me aid you," she offered, hurrying to take his arm.

"I can manage," he declined, brushing her away as she stroked his sleeve. "Don't you got no princessin' stuff to do?"

"My hours are mine own to spend as I please," she answered, moving into the sunlight so that it picked out the glints in her hair. "And I choose to spend them with you."

Lee took a swig out of the jug, then poured some into a goblet before taking a bite out of the bread.

"You have a prodigious appetite, Creeper," she said admiringly. "You must rebuild your strength."

The boy was too busy tucking into the breakfast to answer. Jill lingered in the sunlight a few moments more, but he never once turned to look at her, so she wandered nonchalantly over to the fireplace and ran her fingers over the stonework. When he raised his eyes from the plate, he would see how beautiful her profile was. Lifting her face into a pose that suggested a winsome nymph, she waited for him to notice.

And waited.

"Hey," Lee addressed her at length, when her neck was aching.

She turned round prettily, her eyes sparkling with promise.

"Could you go the washhouse and find me my clothes?" he asked. "I gotta get outta of this Wee Willy Winkie nighty. Gerald mighta liked this kinda thing, but it ain't for me."

Jill was taken aback. "I shall call for a maid," she said.

"Why? You just said you got nuthin' better to do than hang around here. I'm guessing the maids and the serfs are kept real busy in this place, skivvying for the likes of you. Get off your lazy royal ass and be useful."

The girl was at a loss for words. She started walking to the door then stopped and perched on the bed in one last attempt.

"I can be very useful," she said with her most beguiling smile as she ran her fingers through her hair.

Lee drained a second goblet and wiped his mouth on his sleeve.

"Look," he began, "this slut thing you're doin', it's cheap and it's nasty. Baxter told me all about who you was – who all his pupils were. You is Sandra Dixon. He said you was real quiet and smart. Sounds a bit dull, but kinda sweet. Don't you never think about that no more?"

"I am the Jill of Hearts!" she said, not understanding his words. "Shall I prove unto you that I am every inch a princess?"

She ran her fingers provocatively over her bosom and Lee kicked back from the table.

"You want to be a ho," he snapped in annoyance, "that ain't none of my business, but don't try it on me, cos I ain't even window-shoppin' let alone buyin' what you got on discount. I know it's just the way you was writ and that's a shame, cos what I'm seein' here right now is plain desperate, girl. Get some self-respect and dignity. Try bein' better than how that book made you."

The Jill of Hearts' face burned angrily and she jumped off the bed as if it was on fire. She had never been spoken to like that before. How dare he insult the daughter of an Under King this way? She was so furious she couldn't begin to think of a fitting retort. She stormed up to him and raised a hand to strike his face.

"You do that and I guarantee you will lose teeth," he promised her.

"You would not dare lay a finger on a princess!" she exclaimed.

Lee laughed at her. "Ain't that what you was just gaggin' for?"

"Insolent rogue! How...?"

"I'll just say this once," he said in a quiet, calm voice that was more threatening than any fierce shout. "And you can spread the word. You, and the rest of the royals here, ain't nuthin'. If you get in my way, if you so much as say the wrong thing to me, I will mess up your faces real bad. I don't got no time for your crap. I'm gonna be doin' somethin' a whole lot worse to someone with a better family tree than any of you, real soon. So stay clear, you hearin' me? Now take your skank game outta here and leave me in peace."

Jill felt as though she had been slapped. She staggered backwards then hurried away, frightened, humiliated and fuming.

"And send me my goddamn clothes!" he called after her.

It was afternoon by the time the valet returned with Lee's Korean shirt and boots. His underpants and one sock had gone missing and he cursed under his breath. Buttoning his shirt up, he couldn't help smiling at the home-made Nike tick that Maggie had once sewn on it for him. But he mustn't think of her or the others, not now. They were dead. It wasn't easy.

"Remember what matters," he repeated to himself. "Just stay fixed on what you gotta do."

The valet had provided a selection of hose to wear, but Lee threw them right back at him. Finally, because he had to wear something, he settled on a pair of brown leather hunting breeches and was glad there were no full-length mirrors to show how dorky he looked.

After the splendid breakfast and that long refreshing sleep, which had been free from the usual nightmares, Lee was straining to be up and active. Against the Physician's instructions, he left the bedchamber and made his way carefully down the West Tower. The Ismus had not yet appeared, so he went in search of him. The sooner he found out where the Bad Shepherd was, the sooner he could get this thing over with.

The noise and cheers of the joust filled the day and most inhabitants of the castle were out there enjoying themselves. Lee was reminded of the time he had brought Charm here. That too had been a similar day of tournaments, although they never saw any of it. This time it was different; there was no need to hide and sneak about. The few people he did meet bowed, greeting him respectfully as 'Creeper', or merely stared open-mouthed, for everybody knew his identity.

"Guess I'm a celeb," he muttered uncomfortably.

He limped through the empty courtyards and hallways and under the deep arches of the three concentric castle walls. Finally the main gate reared before him. Mauger, the fearsome Guardian, was out of sight, bolted in its barred den. Lee sauntered past the two sentries who kept vigil during the day and crossed the drawbridge. The men nudged one another and exchanged awed whispers from the side of their mouth.

The moat sparkled in the sunshine and the air was thick with the sapphire and emerald flash of dragonflies on the wing. A contented frog lazed on a lily pad, leisurely flicking out a long tongue now and then, and chewed drowsily.

Lee continued on his way, walking through the freshly scythed grass of the long meadow where today's jousts were being held. Colourful, striped pavilions were set up and a berfrois, or grandstand, had been built for the nobility to view the sport from.

A great roar of acclaim went up and, for a vain instant, he thought it was for him. He quickly realised the crowd was cheering some victory at the tilt. The Jack of Clubs had won another contest and a stretcher carrying a wounded knight came hurrying through the throng of common spectators, towards the red and white tent where the Physician was already dealing with two casualties.

Lee halted when he saw the stretcher-bearers. They were Punchinellos. One of them turned a repulsive face towards him as they scampered on their way and those bulging eyes glittered knowingly. The boy recognised him immediately. It was Yikker, one of the sadistic guards in the camp, the one who had dressed as a Catholic priest. Lee's hands curled into fists and he clenched his teeth. The Punchinello gave a high, squawking cackle and continued to the Physician's tent.

"Shoulda brought one of them Kalashnikovs with me," Lee muttered. "Coulda settled some scores before I do the big one."

Skirting round the rear of the crowd, he approached the stand where the nobles and members of the Royal Houses were seated. The Ismus and the Lady Labella sat beneath a black and gold canopy. Between them was a crib in which the infant was sleeping soundly.

By that time, the villagers had become aware of the Castle Creeper's presence among them and they had all turned to stare. A hush fell over the meadow and then the assembled Under Kings and Queens shifted in their seats to gaze on this singular newcomer to the Realm. The Jill of Spades and the Jack of Diamonds eyed him with cold hostility. The Jill of Hearts had conveyed his threat to them and they were incensed at his behaviour.

The Jill of Hearts remained obstinately unaware of Lee's arrival. For her, he no longer existed. She looked this way and that, but never to where he was standing. Her ignoring him would be punishment a-plenty. She waved a slender hand at the Jack of Clubs who was still astride Ironheart, his peerless steed, and was vexed to see that he had lifted the visor of his helm and was also staring in wonderment at the Castle Creeper.

The Ismus had raised his arms in welcome and was leaving the shade of the canopy to go and greet Lee.

"Welcome!" his voice boomed out over the silent throng. "Most welcome to you. This is a great day for Mooncaster. We are privileged to have as our guest the Castle Creeper. Some of you may already have heard of him and his astounding feats."

A small boy from the village could contain himself no longer. "He done saved my life last year on the Night of All Dark," Tully blurted. "The Bad Shepherd was going to dash my brains in, but the Creeper fought him off."

"That's right!" his friend Clover Ditchy called out from the crowd. "He were secret and invisible, but he stopped that horror right enough."

Tully's other young friends, who had been with them, joined in. "He's a hero, that's what he is!" they shouted. "A champion hero!"

Standing at the entrance to Sir Darksilver's tent, Tully's brother, Rufus, remained silent. In the spring, he had been taken on as the knight's esquire – a huge honour and one that had made his mother and grandfather immensely proud. Rufus had much to do this day, making sure Sir Darksilver's armour and weaponry were burnished like mirrors, attending to Flamefoot, his charger, and decking it out with the sable and silver caparison, emblazoned with the badge of Clubs. It was a tough and laborious life but, until recently, the boy had loved every arduous task. Today, however, he was sick at heart and jittery.

Within the tent, Sir Darksilver boomed out for him to finish buckling him into his armour and Rufus hastened to obey, but was all thumbs.

Outside, the rest of the village erupted with joyous yells and grateful praise for the Castle Creeper. They would have surged forward to lift Lee on to their shoulders and parade him round the meadow had the Ismus not intervened and called for calm.

"The Creeper is but fresh out of the sick bed and still convalescing," he told them. "There will be time for celebrations later. Allow him to enjoy the freedom of our Realm at his ease and do not overtire him."

The villagers obeyed and retreated with shy, apologetic and admiring faces.

"You were supposed to stay in bed," the Ismus muttered to Lee, dropping the lordly performance as he led him round the stand and out of earshot. "That leg won't heal if you don't let it."

"I done spent the best part of a year cooped up in small rooms," the boy answered. "Not gonna happen no more. I just need to know where that shepherd guy is right now."

"My agents are hunting high and low. He slinks and skulks about the Realm like a cat's shadow. We are usually only aware of him when he has committed some new heinous act, and then he flits back into hiding. He has not been glimpsed since early in the spring. As soon as his whereabouts are discovered, you will be informed. Perhaps the King of Diamonds will have news when he returns from his hunt later. I suggest you make use of this time by finding the Healing Ruby."

Lee raised his eyebrows. "You think I should be doin' what, for the what?" he asked.

"The Healing Ruby," the Ismus repeated. "Once you have dispatched the Bad Shepherd and rid both worlds of his memory and influence, you must place the Healing Ruby in your beloved's hands. Only that will awaken her."

Lee shook his head in confusion and seized the man by the shoulders.

"What is this BS?" he demanded. "I ain't never heard none of this before. Don't spin me this crap."

The three Black Face Dames had followed them and they acted quickly to take Lee's hands away.

"Back off!" the boy snapped. "I can wipe all of yous outta this story like you never was, so just stay out of it."

They didn't listen and pulled the boy away from their Lord.

"Get your goons off me!" he warned. "Or the deal's off – and I'll come hunting for you instead."

The Ismus laughed. "What a bundle of impotent threats," he said. "You can't kill me. Not here. Not in this world, not any more. You might have succeeded back in the other, if you had thought of it, but not here. And you will honour the bargain. You can only exist in this place now; there's nowhere else for you. Like I said, you're locked in. Besides, you do still want pretty Charm to flutter her lids and drop her aitches for you, don't you? Or have the doe-eyed damsels and buxom wenches of Mooncaster caused you to forget her already?"

Lee could have ripped his smirking head off. He lunged forward, but the three bodyguards held him securely. Eventually his struggles ceased.

"As I was saying," the Ismus resumed, "the Healing Ruby must be placed in Miss Benedict's hands. Only then shall she awaken – after the Bad Shepherd has been dealt with. Don't look so murderous. It's all part of the fundamental rules and magickal lore upon which this domain is founded. It really isn't down to me, I swear on all that is unholy."

Lee hung his head. "Where is this damn ruby?" he asked.

"You shall have to ask that of Magpie Jack," the Ismus replied. "He stole it from under the King of Hearts' pillow, whilst he was sleeping. Such a scoundrel that lad."

"Just tell me where it is."

"I genuinely don't know. Jack was discovered in the royal bedchamber, but the ruby was nowhere to be found; it wasn't on his person, it wasn't under the pillow, it was nowhere in the room. They searched high and low for it, without success. The Healing Ruby had completely disappeared and, even though he went to gaol for it, Jack never disclosed where the jewel was hidden."

Lee uttered a grunt of exasperation. "Don't gimme this," he said. "I ain't one of them dumb Jaxers. This is your book; you know who did what and when and why and what they was wearing when they did it – just tell me where the damn thing is."

"As you observed two nights ago, at the fortress of Battle Wood, there are certain aspects of this domain that were here long before I composed the hallowed text. There are disciplines and governing principles that even I, and the Bad Shepherd, must adhere to. The mystery of the Healing Ruby is one of them."

"You better not be jerking me. What else you gonna surprise me with?"

"Nothing, I vow. You were in no fit state to hear this the other night."

The Ismus signalled for the Black Face Dames to release him. Lee tore his arms free and snorted with disgust.

"Where's the sticky-fingered kid now?" he demanded.

"Watching the joust, with the rest."

"Not no more he ain't," Lee rumbled, stomping off.

"A word of warning, Creeper," the Ismus said gravely. "Remember, this is not the world of *Dancing Jax*, but the furtherance of that world. You will find *Fighting Pax* a much darker, more treacherous domain."

"I'm learning that fast."

"I am in deadly earnest. Though the sun is shining, don't let it blind you. Betrayal and peril are now ripe and ready for the harvest. Have a care. There are other dangers than the shepherd here."

The Jill of Spades and the Jack of Diamonds had left the berfrois and were making their way to the Jack of Clubs' tent, deep in intrigue, when Lee caught up with them.

"Wait up," he said. "You an' me got things we need to discuss."

Jack stared at him in surprise.

"I have naught to say to you, Sirrah!" he snorted contemptuously. "Your infamous treatment of the Jill of Hearts was the conduct of a cur. I will not debase myself by having converse with you."

"You ain't my fave choice of phone a friend either, but seems you's the only one who knows."

"Step aside there," Jack ordered. "Let your betters be about their business."

"Oh, you is so close to gettin' a slap, kid. All I wants to know is where you stashed that ruby."

Jack's expression changed from indignation to amusement and he laughed dismissively. "Is the fellow crazed? Why should I reveal my secret unto you? If that is what you seek, Creeper, then I am overjoyed to deny you."

"I ain't givin' you no choice here," Lee snarled, dragging him behind the nearest tent and pushing him against the canvas. "Tell me, or I'll get all twenty-first century on your skinny ass."

He grabbed Jack by the throat and was about to shake him when he felt cold steel at his own neck.

The Jill of Spades dimpled his skin with her dagger's tip. "Only a fool dares threaten the children of the Royal Houses," she purred into his ear. "And it is an assuredly short-lived folly. If I were to push but a little, your Creeping would be at an end. Which is it to be?"

Lee loosened his grip. He was annoyed with himself for barging in and forgetting the nature of the Jill of Spades.

"I just wants to know..."

"And I said which is it to be? Friend of the Ismus or no, I shall make a fountain of your blood if you do not unhand the Jack of Diamonds. And know this, patience is not amongst my virtues for, in truth, I have none – so be quick."

Lee ground his teeth. Getting embroiled in the petty plots and machinations of these storybook characters was the last thing he'd wanted to do. There was no mistaking the deadly intention in her voice, however. She would stick him deep and think nothing of it.

"This ain't over," he told Jack as he released him. "You will tell me where that red rock is, else you'll lose your own family jewels – you hear what I'm sayin'?"

He pulled away from the blade and stared at the icy chill in Jill's eyes. She was more dangerous than any of the knights here. Jack drew his sword and stood beside her. There was no arguing against their sharp steel.

"You got me this once," Lee admitted with reluctance. "But there won't be no twice. You best lock yourself in your rooms, cos next time you won't see me comin' and I'll get the drop on you. Be my pleasure to smash your heads into something spreadable. I will find out what I need to know. Them torture toys they got in the dungeon here, they ain't nuthin' compared to a going-over, Peckham style. I'll put the fear on you."

The royal offspring laughed at him.

"Creep off," Jill instructed mockingly. "Your threats are as empty as the Waiting Throne."

Lee's temper was close to boiling over. Everything inside him cried out to swipe the derision off their faces, but the sun was glinting on their weapons and he wasn't stupid. He reproached himself for coming out here unarmed. He should have asked the valet for a knife of his own to hang at his belt. That was an oversight he was going to correct straight away.

"Laters," he said with a curled lip. "I'll come looking for you, Jackie boy."

"I welcome it," Magpie Jack replied.

Lee spat on the ground and departed.

"I ought to have challenged him and made an end of it," the Jack of Diamonds declared. "He is a peril to us all. One sure thrust to the heart or through the eye would dispatch him and honour would be satisfied."

The Queen of Spades' daughter disagreed and returned her dagger into the secret sheath up her sleeve. "At least two summers stand against you," she said. "You are not yet thirteen, Jack."

"I am not a-feared. I have bested older knights, and those of greater stature than that tar-skinned felon."

"I shall devise a more subtle plan, one more fitting."

Her lips curled into a devious smile.

"There is an artful way of dealing with him," she said. "A way that would dispatch him with certainty."

"What way is that?"

"He wishes the Healing Ruby, so you must tell him where it lies."

"I will not!"

"Oh, come now," she said. "Your secret, the one that sealed the reputation of Magpie Jack as the peerless thief of Mooncaster, I guessed it long ago. There could be but one explanation to the mystery of what occurred in the royal bedchamber that night, before the warders captured you."

The boy stared at her crossly. "You cannot possibly know," he said.

"It's as plain as the Queen of Heart's face," she answered. "And, if you tell the Creeper, he will surely go questing for it and thereby meet his end."

Jack considered her words. The idea was certainly appealing. But, if others discovered how he had made the ruby disappear from that bedchamber, his renown would tumble.

"A chamber with but one door," Jill mused aloud. "No secret passageway, every hiding place searched four times over... when the answer to that riddle is as clear as glass, oh – but there is no glass in the window of that room. None at all – and what a large window it is."

"The lawn beneath was scoured most thoroughly!" he reminded her.

"Oh, but you did not cast the ruby away," she said. "Someone took it from you. Someone who was passing by outside – or maybe was even in the room with you?"

"Passing by?" he snorted. "At such a lofty height? What stilts are so tall?"

"Not with the aid of stilts, but a hayfork perhaps?"

"Enough!" he demanded. "You dare suggest I am in league with Haxxentrot? Upon mine honour, I swear I did not put the Healing Ruby into that crone's wizened hands."

The Jill of Spades eyed him keenly. She knew she had hit close to the truth of it and was about to press further when a roar went up. Another joust had been won by the Jack of Clubs. This time it was against Sir Darksilver, the mightiest knight in Mooncaster, who had never been bested before. But then he had never been up against the Jack of Clubs before.

Jill particularly wanted to observe what might follow, so she dropped a curtsy and bade Magpie Jack good day. Like a serpent, she wound her way through the crowd and saw the knight being carried to the Physician's tent.

Wrapped in angry thought, the Jack of Clubs strode away.

Moments later, the Jockey emerged from the tent they had been talking so carelessly by.

"Haw haw haw," he chortled softly and went tripping after Magpie Jack. He had a contemptible proposal to put to him, a true test of his talents – and how could the lad refuse, now he knew his secret?

Rufus, Sir Darksilver's young esquire, was hurriedly clearing the tilt yard of his master's shield and broken lance and leading the unmanned Flamefoot back to the stables. When he saw the Jill of Spades moving through the throng, his face clouded over and he grew more anxious than ever.

While the Jack of Clubs was being hailed as the champion of the day, Jill entered the Physician's tent and feigned concern for the wounded knight.

"Pray do not get up," she told Sir Darksilver as the Physician began stitching the slice in his shoulder. "Let the leechmaster attend to his embroidery. I trust your injuries are not too grievous. The Knave of Clubs is unbeatable this tournament. How he topples even the greatest of you."

The knight glowered up at her through his thick, wiry eyebrows. What lay behind this concern, he wondered? This was not usual for the Queen of Spades' daughter.

"The prince is a valiant opponent, Your Royal Highness," he said grudgingly. "He improves with the seasons – and he rides the finest charger in the land. There is no match for Ironheart."

Jill pretended to wince as the needle pushed in and out of his hairy skin, but she had dissected enough creatures herself to be quite unmoved by such grisly work.

"How gallant you are to accept defeat with such good grace," she said admiringly. "If only all knights of the Court were as chivalrous. For a mighty, battle-tempered warrior such as you to be unhorsed by a mere boy, bearing the same badge as yourself... Many of those lesser combatants would have sharper things to say."

"That is so," the Physician concurred, finishing the shoulder and breaking the thread with his teeth. "Sir Gorvain and Sir Eluard have both been under my care this day and they were less complimentary about the Jack of Clubs."

"Any young peasant wench from the village could flick those two from the saddle," Sir Darksilver said scornfully. "They are but two old gossip wives in armour."

"No doubt you are right," Jill agreed. "And Jack's mount truly is a marvellous beast. Yet... it seems most strange to me that, whilst the horses of Mooncaster become mightier, our lances grow more brittle."

Sir Darksilver sat up quickly and popped several stitches, much to the Physician's annoyance.

"How mean you, Your Royal Highness?" the knight asked.

The Jill of Spades appeared alarmed and flustered that she had spoken too freely.

"Heed not my foolish, hasty words," she said. "I know naught of these manly matters; 'twas but a girlish fancy. Tend our old warrior well, leechmaster."

And with that seed sown, she left the tent.

Sir Darksilver's brooding stare followed her until she disappeared from view. The Physician jabbed the needle in once more and the burly knight felled him with one powerful smack.

"Outrage!" the Physician protested, flapping on the floor with a bleeding lip. "Begone, Sir Knight. I shall not tend to you again, though your limbs be hacked and your head fill with green pus, I would not lift a finger to aid you!"

Sir Darksilver rose from the stretcher and went in search of wine and answers.

"And neither shall my leeches!" the Physician shouted after him.

The warm afternoon continued. The best ale was drunk and, when the jousting was done, it was time for the judging of the produce and livestock. As usual, the Ismus was the arbiter and he went from stall to stall and pen to pen to inspect and formulate his decisions.

Then, standing by the large boundary stone, at the edge of the meadow, he announced the results.

Gasps and grunts of indignation and disbelief spread throughout the crowd. For the first time ever, Gristabel Smallrynd, the miller's wife, had not won the bread making. For many years she had been the only entrant. Out of consideration and neighbourliness, no one else in the village wished to trespass on her floury province and so did not compete against her. The mill house also possessed the largest oven. But only last week she had quarrelled with Rhoswen, the stonemason's tiny wife, and she had retaliated by baking the finest loaves the Holy Enchanter had ever tasted. Gristabel was incensed and thoroughly humiliated. She stormed from the meadow, tearing her own, officially second-rate, bread into crumbs as she went and the dogs and ducks ran after her greedily.

There were more shocks to come. Aiken Woodside, the ploughman, had been expected to win a prize for his large and beautiful cabbages, but, at the last moment, young Clover Ditchy entered an onion the size of his own head that he had been cultivating in secret. Nothing could compete with that. The rest of the village grumbled. Aiken Woodside was the local fiddle player. When he was in a bad mood, his music was sharp and spiky – if he could be persuaded to play at all. The night's revels would be spoiled. Aiken's son, Muddy Legs, who was friends with Clover Ditchy, punched the boy on the nose and vowed never to speak to him again, so Clover thumped him right back and blacked his eye. It took four strong men to pull them apart and the boys were led away, hollering dire curses at one another.

Then the livestock caused more upset. Old Edwin's enormous pig managed to break out of its pen, into that of Mistress Sarah's goslings, and trampled two of them to death. Then, startled by the din from the rest, it broke free completely and ran across the meadow.

Some of the children, Benwick, Lynnet, Neddy and Tully, thought it would be a great game to chase it. Benwick even jumped on its back and rode it. Old Edwin huffed and puffed behind them, shaking his fists, while Mistress Sarah followed, shaking her fists at him.

It was all too much for the fat pig. With a squeal, it keeled over and expired.

Arguments and acrimony sprang up like mushrooms, as blame was laid at every door, from the children, to their parents, to the carpenter who built the flimsy fences, to the blacksmith who forged such short nails. Soon everyone was embroiled in a row, old slights and snubs were resurrected and long-buried hatchets were exhumed. Only when the Ismus called for peace did the squabbling stop, and they drifted away, muttering, with sidelong glances.

As a tawny evening settled, young couples sought the stubbly fields and couched themselves among the corn stooks. Soft voices and playful laughter drifted between the scattered bowers, as the stars pinked the deep dark blue of this night in late summer. But even here there was discord and unease. Dulcie, the innkeeper's daughter, had offended Kit, her current Mooncot dalliance, by setting her sights on a handsome gallant from the castle, who was easily persuaded to follow her into the moonlit fields.

Presently the murmurs and giggles turned to yelps and shouts and slaps. One maiden had been pinched too severely, another's hair had been yanked, another had a jug of mead spilled across her face and one squealed when she was bitten.

Their swains were quick to beg forgiveness and pledge ignorance of how such rough play might have chanced to occur. Gentle words and passionate courtship were all they desired and they repented most abjectly if they had caused offence or hurt.

So complete was their imploring, their sweethearts nested next to them once more and the murmurs were even softer.

No one saw four corn stooks rise up on stockinged legs, to go hopping across the field to the next isle of love. Small, pale hands reached out and fumbled through the straw to nip and upset and cause strife between the tangled couples.

The Bogey Boys of Haxxentrot were abroad, doing the spiteful bidding of their witchy mistress.

Further tiffs and tearful bickering broke out, and the Bogey Boys bit their tongues to keep from snickering.

Then a rose-coloured light came floating into the field. At first those who noticed thought it was a will-o'-the-wisp and caught their breaths in fear. But then they saw it was only a heart-shaped lantern hanging from a slender staff.

Cloaked in a hooded robe of purple velvet, the Jill of Hearts stepped through the stubble and made her way round the stooks, staring shamelessly at the couples as she wafted by.

Every lusty lad sat up and winked at her, inflamed with the hope of kissing royal lips instead. But she merely smiled coldly and moved on, leaving their fuming wenches to scold and spurn them and stomp off alone, either to the village or the servants' quarters in the White Castle.

Jill wended her way back to the road. Once that game would have amused her greatly, but now she was weary of it. There were none who compared with the Jack of Clubs. She could have her pick of any lover except the only one she wanted.

Extinguishing the lantern, she walked through the village. Angry voices spilled from every window. Tempers had not been cooled and the scabs of many old scores had been worried and picked at. In The Silver Penny, insults and tankards were thrown, then a table was overturned as a scuffle ensued. Even as Jill passed by, a drunken Kit was thrown out. Cursing the innkeeper, and his faithless daughter, the jilted young man stumbled away.

None of this mattered to Jill. Her thoughts burned with the prospect of what she was going to do that night.

Passing the millhouse, which banged and clattered with hurled pots and pans as Gristabel vented her ire and indignation inside, Jill followed the meandering road through the moon-silvered countryside.

When she felt sure no one had followed her and a coppice screened her from the castle and the village, she took from a pocket in her cloak a golden bracelet. It gleamed and glittered magickally in the moonlight. This was a gift from Malinda.

Jill had ventured to her lonely cottage in the forest to beg a love philtre, but the wise Fairy Godmother had refused. The princess was already the fairest in the land. She could collect suitors like daisies in a garden if she so desired, so there was no need for her magick. Besides, Malinda's wand had been stolen and she no longer possessed her former power.

And so Jill had broken down and confessed the curse placed upon her by the Mistletoe King. The only suitor she yearned for, whose very shadow she would kiss, cared only for his horse and hawk. The hounds in the kennels were higher in his affections than she ever could be. What was she to do?

Malinda had dried those bitter tears and told her the Jack of Clubs' love could not be won with any philtre. His heart and spirit were one with the Wild Wood. To awaken his admiration and quicken his longing, she must make him see her with new eyes. She must appear to him as something wondrous, wreathed in ancient mystery – a goddess of the deep woods.

Opening a small casket, Malinda had taken out a golden bracelet and placed it in the girl's hands.

"Within this bangle," the retired Fairy Godmother had said, "is a force far, far older than any my wand could command. Do but slip this on your wrist and it shall change your shape, and you will be transformed into the most graceful hind ever to dance through the Kingdom of the Dawn Prince. But heed this warning: wear it only when

Jack rides alone, for you will be the greatest prize any hunter has ever seen. The Jack of Clubs cannot fail to fall under your spell. When he espies you, he will stalk through thistle and ditch to feast his gaze. Lead him where you will and, when you deem it right, remove the bracelet. He will be in your thrall till the end of his days."

Jill had thanked her and the retired Fairy Godmother repeated the grave warning.

Now Jill looked down at the bracelet and tried to control her excitement. Dawn was the usual hour Jack rode out on Ironheart. That very afternoon she had overheard him say he would gallop to the waterfall in the East Woods to bathe. That would be the perfect place for him to encounter her. It would be as if they were part of a grand romantic legend.

The girl removed her garments swiftly and hid them, with the lantern, in the coppice. Then, holding the bracelet high so that she could see the moon shining through the centre, she put it on to her wrist.

The leaves of the coppice rustled as a fragrant breeze moved through them. The hedges stirred and the grasses swayed. Wild flowers that had closed with the sunset unfurled and turned their faces. Jill thought she heard faint voices singing on the air.

And then a beautiful scarlet hind was shaking its elegant head and blinking long-lashed violet eyes. It bore a white, heart-shaped blaze and, round the animal's ankle, the golden bracelet glinted.

For a moment the hind seemed unsure and gazed down at its four legs, lifting each one off the ground experimentally. Then it jumped, skittish and light as a cat. With a balletic leap, it cleared the hedge and ran for the East Woods, to be ready for when Jack came riding.

In Mooncot, Tully was having trouble sleeping. He had been sent to bed without supper, for his part in the death of Old Edwin's pig. Lying on his cot, in the kitchen, he heard a tap at the back door.

"Rufus!" he exclaimed when he ran to open it. "What are you doing here? You should be sleeping in the stables, up at the castle. How did you slip past Mauger?"

His brother wrung his hands and wiped his eyes. "They never let him out of his den on this night," he answered distractedly. "With so many serving girls and lads trysting in the fields."

Tully brought his brother inside and sat him down by the window. The moonlight streamed in and he was shocked to see Rufus so distraught and agitated.

"Whatever be the matter?" he asked.

"I got to tell someone," Rufus told him wretchedly. "But you got to swear not to breathe a word to nobody, not even Grandfather!"

"I swear."

"Spit – and wish yourself stone dead if you do."

Tully spat and made this, their most solemn of oaths. Rufus was scaring him.

His brother pulled a small leather purse from inside his shirt and emptied it on to the table. Three bright gold pieces tumbled out. It was the most money Tully had ever seen.

Rufus stared at it shamefully. "I've done a most terrible, wicked thing," he whispered.

18

THE GREAT HALL was noisy with carousing. Lee had sat next to the Ismus and the Lady Labella on the high table, watching the knights and lords and Under Kings get steadily drunker.

A long knife now hung at Lee's side. He had no use for a sword, but the knife he could work with.

Having sat through an appallingly bad performance by Old Ramptana, the useless Court Magician, and listened to enough madrigals to last him forever, he finally glimpsed who he was looking for.

Carrying a sack, Magpie Jack emerged from behind the wooden screen that concealed the way to the kitchen. With furtive glances, he crept through the Great Hall and stepped outside.

Lee rose and followed him.

The Jack of Diamonds hurried through the castle grounds. He ran over the common lawns, through a green door and into the Physic Garden, where he sat at the edge of the ornamental pond and waited.

Presently a noise startled him and he sprang to his feet.

"Is that you?" he hissed to the surrounding shadows. "I have brought what you desired."

"What you got there?" Lee asked, stepping into the moonlight, knife drawn.

Jack went for his sword, but Lee was too quick. He knocked the boy to the ground then hauled him to the edge of the pond where he plunged his head backwards into the water.

Jack emerged spluttering and gasping. Lee did it again. The third time Jack came up for air, Lee said, "If you make me do that one more time, I'll leave you under. Don't think you can mess with me, kid. Tell me where that ruby thing is."

Magpie Jack coughed and heaved for breath.

Lee scowled. "You is takin' way too long," he snarled. "I ain't playing games here. You'll be found floating with the fishes if you don't spill what I wanna know. You got three seconds, then I'm done with you, and you is done with life. You comprende that?"

"I do not know!" Jack protested.

"One," Lee said.

Jack gripped Lee's sleeves. "On my life, I swear it!"

"Two."

"I know not where the ruby is!"

"Three. Too bad for you."

Lee plunged the boy's head in the water for the last time and held it there. The bubbles exploded to the surface and Jack's arms thrashed about.

"You're alarming the goldfish," a new voice observed casually.

Lee looked up. The Jockey had joined them, the creaks of his caramel-coloured leather outfit masked by Jack's frantic splashing.

"Must I be boring and summon the guards?" he enquired. "Let the prince go. I do believe you've made your point."

Lee pulled Jack out of the water and dropped him on the grass, where he choked and retched up pond water.

"You wish to know where the Healing Ruby resides," the Jockey began. "It is secure, in a place beyond your reach."

"Where?"

The Jockey glanced at Magpie Jack, still coughing on the ground. "Haxxentrot has it," he said. "It is in the Forbidden Tower."

Lee swore under his breath. "Couldn't be under a floorboard or in an old shoe," he muttered. "Had to be in the worst place there is – it figures. I hate this crazy-assed dump."

Nudging Jack with his foot, he asked. "This true? That old bag got the ruby?"

The boy was still breathing hard and unable to speak. It gave him the greatest pleasure to agree with the Jockey and he nodded quickly.

"'Tis true," he managed at length. "A Bogey Boy took it from me. The witch has the ruby."

"No sense me hangin' round here no more then," Lee stated, heading back the way he came.

"Surely you do not purpose to enter the Forbidden Tower?" the Jockey asked in surprise. "The perils are too great."

Lee looked back at him. "For her they is," he said grimly. "Frail old lady, livin' in a high rise. She's ripe for a visit. I only got respect for two pensioners: my gran'ma and a cool guy called Gerald. A witch on a stick don't figure nowhere. I've had enough of this fairy-tale BS. No witches or no one else is gonna stand in my way. She don't give me what I want, by the time I finished, she'll wish someone had dropped a house on her instead, like that other mean hag in the movie."

With that, he strode off, out of the garden.

"The Creeper is on his way to an early death," the Jockey remarked.

"That is glad tidings indeed," Jack declared, sitting up and shaking his wet head. "I hope she brews something foul and lingering for him."

"And what news have you for me?" the Jockey asked. "Shall I be pleased in equal measure?"

The boy reached for the sack he had brought.

"I have it here," he said, reaching inside for the strange tambourine he had stolen from a sleeping kitchen maid.

"Do not take it out!" the Jockey cried, clamping his hands to his ears. "I cannot bear it."

Jack wrapped the tambourine tightly again. "I was as stealthy as a phantom," he boasted. "She did not stir when I unhooked it from her person."

The Jockey smiled appreciatively as he took the sack from him.

"You have done well, my knave," he congratulated. "And your reputation is assured."

"What will you do with it?" Jack asked. "'Tis a most curious object."

"Haw haw haw," the Jockey answered. "First I shall find it a new home – in the deepest part of the moat. Then I shall call on Columbine, that grime-smirched hussy of a kitchen maid, and teach her that the Jockey wins every game. He rides everyone at Court in one way or another. Her time has come. Haw haw haw."

His unpleasant laughter hung over the garden as he and the boy left it. When it faded, a small face appeared from behind a rosemary bush.

Nosy Posy, the Constable's daughter, sucked in her cheeks and wondered whom she should tell.

The Jill of Spades made sure the door to her bedchamber was locked, then went to a cupboard and took out a small roll of black cloth. Inside was a slim candle of green wax. Securing it in a holder, she took the candle to the window and set a taper to the wick.

There was a crackle of livid sparks and an emerald-coloured flame started to burn, tall and steady. The warm night breeze that sighed around the North Tower of the House of Spades could not even cause the flame to tremble or waver.

Sitting on a high-backed chair, Jill stared at the window and waited.

Presently she heard a curious sound approaching from outside. It was a droning buzz. Rising, she strode to the window and looked out.

Something was flying over the castle walls. She saw four oval faces, pale as milk, drawing closer. They were Bogey Boys. They were riding upon crowflies, more of Haxxentrot's loathsome creatures. They were larger than ravens, with sharp black beaks, but their eyes were those of an insect and six bird like talons were tucked beneath bodies covered in coarse hairs instead of feathers. Their wings were the same as a great bluebottle and

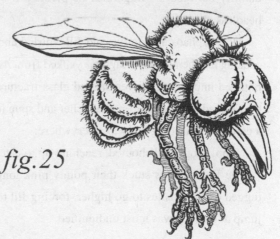

fig.25

they were the cause of the buzzing.

Haxxentrot had bred the crowflies to be swift aerial steeds for her Bogey Boys, but it also amused her to send them to the castle to peck the noses off the unwary.

The Bogey Boys were racing, each trying to be the first to reach the North Tower. Bouncing up and down on their winged mounts, they impelled them with their heels and smacked the tops of those bristly heads.

The Jill of Spades only managed to dodge aside in time. They rushed through the window and whizzed round and round the bedchamber, knocking into furniture, pulling open cupboards, skimming their feet through the water basin and setting the jug reeling so it smashed on the floor. Flying over the fruit bowl, they snatched up apples and scooped hazelnuts from a golden dish and pelted one another with them. Diving between the bedposts and swinging on its curtains, the witch's small, rascally servants chased each other. One made a grab for the fine linen night smock that was laid out on the coverlet and held it daintily between his fingers as he paraded it about the room like a headless ghost.

All was chaos and uproar and Jill whirled about as they circled her causing mayhem. A painting was yanked from its hook, the mirror was bumped into and the silver-backed glass fractured in the frame. Then they seized hold of the iron chandelier and spun it round and round like a carousel, splashing hot wax everywhere.

"Stop! Stop!" Jill shouted, reaching up to catch them.

The Bogey Boys stuck their pointy pink tongues out at her. They tugged on the bristles to go higher, forcing Jill to stand on a chair and jump at them. It was most undignified.

Then, one after another, they steered their ugly steeds downward and zigzagged about the chamber until the mischievous Bogey Boys hopped clear and landed on the feather bed. The crowflies cawed and darted up to the vaulted ceiling, to crawl across the painted plaster and sharpen their beaks on the stonework.

Jub, Crik, Hak and Rott tumbled about like acrobats, flipping and somersaulting from one end to the other. Then they rolled in formation across the bed and, with a flourish, sat cross-legged on the edge – beaming up at the infuriated girl.

Stepping down from the chair, Jill swept a stray lock of hair from her face, incensed that she should be made to look so foolish.

"I did not send for you!" she said crossly and out of breath. "Where is Haxxentrot? Where is your mistress?"

The Bogey Boys smiled even wider, revealing their baby teeth, and they fluttered their ginger-lashed eyes in insolent innocence.

"Answer me!" Jill demanded. "Or I shall have your sickly white heads on spikes and feed the rest of you to Mauger – if he is not repulsed by them."

The Bogey Boys shook their hands in mock terror and rolled their eyes wildly, before falling about, squeaking with laughter.

Jill advanced towards them, reaching into both her sleeves. Then a harsh, cracked voice behind said, "Do not draw thy daggers, my dark little maid."

The girl turned. There, standing by the window, hayfork in her wizened hands, was Haxxentrot the witch.

"My fine, big-headed boys are my most useful spies and attendants," she declared, pinching out the green flame from the signalling candle with her fingers. "Already this night they have been busily occupied sowing disharmony amongst the amorous peasantry, and they have more work ahead yet, have ye not, my pug-nosed, frighty lads?"

The Bogey Boys nodded and delved into the little leather pouches they carried, to show her what they had brought: small bottles, pots, jars and forged letters.

"Distrust, misery and anguish," the hag observed with satisfaction. "Ardent love notes to the Queen of Clubs, in the unmistakable scrawling hand of the King of Hearts, to be discovered by her husband on the morrow. And there, a tincture of toads to add to the water jugs in the Great Hall. One sip and the body will bubble with warts. Here there is an ointment, in the same pot the Queen of Hearts doth use for her salves and aids to beauty, to smooth away the lines of age from her fat face. When she applies this, her skin will wither and wrinkle worse than mine own."

Cackling, she leaned on her hayfork and told her four servants to go about their malignant night's work.

The Bogey Boys stuck their fingers in their mouths and whistled the crowflies from the ceiling. Leaping on their backs once more, they flew through the window and spiralled round the castle, seeking the towers of the other Royal Houses.

"How they love riding their gorcrows," Haxxentrot cackled. "Such an abundance of acrimony and blame shalt flower with the sunrise. Yea, even more than that which already gnaws through the White Castle. Spite and enmity are on the march. Canst thou not feel it, my baneful princess? The lid of the cauldron is rattling; soon the poison shalt boil over and not all of it will be my doing – alas."

"I did not summon you here to listen to your bitter chatter!" Jill told her.

"Summon?" the witch snarled. "Haxxentrot cannot be whistled for, like a crowfly or a hound to heel. Guard thy tongue, child, ere the witch of the Forbidden Tower decides to make cruel sport with you. Do not forget, thine old playmates are in my care. Those same dolls to whom thy vinegar life is spliced and bound. How easy 'twould be to command them to jump into the fire and you too would blister and scorch."

"My pardon!" Jill said hastily. "My words were rash and lacked due respect."

"Such is it ever with you, daughter of the Queen of Spades. What of the bargain we made last year? Thou were to poison all other womenfolk of the castle and bring to me Malinda's wand. Such ficklety and faithlessness."

"The Jockey was to blame that night," Jill explained. "The fault was not mine – and I was on my way to steal the wand when the Castle Creeper beat me to it."

The old witch sucked her teeth and eyed her keenly.

"I know the way of it," she said. "Else one of those treats my Bogey Boys carry would have been for thee."

She gave a foul grin. "It is enough that Malinda hath been robbed of her tawdry walking stick. Now she is even more crippled than ever. First her wings, then her wand. No more than a sorry old dame in the dark forest, whose clumsy spells are waning."

"It is of the Creeper I wish to speak," Jill said as the witch broke into fresh croaking laughter. "He is searching for the Healing Ruby."

Haxxentrot fell silent and glared at her.

"And what would I know of that?" she asked presently.

"Spare me your denials. Magpie Jack was aided by another the night he stole that treasure away. Answer me truthfully: did you not take it from him – at the window? It is the only solution to that riddle."

"Not I," the witch said with a sly wink. "But Jub was in that royal bedchamber that night, nailing nightmares into the King's oafish head. 'Twas Jub who took the jewel from Magpie Jack and escaped upon a crowfly."

"Then you do have it! You have the ruby!"

Haxxentrot shook her head. "When Jub returned, his purse was empty. The jewel had been lost on the journey – and he dawdled and meandered much on the way back to my tower. All my spies have hunted for it since. Gangle Hounds have scoured the land, 'twixt Mooncot and the marshes, and snakes did slither through the bogs and ditches, to no avail. The Healing Ruby remains shrouded in shadow and mystery. I know not where it is bestowed."

"Someone else must have found it," Jill muttered. "A peasant in the fields perhaps, or a serf running an errand across the castle lawns. They have taken and hidden it."

"Thou shalt not find it," the witch commented. "If thou didst seek to taunt the Creeper with knowledge of it, thou hast outreached thyself. He is too great an enemy for thee, my curdled princess."

"I do not fear that dark-faced villain!" she answered hotly. "I am the Jill of Spades. I could put an end to his Creeping whenever I have a mind."

Haxxentrot shook the hayfork at her and pointed a gnarled finger. Every candle flame spluttered and turned a virulent green.

"Do not dare raise thy hand against the Castle Creeper," she warned, as livid shadows leaped about her aged features and the bedchamber was engulfed in a sickly light.

"The doom that drives him will suffer no interference. Though thou be high-born, thou art as naught compared to that one. The Creeper's destiny, and the fate of Mooncaster and beyond, is mapped upon the ancient cards that engine these many worlds. None may prevent the deed he was brought hither to commit."

Jill clutched her throat and staggered backwards. A cold wind began to blow inside the chamber. It raked through her hair and tore at her gown. The bed curtains flapped madly until they were ripped free and went twisting through the blasting gale. Heavy oak furniture rocked and tottered, skidding across the floor in the squall. The large cupboard toppled over and wooden chests crashed against the walls. Even the great bed shook and lifted.

Jill could hardly breathe. Through battered lashes, she saw the witch appear to grow in size, the tip of her conical hat touching the vaulted ceiling.

"Hear and heed me, treacherous daughter of the House of Spades!" her voice resounded above the unnatural tempest. "If thou dost endeavour to hinder or obstruct the Castle Creeper, thy life and much more shall be forfeit. Step away from that path and unhatch thy plots – or accept the direst consequences. This is the solemn warning of Haxxentrot! Ignore my words at thy peril."

The witch lowered her finger and the wind dropped instantly. The bed curtains fell to the floor and the candles burned bright and yellow once more.

The Jill of Spades gasped and stared around her. When she looked back at the window, the witch was gone.

Jill ran to the ledge and leaned out. Haxxentrot was flying over the battlements upon the hayfork.

"So be it," the girl murmured. "Let the Creeper do what he must. There is another whom I would defame. The champion of the day shall not enjoy his victory for long."

Opening one of the wooden chests, she brought out a small silver pot, embossed with the badge of the Heart. Magpie Jack wasn't the only light-fingered royal child. Jill had stolen it from the Under Queen's own boudoir some days ago and knew just the use she would put it to.

Going to another chest, she was relieved that the bottles it contained had not broken. Here were her own noxious concoctions, poisons that could kill an army or make the strongest man as weak as an infant. And then there was this...

Examining a glass jar filled with brown powder, she transferred half of the contents into the silver pot, taking care to hold her head aside, lest she inhale any floating dust. Just a few grains of this compound would put a Punchinello to sleep for a week, or a horse for a day – perhaps a very special horse for several hours.

Choosing the rosiest apple from the floor, she carved a thimble-sized well in its side and carefully poured in some of the powder. Then she plugged it with the piece she had removed.

Wrapping a dark green cloak round her shoulders, the Jill of Spades tucked the apple and the silver pot into a pocket, unlocked the door and crept out.

Returning from the village, Rufus passed the Castle Creeper on the road. Lee was riding one of the spare horses kept for guests or when another was indisposed. Rufus watched him strike out over the fields and scratched his head. The Creeper was no horseman. He had never seen anyone sit so badly in the saddle.

But his thoughts were too full of his own troubles to care much about that. Dragging his feet over the drawbridge, he headed for the stables – where Sir Darksilver was waiting for him.

The knight was wild with rage and fuelled by wine. He had found the pieces of his broken lance and, under close inspection, discovered it had been sawn part-way through before the tournament. Storming to Rufus's bunk in the stable loft, he found, hidden beneath his straw-filled mattress, a small handsaw. The teeth were still clogged with sawdust and flakes of paint that matched the colours of his lance.

Confronted with this proof of his betrayal, Rufus stammered and tried to explain, but Sir Darksilver grabbed him by the throat and hurled him out into the courtyard. Using the largest fragment of the broken lance, he beat the boy, demanding to know who was behind it. Who had corrupted him, to make his master look a prize fool at the joust? The boy dared not answer. Again and again the question was asked and every time Rufus refused, he felt the lance across his back until Sir Darksilver thrashed him senseless.

By that time, every groom and esquire had been drawn from their beds, and sentries up on the battlements were staring down at the torchlit yard. Under Kings and nobles, taking the air before retiring, gathered to see the cause of the commotion and all were aghast to see what he had done. But there were none daring enough to stop him, not even the Constable. Sir Darksilver was a formidable size and, even in the best of moods, his temper was like a sleeping dragon. No one had seen him this incensed before.

Ignoring their timid jeers, the knight knelt beside the unconscious boy and searched him. It did not take long to find the purse. The leather was tooled with the badge of Clubs, beneath a prince's coronet.

Sir Darksilver rose and turned a thunderous face towards the separate stable that had been purpose-built to house Ironheart, and where the Jack of Clubs was also wont to sleep.

He was spared the trouble of calling him out because Jack was already striding across the yard, sword in hand.

"Stand clear!" Jack commanded. "What manner of coward are you, Sirrah, to batter your esquire so cruelly? Such drunken brigandry shall not be tolerated in this Kingdom."

"Coward, is it?" Sir Darksilver roared back, throwing the broken lance at him. "Is it valour to impair the lance of your opponent? Take what name suits you best! Coward! Liar! Cheat!"

A murmur of surprise ran through the watching crowd.

"Aye!" the knight told them. "The champion of the day did bribe my esquire to hobble my chances. Maybe every knight he bested at the tilt would do well to examine the splinters of their lances also – and see how well their esquires jingle."

He flung the purse at Jack's feet and drew his sword.

"My honour will be satisfied," he said with deadly resolve. "Though you be the prince of my house, I will not submit and will not serve such as you."

"This is a thing I counted as missing some while ago," the Jack of Clubs declared, recognising the purse. "I paid no coin to that esquire.

I swear it."

"Who else would gain by it? None but hero Jack. Keep your untruths locked behind your teeth. There is but one way to settle this matter. When you are striped scarlet by my sword, only then shall I be content."

With a furious yell, he lunged and his sword sliced for Jack's head. There was a chime of steel as two blades met and a ferocious duel began.

Moving behind the crowd, the Jill of Spades slipped by unnoticed. She made her way to Ironheart's stable and stole inside.

The last of the untameable steeds, the finest horse in Mooncaster, was restless in his stall. His ears were flicking and those great nostrils were snorting. He knew Jack was in danger and his hooves scraped at the straw-covered ground.

"Peace now," Jill greeted him with a soothing voice as she uncovered a dark lantern. "You know my face. 'Tis I, the Jill of Spades. I am a friend of your friend."

The ringing of swords outside became more intense and the shouts and cries of the crowd grew louder.

Ironheart shook his head and stamped.

"You must not fret, O mighty charger," Jill murmured. "Jack will be back to tend to you soon, I promise. They are but practising out there. Such is the way of boys. It is of no consequence; no hurt nor harm will befall him."

The horse reared away from her as she approached.

"Surely you are the king of your kind – a fine, noble animal. How closely you pair are bonded – more like brothers than horse and rider."

Glancing into the stall, she saw that Jack had moved his cot in here.

"Such devotion," she said. "I wonder, do you share one another's dreams? I have heard such things are possible."

Ironheart shifted from side to side.

"Steady," she whispered. "See what I have brought you. A gift from Jack."

The girl took the apple from the pocket of her cloak and polished it on the sleeve of her gown.

"See how red and bright it is," she said. "Jack bade me give you this. Here, you fine prancer – eat. It is sweet and delicious."

The horse eyed the apple dubiously. Jill smiled up at him. She saw herself reflected in those large black eyes and wondered what Jack would do when they were served up to him. For that reason alone, she hoped he survived the duel she had contrived to bring about. She had toyed with the idea of cutting off the hooves and tormenting him by leaving them in unexpected places for him to find. But hacking them off would take far too long. The eyes would have to do – and maybe the ears also.

The reflection of the apple grew larger as she held it higher. Ironheart's great handsome face swung near and the lips extended to take it from her palm.

The nostrils trembled. He sensed something was wrong. That tantalising sweetness masked something else. With a whinny, he shied away and turned about sharply. His flank knocked into her and Jill was thrown off balance. Stepping on the hem of her cloak, she tripped awkwardly and fell backwards. Her head hit the wall and she dropped to the ground. The lantern clattered down next to her and the straw caught light.

In the yard, Jack was winning. Sir Darksilver's sword was lodged deep in a wooden post and he was struggling to wrench it free. The boy was demanding he yield when he heard Ironheart's frightened neighing.

Jack whirled round and suddenly cries of "Fire!" broke out among the crowd.

Forgetting everything else, Jack rushed to the stable. A sheet of flames already barred the entrance and thick smoke was pouring through the eaves. Jack tried to jump through the doorway, but sensible hands grabbed and pulled him back.

"Ironheart!" he yelled, when he caught a glimpse of the horse rearing in the fire. "I must save him!"

"You cannot go in there, Your Royal Highness!" anxious nobles warned.

The air was filled with noise. Across the yard the other horses were screaming in their stalls and the hounds were barking frantically. Barred inside his den, Mauger roared.

Suddenly the side of the stable burst apart. The most powerful hooves in Mooncaster kicked the wooden wall to pieces. Then Ironheart came charging out. His coat was smouldering and his mane was singed. The whites of his eyes were showing. Whinnying in fear and panic, he tossed his head and galloped through the gawping onlookers.

Jack was overjoyed and called his name, but the horse would not stop. He thundered away, under the gatehouse, over the drawbridge and out across the dark fields.

"Come back!" the boy cried. "Come back!"

Ironheart disappeared into the night and Jack knew he would never see him again. He felt as though he had been knifed through the heart.

"There's someone in there!" a shout went up. "In the stable – look!"

Through the shattered wall, beneath the billowing smoke, they saw a figure lying in the flames.

This time Jack would not be held back. Snatching the cloak from someone's shoulders, he dunked it in a rain barrel then covered himself with it and rushed into the fire. Moments later, he was dragging out the Jill of Spades. The girl's clothes were aflame and Jack smothered them with the steaming cloak. He only just made it in time. Behind him, the stable collapsed.

Everyone gazed down at the Jill of Spades. She was badly burned. Her mother, the Under Queen, had been watching the drama unfold with the aloof detachment she was famed for, but, when she saw her daughter pulled from the blaze, the ice thawed in her veins.

"What is this?" she uttered, looking down on the scorched face in horror and disbelief. "How is my princess here?"

Kneeling, she threw the tatters of a green cloak aside to comfort her daughter. A small silver pot went rolling over the ground.

The young page who fetched it back knocked the lid off accidentally and a brown powder puffed up into his face. The page staggered and dropped like a stone. The Queen of Spades stared at him, then at the pot, and the lid bearing the badge of the House of Hearts.

But now the fire had spread. It had jumped across the roofs and the main stable block was burning. Grooms ran to rescue the horses. Everywhere was tinder dry and floating cinders ignited fresh fires across the castle.

Grabbing as many buckets as they could find, they formed a chain from the well and threw water over the flames, but it was a hopeless cause. Only rain or magick or both could aid them now and they called for the Ismus to aid them.

In billowing black robes, the Holy Enchanter appeared on the top of the Keep, silver wand in hand. He raised his arms and stirred the heavens. Clouds gathered to blot out the stars and, rising into the air, he swirled them round.

Presently a deluge poured from the sky above the castle and the flames were doused. The crowds cheered him, then turned to one another and the feuding began.

High on the Keep, the Ismus gazed out over the land. Another fire was blazing in the trysting field. The jilted Kit had seen the smoke rise from the castle and that gave him an idea to frighten Dulcie and teach her a lesson. Crazed with jealousy, he ran through the field and set light to every stook. But they burned more greedily than he expected and the flames spread out across the parched stubble. Soon the whole field was afire and he was trapped, along with everyone else who had remained after the Bogey Boys had caused them to quarrel.

From his vantage point, the Ismus heard the distant screams and flew as swiftly as his powers could carry him. The rain he summoned this time would not save them all.

Riding over the drawbridge, the King of Diamonds finally returned after a long and bothersome day hunting. When he saw the smoke coiling up from the battlements, he had spurred his horse on and now he came splashing through the puddles and stared around at the sodden, dripping spectacle of the ruined stable yard with knights and nobles of his own house brawling in it.

"What is this?" the Under King demanded. "I am absent for but one day and this is what greets me on my homecoming."

Angry voices shouted their reasons, but he held up his hand for calm.

"I will hear no excuses!" he said sternly. "Fortunately I am in a honeyed temper. The day went ill and every beast we sighted evaded us, but, even as we returned hither, we espied the most ravishing beast in the whole of Mooncaster. Behold what I brought down, with but one true arrow through the side. Did you ever see such a marvellous beast? I will have the hide preserved and the head mounted upon the wall in my chambers."

His servants brought the horse carrying the kill into the yard and removed the covering blanket.

The crowd shrieked and the ladies screamed.

The King of Diamonds blinked in confusion and turned to see what had dismayed them so. Then he too uttered a fearful wail.

Lying naked across the horse, her luxurious tresses hanging loose and her once sultry eyes staring, was the Jill of Hearts.

Soon the White Castle rang with the wrathful clashing of many swords, as battles to the death between the four Royal Houses erupted.

Lee rode through the darkness. He knew in which part of the distant forest the Forbidden Tower lay. His horse galloped unhappily over the fields. Lee was a clumsy and inelegant horseman, but it was an intelligent, good-natured beast and obeyed as well as it could, while doing its best to keep the boy on its back.

When the shadowy sprawl of the forest drew closer, the horse slowed and Lee gazed ahead. A faint, putrid green glow was glimmering in the distance, over the tops of the trees. It was the Forbidden Tower.

For the first time, the boy felt a pang of fear. He was looking at the deadliest place in the whole Kingdom, and his only defence was a big knife and a smart mouth. But he couldn't let his doubts get control. He had to push them aside and keep focused. He'd do this somehow.

"I shouldn't venture much further if I were you," a voice advised suddenly.

Lee jumped in surprise and looked around. He could see no one.

"Who's that?" he asked.

"Just a friendly word of caution," the voice told him. "You'll find this forest filled with all manner of nasty beasties. Haxxentrot has been frightfully busy of late. Time was when you could cut through the fringes of her estate with ease, but not any longer. One daren't sit down for fear of a viper sinking its teeth into one's posterior."

Lee peered in the direction of that suave, cultured voice. There were only the shadows of rocks, not large enough to conceal a person.

"You a goblin thing or somethin'?" he asked.

A velvety chuckle answered.

"No, not a goblin thing."

"What then? Do the rocks talk here too now?"

There was a vague sigh of irritation and two golden eyes opened fully. Then a long-legged, thin, dog-like shape slunk out of the shadows and climbed on to the tallest rock, curling his brush round him.

"The talking fox," Lee declared, to the animal's chagrin. These humans always said the same thing when they encountered him for the first time.

"Wondered if I'd ever run into you," the boy added.

"And I should be a very dull fellow indeed if I did not know the Castle Creeper when I saw his saturnine face. I have to say, you are the worst addition to a horse I have ever seen. It must take practice to be so bad."

"Yeah, well, you ain't nuthin'. I seen plenty of your dumb relatives raiding the bins back home."

"What vulgar vulpines," the fox said sniffily. "One cannot be responsible for the loutish behaviour of one's distant, common cousins. I assure you I do not raid bins – an open window in a pantry or a henhouse however..."

"So what you doing so far out here in this bad neighbourhood?"

"My affairs take me all over the Realm and beyond. Of more pressing interest to me is what brings you, clumping your way like a blindfold, three-legged donkey, to this evil place."

"I got me some business with the witch up there."

"And you have the effrontery to label my cousins dumb? Such ambrosial irony."

"I don't need no attitude from you, rabies breath."

The fox's ears twitched and his brush swished.

"Then what do you need, I wonder? Perhaps knowledge of the whereabouts of a certain pernicious herdsman?"

Lee straightened. "You know where the Bad Shepherd is?"

"Would such information be of value?"

"Friend," Lee said, "you tell where he is and you can have all the family buckets of finger-lickin' good stuff you can handle."

The fox's ears perked up. "I know not what that means, but it sounds appealing."

"So where is he?"

"What of your visit to Haxxentrot?"

"The crabby old girl can wait. She ain't goin' nowhere. It's the shepherd guy I really wanna see."

The fox jumped from the rock and ran into the trees on the right.

"Hey, wait up!" Lee called. "Where is he?"

The golden eyes gleamed back at him.

"Follow me, Creeper," the fox told him. "I shall be your guide this night."

"So where we goin'?"

"To the cave of the Cinnamon Bear; if we make haste, we shall be there by sunrise. Enough talk, now follow!"

Lee urged his horse after the white tip of the fox's tail as it darted ahead of them. This was it. He was going to do what he'd come here for. The final meeting with the Bad Shepherd of *Dancing Jax*. Lee's hand strayed to the hilt of his long knife in anticipation, and his expression became as hard as stone. Nothing else mattered now.

19

ANOTHER CHRISTMAS SONG played over the speakers and Maggie gave a frustrated yell.

"Most wonderful time of the year?" she raged when she heard the lyrics. "Up your rancid bumhole it is! Talk about wrong!"

"Sit down," Esther moaned. "You're getting on everyone's nerves."

"On their nerves?" Maggie shouted. "On their nerves? Really? Me walking from that wall to them bars is getting on their nerves? Not the fact we've been stuck down here for two days with only a bucket in the corner to piddle in? Not the fact we've only got till tomorrow night when we're for the chop? You need to get your priorities in order, you daft cow."

"And you need to stop your whinging!" Esther sniped back. "You make it worse for everyone you do. Why can't you shut your fat gob for a change?"

Maggie glared at her then shook her head. It wasn't worth wasting her breath.

"It's not a fat gob any more," was her only response to that as she stepped away, kicking at the straw on the floor.

"You didn't lose any blubber from inside your head!" Esther called after her. "You're still a two-ton lardy upstairs."

Maggie stomped to the bars and rested her brows between them. She wasn't sure how much more she could take. Not of Esther, she was just irritating, like a small, yappy dog. No, Maggie's eternal optimism had taken a severe battering that she hadn't rallied from. She still believed Gerald was dead, Spencer too probably, and she had no idea where Lee was; maybe he was dead too. She was sure they would be next. It was the manner of their impending deaths that frightened her. She knew she wouldn't be able to guess what the Ismus had planned, but it was certain to be messy and drawn out.

The refugees from the mountain base had been divided into two groups and locked in adjoining cells. Martin was in the one next door and she called to him, but received no answer. If she was despairing then heaven knows where his head was at. He hadn't uttered one word during the trip here. She'd never seen him like this. He'd totally given up. She wasn't even sure if he actually understood her awful news about Gerald. Nothing seemed to register.

"Martin?" she called again. "You still there?"

"Course he's still there!" Esther told her. "Where else do you think he'd be, stupid?"

"Yes, he's here," another voice answered from Martin's cell. Maggie recognised it as belonging to the lad called Drew. "He's not moved and isn't saying anything."

"Come on, Martin!" Maggie shouted with a forced jollity that she didn't feel. "You can't shut down just yet. Still one more shopping day till Chrimble."

"Give it a rest," Esther said irritably. "He's lost it and had a breakdown. Any idiot can see that. I've seen it coming on for ages."

"Liar," one of Charm's girls told her.

Maggie closed her eyes. She almost wished she could join Martin in whatever place his psyche had dipped into. But at the back of her mind she recalled Gerald's words to her, out on the terrace of the mountain base that foggy morning.

"We're not at home to Mr Despair," she repeated to herself and tried her best to believe it.

The journey from the mountain base had been uneventful. They were loaded on to a military helicopter, then flown to an airstrip in South Korea where a jet was waiting to bring them to England. They landed in darkness and were herded into the back of a lorry, like cattle. The last leg of the journey took less than an hour, but they couldn't see where they were being taken.

When the lorry doors were opened, they found they were in a high-walled, cobbled courtyard and discovered, to their horror, familiar faces waiting to meet them.

Captain Swazzle and the other Punchinello Guards from the aberrant camp greeted their former prisoners with merciless grins and the firing of semi-automatic pistols into the air. They were wearing the same costumes as before. Yikker was still clothed as a Catholic priest, Bezuel was a gangsta rapper and their Captain was a squat version of Al Capone. But their outfits had never been cleaned since the first day they put them on and were covered in grime, dried vomit and their own filth.

With dismay, Maggie and the others noticed that their ranks had been augmented by more Punchinellos and those too wore bizarre costumes.

There was a Roman centurion, a Kaiser Wilhelm, with medals, cape and spike-tipped helmet, a Mexican bandit; there was a Mao Zedong with a Little Red Book filled with obscene scrawls, a colonial big-game hunter in khaki shorts and pith helmet, a pirate, a Cossack, Genghis Khan and – perhaps most eccentric of all – one dressed in the away strip of the English football team. They were all chomping on fat cigars and reeked of whisky.

Swazzle and his crew drove the new arrivals through an arched doorway, cursing and goading and spitting at them. Maggie was prodded roughly with a gun barrel and Martin was kicked. Some of the others felt the lash against their legs and Nicholas was hit in the face by a rifle butt when he tried to protect Esther from Bezuel's lascivious hands.

Then they were driven down a steep flight of winding steps to a spacious vaulted chamber lit by flaming torches. The youngest cried out when they realised it was a fully equipped medieval dungeon and the Punchinellos squawked with glee as they showed off the many and varied instruments of torture. But the Jockey had come tripping down after them and scolded the hunchbacked guards, telling them they would have to wait for their fun.

And so the refugees were marched through the dungeon to the cells and had remained there ever since, with only stale bread and water – and a basket of the disgusting minchet fruit.

This was all they had seen of the replica of the White Castle from *Dancing Jax*, but it was enough to tell them it was a faithful copy of the drawings in the book. The attention to detail and commitment to authenticity was astonishing. This wasn't a Disneyfied fibreglass amusement park attraction. This was solid and real. The walls were made of genuine stone blocks and the bars were iron. Only the crispness of its lines betrayed its recent construction – that and the speakers and cameras that were positioned at frequent intervals.

In the other cell, Martin was crouched in a shadowy corner, chin on his knees. He heard Maggie's voice calling to him, but what was the point of answering? What was the point of anything now? Everything he had tried to do had failed and, looking back, just what had he actually achieved? He should have surrendered long ago, instead of fleeing from country to country, trying to warn them of the danger. Not enough had listened and those that did listened far too late. Then there were the betrayals. The resistance group he had organised in Uruguay almost seemed to be getting somewhere; they had organised quickly and bookshops had been torched before *Dancing Jax* had got too strong a hold on the populace. Then one of their unaffected group had sold them out and their base in Montevideo had been attacked by Jaxers from Argentina. Martin and Gerald had scarcely managed to escape with their lives and many of the friends they had made there were shot helping them evade capture.

What had all that struggle and death been for? Martin searched deep within his soul for an answer and the one that kept rearing up horrified him to the core. Were the things that Lee had accused him of true? Had he become addicted to the fame of being the Ismus's nemesis? Had he selfishly revelled in his own celebrity? Was his ego really that out of control? Did so many good people die because he refused to abdicate a position that only existed inside his own deluded head? The Jockey had guffawed at Martin's belief he was in any way significant or unique. He had been just as carried away and out of control as every other Jaxer, except that his madness was of his own making. The realisation caused him to shrivel inside. He wished Mauger had torn him apart that night outside Fellows End over a year ago.

"Mr Martin..." A shy voice broke through his bleak thoughts. "Don't be sad."

Martin raised his eyes slowly. One of the younger children was standing before him. He recognised her as Ingrid, another of Charm's little group. She was eleven years old and in her hands she held a toy rabbit that Maggie had made for her out of a North Korean uniform.

"When I'm sad, I give him a hug," she said, holding the rabbit up for him to see. "You can have a lend if you want."

Martin stared at her for a while. She and the others were too old for soft toys, but DJ had changed that. In the mountain base, the home-made dolls had become important security objects, like Spencer's Stetson.

"You can talk to it," the girl continued, filling the awkward silence. "I do. Sometimes I pretend it's my mum, as she was before, and I tell her how much I miss her. Sometimes it's my dad or sister or nan. Mostly though it's Charm."

Martin's eyebrows twitched.

"Why did you all like her so much?" he asked curiously.

Ingrid smiled. She was doubly pleased: not only had she got him to speak, but he'd asked about her lovely friend.

"She made it better," she answered with honest simplicity. "She wasn't just kind or nice, she was... special. She would have made this place miles better. When I think of her, I don't stay sad. Her heart was big enough for everyone, even them as didn't like her back."

Martin lowered his eyes again. He felt ashamed. Here he was being comforted by a child, one who was handling this situation with far more grace and maturity than him. He bitterly regretted saying those vile things to Gerald about this mysterious Charm. He felt contaminated by the world and his self-pride and wasn't fit to be among these amazing youngsters. Each one had been through just as much pain and anguish as himself and here, at the end of that harrowing road, they weren't wallowing in self-pity.

The girl pushed the rabbit into his hands.

"Who... who do you suggest I pretend it is?" he asked.

"Whoever you like most," she replied with a shrug. "He's a good listener with them ears."

Martin nodded vaguely.

"Thank you, Ingrid," he murmured.

The girl shook her head. "We're using the flavour names she gave us now," she told him. "I'm Dandelion and Burdock; over there is Chocolate Mousse and Lemon Cheesecake. We talked about it and decided that's how we want to go."

"Go?"

"Die. When the Jaxers kill us, we're going to go with her names."

She said it so matter-of-factly it startled him.

The girl turned to go back to her friends. Martin saw them giggling and urging her to say something more.

"You have a flavour name too," she said a little bashfully. "We gave it you."

Martin leaned back against the cold stone wall.

"Go on," he said. "Cat Sick? Rat Dropping? Cough Medicine?"

"Marmite!" she blurted, before running back to the others who laughed as if they hadn't a care in the world – like children.

For the first time in too long, Martin Baxter broke into a smile and the unexpected chuckles that followed lifted some of the crushing weight off his spirit. Letting out a deep breath, he turned his attention to the toy rabbit in his hands and stroked its ears. He was almost tempted. Should he give it a try? He gazed at the button eyes for some minutes then thought, *Ah, what the hell?*

"Carol," he muttered, feeling more than a little self-conscious. "Umm… how are you? Just wanted... I've... Listen, I just wanted to say hello…"

He stopped and set the rabbit down, annoyed with himself. This was stupid. He felt like a total cretin. If he really did have one final chance to speak to Carol, he knew exactly what he'd say to her. He wouldn't be mumbling and fumbling for clumsy words like this. So why couldn't he say them now?

Grabbing the toy again, he stared at it angrily.

"OK, I've been an absolute arse," he stated bluntly. "I'd say I've been juvenile, but having been around these kids so long, that'd be the biggest lie yet and an insult they really don't deserve. These kids make me ashamed of the way I used to think about the ones I used to teach."

He paused and squeezed his eyes shut. "What I really hate myself for though," he said, "is what I've been thinking about you, and the downright nasty feelings I've had. Real appalling stuff: resentment, jealousy – all those dark colours. I got it so wrong. I made this about me, what I was going through, what I had to deal with. What a selfish, arrogant tosser. You did what you had to, for Paul's sake. I knew that, course I did! But I put my hurt pride first, cos that's what failures do."

Bringing the rabbit nearer, he put it against his cheek and whispered into one floppy ear.

"I know I won't get the chance to tell you this in person and, as the High Priestess Labella, you won't want to hear it anyway. But this is for the real you, the determined nurse from Felixstowe, who I drove mad with my nerdy obsessions, but who put up with me anyway. I loved and love you so much, Carol Thornbury. Not a day went by without me being over the moon you were in my life. This past year, I can't begin to tell you how much I've miss—"

The sobs rising in his throat clogged the words and, for a while, he could only hold the rabbit desperately, clinging to it the way he would never be able to cling to his fiancée.

Eventually he said, "Maybe that's why I wanted to be the famous Martin Baxter, in the hope you'd see me on the news, or hear the Ismus talking about me. I just wanted you to know I was still out there. It's warped and twisted, but – I think I did all of this for you."

Hugging the rabbit tightly, he bowed his head.

'Rockin' around the Christmas tree,' another song began. Raucous laughter came echoing from the dungeon down the passage, where the Punchinellos were drinking and telling depraved jokes.

Several hours passed. The festive songs broadcast over the speakers were interspersed with overenthusiastic chatter from excitable radio hosts about the next day's promised incredible events. *Fighting Pax* was going to be unbelievable and, before that, Flee the Beast would be the best entertainment this lousy place had ever provided.

Hungry, and wondering uneasily what the dawn would bring, the refugees waited for the night to drag by. Esther had commandeered the only cot in her cell for herself and Nicholas crouched on the floor beside her, nursing his bruised and swollen face. The others clutched their home-made dolls and tried to sleep.

Maggie remained by the bars, listening to the foul and violent-tempered jabbering of the guards. She almost imagined she was back in the camp. When she rested her eyes, she could practically hear Marcus's voice talking to her enthusiastically about his home city of Manchester. Somehow Maggie slept.

At some point, she was awakened by a loud commotion. The Punchinellos were snarling and yelling and their heavy boots were clumping over the flagstones. But different, new voices were crying out in fear.

Maggie sat up and peered through the bars. Behind her, the others came to investigate.

"Who are they?" a girl asked in amazement.

Maggie's mouth fell open. The Punchinellos were herding a group of at least twenty children into the three cells opposite their own. They were a pitiable sight, being just skin and bone, and their clothes were threadbare rags. Some were very young, perhaps seven or eight years old, and the eldest was no more than fifteen. Their bare and blistered feet dragged as they were shoved into the cells, where they collapsed exhausted.

"Oh... my... God..." she breathed. "They're aberrants, like us."

"Where from?"

"Another camp somewhere."

Esther roused herself from the cot and came to peer through the bars. She cast a disdainful look at the newcomers.

"They look half dead," she observed with a sniff.

As they watched in fascination, Yikker came waddling along, bearing a plastic bucket containing peelings and leftovers. Grabbing great fistfuls, he threw them into the cells and the starving children pounced on the scraps like wild dogs.

"Poor sods," Maggie whispered. "That would've been us if we hadn't escaped."

Captain Swazzle locked the three cells with large iron keys, then twisted about and came swaggering across.

"You!" he barked, jabbing a dirty finger into the cell next door. "Baxter! On feet! You, me, we go."

Rattling his keys once more, he opened Martin's cell and sent Bezuel and the guard dressed as a Mexican bandit inside to fetch him.

Martin was dragged out. When he resisted, they thumped him in the stomach and the bandit bit his arm. Then they pulled his hands behind his back and put them in manacles.

"What's going on?" Maggie protested as they hauled him towards the dungeon. "Where are you taking him? What are you going to do?"

They didn't answer, but Yikker came over and pushed his great hooked nose and chin through the bars as he leered up at her.

"You fat friend of Stinkboy," he drawled, undressing her with his beady eyes. "You not pig-wide now. Yikker like." Licking his lips, he gave her a lusty wink and followed the others from the gaol.

Maggie shuddered. Yikker was the guard who had hated Marcus and called him 'Stinkboy' because of his deodorants and aftershave.

He had made the boy's life a misery in the camp and Maggie despised him most of all. Pushing her hands deep into her pockets, she cursed him and tightened her jaw.

"Hey!" a voice called.

Maggie was too intent on listening out for sounds of Martin getting tortured to respond straight away.

"Hey!" the voice repeated.

Maggie gazed across at the opposite cell. A dark-haired, skeletal boy, roughly the same age as Spencer, was staring right at her. He was chewing half of a blackened raw potato. The rest of the scraps had been devoured in minutes.

"Hello," one of Charm's girls responded. "My name's Blueberry Muffin, what's yours?"

"Lukas," he answered, "You are called funny name."

"It's a delicious name. Where you from?"

"We are from Germany. From prison camp. We are... I do not know how you say in English, Abtrünnlinge – we do not read book or believe fairy tale."

"Aberrant, that's what we are too."

"You too? Is really? Your camp cannot be as cruel as ours. You look well. We do not eat every day."

His remark made Maggie rear her head. "We got away from ours," she told him. "And believe me, it wasn't a jolly picnic. Some of us died in there."

Lukas looked round at his fellow Germans.

"At the start," he said, "our camp had one hundred and seventy children. We are all is left. Yesterday we had twenty-nine more, but they were too sick to travel to England. Before we leave, the devil guards killed them. We thought we too were to die."

Maggie's grip loosened round the bars. She had never suspected just how lucky she and the others had been.

"I'm sorry," was all she could say, but she felt her words were stupidly insufficient.

Lukas waved it aside. By now other pinched faces were staring across at the English children. Horrors Maggie couldn't bear to guess at were graven on their faces and yet they were curious and soon were daring to smile. Charm's girls smiled and waved right back at them and they threw over the bread that was left.

"So tell me, please!" Lukas continued. "That man they took just now. Was he... Martin Baxter, for real?"

"You've heard of him?" Maggie asked.

The boy stared back, astounded, and translated what she had said for the others who didn't speak English. They drew their breaths in shock.

"Martin Baxter is legend!" Lukas told Maggie. "He is world hero. He dares to fight the Ismus. We heard stories of him, we saw his blog, some of us tried to find him before we were caught. In the camp, we get news from German resistance, before they were killed. The idea of him out there, it keeps us alive. He gives hope to all."

It was Maggie's turn to draw a surprised breath. They had never considered how Martin might be viewed by the other aberrants in the world. He really was a big deal. She didn't even hear Esther's snarky comment, or the subsequent squeal when Blueberry Muffin pinched her.

"Yes," Maggie answered, feeling an unexpected swelling of pride.

"That was – is – Martin Baxter, *the* Martin Baxter."

The German children made reverent, marvelling noises. One of them even cheered.

"He is a man incredible, we think," Lukas said. "Tell me, where did the devil guards take him?"

"I don't know."

"Then we will pray for him to return safe."

To the astonishment of the English, the Germans knelt down and clasped their hands together.

"You do not join us?" Lukas asked when he saw they were still standing.

"We've been through too much to believe in that," Maggie said flatly.

Lukas did not understand.

"Not believe?" he said. "But do you not see demons all around? How do you not believe when the evil is in front of you always? That is... that is like doubting water is real when you are drowning."

Shaking his head, perplexed, he led the Germans in a prayer, asking the Almighty to watch over the wonderful Martin Baxter and keep him free from harm.

Maggie and the others were so taken aback that not even Esther made a sarcastic remark. Charm's girls nudged one another and then dropped to their knees to join in.

"It'll take more than prayers to save Martin and the rest of us," Maggie muttered under her breath. "A lot more. If there is a god up there, he pulled his earphones out a long time ago."

Over the speakers, Bing Crosby started dreaming of a white Christmas.

Captain Swazzle's large hand clamped Martin's arm like a vice. He had dragged him through the dungeon, then wrenched him up the winding stairs. When the man stumbled, Bezuel was right behind to shove him on.

At the top of the stairs, the Jockey was waiting.

"Gently, gently, my fine, stumpy warders!" he exclaimed. "We don't want to bruise him, not yet – haw haw haw."

"Thought you and me'd said everything already," Martin spat.

"Ho ho!" the Jockey laughed. "'Tis not I who desires converse with you. But first..."

He reached into the sleeve of his caramel-coloured jerkin and, with a flourish, pulled out a large silk handkerchief.

"What?" Martin shouted when the Jockey tied it tightly across his eyes in a blindfold.

"My command was clear," the Jockey explained. "You're not to see even a glimpse till you get there."

"Where?"

"Haw haw haw."

"This is ridiculous. Get this thing off me!"

Martin felt a Punchinello's fist thump him in the back and he staggered forward.

"That's right," the Jockey said as he danced ahead. "This way, Martin Baxter. Follow my voice. I shall lead you, I shall guide you, over stone and under gap, round the towers and into his lap. Ho ho ho."

Martin blundered in the direction of the mocking voice. He couldn't see a thing. All he experienced of the journey was what his other senses told him. When the cold night air blew across his face, he knew they'd reached the courtyard where the lorry had brought them. That was soon left behind. The reverberating echoes of his People's Army boots on the flags and cobbles described when he passed beneath an archway or colonnade. Then they were in a much wider open space where no walls bounced the sounds back. He could smell freshly cut grass, then felt springy turf beneath his feet. There was the noise of trickling water and he guessed he was in a large garden with a fountain. There wasn't time to stop and listen for any further clues: the Jockey was continually chivvying him along.

"This way – be nimble, trot along, quick – quick."

Martin soon lost track of how long this blind journey was taking. It seemed to go on for hours, but he knew that was merely because his every step was uncertain and cautious. Finally he felt the Jockey's hands catch his shoulders and he was manoeuvred up a series of shallow steps, a metallic-sounding ramp and then bundled into what felt like a small alcove. He heard the Jockey chortling to himself and then Martin was surprised to hear the drone of winching machinery. The floor shifted under him and his knees bent. He was in an ascending lift, but it was open to the elements for the winter wind cut across his face.

After several minutes, the ride was over. The lift gave a judder and the Jockey drew Martin out. He felt boards beneath his feet, then he was turned a sharp ninety degrees and found himself standing on stone.

High winds moved through his hair. The Jockey reached out and untied the knots in the handkerchief.

Martin blinked and his eyes widened as he took in his surroundings and recognised the man standing before him.

"Welcome to Mooncaster, Martin Baxter," the Ismus greeted him. "Is that a rabbit in your pocket or does this place put a strain on your gusset stitching the same way it does mine? Isn't it amazing how much you can achieve on an unlimited budget, with thousands of devoted workers who'll happily break their backs night and day for you and none of that health-and-safety nonsense getting in the way?"

His thin, clever face creased with laughter as he strode forward and removed the stuffed rabbit from Martin's pocket.

"What are you doing with this?" he cried. "How you love your toys. I was only telling the Creeper very recently how 'other' dolls are. You people are so hopeless, lavishing your affections on sewn-up remnants because you're incapable of interacting with one another. I never realised just how powerful the pull of a doll could be. The little animation of myself this week was enormously successful. We were inundated with e-readers because of it. The little chap is going to make some more appearances tonight; everyone will be so pleased."

He waggled the rabbit by the throat, then cast it aside.

"Oh, but do forgive me rambling on," he declared. "I've been meaning to grant you an audience since you arrived; there's been a hundred and one things to do, as you can imagine, and we're still not quite ready. Always so many last-minute details need tweaking, but I think we'll be all right on the night."

He waited for Martin to answer, then smiled indulgently when he saw the other man was speechless.

Martin could hardly believe what he was seeing. There was so much to take in, he felt bludgeoned by it. Firstly, the dawn was breaking.

The sky was a soft grey and darkness was draining from the landscape. Oh – but what a landscape! Taking a sharp, disbelieving and frightened breath, he looked away from it and his eyes roamed instead over the full-sized replica of the White Castle that sprawled about him.

It was a staggering accomplishment and covered a huge area. It was exactly as it had been drawn and described in the book; with three imposing and wide concentric walls with battlements surrounding the central, inner ward and lofty Keep. They were separated by broad expanses of velvety lawn, ornamental gardens and tilt yards. There were stables, brewhouses and stout bastions at every corner, where banners flapped madly. It was built entirely of pale Portland stone that, in the grey half-light of dawn, almost glowed, and the frosty dew made it sparkle.

But it was unfinished. Scaffolding was everywhere, towers were incomplete, with ragged tops, and stone blocks, waiting to be put in place, were stacked in great piles. Industrial cranes besieged the curtain walls. Martin had never seen so many; they were too numerous to count. Their masts formed a forest of vertical steel and their jibs cross-hatched the sky. Temporary plank bridges spanned gaps between the wall walks, or cut diagonally across a corner, bypassing a half-built tower. And, everywhere he looked, there were lighting rigs and remote cameras and tarpaulins covering staging areas for the broadcast. It was a chaotic, ugly mess.

"Of course," the Ismus was saying, "it's not finished and never will be, so you'll have to use a bit of imagination here and there. But then completing it was never the intention. The process was the thing. You have to provide the ignorant masses with a big, shiny project now and then to distract them, like a ball of wool to a kitten. That way they can't take time out to speculate what's actually going on behind the curtains of power. Every king, emperor, dictator, pope, Führer, president or prime minister knows that. Bread and circuses, mob-pleasing bandwagons, jihad, rockets of rampant destruction, storming in to avenge so-called human rights abuses when the sole real motive is to snatch that country's wealth, or to replace one despot with their own glove puppet.

"Sleight of hand and smokescreens, that's what keeps the populace unaware and under control. Give them a cause or a task they can get behind, no matter how absurd or banal, and they'll feel included and happy and won't ask irritating questions. This is no different. Mesmerising as my great work is, the immersive experience is ultimately unsustainable without the necessary smoke and mirrors. The live feed that has documented the build here has been a ratings smash across the world. Don't suppose you ever caught it in your little mountain hideaway? The theme tune is really catchy. I had it as my ringtone for weeks."

Martin said nothing. He hardly heeded the Ismus's familiar, bantering prattle and instead lowered his gaze. They were standing on the expansive flat roof of the Keep, at least eighty metres above the ground. It appeared to be the only structure that was totally finished, but even this was still sleeved in scaffolding and he had been brought up here by a construction hoist lift attached to the exterior.

Once, his enduring love of fantasy and sci-fi would have made him an unwilling admirer and caused him to be captivated by it all, but not even that was left to him now.

"Leave us," the Ismus dismissed the Jockey. "Martin and I want some quality time alone for a private tête-à-tête. Go squeak your leathers in the lift and leave us to it. Don't fret, I've got my bodyguards with me and those manacles really do limit Martin's options if he gets any felonious notions."

The Jockey looked at him peevishly, then tottered back to the lift. Martin had barely noticed the three Black Face Dames standing a little distance away. His full attention was now commanded by the great cast-iron chair that stood in the centre of the flat roof.

"Yes," the Ismus said when he saw his reaction. "It is the very same one. I had it brought from the old home town, along with a couple of other useful odds and ends that you'll get to see later. Looks much better here. I reckon just about everyone out there will get a grand view."

He waved a hand at the landscape and Martin's eyes flicked back at the awful spectacle he'd been trying to avoid.

"Scrumptious, isn't it?" the Ismus said. "I'm so tickled they could shuffle along to my little shindig."

Martin forced himself to stare out across the battlements and ramparts, past the gatehouse and the moat, over the thatched roofs of the replicated village of Mooncot that bordered a quaint, meandering street, and then to the Kent countryside.

His mouth went dry. What he was seeing was impossible.

As far as the encircling horizon, and probably for a great distance beyond that, was a vast ocean of people. The castle was completely surrounded. The only clear spaces out there were the service roads that brought the labourers, stonemasons, engineers, architects, artisans, materials and equipment to this overblown building site every day. If the roads hadn't been fenced off, the Jaxers would have swarmed on to them too. They cut through the human panorama like deep scars while, overhead, pylons carried the current to drive the tools and machinery and to feed the thousands of power points that radiated from the castle. Islands of light showed where e-readers could be charged, and where punnets of minchet were available.

"Not sure of the exact number," the Ismus said. "I'll take a stab at a hundred and fifty million and counting and that's just the ones we can see. But you're the maths guru, you're better at figures than I. There's masses more over the horizon. Good job I had the towns and villages that used to be here flattened, right at the start. Plenty out there have tents or are huddled in their cars or in sleeping bags on the ground, but I shouldn't like to guess how many came unprepared and have already perished in the cold, although the mass body heat generated out there is visible on thermal images from satellites. Fancy that! Those who had the wit to bring supplies will be running out of them by now – and those that didn't will be patiently starving. It must really stink down there; we ought to be grateful it isn't summer. One just cannot provide toilet facilities in such quantities, there aren't enough Portaloos in the world – we checked and decided not to bother."

Taking a platinum-backed smartphone from his pocket, he took a photo of himself and said, "You'll love this – watch. I'm just posting a selfie."

Moments later, the air was filled with the noise of his tweet arriving in hundreds of millions of mobiles. It was like the shrill, suffocating buzz of a plague of marauding insects. Then the colossal multitude answered with a cheer, the like of which had never been heard in the world before. Their voices crashed about the castle walls in a monumental wave of sound. It took Martin's breath away and caused a tear to run down his face. With just a few exceptions, the whole of humanity had been debased to the level of a mindless chorus, hanging on to the Ismus's every banal or evil word.

"Seven billion followers," the Ismus boasted with a wink. "Bless 'em, too excited to sleep. Every creed, every colour, united by my little book. No crime, no hatred, no nationalism, no quarrels of any sort. Peace and harmony reign supreme. The noble ambition of all good-hearted men, fulfilled at last by yours truly. Where there was discord, I brought harmony. Where there was error, I dispensed my truth. Where there was doubt, I gave them faith. And where there was despair, I delivered a new and better life. Yes, it was worth the wait. I never dared dream it would have such an impact, but the world was different in 1936. Minds weren't so plastic and hungry for distraction and this island hadn't devolved into little more than a theme park for wealthier countries with inferiority complexes because they have no class. Dissatisfaction is such a powerful weapon."

Thoroughly broken, feeling hollowed out and empty, Martin stared at him, grasping for words. He had no fight left. It was over. He was defeated. On that high platform, they faced each other: one utterly crushed, the other triumphant.

"You've won," Martin said in a stricken, dead voice. "You got the entire world worshipping you. No free will anywhere – you've done it. What now? Throw me off here – or chuck me out among them so they can tear me apart? I don't care any more. Just get on with it and stop posing."

"That bleating livestock out there, my avid readers, don't deserve you," the Ismus answered with a tut. "And how could you think I'd do something so unsporting? No, you're not going to die just yet. There's still the broadcast to go and you're going to be a highlight of that, Mr Baxter. Your big starring moment awaits you."

"I'm not going to jump through your hoops. Finish me now."

"Yes, yes, blah blah. Token protest over with? Good, because we both know you'll do exactly what I want, when I want, because I hold all the cards, especially two very dear to you. But don't look so crestfallen. To make it even more amusing for me, I'm not just going to threaten them, I'm going to make you an offer you'll jump at."

"There's nothing..."

"Oh, but there is. My Lady Labella and Magpie Jack – did you know I have it in my gift to excommunicate them? Actually I think 'unfriend' is a more apt modern term. I can remove them from the world of *Dancing Jax* as easily as that and they'll remember who they really are and who you are to them. Wouldn't you just love such a happy reunion? Bound to be good for a few tears. It would make excellent television. Viewers love overwrought displays of snot."

Martin's eyes narrowed. "Why would you do this?" he asked suspiciously. "Carol and Paul are two of your prime characters. You wouldn't let them go as easily as that."

"There's always someone ready to replace them, just as your Carol replaced Shiela. You remember her, your former pupil and my... old flame?"

"Course I do. What did you do with her? Is she here?"

The Ismus grinned and ran his hands over the cast-iron chair as he recalled the girl's grisly fate. "Gone, I'm afraid," he said. "The man Jezza always said smoking would be the death of her."

Martin hung his head.

"And Lee?" he asked. "You said you've seen him, your Castle Creeper? Is he over in that other place? I know what you wanted him to do. Has he done it?"

"Not yet, the Bad Shepherd is notoriously elusive. But I'm confident the Creeper will track him down today and accomplish what is required. He's got a nice, big, sharp knife ready and waiting."

"You sick maniac."

"Now don't be so churlish. The Creeper is more than happy with his little commission. He'll get to be reunited with his vacuous girlfriend once the deed is done. I'm offering you a similar proposition here. Show a little gratitude. You do something for me and in return you get your nuclear family back."

"Something for you? What?"

"All in... bad time. You'll find out tonight. It's going to be an incredible, unmissable show – followed of course by the publication of *Fighting Pax*. I'd love you and yours to witness that. You've squirmed and wriggled against my plans for so long and come so far, daring to be a Daniel, you deserve to be here at the grand finale."

"And you'll let Carol and Paul be themselves, even after? If there is an after?"

"That depends on how good a performance you put on. You have to earn their continued freedom by giving your all. Break a leg, as they say. Eyes and teeth and all that, Martin. Show us what you've got – be convincing."

Turning to one of the Black Face Dames, he said, "Escort him back to the lift. The Jockey will see he returns to the gaol."

The bodyguard took Martin by the arm.

"Wait," Martin said. "I can't go back without that rabbit. It belongs to a little girl. Please, give it back."

The Ismus regarded him for a moment with undisguised derision. Then he picked the stuffed toy off the floor and pushed the ears into Martin's mouth.

"There's a good gun dog," he said, patting his head. "Now get going and I don't want to hear any complaints about the costumes you'll be wearing tonight. Oh, yes, there are costumes – no expense spared in this extravaganza. I'm not having it spoiled by the sight of your beggarly rags. If I hear of anyone refusing to put the outfits on, I shall let Captain Swazzle do some sums of his own. He'd just love to discover how many times his sword can go into one of you. He adores a long division. Be sure to pass that information on."

With the rabbit dangling from his teeth and, due to the manacles, having no way to remove it, Martin was forced to carry it like that all the way back to the dungeon. The Jockey hooted and taunted him for the whole journey.

Martin paid no attention. His mind was burning with the Ismus's proposal. Was he really going to be allowed to see Carol and Paul tonight? Could he believe what that evil man promised? Would they truly be released from the dark spell of *Dancing Jax*? And just what exactly would he have to do to buy them that freedom? It was certain to be something foul and horrific and an ultimate degradation. Martin told himself that, whatever it was, he would simply have to get on with it. If there was the slightest chance the Ismus wasn't lying... Carol and Paul were the only things that mattered now. He couldn't back down; he couldn't be squeamish about anything. Whatever the Ismus told him to do, he'd jump at it and perform like a trained seal. Even if it meant the loss of his own life, it'd be worth it. Everything else he had tried had failed; maybe this last act would partly atone for his countless mistakes. Perhaps, deep down, he felt as though he deserved whatever ordeal the Ismus had prepared for him.

On the roof of the Keep, the Holy Enchanter of Mooncaster stared down over the huge construction site of the castle. He watched the Jockey lead Martin back through the inner gateways and lawns towards the courtyard that led to the dungeons. The crooked smile played across his face and he stepped back to the great iron throne.

"Tonight, my Lord," he addressed it humbly. "Tonight You shall reclaim Your rightful place amongst us. Your kingdom is well prepared and the way shall be opened."

Turning his attention to the encircling landscape, his dark eyes glinted and the smile grew wider. "Nothing has been left to chance and the pieces are primed and set."

Even as he indulged in the appalling spectacle and anticipated the magnificent victory ahead, a fragment of doubt prickled in his mind. There was something, the remotest possibility of the meticulously planned broadcast going awry. It was so minuscule and improbable that he refused to consider it. And yet overconfidence had been the downfall of so many before now.

"Austerly Fellows leaves no loose thread hanging," he announced decisively. "No matter how slender. Tonight's programme of events will be a stupefying success and the Prince of the Dawn shall be restored."

Bracing himself against the great chair, he tilted his head back.

"But just to be doubly certain..."

Taking a deep breath, he closed his eyes. The skin of his face became peppered with dark spots that spread and bloomed rapidly, until the flesh was consumed and hidden beneath a foaming carpet of writhing black mould. Then his mouth opened horribly wide and he exhaled.

A stream of spores like a cloud of sooty thistledown erupted from his throat and went flying into the winter air. The strong breeze snatched them and they were carried out across the battlements, into the breaking day.

"Bon adventure, my dark seeds," he said once the mould had retreated from his features. "May you find fertile soil."

Straightening, he turned to his three bodyguards and was irritated to find them overawed, even after all this time.

"Come," he ordered. "We must make ready. There is still much to prepare before *Fighting Pax* is released. We have the final technical run to get through. Bring me the director – I want to make sure every spring trap is working, that aerial cam still isn't gliding smoothly and get those dancers rehearsed until their feet bleed. I want those royal replacements standing by to take over at a moment's notice, no cock-ups. This broadcast is going to be called 'diabolical' for all the right reasons."

20

GOOD MORRRRRNIIIIING, *Dancing Jax*! Yes, it's finally here, the twenty-fourth of December – Christmas Eve. Tonight *Fighting Pax* is going to be released to every e-reader everywhere. The suspense is excruciating. Our time in this grey dream will be over and we shall never have to think of this boring place again. The spectacular kicks off at 9pm GMT. Everyone is here, everyone is ready. Get set for the most fantastic Christmas! Blessed be.

Now heeeeeeeere's Slade...

When Martin returned to the cells, he was astonished and then discomfited to learn how much the German aberrants revered him. His unease was compounded by the fact that a second batch of arrivals had turned up in his absence. They were thirty-four teenagers from America and they too considered him to be some kind of superhero. Reaching through their bars, they begged him to help them.

"Please!" they cried. "Save us."

Captain Swazzle shoved Martin roughly back into his cell and removed the manacles. Rubbing his aching wrists, Martin returned the rabbit to Dandelion and Burdock, who hugged it desperately. Then he gazed over at the newcomers with an overwhelming sense of his own helplessness.

"Martin Baxter!" they implored.

The Punchinellos growled and bawled at the children to keep quiet. Darting up and down in front of the cells, they struck out with the lash until every hand and face was withdrawn.

"I can't help you," Martin said apologetically. "I'm just a man, not a legend. There's nothing I can do. Nothing."

"He useless," Swazzle cackled. "No cry out to him. Save cries for later. You will need them – oh, yes."

Hungry and afraid, the young aberrants settled down. No one dared speak until the guards had departed and could be heard carousing in the dungeon. Then, gradually, hushed conversations began to spring up between the different groups. The Americans were the gleanings of three different camps in the US and they had been just as ill-treated as the Germans. Everyone had horror stories to tell, but no one wanted to darken this final day any further and so they spoke of the times before *Dancing Jax* and Martin answered as many of the new arrivals' questions as he could. They drank in his words and waited for the hours to pass.

It was a Christmas Eve like no other. Most of the population of Britain had made the pilgrimage to Kent, or were still trying to get there. The tailbacks on the motorways were unprecedented, but no one in the gridlocked vehicles was getting angry. They were just waiting: for the traffic to move or the release of *Fighting Pax*, whichever came first.

Hospitals, care homes, farms, prisons and zoos had been abandoned by their staff, and patients and animals were left to die in their beds or barns or be eaten by creatures that crept into the neglected wards and through the fences. Fires raged out of control in most towns and cities, and airports still boomed with exploding fuel as planes continued to try to land.

In Felixstowe, the sea and the sky were an angry red. Across the harbour, Harwich was ablaze and the immense pall of black smoke kept the dawn at bay.

Standing in the front garden of the Duntinkling guesthouse, Spencer viewed the distant glare and reek in mournful silence. The world was ending. Adjusting the brim of his Stetson, he glanced back at the house. Having slept deeply for the first time since he could remember, he was impatient to set off. He'd forgotten what sleeping in a real bed was like. And then, this morning, Gerald had cooked the best breakfast he'd ever eaten with the provisions they'd looted on the way from Stansted. But time was running out and he was itching to get down to Kent.

Inside, a sweet and beautiful tune was being tentatively played on the piano.

Two hours previously, Chung Eun-mi had awakened in one of the guest bedrooms with a pain-filled cry that could be heard in every part of the house. Shell-shocked by the terrors of the night, she crawled into a corner and they found her curled into a ball. Gradually, with gentle words and patient coaxing, Gerald drew her out and led her downstairs. After Eun-mi had been encouraged to eat some toast and drink a cup of green tea, in a faltering, weak voice she thanked them for helping her.

But that was all she would say about what had happened and, when Estelle's name was mentioned, Eun-mi quailed and dropped the teacup.

Now, after a shower, with her uncannily white hair turbaned in a towel, she sat at the grand piano.

Her mother had been a beautiful, talented pianist who had played in the State Symphony Orchestra before her marriage. The most beloved memories Eun-mi had of her were when she played the piano in their home, when the General was away. Often, as a small child, she'd sit beside her mother and watch, entranced by the fluid movements of her graceful fingers over the keys.

The tune that Eun-mi was trying to play was the only one her mother had taught her. It was called 'Arirang' and was the spiritual music that beat in every Korean's heart and the unofficial anthem of the whole peninsula. It was an ancient folk song, with many versions, and the notes flowed through the people's veins. It was a symbol of their identity and now, more than ever, Eun-mi needed to hear it.

She had never understood why, sometimes when she played it, her mother had wept and her tears would splash on to the ivory keys. The song was about the bitter yearning after two lovers part and had become a powerful metaphor for their divided country.

"Man's heart is like water streaming downhill," she sang softly. "Woman's heart is well water – so deep and still."

And then, abruptly, she was transported back. One of those memories she had locked away and had never dared approach broke through the barred door she'd created in her mind.

It was the day she returned home from school to find her mother slumped against the piano. The keys were awash and dripping with vibrant red blood. She had slashed her wrists and sat down to play one last time. Eun-mi tried in vain to wake her, calling and imploring, hugging and kissing her cold skin. Finally she backed away. Nabi was crying in the next room and, mechanically, she went to comfort her, covering the baby's clothes in their mother's blood as she held the infant closely, promising to protect her, promising to be strong, promising to never show weakness, promising to never leave her. Hours later, this was the scene their father encountered when he returned home.

Eun-mi's own tears fell on to the keys of Gerald's piano and she sat there, shaking, wracked with fresh agonies of grief.

Outside, Spencer kicked his heels. What was Gerald doing? The old man had disappeared into the attic some time ago and, inexplicably, had rooted through boxes of Christmas decorations. Then he'd vanished into his shed for a while and was currently getting changed upstairs.

Spencer checked the car one more time. Everything was in there: rifles, ammunition, grenades. Catching his reflection in the wing mirror, he noticed, with some astonishment, that his complexion had cleared up considerably. Whatever strange rays had bombarded his skin in Fellows End seemed to have done it the world of good.

"Bit late now," he mumbled.

He was getting anxious: would they be able to get to the White Castle before nine o'clock? Would they even get there at all and, if so, how could they find that master console? Just what did Gerald have in mind? He hadn't explained his "silly idea" any further and so far Spencer hadn't understood what he had meant by having left someone behind. There was nobody here. Felixstowe was completely deserted and it was obvious that nobody had been inside the guesthouse for over a year.

However, his questions were soon to be answered and Eun-mi would be jolted out of her despair when Gerald came downstairs.

The day wore on. In the gaol of the White Castle replica, around five in the afternoon, the aberrants were stunned when all the guards came waddling in, carrying five trestles that they set down in the centre of the chamber. Then they scurried away, while the Mexican bandit unfurled two long tablecloths, decorated with holly and poinsettias, and covered the trestles with them. Then the others came scampering back, bearing large wooden bowls. Some of them were steaming and smelled fantastic and the belly of every child whimpered pitifully.

The aberrants pressed close to the bars, their gaunt faces fixed on the feast that was being laid on the table before them. There were five bowls of pasta in tomato sauce, three baskets full of loaves still warm from the oven and another filled with bagels and pots of peanut butter to slather over them.

The Punchinellos spent half an hour scurrying to and fro, bringing fresh dishes and jugs of water and flasks of hot coffee.

There were baked potatoes, fruit, deep vessels brimming with nuts and seeds, tureens containing kedgeree, yoghurt in ceramic urns and a large oval plate piled with cooked chicken breasts.

When the trestles could take no more, the Punchinellos stood back to admire the mouth-watering banquet and exchanged sly glances.

"The sadists," Maggie murmured under her breath. "They're going to stuff their foul faces right in front of us."

But she was wrong. Captain Swazzle unlocked the cells and ordered everyone out.

"Dinner time," he squawked. "Eat up – is good. Plenty for all. Much yummity."

Warily the children crept forward and approached the long table as if it was laden with bombs. The aberrants stared at the irresistible feast uncertainly. It was the most food any of them had seen in over a year. They were so hungry, some of them were crying, but they didn't dare touch the incredible spread. There had to be a trick. Was it poisoned?

"What is this?" Martin demanded. "What cruel game are you playing?"

"No game!" Swazzle answered, seemingly offended by the slur. "Is good scoff. Get down neck."

"You forgotten what you fed us that last time in camp?" Maggie snapped. "Cos we bloody haven't."

The Captain bowed and Charm's girls saw a foul smirk creep over Bezuel's face.

"Is a gift from Ismus," Swazzle said. "You eat – you not eat. You make choice."

He and the guards withdrew, back to the dungeon, leaving the aberrants gazing miserably at the bounty spread before them. Slowly their eyes left the food and they looked to Martin for guidance.

"I think it's all right," he said. "It doesn't make sense for them to kill us like this. No, I know what this is about. I'm afraid this is the last hearty meal of the condemned."

"So just real food, Sir – yeah?" one of the Americans asked. "No crap, no funny business?"

"I really..."

The rest of Martin's words were drowned out by the squeals of delight as everyone dived at the feast. They didn't even care when some of the guards came back to watch and made oink oink noises at them.

A little while later, Maggie wandered away from the table to join Martin who was sitting back in his cell.

"Hiding from your fans?" she asked in amusement.

"I never expected any of that," he said. "How mad, here on the last day!"

"I reckon it's brilliant. Us lot didn't stop to think about it, but you're a star."

"Believe me, I'm not. I'm nobody."

"Shut your face. You gave hope to those kids out there and lots more besides — thousands that we'll never know about cos they didn't make it. But them out there, you saved their lives, Martin. That's gobsmacking awesome that is."

"Saved them for what though? For this? For whatever's going to happen to them tonight? They'd have been better off..."

"Oi! None of that. Gerald would tear you off a strip if he heard you talking that way. Keep on going, keep on fighting, that's what he'd have said."

"Hell, I miss him."

"He was the wisest and funniest person I've ever met."

"I wish he was here right now; he's the one who kept me going all this time. It's him those new kids should be idolising, not me."

"Well, he isn't here, so you'll have to like it and lump it. Just stop with the humble, it really gets on my wick, and I'll kick you up the arse if you carry on."

Martin suppressed a laugh.

"You didn't eat much just now," she observed.

"I had enough," he answered.

"Time was when I'd have hoovered up everything in sight," Maggie said. "But that was another life ago. Besides, what you said about the hearty meal, that wasn't quite right, was it?"

Martin looked at her. "How'd you mean?"

"Any hearty meal would've been full on Mooncaster stuff: roast goose and turnip pudding or something hey nonny nonny, not sodding pasta and definitely not coffee. It's not even remotely Christmassy, apart from the tablecloth."

"What are you getting at?"

"I thought it was weird when they fetched it all out, but I didn't catch on till I saw what was in that hamper at the far end. You didn't stick around for that, did you? Here."

She took from her pocket a modern cereal bar, still in its wrapper.

"What they've served up to us, Martin," she said, waving the bar and nodding at the banquet, "is a load of energy food: carbs, cereals, caffeine. That's the sort of blow-out athletes eat hours before they run a marathon. Looks like we're expected to do a whole lot of running tonight."

"Oh, God!" Martin muttered, aghast. "Of course, Flee the Beast... so that's what it means."

"No prizes for guessing who'll be doing the fleeing, but what sort of beast will it be?"

"We'd better stop these kids gorging," he said, jumping up. "If they stuff themselves stupid, they're not going to be able to move, never mind run."

It was only Martin's hero status that made the children pay attention. They would have continued to eat until there was nothing left, but they listened to what he said and abandoned the banquet. Esther lingered wilfully to pick at the nuts and fruit. She made a show of sauntering round the table, picking up a bagel or a potato, sniffing them, putting them down, dipping a spoon into the yoghurt and licking it clean.

When Martin shouted at her to stop taunting the others, she laughed and ignored him. Those foreign kids might think the sun shone out of his backside, but she knew he was just a crappy teacher and said as much. Turning her back, she scooped up a handful of pumpkin seeds to nibble on and raised her eyebrows at the other children who were glowering at her.

Maggie saw red and stormed over, grabbed the girl by the hair and dragged her to the cell. Esther howled and lashed out, catching Maggie across the face with her hand and the animosity that had been simmering for months finally boiled over into a fight.

"It's beginning to look a lot like Christmas," Perry Como sang as the chamber rang with shouts and jeering. The two girls punched and slapped one another and yelled insults. But it wasn't a fair contest. Maggie was two years older and, even though she'd trimmed down, still had the bigger build. Esther was on the floor in no time and Maggie was about to pounce on top of her when Martin pulled her away.

"Stop it!" he ordered. "The pair of you! Tonight you're going to need every bit of energy you have."

"She's mad she is!" Esther cried, rubbing her scalp gingerly. "I'm going to laugh my head off when you get killed later – you cow!"

"Keep her nasty mouth quiet," Martin told Nicholas as he led Maggie away.

The boy reached down to help Esther to her feet, but she smacked his hand clear and strode to her cot where she sat down with her arms folded, fuming.

"What is it with you two?" Martin asked Maggie. "Do you have to keep snapping at each other, even today? I know she's a royal pain, but you're better than this."

The girl sighed and shook her head. "I dunno," she said. "She just knows what buttons to press. You know, back in the camp, at the start she was OK. We worked in the kitchen together and we got on fine – at first."

"So what went wrong?"

"Buggered if I know. But she started listening to spiteful rumours about me, and that drippy Nicholas drew a cartoon of me as an elephant. She turned sour and deeply unpleasant and has been stuck in uber bitch mode ever since."

"Maybe it was her way of coping with the regime there? We all find different ways of dealing with what's happened and trying to stay sane. I'm not proud of mine. Sometimes it's easier to lash out and be unpleasant than risk losing someone you care about."

Maggie pulled a face. "I'll try not to wallop her again," she promised. "But if you think we're suddenly going to be best pals then you've got your sums wrong."

"If only life was as simple as mathematics," Martin murmured.

Everyone was glad when the Punchinellos eventually came to remove the food. It was a torment to have it in front of them. Even though they'd eaten more than they had in ages, there was still room for extra and they'd got into the habit of eating as much as they could, whenever they could, because they had no idea when they'd see the next meal.

"Only three more hours till Flee the Beast," the speakers heralded. "All the e-readers are out there now. Well done to everyone who donated. You've made the hopes of everyone in this grey place possible and we'll all soon be leaving it together. Now make sure they're fully charged and get yourselves to a TV screen or your Internet device of choice. You won't want to miss a second of this."

After the feast had been taken away, the children were permitted to wander freely about the gaol chamber. Yikker had whispered to Maggie that she could visit him in the dungeon if she wanted.

"In your dirty dreams, padre," she replied, reaching into her pocket. "And, if you so much as touch me, I'll kill you. That's a promise."

Yikker sidled away, licking his teeth.

The next time they saw the guards, they had changed out of their bizarre and filthy costumes and were wearing brand-new versions of their red and yellow Mooncaster uniforms.

Headed by the Jockey, they came stumping in, hauling eight clothing rails after them. Peculiar-looking garments were swinging on the hangers. Maggie saw a lot of white fleeces and some bulky, furry costumes with floppy feet that looked suspiciously like pantomime horses.

"Gather, gather!" the Jockey called, clapping his hands and summoning the children round. "Here are your outfits for tonight. Also, you will find, taped to the front of each rail, a list of names, and each name has a number that corresponds to an item of apparel. The Holy Enchanter has been most specific, so do not deviate from his instructions. That would be most unwise, would it not, Mr Maths Teacher?"

Martin nodded. "Best do as he says. Don't give the guards any excuse to use their swords."

"Gah!" Bezuel grunted in disappointment.

"So be quick, be quick!" the Jockey commanded. "Don your outfits without hesitation. Then the warders will escort you to your positions about the castle, in readiness for the great broadcast. This world awaits you. Such merry sport it will be! Haw haw haw."

The aberrants stared at him dumbly and eyed the odd collection on those rails with dread. The hour of the broadcast was getting closer – the time when they were expected to 'Flee the Beast'. But was that the only performance they were expected to give, or was there more to it?

"Here goes," said Maggie, inspecting the lists. "Let's see what tasteful number they've saddled me with. Hope it's not too tarty, unless they've provided a good push-up bra as well. If it's the back end of a horse, I will not be happy."

"That'd be typecasting," Esther said cattily.

"Drop dead," Maggie answered under her breath. But, remembering Martin's words, she turned and gave Esther a fixed, beaming smile, which the girl found unnerving and she moved closer to Nicholas.

Following Maggie's lead, the others closed round the rails and began searching for the costumes they'd been allocated.

Tripping across to Martin, the Jockey wagged a scornful finger at him. "You will not find your vestments here," he said. "Your special contribution to the night's entertainment is quite separate. Trot along with me. I shall lead you to your new wardrobe. This way – this way."

He shooed Martin from the gaol and the young aberrants watched him leave.

"Are you coming back?" Maggie called uncertainly.

Martin looked at the Jockey and that florid face moved from side to side.

"Alas and alack, no. Make your last farewell brief and swift."

Martin turned to the children and raised his hand. He intended to merely wave and go, but they deserved more than that.

"Everyone," he addressed them, "it looks like this is it. I won't see you again, so I wanted to tell you... no, I have to tell you that you've been amazing. You've been so strong, so brave. You should be extremely proud of yourselves. You're bloody fantastic. Whatever happens tonight, whatever you have to face, remember that. Remember how great you are. You've suffered more than most adults could ever cope with, endured the worst horrors this world, or any other, can throw at you, and yet you're still here. You never gave in; you never forgot what it is to be human beings. Your world was smashed, but you're not broken. Now I know I don't have to tell the older ones to look out for the others, you've been doing that long enough already, but tonight will be the worst time yet, so you have to be stronger and tougher than ever. Keep fighting, keep looking out for each other and most of all... I want you to run as fast as you can. Whatever comes after you, get the hell out of its way and try and stay safe, try and stay alive. You're phenomenal, you really are, and I'm so very proud to have known you. I just wish I could've got to know you better, but, if humankind makes it through somehow, future generations will know your names. I'm one hundred per cent sure of that – you're heroes, each and every one of you."

Tears were glistening in many eyes. Maggie wiped her nose and Charm's girls held hands.

"Good luck," he said warmly. There wasn't anything more to add and the Jockey was chivvying him along. Martin followed him through the dungeon and up the steps, to whatever humiliating fate awaited.

"God bless you, Martin Baxter!" Lukas shouted.

"Martin!" Maggie yelled sorrowfully. "Take care, you bloody marvel – and thank you!"

Suddenly everyone started clapping and cheering. Crossing the courtyard, Martin could still hear their applause.

The Jockey halted in surprise.

"Such riotous acclaim," he observed. "In truth, I do not see how it has been earned."

Martin smiled. "Nor do I really," he confessed. "But that's one thing your Ismus can never take away from me – and he'll never be treated to anything so spontaneous or freely given."

The Jockey scowled and pushed him onwards.

Down in the gaol, the Punchinellos drew their swords and pounded their spears on the floor, squawking for silence.

"Put on clothes!" Captain Swazzle barked. "Or we put them on you."

"Me likey do that," Yikker cackled and Bezuel agreed.

The children ceased clapping and hurriedly returned their attention to the clothes rails.

The costumes were highly unusual. The fleeces were the most numerous and, when they were taken down, were found to be sheep suits and came with ingenious hats shaped like sheep's heads. They were for the youngest children, which included Charm's group of girls, who, in spite of everything, couldn't stop giggling at each other as they put them on. Then there were two dozen red cassocks with white surplices for the boys. Maggie was nonplussed to discover she was supposed to wear a drab-coloured robe like a dressing gown that came with a headdress, sandals and a shepherd's crook. Six of the other older children had the same outfit.

Esther sniggered. "Oh, dear," she said sarcastically, "tough luck. You're going to be the Bad Shepherd. They'll have something really special lined up for you."

Maggie did her best to ignore the urge to yell at her. Still, she wasn't convinced Esther was right. Why would there be more than one costume for that character? Looking around, she saw Lukas and Drew clambering into what she had assumed was a pantomime horse. It wasn't.

"That's a camel!" Blueberry Muffin gurgled in recognition. "He's gorgeous – awww."

There were three camel outfits. Maggie's eyes roamed from person to person and she began to understand. They weren't dressing up as characters from *Dancing Jax* at all. Changing into her shepherd's robes, she was relieved to find it had a pocket and surreptitiously transferred the sewing scissors she'd brought all the way from North Korea in her greatcoat into it.

"What are you?" Esther asked Nicholas.

The boy shrugged. "Another shepherd, I think," he answered. "But I can't find my stick thing. How about you?"

"I've got a frock," Esther exclaimed happily, examining what was on her hanger. The long-sleeved dress was of creamy linen and there was also a deep blue veil. "Hang on, I think I'm a nun! There aren't any nuns in the book, are there?"

Then she found a curious, padded square with Velcro straps and held it up, puzzled.

"What's this then?"

"It's to go round your middle," Maggie told her. "It's to make you look pregnant."

Esther snorted. "You don't get pregnant nuns, stupid."

"You're not a nun," Maggie stated. "Haven't you worked it out yet? Open your eyes. All we're missing here are three wise men."

It took some moments for Esther to grasp what she meant. Soon everyone realised what the theme of the entertainment was going to be.

"Big funny!" Swazzle crowed and the other Punchinellos grinned hideously.

"Away in a manger," sang the St Paul's Cathedral Choir over the speakers.

21

9pm, 24th December

THE SCREEN WAS BLACK. There was no sound. An expectant hush had fallen across the world. Everyone on the planet was tuned in, via satellite or live streaming, to their computers, tablets or phones.

Then, almost imperceptibly, the silken sound of violins began playing the same incessant four notes. The music swelled with extra strings, then choral voices and crashing cymbals. It was an intense, strident and frenetic rendition of the Ukrainian 'Carol of the Bells', charged with all the pressure and panic of a traditional Christmas Eve – the last-minute race around, before the shops closed, and the battle to get everything ready for the big day.

> *"Hark how the bells,*
> *sweet silver bells,*
> *all seem to say,*
> *throw cares away*
> *Christmas is here..."*

The replica of the White Castle was in darkness. Suddenly arc lights snapped on and the Keep leaped starkly into being.

A noise like violent thunder drowned out the orchestra and choir as the uncounted millions of Jaxers surrounding the construction site roared and stamped their feet with unbridled ecstasy.

"Oh how they pound,
raising the sound,
o'er hill and dale,
telling their tale..."

Then, in time to the relentless pace of the tune, the inner wall flashed on, out of the gloom, followed by the second and then the main outer wall. Gaudy coloured spotlights played over the Portland stone and the forest of steel cranes danced in and out of the garish hues, casting web-like shadows across the walls and grounds. Beside the Keep, rising high above the walls, a forty-metre-tall Norwegian spruce sparkled and glittered with thousands of fairy lights. Searchlights fanned the sky and floodlights blazed above the moat.

The establishing long shot cut to a bewildering barrage of different views and angles. In and around that site over seven hundred remote cameras had been installed, controlled from the mobile edit suite in the postern car park. The most dynamic views were from the camera mounted on a motorised trolley-like device attached to two overhead cables that ran from high on the Keep, right over the castle and out across the recreated village of Mooncot. The technicians had called it witchcam, because the sweeping aerial views were suggestive of Haxxentrot riding her hayfork above Mooncaster.

Hurtling from the keep, plunging between the towers, witchcam passed over the gatehouse in perfect time to capture the pair of large iron braziers, either side of the drawbridge, erupt with soaring flame. Then it sped over Mooncot, sailing first over The Silver Penny tavern. Strings of multicoloured bulbs popped on in sequence down the street and each little cottage was illuminated in turn, ending at the mill, where witchcam swivelled round and came flying back again.

"Merry, merry, merry, merry Christmas,
Merry, merry, merry, merry Christmas."

Inside the walls, ten industrial snow machines began spraying a blizzard high into the air and golden fireworks exploded around two of the towers, sending glittering spangles far over the castle. Then, from the archways in those towers, high-kicking in unison, streamed 200 leggy chorus girls in skimpy red velvet skirts, trimmed with Arctic fox fur, with matching, low-cut waistcoats, shoulder-length capes and adorable Santa hats.

The 'Carol of the Bells' continued and the two lines of dancers progressed round the sentry walks like a musical number from a Busby Berkeley routine of 1930s Hollywood. Smiling into the lenses of the cameras they passed, they converged at the front of the battlements, over the inner gatehouse, where their scarlet, sequined tap shoes contributed to the music's urgent pulse.

Then a new tune started up, to disrupt and join with the first. It was the *Danse Macabre* by Camille Saint-Saëns. The discord raged briefly, then blended into a new and chaotic, sinister rhythm. A further 200 figures, dressed as horned skeletons, went clambering up the scaffolding that covered the curtain wall, with pitchforks in their grasp. As the glamorous chorus girls continued, waving their arms, bobbing their heads and clattering their heels and toes, the skeletons leaped on to the parapet, grabbed each one by the throat and plunged the pitchfork into their back. Casting the bodies down, they began their own jerky choreography.

> *"throw cares away*
> *Christmas is here.."*

The squeal of an electric guitar suddenly blared over the battlements. A fountain of Roman candles whooshed up and rockets shrieked into the sky, exploding into gigantic, glimmering flowers that lit up the countryside. Spotlights swept upwards, picking out a solitary figure suspended from the jib of a crane, descending on a cable.

It was the Ismus.

Dressed in skintight, reindeer blood leather, with antler buttons and cream velvet trim at the cuffs and collar, the Holy Enchanter of Mooncaster came gliding through the winter night, silhouetted against snow and fireworks. There was a red velvet scabbard at his waist and a chaplet of holly leaves, with clusters of bright red berries, sat lightly upon his head. An electric guitar, shaped like an Ace of Spades, was slung low at his hip and he tortured it and made it scream.

The incalculable crowd went wild. Their fanatical shrieks obliterated every other sound and the Ismus alighted on the roof of the gatehouse, strutting left and right.

Throughout the pandemonium he continued to play and the ninety-piece orchestra that was concealed in an enclosure around the rear of the castle, by the car park, was his backing group. For twenty minutes the guitar screeched and blasted out the victory of Austerly Fellows, the ultimate conqueror of the human race. When the music reached a crescendo, around the ramparts fifty cannon fired, with one booming voice. Three hundred archers appeared on the inner curtain wall and fired flaming arrows into the night. Fiery streaks shot over the outer defences in unbroken formation and exquisite symmetry, plummeting down into the moat with a unified hiss. Then the Ismus hurled the guitar into the air, where it burst into flames and went spinning down into the water after them.

The skeleton dancers leaped around him and went jiggling off into the towers. The archers disappeared once more and the Ismus was alone on the roof of the main gatehouse. A large Bakelite console was behind him, its dials barely glowing.

Smiling raffishly, he stared into the nearest camera and opened his arms in welcome.

"Ladies and gentlemen, boys and girls – and everything in between!" he exulted. "A most heartfelt greeting to you all. Here we are – we made it: the night before Christmas when, all through the house, everyone will be reading *Fighting Pax*!"

He waited for the ensuing uproar to die down then continued. "But, before that glorious time when we depart this dungheap dream world forever, let's paaaaarty!"

The audience's appreciation shook the ground; the words Flee the Beast came blasting across the screen with a riot of computer-generated lens flare.

"All your favourite courtiers are here tonight!" the Ismus exclaimed as the cameras cut to the Great Hall inside the Keep where chandeliers were ablaze with candles. Under Kings and Queens, lords and ladies and knights in burnished armour were seated round the feasting tables, banging their fists, making the dishes jump, or inclining their heads in a stately fashion. The Limner was also there, making sketches of everyone on this most auspicious occasion.

"At the very top of the Keep – keeping a watchful eye over everything and stationed either side of the Waiting Throne – are the Harlequin Priests!"

Back outside, the picture panned up to the flat roof of the Keep where the two men in colourful, diamond-patterned robes pointed to the yellow patches with their iron pokers to show their pleasure and bowed.

"Over by the East Tower are the Dancing Jacks themselves. Let's hear it for the Jill of Hearts, that lusty beauty!"

The spotlights went sweeping over to the inner curtain wall where a stage had been built in front of an incomplete tower. Sitting on carved and gilded chairs, behind a table draped with embroidered velvet, were the four Jacks and Jills, wearing their finest royal robes. At the mention of her name, the Jill of Hearts rose and blew a kiss to the camera.

CGI hearts bombarded the screen like fluttering rose petals and morphed into a romantic oil painting of her wearing a diaphanous gauzy gown and reclining among a bed of flowers, eating suggestively from a bowl of cherries.

"The Jack of Diamonds! Let's hear it for Magpie Jack!"

The youngest of them stood and bowed, winking as he rubbed two gold pieces in his fingers. An avalanche of CGI diamonds obliterated the screen and an animated Magpie Jack was shown tiptoeing behind their distorting facets, carrying a bag of booty.

"Give me your jools!" he demanded into his microphone.

"Now here's everyone's champion! The dashing and courageous Jack of Clubs!"

The golden-haired lad sprang up, drew his sword and put his foot on the chair, striking a heroic pose. Shields bearing the badge of Clubs came spinning in. Interlocking, their dark outline transformed into rolling hills and then Jack was there, riding Ironheart into battle across them.

"Is it blood in her veins or water? Look out – it's the Jill of Spades!"

The dark-haired girl at the end of the table reared her head and her eyes flashed. Spades came slicing down the screen like daggers, razoring through the picture, revealing a portrait of her made entirely of intertwining vipers.

"Are you ready, Jacks?" the Ismus shouted.

They nodded or gave regal waves.

"Then let's get in the xmassy mood," the Ismus addressed the viewing billions. "Drape yourself in tinsel, settle down with your eggnog whilst your chestnuts pop on an open fire and roll Zsu Zsu's petals in your Rizlas an' smoke 'em. Feel the thrill and tingle of the holiday and I will tell you the greatest story ever told."

His face grew serious and he bowed his head, putting his hands together before him as he composed himself.

"Noel, Noel," he began gravely. "And it came to pass that on this most special night, many years ago, Bruce Willis was trapped in a tower, in a sweaty vest, shooting terrorists and throwing villains out of high windows on to the cars of fat policemen. Single-handedly, and without the aid of footwear, he saved Christmas and henceforth Ebenezer Scrooge was a changed man and made sure that the Cratchits were properly goosed in the morning. God bless us, every one."

The Ismus broke into jeering laughter. He looked up and witchcam was directly above him. "That's as believable as that other trite bilge they peddle at this time of year," he declared. "But still, when in Rome... let us continue."

He gave an elaborate wave of his hand to send the aerial camera on its way and it went whizzing down over the village once more.

"Imagine if you will," his voice-over continued as the orchestra softly commenced playing 'Oh, Little Town of Bethlehem', "that our happy hamlet of Mooncot is a small area in the stony hills of Judea, two thousand years ago and about six miles outside Jerusalem, where two weary travellers are nearing the end of a long journey on a dusty road."

At the mill, there had been some swift scene-shifting. Fake palm trees had been put in place around the pond and a real donkey had been led out on to the newly sand-scattered road.

Esther cracked her knuckles. She was balanced uncomfortably on the animal's back. Standing beside her, Nicholas held the reins.

The din of the immense audience, the dazzling lights and the impending unknown terrified her. She was shaking. The Punchinello that had brought them here had said that all they had to do was make the short journey through the village and enter the castle across the drawbridge. After that, they could return to the cells. But he had said it with a wicked grin on his foul face.

They'd been instructed to wait for the camera to come flying overhead. That would be their cue to set off.

"It's there," Nicholas hissed as witchcam came racing into view above the village. "You ready?"

"Hurry up and move," Esther whispered unhappily. "Just get it over with."

Nicholas pulled on the reins and the compliant donkey began plodding along, flicking its long ears.

"There they go," the Ismus intoned. "The blessed couple. They have trudged eighty miles from Nazareth, because Augustus Caesar has decreed that everyone must return to their ancestral home, to take part in the tax census."

A large X appeared across the screen, together with a sound like an electric raspberry and the stop-motion puppet of the Ismus that had made the appeal for spare e-readers earlier in the week hopped in from the side. It was the first of several specially filmed segments. The character was wearing an old-fashioned schoolmaster's gown, mortar board, pince-nez and was pointing at a caricature of a Roman patrician drawn on a blackboard.

"The only census in that area around that time," the puppet proclaimed, tapping the board with a baton and poking the snooty nose with it, "was undertaken by Quirinius, the governor of Syria in the year six AD. Roman censuses only recorded Roman citizens, not Jews, and nobody was required to go anywhere."

The scene with the puppet spun round and was replaced by the shot

415

of Esther and Nicholas moving slowly up the street of Mooncot.

The girl looked warily at the cottages they passed. Beneath the eaves, where the strings of coloured bulbs shone brightly, shutters covered the windows and no chink of light showed through them. She didn't realise they were just empty shells and not real dwellings. The crowd beyond the barriers had grown still and quiet and her anxiety mounted. They weren't even halfway yet.

"Make it go faster," she muttered to Nicholas.

The boy tugged on the reins, but the donkey refused to be hurried.

"I can't stand this," Esther said. "It's not right; something is going to happen, I know it – something terrible."

"It'll be fine," Nicholas assured her. "The Punchinello said we'd be OK if we reached the castle. Don't panic, it's going to be sweet."

"You don't trust anything they say, do you?" she asked. "Are you a moron or what?"

"It'll be fine," he repeated, but it was really himself he was trying to reassure.

"What an arduous journey on such a dark December night," the Ismus's voice-over said.

Another X covered the screen and the puppet jumped in again. This time a calendar was pinned to the blackboard.

"Hooey!" he cried, tearing the months away with abandon. "Nobody knows the season this baby was born in, never mind the month or day – or even the year! The twenty-fifth of December was chosen to usurp the old pagan festival of Saturnalia – now that was a whole lot of fun! Good times, fellas!"

A pair of stop-motion, nubile nymphs with ivy and mistletoe in their long woollen hair skipped into shot and dragged the puppet Ismus off screen as he let loose a roistering laugh and kicked one leg in the air.

"Ooh, ladies!" he cried. "You might've warmed your hands!"

The live coverage of Esther and Nicholas returned. The donkey had not appreciated the efforts to speed it up and had stalled.

"Make it move!" Esther insisted. "Shift it!"

Nicholas tried patting the animal's head and leading it from the front, but it refused to budge. Esther dug her heels in its side, but it made no difference.

"I'm going to get off and walk," she muttered. "Not sitting here all night."

"You're supposed to stay on the donkey," the boy told her. "That's what the guard said."

"But it's not going anywhere! Four-legged dog meat, that's what this is."

"Shh! They're filming, don't wreck it – and don't look so angry. Remember who you're supposed to be! Try smiling and looking holy or something."

The picture cut back to the real Ismus on the gatehouse. A mischievous glint was in his eyes.

"So what have we got?" he asked, twinkling into the camera. "A story with no basis in historical fact. And, what's worse, it's a bit tedious, innit? Let's shake it up. What this scene really needs is a bit of Mooncaster spin and a lot of oomph. Yes, dear viewers, it's time to play the first round of Fleeeeeeee the Beeeeeeeeeeeast!"

The same titles as before flashed by, accompanied by a bombastic theme tune. Then sophisticated computer graphics came tumbling and spinning in. They whirled about busily, colliding and exploding until the screen was divided horizontally in two. In one half was an image of a Doggy-Long-Legs; on the other was the frightening face of the Growly Guardian of the Gateway – Mauger.

"The choice is down to you!" the Ismus shouted enthusiastically. "At the bottom of the screen is the address of our website. Visit the 'Beasts' page and vote now for the creature you most want to see released into that street this very moment. There's also a phone number: just text 'Doggy' or 'Mauger'. Come on – what do you want to see chase Mary and Joseph down there? I know which one I want! Get texting and voting and let's play Flee the Beast!"

The theme tune came crashing in once more and the Ismus gyrated his hips to it. Superimposed on either side of him, the face of Mauger and the Doggy-Long-Legs began revolving and beneath each one was a blue bar that started filling up with sparkling red light as the votes came flooding in from around the world.

The picture cut to the Jacks and Jills and the Ismus asked which

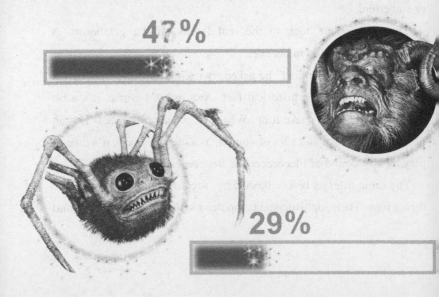

beast they would vote for.

"Mauger, my Lord," the Jill of Hearts answered breathily. "He's so strong and brutal."

"Look at these results," the Ismus shouted like a race commentator. "Mauger's in the lead. He's going to be the clear winner. Wait! No! The Doggy-Long-Legs is catching up! It's neck and neck! The Doggy-Long-Legs is nudging past. It's going to... yes, it has! You've picked the Doggy-Long-Legs! The Gangle Hound, pet of Haxxentrot the witch, is the winner!"

More fireworks exploded and, directly beneath the Ismus, in the kennel of the gatehouse, the Mauger demon let out a ferocious roar.

"Poor Mauger," the Ismus said consolingly. "You'll get your turn next time, old lad."

The crooked smile slid across his face and he crept towards the camera.

"Now," he began, "I'm not going to release one Doggy-Long-Legs. I'm not going to release two or even three. I'm not going to release ten or twenty or even sixty. What do you say to five hundred of them?"

The audience screamed their approval and the Ismus raised his arms.

"Release the beasts!" he commanded.

Inside the mill, two Punchinellos were watching on an eighty-four-inch HD TV. They waddled quickly to a control desk and flicked some switches. Then they dashed excitedly to the windows to witness the imminent sport for real.

Esther was holding on to Nicholas's arm. The donkey hadn't liked those fireworks and was stamping and swaying in agitation. Then, suddenly, it stood stock still. The long ears twitched and its nostrils snorted the cold air. Esther felt it shudder.

Along the street behind them, secret doors were opening. A stack of artificial logs outside the blacksmith's forge swung apart, revealing the entrance to a small, sloping tunnel. A concealed panel, built into the faux wattle and daub of Mistress Sarah's cottage, slid open and a barrel outside the neighbouring Ditchy home split in half. The stone steps leading up to Aiken Woodside's onion loft angled down into the ground and trapdoors in the meadow near the pond flipped up, casting off the camouflaging turves.

"Did you hear that?" Nicholas hissed. "Back there..."

Esther pulled the drape of her dark blue veil aside and listened. She couldn't hear anything except the expectant murmuring buzz of the crowd.

In those dark openings, many eyes glittered and long, stick-like legs came reaching. Furry bodies jostled and barged against each other and the Doggy-Long-Legs poured from the hutches they had been penned in for days. They were hungry and fierce and they charged out, yapping and snapping, biting anything in their path.

The donkey tossed its head and bucked, throwing Esther to the ground. With a kick of its hind legs, it bolted.

"It almost kicked my head in!" the girl cried crossly. "I never knew they could run like that! Bloody dangerous, could've killed me!"

She raised a hand for Nicholas to help her up, but the boy was backing away, his face white with terror. Then Esther heard them. She turned and saw a dark mass galloping on to the street, issuing eagerly from the sudden holes. Their bulging eyes were glaring at her and their fangs were dripping.

Shrieking, Esther jumped up, hitched her linen skirts and ran after

Nicholas who had raced off. The Doggy-Long-Legs came surging in pursuit.

"You left me!" Esther yelled, slapping the boy about the head when she caught up with him. "You left me! Coward!"

"Shut your face and run!" he bawled.

Dashing to the door of the next cottage, he wrenched at it, but it was screwed into the frame. Esther tried the one across the way. That wouldn't budge either. They had to get off the street, into shelter. Glancing back, she saw that the vicious terrors were gaining swiftly and she knew they weren't going to make it to the drawbridge.

In a moment, the decision was made and she ran at Nicholas, shoving her shoulder into him violently. The boy gave a startled yell and went crashing sideways. He blundered over a low wicker fence and fell headlong into mud.

Esther closed her ears to his screams as the pursuing Doggy-Long-Legs swarmed over the fence and the boy was buried beneath them. But there wasn't enough of him to feed five hundred. The rest swerved back on to the street and their famished yammerings drowned out Nicholas's failing cries.

Esther ran for her life. The castle was tantalisingly close. She could see the flaming braziers either side of the drawbridge and saw the donkey trotting across to safety. But the Doggy-Long-Legs were almost upon her. She howled when the foremost did a flying leap and hooked its clawed legs in her gown. She felt its weight swinging from side to side at the back as it clambered higher towards her neck. When it reached her veil, she tore it from her head and threw it down. The creature screeched and fell in a tangle and the others flowed over it.

Another came biting at her heels. Esther felt a sharp fang lacerate her ankle. Another clamped its jaws round the hem of her gown and started shredding the cloth in a snarling frenzy.

The girl knew she was finished. Very soon they would overwhelm her.

And then, even as she despaired, she saw, to her amazement and monumental relief, the illuminated windows of The Silver Penny tavern at the end of the village. The top half of the main door was open.

"YES!" she yelled.

Exhilarated by this incredible chance, she sprinted faster than ever and threw herself at the door, swinging her legs over.

"Oh, nay nay nay!" Captain Swazzle's voice squawked suddenly as he jumped up behind it like a jack-in-the-box and shoved her back out.

"Let me in!" she shrieked in terror and panic. "Please!"

A vile cackle came from the Punchinello's lips as he looked past her shoulder, to where witchcam was suspended above the street. Clearing his throat, in an affected, actorish voice, he delivered the line he had learned for this cameo role.

"No room at the inn!" he pronounced with hammy relish. And he slammed the top half of the door in her face. Hammering frantically on it, Esther heard the bolts being dragged across on the other side.

Trembling, the girl turned and pressed her back against the entrance. Hundreds of Doggy-Long-Legs were in a great semicircle around her. Tensing, they bobbed and swayed, and in those protruding eyes she saw the reflection of her own terror.

Burying her face in her hands, she slid helplessly down the door and the savage Doggy-Long-Legs rushed forward.

A fanfare blared over the battlements and trumpeters announced the end of the first round. The audience applauded, sounding like a ferocious sea tempest, and the choir began singing 'Ding Dong Merrily on High'.

Witchcam came whizzing back up the cables to focus on the Ismus who was gazing down at the dispersing Doggy-Long-Legs. The drawbridge had been raised so they couldn't enter the castle and they went hunting other prey. Some of them chewed their way into the enclosure for the orchestra and there were more than a few bum notes in the carol for a while until they were dealt with. Others scaled the crane masts and started spinning dirty webs between the steel struts, while the majority turned back down the village street and went prowling towards the barriers that kept out the crowds.

The Ismus was revelling in it. He twirled about and stared down the lens.

"More of that later," he promised. "Now let's find out what our panel of Jacks made of our two performers."

The picture cut to the Jacks and Jills for their verdict. In front of each young royal was a small golden casket containing two playing cards. One had a large X painted across it, the other a smiling moon face.

The Jill of Hearts held up the card bearing the X. "How shrewish and ill-favoured the wife was," she commented. "'Tis my judgement 'twas best she died, ere her face became crabbed from so much scorn and anger."

The Jack of Clubs reached into his casket and took out a card bearing the same symbol. "The lad was no gallant," he said. "He should have fought those Gangle Hounds and defended his lady to the death."

"I do not agree," the Jill of Spades declared, brandishing the moon face. "I commend her guile. I would have done the same as she."

Magpie Jack tutted and showed the X. "She should have crept into the tavern round the back," he said critically. "Or slipped in through a window, like a thief."

"Three to one against then," the Ismus said. "Let us continue with our tale. Unlike our hapless holy couple, the one in the story found shelter in a stable and it was there that the blessed infant was born and laid in a manger."

The picture cut to the puppet Ismus once more. This time his clothes were unbuttoned and hanging off him, his hair was mussed and his face was covered in lipstick kisses.

"Saturnalia," he said, whistling through his teeth and swaying unsteadily. "Yowza! Oh, what have we been missing out on! You have got to try some of that at home! Bad, bad ladies – so naughty! I'll never be able to look at a candy cane in the same way again."

The eyes rolled in his head and his lips quivered dreamily. The Captain Swazzle butler came trotting in with a scowl and nudged him to get on with it.

The puppet Ismus pulled himself together and coughed. "There is no mention of a stable or cave, or even a Holiday Inn, anywhere," he said. "Manger is all we get, not even any confused oxen wondering what'd happened to their dinner!"

Another fanfare trumpeted and the live coverage was back.

"Are you ready for round two?" the Ismus asked. The viewers roared. "Let's see if our Jacks are ready."

The four royals confirmed that they were, but the Ismus tapped his earpiece and said he couldn't hear them. They repeated themselves, but he still couldn't hear them.

"This will not do," he said playfully. "I think you should come join me here. There seems to be a fault with the sound. Come on, keep your Holy Enchanter company. It's getting a bit lonely – and don't forget to bring your voting caskets."

The Jacks and Jills rose, taking their golden boxes with them. A Punchinello warder stepped up to usher them along the castle walls.

"Is quicker this way, Your Highnesses," Bezuel said, bowing low. "Just a moment, m'Lord Magpie Jack, your mama likey a word with you."

"The Queen of Diamonds?" the boy asked in astonishment. "Why should she wish to see me? It will have to wait. The Ismus has requested my presence – he has precedence, as well you know."

"'Tis most vital you see her," Bezuel insisted, blocking the wall walk with his squat bulk. "'Twould take but a sliver of thy time."

Jack frowned with impatience and put the casket back on the table. The guard grinned and led him down a flight of steps, through a colonnade, to the entrance of a drum tower. The bodies of the chorus girls had already been removed. It wouldn't do for there to be any distractions in the entertainments.

"Her Majesty awaits within," he said, bowing again and opening the door.

As Jack crossed the threshold, the guard pushed him through and pulled the thick oaken door shut again. He locked it with a great iron key and loosed a foul, gargling laugh.

"What treachery is this?" Jack cried in the absolute darkness of the tower. "How dare you!"

He despised and feared the Punchinello warders. They were always trying to sniff him out on moonless nights when he was on a spree to steal away a jewel or trinket. He had slain one of them once. Perhaps this was revenge for that?

"The rogue shall swing or be drawn for this outrage!" he shouted indignantly. "I'll have him thrown in irons! I'll have the skin flayed off his crooked bones!"

It was then he became aware of the appalling stink in the place and he covered his nose with his hand. Something was in here with him, some vile creature that reeked of the midden. He heard heavy chains clinking and he reached for the dagger at his side.

"Paul?" an uncertain voice addressed him from the pitch-dark. "Paul, is that you?"

22

ON THE WALLS, the three royals processed in single file, bearing their caskets before them.

The Ismus tapped his nose at the camera and stepped behind the Bakelite console.

Leading the way, the Jill of Hearts saw that the wall walk was incomplete and the planking that bridged the gap had been removed.

"We can go no further," she informed the others.

The Jill of Spades looked round sharply.

"Guard!" she called in irritation. "Guard!"

"Here, Your Highnesses!" a squawky voice shouted up at them.

Gazing below, they saw Bezuel on the ground, holding a lantern aloft and beckoning keenly.

"There is a narrow stair here!" he declared. "Have a care. Come down. I will lead you to the main gatehouse."

As they descended, the Ismus adjusted the controls and studied the dials on the master console, playing like a virtuoso over the knobs and switches.

Bezuel bowed and tugged at his eyebrows in humble respect as he guided the three royals through an arched opening in the twelve-metre-thick stone wall.

Beyond was a cobbled area leading to the expansive castle tilt yard. It was steeped in shadow.

"This is not the way to the main gate," the Jill of Spades said tersely. "What Jockey-coined trick are you ha—"

She stopped speaking when she saw the vague shapes of three strange animals lying on piles of straw at the edge of the jousting area.

"What sorry beasts are they?" Jack asked, striding over. "They do not seem..."

He gave a shout and laughed merrily when he realised they were not real, but camel costumes.

"Why, they are part of this curious pageant here!" he declared. "They are mere comic masquerades."

Bezuel nipped forward and took out his lash. He cracked it across a camel's hindquarters and one of the aberrants within cried out. They had been waiting there for hours and had found it impossible to remain standing in the suffocating, uncomfortable costume.

"Don't!" Drew pleaded through the faux fur. "Please!"

"Yarr!" Bezuel shouted, kicking the one the voice came from. "On your lazy feet, you mangy, humped nags. Don't you know there's royalty 'ere?"

The Jill of Spades enjoyed watching him whip the foolish thing, but she had no time for the mummery of peasants.

"Let us be on our way," she ordered. "We must go to the gatehouse."

"Take these 'ere no-good camels, Your Highness," Bezuel suggested. "Ismus wants to see they as well – most muchly."

"I am the daughter of an Under King!" she replied, grossly insulted. "I am not one to be seen with such vulgar oafery!"

"It was Ismus's especial command," the guard warned and she glowered at him for the implied threat.

Jack came to her rescue. "I shall take the reins of two of these noble mounts," he chuckled. "Will my Lady of the House of Hearts take the third?"

The Jill of Hearts smiled at him. He could make her do anything.

"You look absurd!" the Jill of Spades told them. "A pair of clods! You debase your high-born blood acting thus. How can you shame your noble houses in such a way?"

She turned back to the guard to demand he cease this tomfoolery, but the Punchinello had covered his lantern and retreated into the shadow of a deep alcove in the stonework. The alcove revolved silently and he was conveyed to a passage that ran clean through the centre of the wall – protected from the imminent danger.

"I will thread his eyes as beads upon my purse string," she cursed. "Where is the insolent—"

Suddenly there was a crackle of light, high overhead. Hanging from the tallest crane, a large neon shape shone above the castle.

"What is that?" the Jill of Hearts wondered aloud.

"'Tis fashioned like a star!" Jack declared.

On the gatehouse, the Ismus rubbed his hands together.

"And so three kings came from the East, following a bright star," he said. "All right, all right, we don't have three kings down there; the Under Kings are too dull and slow for what I have planned. You don't need my puppet to tell you the wise men weren't really kings anyway.

429

They were astrologers. We don't even know how many there were."

A smirk like that of a schoolboy appeared on his face.

"Christmas is a time for games and surprises," he said. "Now watch, very – very closely..."

In one smooth motion, he slid a control all the way down to the end stop and four indicator lights went out.

"Unfriended," he muttered callously.

At the tilt yard, the effect on the Jacks and Jills was immediate and alarming. They dropped the caskets, clutched their heads and doubled over. The Jill of Hearts screamed and fell on the ground. Jack shuddered and tore his hair. The Jill of Spades shook violently and grasped her stomach. It felt like they were being ripped apart.

The global audience held its breath. What had the Ismus done to them? Was it poison? Why would he do this? Then, amazing sensation! In the blink of an eye, they weren't there – a miraculous substitution had taken place. The young people calling out in pain were total strangers. Who were they? Where had the celebrated young royals gone? What a marvellous feat of magick by the Holy Enchanter! Hurray!

Conor Westlake coughed and spluttered. He gasped for breath and hunched over until the spasming cramps subsided.

In their camel costume, Drew and Lukas didn't know what they were supposed to do. Was this part of the performance? They had been told nothing. Lukas looked out through the restricted view afforded by a patch of gauze in the camel's neck.

"We help them?" he asked.

Behind him, Drew was still smarting from Bezuel's lash.

"No! Don't interfere," he urged. "That might be part of this. Keep well out of it! It's not you who got whipped and kicked."

The Germans and Americans in the other camels were also wondering what to do.

"What the 'ell is goin' on?" Emma Taylor demanded, wiping her sweating face and running her disbelieving eyes over her gown of sable velvet and green taffeta. "What is this mingin' emo frock? Where the sod am I?"

She stared at the other girl, who was whimpering like a frightened animal.

"Sandra cowing Dixon!" she spat, knowing her from school. "What you done to me? You dropped a tab in my breezer? I'm gonna knock your teeth down your throat, you titless mare!"

"Don't you touch her!" Conor shouted.

Emma rounded on him. Then everything that had happened since *Dancing Jax* had stolen her life came slamming back in a car crash of memories and she staggered into one of the camels.

Sandra sobbed in despair; she too remembered. Her mind revolted and her skin crawled at what she had done.

Conor took great lungfuls of the biting winter air as the horror of it all flooded his mind. "What's going to happen to us now?" he asked.

The picture cut back to the East Tower where their replacements were already sitting at the table, wearing identical garments. The audience instantly recognised them as the Jacks and Jills of Mooncaster. What a fine trick the Ismus had played.

"The wilderness is a dangerous place for three people to be travelling on meaty camels," he said. "They really aren't very wise at all. Yes, you've guessed it; at any moment they'll have to Fleeeeeee the Beeeeeeast!"

The computer-generated titles flashed across the screen again. The theme thumped and the image of Mauger came revolving into view. Alongside that rolled a close-up of a bloody claw and the same blue bars as earlier appeared beneath them.

"This time, Mauger is competing for your votes against the ravening jackals of the ancient deserts. Which of them shall win? Only you can decide. Vote now or text 'Jackal' or 'Mauger' and let's play!"

As the world obeyed and the red levels went shooting up, Emma Taylor was shaking her head in the tilt yard.

"This is mental," she shouted belligerently. "All of it. Just mental! And what's them supposed to be? Scooby Doo roadkills?"

She gave the nearest camel a push with her foot and Lukas threw the furry head off.

"Stop that!" he told her angrily.

"Who you talking to, skinny?" she bawled.

Drew lifted the skirt of the camel's body and peered out. "What's going on?" he asked nervously. "Is this the thing now? Are the cameras on us? Put the head back on quick!"

"What you doing down there?" Emma cried. "Sniffin' his bum? You dirty pervs!"

"This is not right," Lukas said, looking around, afraid. "Is too open here."

Conor agreed. "We should move; this place is an arena."

"Bog off, Westlake," Emma told him. "You ain't no prince now. Poncin' about in them tights. You bloody loved it, didn't yer?"

She was silenced by the frustrated roar of Mauger in his kennel. The world had chosen 'Jackal'.

The aberrants and unfriended royals heard the millions of voices cheering around the castle and their blood ran cold.

"Martin Baxter said we must run..." Lukas said.

"What, boring Baxter our old maths teacher?" the girl sneered.

Within the deep arch of the curtain wall, the sound of an iron grate pulling across stone was almost lost in the uproar. Conor caught it and knew what it meant.

"Get out of those!" he told the camels urgently. "Take them off! Quick!"

Lukas was already unzipping the front of the body that attached him to Drew and was feverishly pulling off the furry legs and floppy feet. The other two camels were wrestling with the zips. The hands of the lads inside were panicky and shaking.

Suddenly, out of the arch, burst a pack of twelve demonic jackals.

They were larger than mastiffs and hairless. Monstrous, with cracked, blotched skin and bunched sinew, unwieldy heads and vicious jaws and their backs were corrugated by bony spines.

Yipping and snarling, they raced out, claws clattering over the cobbles. Their bloodshot eyes were fixed on the aberrants and they charged towards them.

Conor grabbed Sandra's hand and yanked her to her feet.

"Leg it!" he yelled at the others as he dragged her after him. "Make for that wall over there. Climb the scaffolding!"

The teenagers tore over the tilt yard. The loose soil had a light covering of snow from the industrial blowers and their feet left dark prints as they pelted for safety. The ones still struggling out of their camel suits weren't quick enough. Three jackals leaped on each costume, then dragged it and shook it in their great jaws. They ripped through the fake fur and did the same to the flesh inside.

Running as hard as he could, Drew was still wearing his furry legs. The outsize feet slapped the snow in an absurd, darkly clownish manner. They were the reason he didn't make it. Two jackals lunged. One leaped on to his back, the other snapped at his calves and the boy was brought down.

Emma was the first to reach the wall and she was already clambering up the scaffold when she heard his screaming.

Glancing back, she uttered coldly, "Seen it all now – death due to camel toe."

Conor was shaking Sandra and telling her to snap out of it. He had hauled her this far, but could do no more.

"If you don't climb," he yelled in her face, "you're dead! I can't pull you up there. You understand?"

The stricken girl's eyes stared at the carnage behind and saw that the other jackals were almost upon them. Shrieking, she threw herself on the scaffold and began scaling it. Conor was right behind and Lukas was catching up with Emma.

The scaffolding juddered as the fury of the hellish creatures thundered into it. They leaped up, scrabbling furiously at the horizontal and diagonal poles, but they couldn't get higher and dropped back to the ground. Incensed, they saw their prey escaping out of reach and they prowled between the uprights, baying and bellowing, seeking a way up. An infernal intelligence burned behind those eyes. They were assessing, calculating, deciding.

Some started chewing the metal with their powerful teeth, puncturing and mangling the aluminium. Then two began excavating the earth beneath one of the base plates while others attacked all the joining couplers they could reach, crunching down on the bolts and shearing through them.

The scaffold trembled then buckled. With a thunderous clanging, it sagged and collapsed across the tilt yard. The jackals scampered clear, then sprang back to devour whoever would fall.

Emma and Lukas had already reached the parapet at the top and were breathing hard when the tubes and boards went crashing down. Conor was halfway over the wall and heaved himself up just in time. But where was Sandra?

He turned to see her fingertips clutching at the edge. Before he could rush to help, her grasp slipped and she fell.

"No!" he shouted.

But a pair of hands had flashed out and grabbed one of her wrists. With a face almost as fierce and determined as the jackals, Emma Taylor saved her.

The hellish animals yammered and barked below.

"Don't just sit there gawping!" Emma ranted at the boys through clenched teeth. "Give me a bloody hand before I drop the slutty munter!"

Moments later, Sandra was hoisted on to the top of the wall and lay there, shivering with terror and panic.

"Th–thank you," she said.

"Stick it, you dozy bint," Emma told her. "Didn't do it for you, did it for me. You wouldn't understand."

Lukas gulped for breath. He was too frail for this much exertion. He was relieved he hadn't overeaten earlier, but he was weak and needed rest. Clasping his hands, he gave thanks for being saved, but the prayer went unfinished and he raised his head slowly. The jackals had stopped barking.

Conor noticed it too and they both stared over the edge of the parapet. The ground below was empty. Where were they?

"Oh, that's brilliant that is," Emma muttered when she spotted them.

Further along the wall, blocks of unused stone had been stacked in a neat, sloped pile. Six of the jackals were climbing it stealthily.

"Good as a bloody staircase!" she declared.

"We can't stay here!" Conor said quickly. "Soon as they reach the top they'll come right for us."

Emma threw him a disbelieving look. "We know that, you bell end!"

"But where can we go?" Sandra cried. "There's nowhere! If they don't get us, the guards or the Ismus will – or them out there. Oh, God, can you hear them? All those mindless people!"

"If we can reach one of the plank bridges," Lukas suggested, "we might kick the wood clear when they are crossing."

"Great idea," Conor said. "There's plenty of them ahead."

"Long as I don't end up as some hell dog's dinner that'll do me," Emma said, running along the high walkway. "Oh, balls!"

Beyond the next drum tower she had seen a second pile of stones. Skidding to a standstill, she watched two jackals come stealing round the tower.

The teenagers were trapped.

Sandra screamed and Emma slapped her. Then she did it again, because at least it made her feel better.

"Don't just stand there, Westlake!" she raged. "You've got a bloody sword! Use it, you moron – or give it here!"

Conor was already reaching for it. Drawing the blade and holding it artlessly in both hands, he realised with a shock that the skills and prowess he had possessed as the Jack of Clubs had deserted him. The sword felt heavy and he couldn't find the balance. He waved it about gauchely, struck the wall and almost dropped it.

"You don't have to be flaming Zorro!" Emma yelled. "Just hack the buggers to bits!"

The boy knew she was right. Squaring up to the six that were sneaking up behind them on that high, narrow way, he hollered at the top of his voice and thrashed the blade in front of him.

The jackals eyed the bright steel dubiously, then growled and came bounding on.

Emma's features set hard and grim as she faced the other two. Reaching into her sleeves, she pulled out two thin daggers. She was grateful the Jill of Spades never went anywhere unprepared. She wondered whether to give one to the German lad, but he was so flimsy he'd be no use at all.

"Here," she told Sandra. "Take this and stop being such a liability. Your damsel days is over. You got to toughen up and kick arse right now, girl."

Sandra received it shakily. She swallowed hard and took control of herself.

"The two Jills together," she said with a faint and frightened smile. Emma nodded. "Double trouble."

The jackals attacked.

Emma was thrown against a stone merlon and the beast lunged for her throat. Sandra lashed out and stabbed it repeatedly in the neck. The hide and muscles were tough. Only when Emma drove her own dagger up through the creature's jaw did it tear away, yowling – taking Emma's blade with it. The girls lost no time and kicked it off the wall. Before it hit the ground the second one had already pinned Sandra to the floor and her dagger went clattering out of reach.

Emma would have ripped its ears off, but its bear-trap jaws snapped at her hands and she almost lost them.

"Quick, close your eyes and turn away," she yelled at Sandra.

The other girl obeyed without hesitation.

"All right, Scrappy!" Emma shouted. "Cop a load of this!"

Flipping back the large emerald on her finger, she threw the powdery contents of the deep setting straight into the jackal's eyes. At once they started smoking and the brute toppled from the parapet, black fumes pouring from its sockets.

"Don't you screw with me!" she crowed, dusting her hands. "The Jill of Spades might've been sly an' deadly, but she weren't no Suffolk girl. We ain't subtle!"

Helping Sandra up, she looked back to see how Conor was faring. Three severed heads already lay at the boy's feet and the jackals had learned to fear his sword. Lukas was cheering him on.

"Get on with it," Emma shouted.

"You three get going," Conor called back.

"No!" Sandra objected. "We can't leave him."

Emma looked down into the tilt yard. The jackals that had killed

Drew and the others had left their mauled corpses and were now sniffing the air and eyeing the ramparts.

"Oh, yes we bloody can!" she said when she saw them loping towards the stacked stones. Snatching up the remaining dagger, she rushed along the parapet and Sandra and Lukas followed.

On the gatehouse, the Ismus grinned into the camera.

"You should have voted for Mauger," he berated the viewers. "He'd have seen them off. Don't worry, they won't get far. There's more surprises just around the corner for them. Now let's crack on with our spiced-up telling of the Christmas story. When those not-so-wise men visited Herod and told him they were going to pay homage to the newborn King of the Jews, he ordered the killing of every male child in the vicinity of Bethlehem. Sounds like my kinda guy."

"'Scuse me!" the puppet Ismus interrupted as the picture cut away to another pre-filmed sequence. "I feel I should point out here," he said, now dressed like a Victorian undertaker, standing next to an upended, open coffin, in which the Swazzle butler was pulling faces, with pennies covering his eyes, "that Herod the Great had karked it back in four BC, nine years before the census of Quirinius. Problematical? Not half!"

The live footage returned and the real Ismus cupped an ear with his hand.

"Hark," he said, "what heavenly music is this? Whoever can it be?"

The choir had begun to sing 'The Coventry Carol' and witchcam flew over the gatehouse and drawbridge. It swivelled about to show the castle side of the moat. A tiered stage had been built on the grassy bank there. Standing on it, miming badly to the real choir, who were hidden with the orchestra round the back of the castle, the young aberrants dressed in surplices held hymn sheets in trembling hands. This was their time.

> "*Lully, lullay, Thou little tiny Child,*
> *Bye, bye, lully, lullay.*"

When the picture cut back to the Ismus, he was wearing a richly decorated purple surcoat and a crimson, pillbox-shaped crown, rattling with small gold discs and beads. The very image of an ancient ruler of Judea.

"Go get them, lads," he whispered.

> "*Herod, the king, in his raging,*
> *Charged he hath this day*
> *His men of might, in his own sight,*
> *All young children to slay.*"

Out on to the banks of the moat, ten Punchinellos, led by Captain Swazzle, went berserking, with spears and swords in their fists. Squealing barbarously, they set about doing what they loved best of all. The young aberrants tried to run, but it was no use.

The Ismus threw back his head and hooted. The central dial on the console began to glimmer. One of the ancient symbols lit up and the needle jerked round a degree.

In the unlit formal gardens of the castle, Maggie couldn't blot out the harrowing sounds of slaughter. She and the other shepherds had been waiting in the cold and dark for hours. Weeping in silence, her hands covering her ears, she tried not to imagine what was happening outside the walls, but it was impossible not to and every mental image gushed with blood.

The Germans and Americans were on their knees, praying and sobbing, and she almost joined them. But she had her own charges to think about. With a tremendous effort of will, she forced herself to think about them and only them. Their moment was nearly here, the time they'd been dreading – when they too would have to Flee the Beast.

23

ONE OF THE many remote cameras inside the castle walls panned right, over the ornamental hedges and flowers of the Gentle Garden. It was swamped in deep shadow. There was a crash of cymbals and blue-tinted lights flooded the entire area, making it appear bathed in a frosty moonglow.

Next to one of the fountains, Maggie and the other teenagers who were dressed as shepherds were startled by the sudden glare.

"In the fields of Judea," the Ismus's voice-over began, "shepherds were tending their flocks by night. Not that they'd do that in the middle of winter, but never mind, we've already established what drivel this is. Wait a moment, oh, dear, where are those flocks? Can you see them? Not a baa-lamb in sight. What good-for-nothing shepherds! We don't like shepherds in Mooncaster, do we?"

Around the world the audience booed and shook their fists at their screens. The Ismus chuckled.

The girls dressed as sheep had been taken from the cells before anyone else, and Maggie had been fretting about what had happened to them. She had made a promise to Charm to look out for her girls – but where were they?

Yikker had brought her and the six lads here and ordered them to keep silent and still. He warned that they could only move when the lights came on and no earlier. If they disobeyed, he would bury his spear in their guts and tear out their livers. And they believed him. He was enraged to have missed out on the massacre, so was itching to make up for it.

Squatting on a stone bench, blocking the exit leading to the common lawns and courtyards, and looking like the most grotesque garden gnome imaginable, the Punchinello squinted up at the harsh lights, then gave the order.

"Go seek your lambies. Noble gardens only."

Maggie didn't need any further prompting. She and the others ran over the grass, calling the girls' names.

There were three formal gardens in this part of the White Castle, between the two inner curtain walls. The Gentle, the Lordly and the Physic were linked by pleasant walks along meandering pathways that passed through arches of yew and climbing roses. It had taken 350 Jaxers a month to hard landscape and install the statuary, water features, fruiting trees and hardy plants. The last of the out-of-season flowers for the herbaceous borders had only been removed from greenhouses and planted that afternoon. The gardens were stuffed with summer blooms, most of which wouldn't survive that night's frost.

Maggie called out desperately. Why didn't they answer? Were they gagged? Those evil guards were capable of anything and her fears multiplied. Jumping over low box borders, she searched the Gentle Garden, where only the Jills and Under Queens were permitted to stroll. Frantic, she looked behind the rose arbours, trellises and wicker hurdles. Using her shepherd's crook, she probed the bushes and parted the blousy profusion of flowers. The girls weren't there. Dashing under the next archway, she raced into the Lordly Garden.

This was more masculine in design and cloistered on three sides, with a stone terrace and wide steps to different levels. Carved, fiendish faces projected from the walls and featured on the terracotta urns that topped square pillars. The hedging was geometric, with uniform topiary of slender obelisks sitting on spheres, and the plants were architectural and robust.

Maggie and the other shepherds searched every nook and corner.

"No sign?" she asked them. The six boys shook their heads anxiously.

The girl ran through a pleached alley leading to the Physic Garden. Gravel crunched under her feet. This garden was filled with plants and shrubs of medicinal virtue, from aloes and angelica to valerian, vervain and yarrow. A large, circular pond was in the centre and Maggie approached it with a gut-wrenching sense of dread. What if those girls had been drowned in some murderous pretence of sheep dipping? Anything was possible in this barbaric lunacy. Gazing down at the water, she swept aside the lily pads and was relieved to see only goldfish in there.

A high wall, covered in jasmine and honeysuckle, marked the boundary. There was a green wooden door in the centre and Maggie hurried over to it. The door was locked. Whirling round, she didn't know where to think of next. She ran to the straw beehives and tipped them over, but there weren't even bees inside, and there was nobody trapped under the woodpiles.

The boys were just as distressed. What could they do?

"We look again!" Maggie shouted. "Check for hidden doors, panels – anything like that. We've got to find those girls before it's too late."

The cameras zoomed out and a high-angled shot showed them running through the gardens like mice in a maze.

When the picture returned to the Ismus, he had cast off the Herod costume.

"Dear oh dear," he said. "If only they were more familiar with the sacred text, they would remember that there is still one more garden within the confines of the White Castle. You out there know that, don't you? Yes, the Queen of Hearts' very own private retreat – the Garden Apart. Let's have a sneak peek inside there, shall we?"

The scene switched to a walled garden, where topiary animals cast deep shadows across ugly plants. Six ornate wooden dovecots, set up on tall posts, formed a circle round the central minchet shrub that had been trained into the shape of a heart. Huddled about that were the young aberrant girls, in their sheep costumes.

They had heard Maggie and the others call their names, but a Punchinello was holding a knife to Blueberry Muffin's throat. If any of them cried out, she would die. The petrified children hugged each other. It wasn't just the threat that instilled them with despair, but, overhead, they could hear something scratching inside the dovecots, trying to get out.

"Poor lost little lambs," the Ismus said. "A heavenly host is about to descend upon them – Mooncaster style. Will their shepherds find them in time? Let's play Fleeeeee the Beeeeeast!"

The viewers' jubilant cries and wild foot-stamping sent tremors through the landscape that broke the surface of the moat, scattering small waves against the blood-soaked banks. Inside his barred kennel in the gatehouse, Mauger gave a mighty, demonic roar.

As the theme tune played, the same image of him zipped across the screen, accompanied by a picture of a creature with a sharp black beak and great transparent wings.

"Crowflies or Mauger!" the Ismus exclaimed. "Which is it to be this time? Won't our Growly Guardian of the Gateway ever get released? Show him some love, people! Vote now or text 'Crow' or 'Mauger' – and let's see what little sheep are made of."

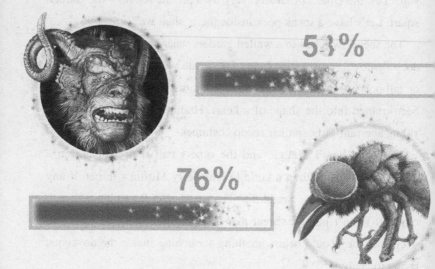

The world gave its attention to the voting and the red levels shot up the blue bars. Once again it was a close-run race. Once again there came a disappointed bellow.

"Release the flying steeds of Haxxentrot's Bogey Boys," the Ismus commanded.

In the Garden Apart, the Punchinello pushed Blueberry Muffin to the ground, then went up to the tall, supporting poles of the dovecots and hastily wound a lever on each one. Their conical roofs furled up like fans and out of every high, whitewashed hut flew three crowflies.

Swooping and zigzagging about the garden, they croaked and cawed. Their wings buzzed loudly and their bird-like talons scratched the air. Then their heads turned to the children dressed as sheep and they came zooming down to harry and snatch them.

The girls screamed and scattered and the crowflies attacked in groups. They clustered round a victim, biting and clawing. The hats shaped like sheep heads were torn off and savage beaks nipped in to pinch and pierce exposed necks. Ears and eyes were targeted and the beaks darted and pecked to get at them.

Four crowflies swarmed about the girl called Dandelion and Burdock. One flew at her face while another perched on her head, clinging to her hair and raking its talons through her scalp. The others bit the fingers that covered her ears. The girl charged through the garden, crying out for help.

The Punchinello that had released them watched appreciatively.

"Nicey gorcrows," he warbled. "Gobble your ickle crumbs and wormies."

Suddenly one of them dived at his hooked nose and impaled it. The strong beak drove right through the fleshy cartilage and the guard squealed shrilly. Grabbing the creature, he ripped it clear and the crowfly lashed out with all six legs. The Punchinello howled when one of those claws slashed his left eye. Snarling, he wrung its neck and threw it down. Then a second bombed into his face.

Maggie and the boys had run through the Lordly Garden and into the Gentle the instant they heard the girls' screams. They cast around, but they were still nowhere to be seen.

Yikker was still sitting on the stone bench, a hideous smirk on his face. They pleaded with him, but he wouldn't give any hint or clue as to where the Garden Apart was situated.

"Curse you!" Maggie spat. "If they're harmed, I'll keep that promise and kill you. You hear me?"

"Sexy Bo Peep," the guard hissed lustily, waggling his tongue at her.

Maggie turned away in disgust.

"Over here!" Ryan, one of the American lads, shouted. "They're behind this wall."

"What?" she cried. "There's no door! How'd we get in?"

Three of the boys tried to scale it, but the wall was covered in climbing roses growing from ornate lead troughs. Their cruel thorns cut like razor wire. It was no use. They couldn't do it. Frantically they attempted to clear the woody stems aside with their crooks, but they were tethered firmly to the brickwork. The screams beyond the wall continued.

Maggie couldn't bear it.

"Listen to them!" she wept, distraught. "Oh, please – no!"

Despairing, she looked back, over the Gentle Garden; if they pulled a trellis down, they might be able to use it as a ladder... Then she noticed something she hadn't spotted before. The badges of the Royal

Houses had been clipped into the box hedges; spades, diamonds, clubs and hearts, each of the four was equally represented. Why then was the heart the only sign to feature prominently on a statue?

The marble sculpture she was staring at was a voluptuous naked nymph called Chloris, whose right arm was laden with a bouquet of flowers, but the other extended in a graceful gesture towards the wall. In that hand was clasped a silver heart that gleamed under the blue lights.

Maggie ran to it and reached up. Glancing at Yikker, she saw his expression change into an exasperated scowl and she knew she was right. Seizing the silver heart, she pulled and it twisted on a secret pivot.

Immediately there came the sound of stone over stone. The middle section of wall and the lead planters at the base were opening outwards.

Before Maggie and the boys could dash into the widening gap, a squealing guard burst through, thrashing his short arms above his head. Dark blood was streaming down his face. Squatting on his hump, a crowfly was greedily gulping down his remaining eye. Maggie and the others didn't waste any time or pity on him. He blundered past, shrieking and yowling, into the Gentle Garden and Yikker's displeasure intensified.

There wasn't time to be horrified at the scene beyond that wall. Shouting and yelling, the seven shepherds stormed into the Queen of Hearts' hidden retreat and dashed to the aid of their flock.

Most of the girls were cowering on the grass, their heads and limbs tucked in as tightly as possible. The crowflies were buzzing all around them, scraping and pulling at the fleecy costumes. Maggie barged over, wielding her crook with fury. No one fought more fiercely. She caught one of the foul creatures by surprise and struck it across the head. It went spinning to the ground and a German lad stamped its brains out.

The other crowflies were too fast; they darted away and hovered just out of reach, croaking and screeching.

"Stay up there!" Maggie threatened. Looking down at the girls, she promised them it was going to be all right. She wouldn't let those things hurt them any more.

"Crowd together," she said. "Everyone OK?"

The girls were badly scratched and bruised, and horribly afraid, but not too badly harmed.

"Wait," said one of the shepherds, who had been doing a quick headcount. "They're not all here!"

"Blueberry Muffin!" Charm's girls cried in dismay. "Where is she?"

Maggie spun round. There was a croaking commotion behind one of the large shrubs. As she watched, four of the crowflies rose up, buzzing and cawing, and their talons were hooked into the missing girl's fleece. They lifted her, kicking and wailing, from the ground and other crowflies joined them, carrying the girl higher into the air.

"No!" Maggie screamed. Bulldozing through the flower beds, she leaped up to catch hold of the girl's legs, but the crowflies hoisted her out of reach.

Blueberry Muffin called for help. The crowflies rushed her across the garden, gaining enough height to convey her over the wall.

Maggie raced after, lifting her shepherd's crook as high as she could.

"Grab on!" she shouted.

The girl strained to reach it, but couldn't and her heels brushed against the top of the wall as they bore her away. Determined not to lose her, Maggie yelled at the lads and four of them gave her a boost.

"Now, sweetheart!" she instructed.

Blueberry Muffin squirmed and twisted and pitched herself forward. Her fingers closed about the curved handle of the staff and Maggie pulled hard.

The crowflies screeched as they were dragged down. Their wings buzzed louder than ever, but Maggie and the boys wrenched at the crook and the little girl was soon in her arms.

Maggie's fist clouted the creatures away and she hugged her tightly.

"I knew you'd save me," Blueberry Muffin said, throwing her arms about her neck.

"Right," Maggie announced with dogged resolve. "We're getting out of here."

Like a determined hen with chicks, she led the girls to the secret entrance in the wall and the boys followed closely, keeping the angry crowflies at bay.

Running across the Gentle Garden, they discovered the blinded Punchinello lying dead in the grass. His head had been hacked off.

Before they had time to react, a dirty laugh sounded and Yikker stepped from behind the topiary. His spear was in one hand, a drawn sword was in the other and it was drenched in blood.

"Me no likey Mizcha," he said, staring down at the decapitated Punchinello. "Him yap yap too much. Him no yap no more. He no use with no eyes – is better this is."

His own eyes slid up at the aberrants and even under the blue lights they saw his cheeks were flushed. His infernal bloodlust was burning. He'd missed out on the massacre beside the moat and now he was determined to make up for it. He scythed his sword through a clump of plants and they gave off an aromatic, minty scent. His great nose inhaled deeply and the blade turned in his grasp as he looked from one child to the next.

"Yikker want lamb chops," he drawled. "Cutlets and mint sauce – juicy tasty."

"You will not touch them!" Maggie warned, holding her crook before them protectively.

"Touch, slice, skewer, rip, chew – Yikker do all this – yes."

The other shepherds joined her, shielding the girls, and the Punchinello laughed at their reckless bravery.

"Nicey," he said with a snicker. "You give Yikker plenty fun."

Maggie's knuckles blanched as she gripped the crook tighter than ever. She stared into the guard's ugly face and read the deaths of each one of them there. They wouldn't be able to stop him. His appetite for killing had been roused and they would all die brutally. Their hapless resistance was just sport to him. But what else could they do?

"Wait," she said abruptly. "You don't have to do this."

"Yes, Yikker do."

"Listen to me. You let them go and I'll give you something you want."

"What you give?"

"Me."

The Punchinello's bristly eyebrows twitched with interest and he leered at her keenly.

"You?"

Maggie nodded, trying to stop the revulsion showing on her face.

"Yes. You let them go and you can have me. You want me, I know you do."

Yikker licked his chapped lips. "Give self to Yikker?"

"Willingly," she promised. "You and me, on the grass, surrounded by flowers..."

Behind her, the girls uttered cries of protest and the other shepherds were horrified at what she was saying.

"We can take him down!" Ryan said confidently. "He's just one. There's seven of us."

"Don't be stupid," Maggie told him. "You know how strong they are. He'd cut through us like butter. This way you'd have a chance. Take it and shut up."

"Yikker not agree yet!" the Punchinello interrupted.

"Oh, but you will," Maggie said, laying her crook on the ground, then removing the headdress and shaking her hair loose. "We both know it, sunshine. Don't start playing hard to get. That's a waste of everyone's time."

"You can't do this!" another boy cried.

"Take the girls and go," she hissed. "Now!"

"Maggie!" Charm's group wept. "Don't!"

453

"Get out of here," she told them. "Go – and don't you look back!"

The lads eyed the guard and he grinned, showing all his dirty teeth. With a jerk of his head, he gave them permission to leave. Quickly they hurried the girls past him and out of the Gentle Garden.

"Nicey," Yikker purred when they were alone. "Me likey."

Maggie began unbuttoning her robe. "Take your hat off, Tiger," she invited. "And get over here."

Yikker threw his hat into the bushes and came waddling over, dropping his spear and sword.

"Oh, you frisky devil!" Maggie exclaimed through clenched teeth. "What a handful you're going to be."

Overwhelmed with bestial passion, Yikker reached up to pull the robe from her shoulders and Maggie caressed his great bony skull. Forcing a laugh from her lips, she pulled his face into her chest so he didn't see the glint of steel in her fingers as she drew her arm back. Then, with all her strength, she drove her scissors deep into his ear canal, piercing the drum and beyond.

There wasn't a chance for him to struggle and fight. Clutching him close, she felt his body convulse and she slammed her palm against the handles – again and again, hammering them well and truly home. Then she wound them round like a key, unlocking the life from his body.

"That's for Stinkboy!" she snarled, letting his body sink to the grass. "And for the rest of us who didn't make it – you piece of filth."

Stooping, she snorted to summon enough saliva to spit in his dead face. Then, with a sickening jolt, she realised what she was doing and stumbled away – ashamed. Wiping her eyes, she snatched up his sword and spear and ran after the others.

Cawing and buzzing, the crowflies swooped down and feasted.

Jumping over the stone bench, Maggie raced across the lawns and through courtyards, calling for Charm's girls.

She found them by the brewhouse, anxiously wondering where to turn next. Everyone was overjoyed and they embraced her desperately. They didn't dare ask what had happened or how she had escaped. They saw she was carrying Yikker's weapons and that was enough. But their elation was short-lived.

"Where we headed?" Ryan asked. "There's no way outta this place. There's, like, waaay more guards than him – and then there's everything else out there. We're stuck. Just going round in circles in a stone cage, till we run into something we ain't never gonna get away from."

At that moment they heard the baying of the jackals. The sound was nearby and it bounced and echoed eerily around the high walls, making it impossible to know which direction it came from. One thing was sure though – it was getting closer.

"We keep on running," Maggie said resolutely, as she gave Ryan the spear, because he was the eldest, and kept the sword for herself.

Leaving the brewhouse behind, they hurried over the cobbles and were soon confronted by washing lines strung between the walls, hung with prop laundry.

"We're near the back door of the castle," Lemon Cheesecake said. "The wash-house isn't far from the postern gate. It says so on the maps in the book."

Maggie could have kissed her. Could they really escape? Was it possible to actually get out of here? The idea was so incredible she almost felt giddy. They hadn't seen the size of the terrifying crowd beyond the walls and had no concept of what exactly was going on. Their minds burned with the prospect of escape and they dared to hope.

Suddenly the laundry yard was filled with savage barking and the jackals came tearing round the corner. At first Maggie and the others couldn't see them. Multiple lines of washing were in the way. They just heard the ferocious din and Maggie yelled for everyone to turn back.

"Get the girls out of here!" she bawled. "NOW!"

Gripping the heavy sword uncertainly, she stared at the squares of linen and damp garments hanging across the yard. She couldn't see any movement in the shadowy gaps beneath. Then, to her horror, the largest sheet punched outwards and, for a ghastly instant, took on the form of the beast leaping towards her. The fabric swept across its powerful limbs, then over the large, vicious head. Maggie wailed and the jackal dived straight for her.

She only just managed to dodge aside in time and she brought the sword swinging down, striking sparks from the cobbles. Before she could even lift it again, the demonic creature spun about and sprang for a second attack. It lunged right for her throat. Then it yowled as the spear plunged deep into its side and it crashed to the floor yelping and writhing. Maggie raised the sword and finished it.

Breathing hard, she turned to the boy who had saved her, to thank him. The words hadn't left her lips when a second jackal came bounding through the washing. As it sailed through the air, its wide jaws snapped shut round Ryan's head and felled him.

Maggie shrieked and rushed at it. The jackal growled at her menacingly. Then its ears caught the sound of the others running away and its eyes blazed with malice. It didn't want to fight, it wanted to kill.

With a scrape of its claws, it wheeled about and pursued them.

Maggie glanced quickly at the boy. She couldn't do anything for him and there wasn't time to grieve. But that nightmare wasn't going to get her girls, not while there was an ounce of strength in her body.

Yanking the spear from the dead jackal's ribs, she charged after the other, yelling at the top of her voice. This was why she'd lost so much weight and exercised daily on the terrace of that mountain. She'd known a moment like this would eventually come.

The girls and five remaining shepherds had run back to the brewhouse when they heard the beast chasing after them and Maggie's fearless cries close behind. Running was no use here; they couldn't escape that monster. Frantic, they tried the doors of the brewhouse, but they were locked. Then they saw a narrow stairway leading to the battlements.

"Up there – fast!" the shepherds urged their sheep.

The girls rushed to the steps, but halted when they saw a figure charging down towards them, bearing a long blade.

"Jaxer!" Dandelion and Burdock cried.

The lads glanced up fearfully. They were caught between the jackal that was almost upon them and now this new enemy. Staring upwards, they saw it was a boy not much older than themselves. With a start, they recognised his famous face instantly. It was the Jack of Clubs.

"It's all right!" Conor Westlake shouted as he rushed down to meet them. "I'm not part of it any more. Get up here, all of you!"

"Is real!" Lukas's voice called down from above. "He's a good guy. Quick!"

The girls charged up the steps and Conor jumped down, just as the jackal tore into their midst. For several awful minutes there was chaos and screaming. The jackal lashed out with claws and teeth, snapping and swiping. But the boys defended their flock valiantly. With renewed vigour, they surrounded the beast, smiting the ridged spine with their staffs and ramming them into its jaws. The jackal crunched through the wood and ripped the crooks from their hands. Then, as it rounded on them, Conor struck with his sword. It sliced deep into the muscular shoulder. When the jackal twisted round, he drove the steel down the gaping throat – right to the hilt.

The beast quivered and the sinewy legs collapsed under it. Moments later, Maggie came running up, in time to see Conor wiping his sword on its carcass.

"Great job," she panted gratefully, despite being annoyed with herself for not getting here sooner. "Well done."

Conor regarded her in surprise. Armed with spear and sword, she looked like some ancient warrior. She was staring at him equally curiously.

"Hang on!" she exclaimed in alarm when she realised who he was. "You're him! The proper Jack of Clubs. What...?"

"I'm not him any more," he assured her. "We got kicked out, or something – I dunno what. I'm just me now. Call me Conor."

"You don't look as daft as you used to on telly."

"Oh – cheers."

"Hey," one of the Americans asked. "Where's Ryan?"

"He didn't make it," Maggie answered. "He took out one of those things first though. Saved my life."

The shepherds hung their heads.

Maggie raised hers to watch the girls running up the steps and being met by Lukas, Emma and Sandra.

"We were headed for the back gate," she said to Conor. "Any chance of us getting out that way?"

"You crazy?"

"Probably, but try answering the question."

"Have you seen what's outside these walls? You don't have a hope."

"There's always hope."

"Forget it. We're trapped in this castle and there's four more of those devil dogs on the loose somewhere. That's the entertainment, watching us get killed."

"Yeah, well, I don't give up so easy," she told him. "Come on then, handsome, show me what's so scary beyond them walls."

Conor followed her up the steps. "Brace yourself," he warned.

On top of the main gatehouse, the Ismus gave an amused chuckle as the camera zoomed in on Maggie's awestruck face when she stared out over the battlements.

"Such resourceful shepherds," he declared. "They've survived far longer than I anticipated. Again, if you'd have voted for Mauger... ah, well. I think our Growly Guardian is beginning to feel unloved. Now aren't you a little curious to see what happened to Magpie Jack...?"

24

THE SCREEN CHANGED to green-tinged night vision as it showed a recording of when the Jack of Diamonds was pushed into the pitch-blackness by Bezuel.

"Paul?" the voice had said. "Paul, is that you?"

The cameras inside the tower made the boy's eyes shine strangely. Covering his nose and mouth, he answered haughtily, "Who is there? What foul corruption abides within these walls?"

"It's me, Paul," the voice answered gently. "It's Martin."

"Do turds now speak and take names unto themselves? For no other thing in Mooncaster could stink so mightily. This is witch's work and I'll not fall prey to so noisome a spell."

Heavy chains clanked as the man reached out in the direction of that young, arrogant voice.

"Think, Paul!" Martin begged. "Remember me! Remember Carol, your mother."

"My mother is the Queen of Diamonds and my name is Jack, not Paul. That was a pauper's life I dreamed once when I was a child."

"No, that's your real life. What you think you are now, this is the dream – the mad illusion. You're Paul Thornbury. You, me and your mother lived in Felixstowe. You must remember!"

"Must is not a word for princes. Speak no more unto me, stench ogre. I must needs find a way out of this putrid pit ere my nose rots."

The boy resumed hammering on the door with his fists and yelling oaths.

The remote camera panned away and focused instead on the chained, ragged man in the centre of that fetid darkness.

Martin Baxter was shaking his head and clenching his fists. Pulling on his shackles, his anger mounted and his temper exploded.

"This isn't what you promised!" he raged, turning wildly. "You said he'd remember! And where's Carol? I should've known not to trust you!"

His voice thundered around the empty tower. When the echoes faded, the Jack of Diamonds gave an agonised cry and fell to his knees. Outside, the Ismus had 'unfriended' the four Dancing Jacks.

"Paul?" Martin called in alarm. "Paul? What's happened? Are you all right? Answer me!"

The boy was shrieking and clutching his head. It felt as though it was splitting open. His legs thrashed uncontrollably and he rolled around on the floor. Then, abruptly, he fell silent and his limbs pulled in as he curled into a ball.

"Paul?" Martin cried, leaning as far as the chains permitted. "What is it?" He wondered if there was something else in there with them, something that had attacked the boy in the blackness. "Paul – Jack, are you OK?"

For some time the only sounds he could hear were anguished sobs – and then...

"Martin...?" a small, frightened voice uttered. "Martin, is that you?"

Martin spluttered and almost wept with joy. He could tell at once that the madness had lifted. All traces of royal pride had left that voice. It was just a boy, timid and afraid.

"Yes, yes, it's me!"

"W–where are you? I can't see a thing."

"Over here. Be careful; the floor is raised and there's lots of chains."

"And a shocking pong. What is that?"

Martin laughed out loud. "That's me!"

"Blimey, let yourself go a bit, haven't you? I'll have to get you some more Tardis bubble bath for Christmas. Use it this time, don't just keep it in the..."

Paul faltered. He recalled what he'd done to Martin's prized collection of sci-fi memorabilia. In a violent rampage as the Jack of Diamonds, he had smashed the lot.

Martin knew exactly what he was thinking.

"Hey, none of that matters," he said. "That was just stuff."

"It was fantastic stuff. You loved it."

"I love you and your mum more."

The boy shuffled cautiously across the tower to find him. There was some sort of metal stage in the centre. He clambered on to it then almost tripped over the iron hoops the chains were attached to.

"Steady," Martin said. "And don't touch me – I'm covered in pig... erm, poo. That's what the stink is. They plastered me with it."

Hearing him so close, Paul hurried towards his voice and threw himself blindly into Martin's arms.

"I don't care!" he cried joyously. "I can't believe it! I missed you – I missed you!"

Martin held him fiercely and tears ran down both their faces. The camera lingered on their emotional reunion, capturing every detail in voyeuristic close-up.

"I'm sorry!" the boy said desperately. "So sorry for what I put you and Mum through."

"Wait! It wasn't your fault! I should've listened when you tried to tell me what was going on. Right back at the start, you saw it and I took no notice. I've been such an idiot about everything. You did absolutely nothing wrong. You've got no reason to blame yourself — none whatsoever. The book was too powerful. Nothing could have stopped it."

"But it didn't affect you! Why?"

"No one knows. It just didn't work on me and a few others."

"So... why me now?" the boy asked. "How come I snapped out of it? I don't understand."

Martin held him a little closer.

"Because I made a deal," he said. "I get you and Carol back."

The boy pulled away. "What sort of deal? Who with?"

"The Ismus."

"What?"

"I know, I know, believe me. It was the only way."

"So what does he get out of this deal? What did you have to do for him?"

"I don't know that yet. I'm still waiting to find out. Dressing me up as the dungy guy from the book won't be enough. There's more to this than putting me in rags covered in pig muck."

"You shouldn't have agreed."

"I'd do anything for you two. Nothing else matters."

"Where is Mum?"

"I don't know. I haven't seen her. Maybe they'll bring her in here too?"

At that moment the door was unlocked and, after the total blackness in there, the light that flooded in from outside was painful to look on. As their eyes adjusted, they saw a shape silhouetted in the arched opening. For an instant, they both expected it to be Carol.

"I'm taking the boy," the Jockey's voice said gruffly.

"No!" Paul shouted. "I'm not leaving Martin!"

"Don't take him!" Martin pleaded. "Not so soon."

"Haw haw haw," the Jockey laughed. "The rascal can't go where you're bound, Mr Maths Teacher. Assuredly 'twill be safer for him. I have been instructed to guide him to my Lady Labella and leave him in her gracious charge."

"I'm not moving!" Paul objected.

"Wait," Martin told him quickly. "Carol is Labella. Go – go be with her."

"Does she know who she is? Is she back to normal too?"

"I don't know. Maybe. But you belong with her. Go on, Paul, please."

Paul didn't know what to do. He wanted to stay with Martin, but he was also anxious to see his mother. If he left with the Jockey now, he'd feel like he was abandoning and betraying the person he loved as a father.

"Dad!" he cried wretchedly.

"I want you to go to her," Martin urged. "Do it for me."

The boy hugged him one last time. Stepping away was one of the most difficult things he'd ever done and he walked slowly towards the door, where the Jockey was waiting.

"Paul," Martin said. "Give your mum a great big kiss from me and tell her how much I love her – in case I don't get the chance to do it myself."

Paul halted and turned for a final glimpse of him, caught in the wedge of light that spilled from the door. The boy couldn't find any words to say goodbye and thought they'd stick in his throat anyway, but he had to say something. He tried to remember a line from one of Martin's favourite films that would convey his feelings better than anything he could come up with and almost attempted "I'll be back", in the stilted style of Arnold Schwarzenegger. But he didn't believe it and it would sound forced and phony. In the end, he simply raised his hand and made the Vulcan salute from *Star Trek*. Although he didn't think there was any chance of either of them living long and prospering.

The chains rattled as Martin tried to do the same, but they were too short. Paul departed with the Jockey and the door of the tower closed, sealing Martin in complete darkness.

Once again the night-vision camera closed in on his face as he broke down.

"Is there no end to that man's tears and self-pity?" the Ismus asked dryly when the screen cut back to him. "That was a little while ago.

Let's see how the notorious Martin Baxter, self-proclaimed champion of the aberrants and tedious blogger extraordinaire, is faring now. Time he stopped skulking and sulking in the shadows and finally joined our merry festivities. Bring him up into the open! Raise it!"

The command was for Bezuel, who was sitting at a control desk inside one of the stables. The Punchinello turned from the TV monitor and pressed a red switch. It sent a signal to the orchestra to commence playing 'Once in Royal David's City', then Bezuel pulled a lever.

In the blackness of the drum tower, Martin was sitting, hunched over and despondent. He had tormented himself wondering what each new roar and jeer of the immense audience out there signified and hoped Paul had found Carol safe and that she knew him. Then he began to suspect that those brief minutes with Paul were all he was going to get and he wouldn't see Carol at all. The doubt and anxiety were crippling.

Suddenly the metal plating beneath him juddered as power snapped through to the hydraulics below. Then, with a mechanical whine, the circular dais began to rise and Martin realised he was chained to a platform lift. Smooth and steady, he felt it elevate higher up inside the tower – up and up. Gradually he heard the noise and echoes of the machinery alter around him and guessed the ceiling was getting very close. The lift showed no sign of stopping.

Martin flattened himself against the metal floor. Was this it? Was the Ismus going to squash him like an insect? That didn't ring true somehow. That would be too quick, too private, in this all-engulfing dark. There had to be more to it than this. Yet he was still terrified when the back of his head touched the ceiling and he screwed up his face, expecting to be crushed.

But no, the ceiling was soft. It was just a stretched tarpaulin, pre-cut across the centre and gaffer-taped together. The rising scissor lift pushed Martin right through it and he was thrust up into the outside world. Lurching to his feet, he blinked in the harsh glare of the spotlights and the lift came to a stop.

"Behold!" he heard the amplified voice of the Ismus proclaim. "Martin Baxter as you've never seen him before. He's come as Dung-Breathed Billy the Midden-Man. Was there ever a dirtier, filthier, more despicably base cockroach? I'm glad I'm upwind!"

The crowd hissed and booed. In the book, the midden-man was an unpopular character and had been cursed to receive fifty kicks a day from the villagers of Mooncot. Martin didn't even notice their heckles. He was too busy staring around him, at the castle that spread out in every direction. This tower was part of the second curtain wall and he searched desperately for any sign of where Paul had been taken.

The huge structure of the Keep loomed away to the right and he saw the windows of the Great Hall blazing with candles. Had the boy been taken in there? That's where Carol would be as the Lady Labella.

"Where are they?" he shouted. "Where are they?"

His cries were answered by the Jockey who came scampering across a temporary plank gangway that linked the unfinished drum tower to the sentry walk of the outer battlements. He was accompanied by two of the Black Face Dames: stern and ready to punish any sign of rebellion or resistance with violent force.

"What a commotion!" the Jockey declared. "Have patience. I am tasked with coming to fetch you to the Holy Enchanter. Your part in the entertainment is about to commence. Unfetter him, unfetter him."

The bodyguards moved in to unlock Martin's chains. The Jockey's face wrinkled at the smell, but their blackened features remained fixed and severe.

"Where did you take Paul?" Martin demanded. "Where is he? Where's Carol?"

"Follow me and these things, and more besides, shall be made known to you," the Jockey replied, skipping back along the planks.

When the last iron cuff was unlocked from his wrist, Martin complied. There was nothing else he could do. But what was the Ismus going to demand of him? What further humiliation could be in store?

"While he wends his grubby little way towards me," the Ismus addressed the camera, "let's get some vox pops down in the crowd and see how you're enjoying the show. Your opinions matter so much to me, they really do."

The picture cut to a section of the barricade that surrounded the castle. It was a puny fence to keep out such vast numbers, but no one would disobey the Ismus by breaching it. The American reporter, Kate Kryzewski, had flown in to deliver her last story, with the biggest ratings any newscast would ever have.

Beneath an Armani Puffa jacket, designed to keep out a New York winter, she wore the patched rags of the kitchen girl, Columbine. A tambourine rattled at her hip and her feet were bare and blue with cold.

With a microphone in her hand and a cameraman walking backwards in front of her, she roamed the nearside of the barricade, speaking to the people at the front. They were all watching the evening's spectacular on their phones or tablets or laptops and were full of praise.

"It's good to see aberrants put to such a good use," a group of middle-aged women dressed as wenches said. "Watching them try and run away from the beasts is the best fun we can remember here in these dreams."

"Ooh, when the Jacks and Jills did that swap! What a brilliant trick that were. Our Ismus is so incredible. What'll he do next?"

"Wish I had some of that minchet ointment. I'd fly up there and show him exactly what he could do next!"

The women whooped with raucous laughter.

"I keep voting for Mauger," said a student, wearing one of the plastic suits of armour that had been a bestseller in Topman throughout the past year. "It sucks he never wins."

"And what about you, Ma'am?" Kate asked an elderly woman, wrapped in a car blanket, sitting in a deckchair.

The woman didn't answer. She'd been dead for three days. The reporter gave a light, professional laugh and breezed on to the next group.

"Can't wait to get our hands on *Fighting Pax*!" declared a couple dressed as an Under King and Queen. "To be in Mooncaster and never come back here... can't happen fast enough. First thing I'll do is order a feast from the kitchens. I feel as though I haven't eaten for a week."

"Well, not long till midnight now, Sir," Kate told him. "Then we'll all go together and I'll get that feast sorted for you. There'll be lots of geese to pluck and onions to peel for me tonight, that's for sure. But what a send-off, huh? What a great show."

"My best bit was when the spider things got the shouty girl," said an eleven-year-old boy done up as a page. His face was pinched with cold and starvation and his voice was frail. "I wish the big jackals had eaten more of them shepherds. Is it time to go yet? I've got so much work to do at the real castle."

"And what do you think of the Christmas story being told here tonight?" Kate asked a man sitting in front of a small tent.

"Load of tripe," he answered. "Didn't some people here used to believe that guff? Were they moonkissed? I've grown cabbages with more brains. Total codswallop. If they can't even get the start of that story right, what other lies come after? If it weren't for the Ismus doing it his way, it'd be unwatchable. I'd rather have seen him do the one with the terrorists and the guy in the sweaty vest though, to be honest. That would've been excellent."

"Did you never celebrate this Christmas holiday here?" she asked.

"I can't really remember. I think so. Yeah, I think I had three young kids in my dream family, so I guess I would've. No idea where they are now. I just want to get back to my strip of land and bring in the parsnips – and down a big bowlful of stew."

Kate thanked him and turned her back to that ocean of faces.

"So there we have it. A unanimous thumbs up for tonight's broadcast, but not so much for the Nativity baloney. I'm inclined to agree. I was never into half-baked fantasy either. This is the Two of Hearts, Columbine, signing off for the final time as Kate Kryzewski. Blessed be, everyone. See you real soon in the one true world – the Kingdom of the Dawn Prince."

As she said goodbye, a slight commotion was rippling through the massive crowd. Something was travelling down one of the service roads and astonished voices were whispering the name Malinda.

25

IN THE REALM of the Dawn Prince, behind the encircling hills, dawn was creeping into the late summer sky. Upon Judgement Hill, rising far above Battle Wood, the octagonal tower of the Black Keep reared into the early morning. On its lofty summit, beneath the illuminated dome, the four silent, robed figures continued their age-old game.

The creature called Grumbles appeared from the hatch, bearing his silver salver, to collect the spent cards. Gazing out beyond the withered forest, across the plain, he saw the threads of smoke rising from the White Castle and the scorched fields behind the village. Thoughtful, and pondering on the meaning of these forbidding signs, he chewed the inside of his cheek.

Big events were transpiring over there. They would never impact on his life in the tower, but he still wondered what they were. The Ismus would be sure to tell him, next time he called.

Grumbles studied the sky. The strongest stars were failing with the climbing dawn. He lamented it had not been a better night for catching bats, and he smacked his lips hungrily; he'd fancied a fritter or two. He told himself he'd better be quick about gathering up the scattered cards:

another day of fetching and cleaning lay ahead of him.

His goat-like hooves trotted nimbly to the stone table and he was soon busily occupied. The robed figures made no movement. As usual, they didn't acknowledge his presence, but he knew just how important he was to them. Without their Conservius, the players would not be able to continue the game for long, oh, no.

Humming softly to himself, he glanced idly at the cards in the players' skeletal hands and almost dropped the tray.

Two of the cards in that new deck were decorated in gold leaf. That made them the rarest and most powerful of designs. To his knowledge, in the entire history of the game there had only ever been seven gold cards in all of the countless packs that filled the floors of the tower. Fascinated and apprehensive, he edged a little closer in order to see what the nature of those cards were. One was the image of Sacrifice, but he could only see a gilt corner of the other.

Grumbles stepped away from the table and leaned against one of the pillars fearfully.

In the past, every time a golden card had been played the consequences had been catastrophic. They had changed worlds. And here were two of them! He lifted his eyes to the fading stars once more and pulled on his side whiskers anxiously. Doom and disaster were drawing nigh. Turning back to the game, he saw the bony hand of the figure that had turned to look at Lee cast the hidden card down.

Betrayal.

In the county of Kent, that ravaged terrain once called the garden of England, midnight was drawing closer.

"Did I hear somebody say they were hungry?" the Ismus called out. "Shall we take a break for sustenance before we hunker down and read *Fighting Pax*?"

The volume of the answering roar blasted painfully in the ears. The Ismus revelled in it and strutted round the console.

"But how can I provide for all of you out there, my dear subjects?"

This was the cue for a small child to step up on to the gatehouse roof and trot over to him. It was little Nabi. She had been given a costume to suit her character in *Dancing Jax* and in her hands she carried a large basket.

"Please, Holy Enchanter!" she piped up, tugging at the tails of his leather jerkin as had been rehearsed. "I could not help but overhear. I am taking this to my father, the Constable, for his supper, but you may have it if it will help."

"Why!" the Ismus exclaimed. "It's Posy, the snoop. How generous you are. But what is in the basket, dear child?"

"Five loaves and two fishes," she said smartly.

The Ismus gave a knowing look into the lens.

"Sounds familiar," he said with a wink. "Although they couldn't even agree on how many loaves there were in that book of lies: five, seven – who cares? Let's see what we can do with some fish and buns."

The trumpeters played a fanfare. When the blaring notes ended, the sound of helicopter blades could be heard in the sky. Searchlights swept up and a fleet of 200 aircraft moved in from every direction. Hovering over the vast crowds, they disgorged millions of small boxes. Tumbling through beams of light, the containers fell into countless eager hands on the ground below.

"McManna from heaven," the Ismus laughed as the lucky ones wolfed down Filet-O-Fish. Then he put a hand to his nose and coughed. "Oh, dear, what is that terrible smell?"

"It's him!" little Nabi cried, pointing at the dishevelled, filth-covered man stepping on to the gatehouse roof, behind the Jockey and two of the Black Face Dames.

"Mr Baxter!" the Ismus greeted. "You'll understand if I don't shake hands."

"Is he the midden-man?" Nabi asked. "I must kick him."

"Later, child," the Ismus told her. "This one has been kicked quite a lot already. Is that not so, Martin?"

Martin gazed out at the unimaginable numbers beyond the barriers and raised his eyes to the helicopters that were still circling and dispensing boxes to the starving mass of people.

"One last sick joke?"

"Rather like myself in skintight leather, Martin, it was impossible to resist. But there is a very serious and sensible purpose behind it. My worshipping public will need some strength in them, once they've finished reading. They've got to be strong enough to fight."

"Fight? Who or what?"

"Each other, naturally."

Martin stared at him in disbelief and revulsion.

"I've always maintained that wars don't work. This is my final solution. For maximum lasting impact, you don't turn country against country, you don't march crusading armies into battle. The deepest, cruellest wounds are personal. You turn one person against the next, neighbour against neighbour, sister against brother, father against daughter, husband against wife, friend against friend, child against adult, blood against blood, suit against suit, number against number. They're playing cards in the cut-throat game of my devising. And then..."

"Then?"

"Then the survivors, the ones left standing or merely unlucky enough to still draw breath, those murderers with blood on their hands are all unfriended and they suddenly realise what they've done. In a world without hope, where only despair and horror rule, what do you think they'll do? Should be even more entertaining to watch."

Martin felt sick.

"But you and Carol and Paul will be fine," the Ismus assured him. "Don't worry. I'll guarantee your protection."

"Expect me to believe that? You're madder than you sound and that's a real achievement."

"Would you like to see your lady love?" the Ismus asked curiously. "See her and Paul together, mother and son at last?"

"Don't taunt me, you son of – well, no one knows what you're the son of, do they? You were the Devil's cuckoo in the Fellows' nest."

"Don't be boorish, Baxter. You already said all that in your monotonous blogs and ranting interviews. Such tinfoil-hat-worthy ravings, most amusing. Did you ever pause to consider how delusional and paranoid you sounded? You gave *Dancing Jax* fantastic publicity. I couldn't have wished for a better global marketing campaign. I was delighted. So just answer me – do you want to see them or not?"

Martin nodded.

The Ismus grinned and strode to the centre of the roof, waiting for witchcam to come flying down for a close-up.

"And so, my friends," he addressed the world one last time, "the moment, long anticipated, is here. The time of rapture, when, together, we shall read the furtherance of the hallowed text and the way shall be opened. Never again shall we dream of this depressing place. But, before the manuscript goes live for you to download and awake eternally in Mooncaster, let us conclude this night's entertainment with a final look at the colossal lie at the heart of this farce they called Christmas."

He clicked his fingers. High overhead there began the clanking and squeaking of metal and machinery. The jib of the crane, from which the neon star was suspended, started to turn. It angled away from the eastern section of the castle, out towards the west. On top of the West Tower where, in the book, the House of Hearts dwelt, arc lights suddenly flashed on.

Martin darted forward at what he saw there, in the distance, but the Black Face Dames restrained him.

The harsh glare of the lights revealed a rustic-looking structure built on top of the tower. It had a narrow, pointed roof, covered in mossy tiles. There were no walls, just four square posts at each corner. Beneath the roof was a manger. It was a life-sized Nativity scene, but there were only three figures. In a costume identical to the one Esther had worn earlier that night was Carol Thornbury. At her side, her eldest son, Paul, had been divested of his royal robes and was now dressed as a drummer boy.

Leaning over the manger, with a knife poised above it as a warning, was a Punchinello. When the lights came on, the guard put the knife away and stepped out of the tableau. Carol and Paul were free to move and speak.

Carol immediately reached in and took her infant son from the straw-filled ox stall and held him desperately. Then she turned to see where Paul was pointing, down over the battlements to the gatehouse.

"Martin!" they shouted at the ragged man. "Martin!"

Martin couldn't hear them above the din of the departing helicopters and the excited multitude. But he saw them and his heart leaped.

"Carol!" he yelled. "Carol! Paul!"

The woman rose. She wanted to run down there and press the baby into his arms, then kiss him and never let go. But the Punchinello was lurking behind the lights. They weren't allowed to leave this spot.

Carol held out the swaddled baby. "He's yours, Martin!" she cried. "He's yours! This is your son! I love you so much!"

"He can't hear us, Mum," Paul said. "He can't hear us."

Holding on to one another, they stared down at the gatehouse.

"Let me go to them!" Martin raged, straining to get free of the Black Face Dames. "I've got to see her! You promised!"

"Ah ah," the Ismus warned. "Not yet – you still haven't given your party piece. That's coming up next. Whilst the world is reading *Fighting Pax*, your performance is going to be my own personal diversion. So remember, you have to give your all. I'm looking to be impressed here. I'm a very harsh critic and won't be satisfied with any half-hearted effort."

"What've I got to do?"

"One moment, Mr Baxter. I do believe..."

The orchestra struck up a rousing fanfare and the chimes of Big Ben were broadcast live from London.

"Midnight!" the Ismus proclaimed as an even greater barrage of fireworks than earlier boomed in the sky, creating a canopy of brilliant, jewelled fire, high over the castle. "The new text is now released to every one of my servers around the world. Good people of Mooncaster, are you sitting comfortably? Then let us end this grey dream once and for always. I, the Holy Enchanter, give you... *Fighting Pax*! Download it and welcome home!"

The cheers and roars of jubilation jolted through Martin's bones more violently than the exploding rockets. It was staggering and terrible; the world was spiralling towards the end of everything.

And then, abruptly, the deafening riot ceased and the last falling sparks were extinguished in the moat. The unnatural silence that followed was even more frightening. Stillness gripped the planet. It happened so fast, it was as if an iron fist had smashed the world's voice and Martin's ears rang with the loss.

Dragging his eyes away from the West Tower, he gazed out over the countryside and saw the ghostly glow of over a hundred million hand-held devices, stretching to the horizon. It was like moonlight on the ocean, and that illusion was reinforced when the lights began to move, rippling like waves. Martin knew the people were rocking backwards and forwards as they read. The haunting image imprinted on his soul. The population of the earth was reading *Fighting Pax*. Seven billion minds were entering that strange other world.

The faint shouts of Carol and Paul made him wrest his eyes away. Finally he could hear them.

"We'll be together soon!" he called.

"Martin!" Carol cried out, holding the baby up again. "He's—"

The noise of an explosion blotted out her words. But this was no firework. A fireball erupted in the great distance, among the crowd.

"Dear, dear," the Ismus tutted. "That pilot really should have waited to land before starting to read."

Another explosion followed, then many more. Fiery roses blossomed across the glimmering landscape as other helicopters dropped out of the sky.

"Such impatience, not like my Black Face Dames and the Harlequin Priests. They have selflessly vowed not to dip into the manuscript until my night's work is complete."

The Jockey stepped forward. "What of me, my Lord?" he asked humbly.

The Ismus smiled indulgently. "Of course. Take yourself away to the Great Hall and enter the furtherance with the rest of the Court there. You have behaved yourself well this night, my caramel-coloured jackanapes. I thank you for that. Go and find your deserved reward – and take Posy here with you. I'm sure she is also anxious to read *Fighting Pax*."

"I want to get home and be partic'lar nosy!" little Nabi declared with an emphatic nod. "I want to hide behind tapestries and under tables, and spy through keyholes and listen at windows."

"Be off with you then. Very shortly you shall uncover the best secret of them all."

Nabi clapped her hands joyously. The Jockey pointed a toe and bowed. Then they descended the steps and headed for the Keep.

The Ismus moved to the Bakelite console and was pleased to

discover two more symbols illuminated. His fingers eased a control along its slot. Then he unhooked a horn-shaped microphone that hung at the side.

"Swazzle," he spoke into it. "Be an angel: round up the stray sheep, shepherds and wise men and take them to the crib. It's far too bare up there at the moment. Use whatever force you deem appropriate."

The Punchinello's answering voice snickered foully.

"And no, I haven't forgotten you, Martin," the Ismus muttered, not looking up from the dials. "Do you recall this morning, when I said I'd brought a few things from home? This is one of them. I know how much of a sci-fi freak you are. Isn't it ravishing? And still way ahead of its time. My sister, Augusta, helped me devise it; she was a genius with a cat's whisker. Another souvenir of home has been built into the side of the Keep. Can you guess what it is?"

Martin shook his head.

"No matter. I doubt you'd appreciate it. Now where were we?"

Looking up over the top of the console, the crooked smile stole across his face.

"I reckon my avid fan base have about twenty minutes before they put down their e-readers and begin killing one another. Barely time enough for you to save the ones who are left, if you have the courage, and if you want to join the happy Nativity scene on the West Tower."

"Save them?" Martin asked in confusion. "How?"

The Ismus turned his face towards the unlit South Tower. He flicked a switch and a single spotlight shone on the top of the turret.

Martin narrowed his eyes. Was that a bench or a table up there? No, it was a person lying on a medical bed, covered in a pale green sheet.

Monitoring equipment and a stand holding a saline drip were close by. It was too far away to see who that patient was.

"Regardez our Castle Creeper," the Ismus enlightened him.

"Lee?"

"Yes, the Peckham hard nut or should I say 'Brazil nut'? is sleeping, deep as death. Since I shipped him from North Korea, his earthly body has been kept safe and well, as I promised him it would."

"So what's he doing up there?"

"That, Martin, is your party piece. Even as we speak, in that other Realm, the Creeper is approaching the cave of the Cinnamon Bear, where the Bad Shepherd has been hiding. It won't be long now before he accomplishes his part of the pact. He loves his girlfriend so much he's going to commit one of the most heinous deeds in creation. I sooo admire him for that. You do comprehend the significance of what he's about to do, don't you?"

"I know who the Bad Shepherd is supposed to be."

The Ismus snorted. "Oh, he's not just the Bethlehem birthday boy! The Bad Shepherd is the embodiment of every prophet. Not only the ones with top billing. I was very thorough when I compiled the sacred text, you see. I created a watertight contract and nothing was left to chance; there are no loopholes or get-out clauses. When the Creeper kills the shepherd, the laws that govern such things will erase all knowledge, all memory, all writings of those intolerant advocates. It will be as if they never existed here. Every place of worship shall disappear; religious art and music will vanish and be forgotten."

"Isn't what you've already done enough?" Martin asked. "What's the point?"

"Pay attention at the back, Baxter. When my murderous readers are finally unfriended and realise the brutal horrors they are guilty of, there will be no quarter, no sliver of hope, no forgiveness for them, no one to pray to – only intolerable despair. Those woebegones will seek to make an end of it and, before sunrise, there won't be very many people left in the world at all. Naturally, human nature being what it is, not everyone will be overcome with remorse and embrace suicide as the only option, but what an interesting place it will be, populated with such psychotic detritus. I'm really looking forward to it."

"Not much of a kingdom for you to rule over."

The Ismus looked disappointed in him. "I haven't done this for me, Martin. But, if you don't wish to live in a world of psychopaths, I'm giving you the chance to make it less bleak."

Reaching for the golden dagger at his hip, he drew it from the red velvet scabbard and held the hilt towards Martin.

"Take it," he said. "Go on, I brought it specially for you to use."

Suspicious, Martin reached out and grasped it, sliding the glittering blade out of the Ismus's hands.

"Don't get any impulsive ideas," the Holy Enchanter warned when he saw the man glance quickly at the Black Face Dames and read his intention. "They'd rip your arms off. Besides, you can't use that puny weapon against Austerly Fellows. I'm beyond the reach of such things now."

"Why don't I find that out for myself?"

"You're wasting time. In roughly fifteen minutes, when my readers emerge from *Fighting Pax* and go berserk, do you want to save the guilt-ridden survivors or not?"

"How am I supposed to do that?"

"Add it up, Martin, add it up. The Castle Creeper is going to kill the Bad Shepherd, yes? So all you have to do... is get to the Creeper first and prevent him. That's what the dagger is for."

"What?" Martin cried. "Kill Lee?"

"It's the only way to stop your precious prophets from being erased. Who will my unfriended readers turn to in their darkest moment if not to them? Think of the billions of suicides you'll be preventing."

"You're seriously asking me to murder Lee?"

"Not asking you at all, no. I'd prefer it if you didn't, but I'm offering you a chance to be the saviour you always wanted to be, Martin. This is the performance I want from you tonight; this is your speciality act, your golden opportunity to shine. If you pull it off, just look at what you'll win: possibly half the population of the world rescued from the pits of anguish and, best of all, you get to play happy families with Paul and Carol... and your baby son."

"My son?"

"Yes, Martin. That bonny infant playing gentle Jesus so convincingly up there is your flesh and blood. I should have asked Swazzle for one of his ostentatious cigars for you. Congratulations."

"My son..." Martin repeated, staring at the West Tower, where Carol and Paul were gazing down at him.

His mind was in turmoil. Months ago, from the moment he'd learned about the pregnancy, he'd never dared dream the child might be his. He couldn't begin to process the emotions that were battering and smashing against him. He felt like the smallest of boats, floundering in a tempest. But, up there, Carol, Paul and his baby, they were his beacon. They were the guiding lights of home. He would do anything to be with them. Anything.

"It's not as if you even liked the Creeper," the Ismus continued. "He was council-estate scum – a mindless thug from a violent gang. Weren't you two always at each other's throats in that draughty mountain? He won't feel a thing, you know. One swift thrust in the chest or neck will do it. He's just lying there, in a vegetative state that he'll never recover from. He may as well be dead already. It would be a mercy – and think of the atrocity he's about to commit in that other Realm. You'll be saving Jesus Christ himself, not to mention all those other sandalled seers. You'd be a bloody hero, Martin – a bona-fide saviour of the race."

Another symbol illuminated on the dial of the console.

"What's the quickest way there?" Martin demanded.

The Ismus grinned. "Through that arch, turn right, then up the first flight of steps that takes you to the top of the inner curtain wall. Follow the sentry walk around, till you come to the tower, and climb the spiral stairway within. But you must run, Martin. Run before it's too late – before the Creeper kills the Bad Shepherd."

Martin Baxter was already leaping down the gatehouse steps. The Ismus threw back his head and laughed. This was better than he had hoped it would be.

He watched the man charge over the courtyard and heard his footfalls echo beneath an archway. Then his amusement changed to sneering contempt.

"Covered in the excrement of swine and rushing to kill a boy in a coma... the famous Martin Baxter. Could you have sunk any lower?

The rest of the world is under the spell of my book and can't help themselves. What's your excuse? You're worse than all of them. I didn't expect it would be so easy. You disgust even me. How readily you became a beast to flee from."

"Still," he said, "at least Jangler will be avenged."

Returning his attention to the console, he examined the meters. The levels were rising. Out there in the vast crowd the first whimpers of distress were beginning, as the readers experienced the traumas of *Fighting Pax*. The Ismus judged it was time for the next phase. Making the necessary adjustments, he whirled about to view the forest of cranes surrounding the castle.

The valves within the console began to hum and pulse. There was a pop and a spit of sparks and streaks of energy crackled along the cables that snaked from the back. Ribbons of blue light raced through the connections. Moments later, arcs of electricity were travelling up the steel masts.

"Such magnificent antennae," he declared proudly. "The signal shall be strong and clear."

Forks of lightning began to lick out from the jibs overhead. The neon star shattered, and fizzing sparks showered down on to the roof of the Nativity scene. Some bounced down on to the straw and set it alight. Paul rushed to stamp out the flames. Carol returned the baby to the manger and helped him. Across the castle, arc lights were exploding.

The crane jibs began to move. Turning inwards, they changed position, grazing and scraping over themselves with the sounds of squealing metal. Each one had been placed with extreme accuracy and the path they traced had been carefully calculated. In that shifting cat's cradle of steel, a pattern was beginning to form. The jibs started to align, creating long diagonals, criss-crossing high above the castle until, finally, it was done.

"Yes!" the Ismus shouted, gazing up in feverish excitement.

Dominating the sky above was an immense pentacle, and the lightning ripped and raged about it.

At the base of the Keep, close to the forty-metre-high Christmas tree, the other souvenir from Felixstowe was quaking and deep cracks radiated through the cobbled yard from it. The old wartime bunker that Austerly Fellows had built on the shoreline had been carefully excavated and removed in one massive piece and transported here. The castle stones had been laid around it and the wall of the Keep constructed on top. It was the only way to bring the Dark Door, which was set into it, here – for that great iron barrier was impossible to open from the outside. Now its rusty surface was bristling with whiskers of branching energy and tremors juddered through the concrete surround. There was a splutter of fire and a thin line began to burn over the metal's surface, drawing a glowing symbol of a serpent and a crescent moon.

The Norwegian spruce's thousands of fairy lights popped and banged like rapid gunfire and the tinsel-draped branches began to whip and flail the air as a windstorm came gusting through the archways.

At the console, the Ismus watched the levels rise on the gauges and he teased the controls around.

"Abase yourselves," he commanded the Black Face Dames. "He is returning! The one true Majesty."

The three bodyguards dropped to their knees and bowed their heads.

"Hail to the Dawn Prince," the Ismus proclaimed. "The Bearer of

Light! The Shining One, He who was cast down. The term of Your exile is over. The way is open. Come amongst us once more – in this realm I have prepared."

Lightning scored the night and the castle jumped in and out of the stark, shivering flashes. Beneath the earth, a monstrous roar sounded. The ground shook. Scaffolding collapsed and loose stones went toppling from the walls.

With a thunderous blast, the Dark Door crumpled like tin and shot across the fractured courtyard, clanging like a discordant bell, tolling the cataclysmic end.

The shadows within the concrete bunker were churning thickly. Streaks of blood-red flame came flying out. At once, the huge Christmas tree ignited and fire engulfed every branch.

Then from the gaping doorway burst a shining crimson shape. It flew to the burning spruce and spiralled swiftly up the trunk before leaping back to the scaffold round the Keep. The steel poles turned a cherry red as it climbed and the boards turned to ash.

On the roof, the Harlequin Priests observed the pinnacle of flame the tree had become and heard the roar of He who was returning. Raising their arms in adoration, they turned to greet and worship Him.

A glare, like an angry dawn, rose over the roof's edge.

The Harlequins' eyes shrivelled like raisins. Their faces charred and flaked away, as their bodies became torches.

Lucifer ascended the Waiting Throne.

26

DESPITE BEING OVERAWED by the sight of the audience beyond the castle walls, Maggie had still insisted that finding the postern gate was their only chance. Conor argued strongly, but she was adamant. He tried to make her see sense. There was no way they'd be allowed to get out of here. But she was determined to lead Charm's girls to a place of safety. The other shepherds and Lukas had total faith in her. Emma and Sandra wanted to break out too and, as Conor couldn't suggest an alternative, it was decided.

While Martin Baxter was being led to the Ismus, they were hurrying along the walls towards the rear of the castle, running round incomplete towers and over plank bridges. Passing the great, glittering Christmas tree on their left, they made their way behind the Keep and were overjoyed when, up ahead, they saw a flight of steps leading down to the largest door any of the aberrants had ever seen.

"That's it!" Blueberry Muffin cried out gleefully. "The back door, the back door!"

The other girls took up her cries and surged forward, running heedlessly into the shadows of a covered walkway that ran between them and the stairs.

"Not so fast!" Maggie called as they charged past her and the other shepherds. "Be careful!"

The little sheep didn't listen.

"Wait!" Conor shouted. "Come back."

"Oh, let them have a laugh," Emma told him. "Poor little sods."

"There's still jackals on the loose," Conor answered. "Been too long since we've seen or heard them. They could be lying in wait in there."

Suddenly Blueberry Muffin let out a scream, swiftly followed by her friends.

Gripping their swords, fearing the worst, Maggie and Conor rushed into the covered walk. The other teenagers raced after them.

Moments later, when they reached the girls, they were astonished to find them laughing.

"Webs!" Dandelion and Burdock explained. "There was webs all across here. We ran into them."

"Doggy-Long-Legs?" Maggie asked urgently, glaring around at the gloomy corners.

"Not them, silly," Lemon Cheesecake told her. "Just ordinary spiders' webs."

"They're still horrid and scary when they wrap round your face," another girl put in.

Maggie and the others almost wept with relief and they hugged the giggling flock and ruffled their hair for frightening them.

The spiders had arrived from greenhouses, with the out-of-season plants for the ornamental gardens. They'd tried to escape sudden exposure to the winter cold and had spun large webs, but they hadn't survived a day. Maggie glanced up at the long wooden ceiling, where many small, curled-up bodies dangled from broken, frosty threads – and something else. It looked like a large smut or fuzzy speck of black fluff, snagged on a gossamer strand.

"We go extra careful from now on," she cautioned everyone. "Lambs stay behind us older kids, yeah? No running off without us."

The girls promised.

And then the clock had struck midnight. The fireworks erupted overhead and the chimes of Big Ben were broadcast over the speakers.

They didn't understand what any of it meant, but it was the best possible diversion.

Conor and Maggie were about to lead the way down the steps when the eerie hush descended, as the world began reading *Fighting Pax*.

Forgetting the stairs for the moment, everyone crowded to the embrasures to look out and see what was happening. Staring out from the battlements, they witnessed the huge expanse of e-readers glimmering across the landscape and wondered what was going on.

"Doesn't matter," Maggie muttered, alarmed by how loud her voice suddenly sounded in that profound silence. "As long as them zombies are stuck in Mooncaster, we can get past them."

"It is the answer to a prayer," Lukas breathed, crossing himself.

Conor nudged Maggie. "OK, I take it back," he admitted. "This mad idea of yours might just work!"

"Course it will," Blueberry Muffin told him. "Maggie's chuffing brilliant."

"I think you're right," he said, smiling. "Bit bossy though."

"Bloody hell, Westlake," Emma hissed. "Give your codpiece a rest."

"Makes a change from when he was the Jack of Clubs," Sandra added with a laugh. "He wouldn't look at anyone who didn't have four legs."

"Well, I've had better," Maggie stated flatly. "So he's wasting his time if he is."

"Oi!" Conor objected, but it was all good-natured teasing. Their spirits were high. At last escape from this harrowing place actually seemed possible and they dared to let themselves hope.

Then the helicopters began to crash into the crowds and they remembered there was still a very long way to go before they would ever feel safe – if they ever would.

"Down the stairs," Maggie whispered grimly. "Time to ditch this dump."

Conor went first, then Emma and Sandra. The little sheep followed, with Lukas and the shepherds. Maggie counted everyone down. Before joining them, she glanced back warily, along the shadowy covered walk. Nothing was prowling behind them, except...

That unusual black fluff caught her attention again. Now it was bobbing and jiggling about on the spider's thread. It wasn't caught in a breeze; the other strands of broken web around it were barely moving at all. It was as if this dark fleck was trying to free itself.

Curious, she stepped beneath it for a closer look. It was more like a seed head – like sooty thistledown.

Maggie reached up.

The postern gate was a huge arched double door, several metres wide and tall enough to drive a lorry through. It made Charm's girls feel as small as Lego people. The iron hinges were longer than Conor's arms and the timbers were covered with studs the size of his fist. Three bolts, as thick as his wrist, were drawn across the centre and he began wrenching the first aside.

The others were tackling the stout wooden beam that barred the door, sliding it along the runners, when Maggie joined them.

Her face was so ashen, Conor stopped what he was doing and asked if she was feeling all right.

Blueberry Muffin tried to hold her hand, but Maggie pulled away.

"I'm fine," she said. "Had a funny turn up there just then, that's all. I should've ate more earlier."

"You sure?" the boy persisted. "You look half dead."

Emma rolled her eyes. "Killer chat-up line, Westlake," she said sarcastically.

Conor frowned and started pulling the second bolt back.

Charm's girls stared at Maggie, their young faces creased with concern. She didn't look at all well.

"What's that?" Sandra said suddenly. "Listen..."

Everyone froze, expecting to hear the clattering of jackal claws on the cobbles. Instead they heard a delicate clip-clop. It was too dainty a sound for a horse.

The little sheep had heard it before.

"Open it!" they cried to Conor as he struggled to reach the final bolt that was high above his head. "It's the bones. The bones are here!"

Conor didn't know what they meant. Jumping up, he tried to knock the bolt back, but it wouldn't budge.

"It's stuck!" he said.

"No, it's you," Emma berated him. "You're useless. Give me a bunk-up – I'll do it. And watch where you put your hands!"

Before he could lift her, they heard the steady pace of the light hoof falls turn into a trot. Everyone stared at the deep shadows, where that outer wall met the ground, and saw a hideous shape cantering towards them.

It was the unicorn skeleton. The Ismus had let it patrol the castle's rear walls as a guardian of the postern gate.

Charm's girls screamed and pulled the others away.

"You can't fight that!" they cried when Conor reached for his sword and the shepherds braced themselves.

Shaking its macabre head, the skeleton ran at them.

"Back to the stairs!" Conor yelled fiercely.

The girls spun round. To their horror, they saw that Captain Swazzle and his Punchinellos had gathered silently in the courtyard behind them. Bezuel was now standing at the foot of the steps and the four jackals were by his side, snarling menacingly. There was no possible escape.

The unicorn's jaw opened and it emitted an unearthly shriek. It barged in front of the great wooden door and the children fell back from it in terror. Rearing up, the skeleton thrashed its front hooves in the air.

"That's the way to do it!" Captain Swazzle crowed. "Oh, yes, oh, yes!"

The other Punchinellos snickered, their beady eyes flicking from one petrified face to the next.

"We fetch you," Swazzle barked. "Ismus want. You come."

The aberrants couldn't believe how near they'd got to escaping.

Just a minute or two more and they would have succeeded. It was devastating. Sandra couldn't bear it.

"We were so close," she uttered bitterly. "So close."

"Now!" Swazzle bawled.

The sheep stepped falteringly towards him. The shepherds followed.

"You can sod right off," Emma shouted defiantly. "I'm not shifting. I'm done – that's it. Show's over!"

"Emma!" Conor warned her. "What are you doing?"

"They won't be taking us nowhere good, Westlake," she said. "I'm not gonna make it easy for them. I've had it. They want me, they'll have to carry me."

A horrendous grin split Swazzle's face. He had been hoping for some resistance. He had expected it to come from the mouthy female shepherd, but she was unusually quiet. At last she had been cowed.

Swaggering up to Emma, he bared his mottled teeth.

"You no obey?" he asked, just to make certain.

"Swivel," she said.

"Swazzle," he corrected.

"No," she told him, raising her hand. "I meant swivel – on this."

His eyes bulged in astonishment and he shuddered. Then he staggered back, away from the dripping dagger in her grasp. Clutching his throat, he collapsed, his stumpy legs flailing, as founts of dark blood spouted over the cobbled yard. Gargling hideously, Captain Swazzle died.

"Now *that* is the way to do it," Emma complimented herself.

The other Punchinellos gaped at their dead Captain in shock, stunned that anyone would be so bold – and stupid – as to kill him.

"You're crazy!" Conner bawled at her. "What did you do that for?"

"Oh, wake up, you tool. We ain't getting out of here, and I wanted to take one of them evil gonks down before I kark it."

"Still only thinking of yourself," he said angrily. "What about these kids?"

"They was on their way to the abattoir anyway. So stop whining and get stuck in with that sword."

"Don't have a choice now," he seethed.

"You too," Emma told Maggie. "Carve up as many as you can."

As one, the Punchinellos screeched shrilly. Brandishing their blades and squawking vengeful oaths, they charged – leaping over their Captain's body and splashing through his blood. Bezuel ordered the jackals to attack and lunged after them. The children huddled together. The unicorn skeleton stamped its hooves and lowered its head.

Sandra was so petrified, the world seemed to slow down and she perceived everything that happened next in minute detail. She saw the savage faces of the advancing Punchinellos contort into endless vicious forms with each new scream for death. She witnessed the powerful muscles of the demonic jackals flex and quiver as they leaped to tear the aberrants apart. Hearing the unicorn's baneful screech, she turned and saw it lunging for her.

Then the timbers of the door behind it rippled and a brilliant flash of light shone between the widening joints. The wood splintered. The unicorn fragmented and a blast of sound slammed into her.

The explosion threw her off her feet. Everything was spinning. Sandra saw the young girls flying past her. Punchinellos were tumbling and jackals were rolling through the air. Then she struck the ground.

Everywhere was noise and smoke and confusion, yelps and groaning.

Children and Punchinellos were sprawled on the cobbles, among splinters of burning wood. Conor raised his head. A trickle of blood ran through his blond hair. He reached for his sword, but it had been hurled across the yard. Emma had cut her hand on her dagger and she swore loudly. Charm's girls were already sitting up and tapping their ears. The bang had been deafening. The shepherds crawled to them and checked they were OK. Maggie was lying face down. Lukas nudged her gently.

Maggie muttered under her breath and turned over.

She looked on the wreckage of the postern gate. It was in shattered pieces. The large hinges were swinging at angles, with only split shards of wood attached. Smoke was billowing through the ragged gap. Shifting her gaze, Maggie saw the unicorn's smashed and scattered bones strewn about the yard. A jackal lay on its side, whining, impaled by the twisted horn, and another had been killed by the flying shrapnel of an iron stud. The other two were dazed and staggered drunkenly when they attempted to stand.

The Punchinellos were croaking and gasping. Bruised and jarred by the explosion, they picked themselves from the floor and retrieved their swords.

A sliver of unicorn bone was stuck in Bezuel's chin and he tore it out with a squawk. None of them knew what had happened, but they'd had a bellyful. It was time to butcher these aberrants.

"Throw down your weapons!" a hectoring female voice commanded beyond the ruined gate. "Down, I say!"

Bezuel glared at the swirling smoke and shook his fist defiantly.

"Stand and disclose," he demanded.

"I won't tell you again!" the unseen woman warned. "Put the swords down and step over to the wall, with your hands behind your heads."

The Punchinellos glanced at one another in bemusement. Who was that out there?

The children peered at the doorway and held their breaths as a tall figure came swishing serenely through the smoke.

"You gotta be kiddin' me," Emma breathed.

The little sheep clasped their hands to their mouths in wonder.

Thoroughly startled, Bezuel and the other guards blinked – and then broke into mocking laughter.

Stepping into the courtyard, Gerald Benning's alter ego, Professor Evelyn Hole, arched her finely drawn brows and, over the rims of her spectacles, regarded them severely.

She was dressed as Malinda. A beautifully made costume, with a full crinoline dress of ruched gold silk over layers of peach tulle, was a relic of her one and only foray into pantomime as Mother Goose. With a shawl of silver lace, sprinkled with sequins, it was perfect for the retired Fairy Godmother of *Dancing Jax*. Bandages wrapped round folded paper plates, splashed with red ink and stapled to the back of the bodice, formed Malinda's mutilated wings. A length of aluminium tubing, bent at one end where a plastic Christmas star was glued, made a fine magic wand to complete the outfit – and it had all worked like a dream.

Malinda was one of the most important Aces in the book. No one would dare challenge her. Evelyn had sailed through every security check on the way to the castle without hindrance.

The Punchinellos could scarcely believe what they were looking at. As Evelyn, Gerald made a very convincing, slightly comical, elderly woman and the guards didn't realise they were staring at a man in drag. The sight of Evelyn was so unexpected and out of place, and her manner so imperious, they couldn't help but jeer and snigger.

"Get behind me, children," Evelyn's clipped voice instructed, beckoning them with the wand. "What funny little lambs. I shall feel quite like Marie Antoinette at the *Petit Trianon*, playing at being a shepherdess."

The girls didn't know what to make of her and hung back shyly. She looked so incongruous and surreal. Conor was totally confused and Sandra thought she'd hit her head and was hallucinating. Then Lemon Cheesecake saw through the wig and make-up and squealed with delight.

"It's Gerald!" she cried. "Maggie – it's Gerald. He's not dead!"

"Don't speak to me about Gerald," Evelyn upbraided her. "The lazy old fool decided to stay in Felixstowe, leaving me to do all the dirty work. What a muddle he's made of everything! It's a good job I've assumed command to sort out this mess."

The girls rushed to her in delight. Evelyn summoned the older ones and they approached with baffled faces.

"You too," Evelyn called to Maggie who was still on the ground. "Don't dawdle, dear."

The Punchinellos stopped laughing. This joke had gone on long enough.

"You no go no place," Bezuel ordered. "The rejects is ours."

Evelyn straightened her back and glared at him witheringly.

"You're supposed to be standing against the wall, you odious little gnome," she said. "You had ample warning."

"What you do about it?" he snarled.

"You leave me no alternative. I shall have to destroy you."

The guards hooted once more. "You, fairy queen? You and what army?"

A second figure strode through the ragged doorway. It was a young, fierce-looking woman in a khaki uniform, her bright, platinum-blonde hair tucked under a military cap.

"Korean People's Army!" Eun-mi yelled, raising the Kalashnikov she carried.

The Punchinellos gaped when they saw the General's daughter. Cursing their primitive, medieval weapons, furious they didn't have their own firearms that night, they rushed forward, slashing with their swords.

Eun-mi opened fire and Evelyn reached for the assault rifle that had been slung discreetly over her own shoulder. Standing side by side, they mowed the guards down. The two muzzles spat light and noisy death and the Punchinellos jumped and jittered as bullets pumped into them. Before the two jackals could turn to run, Eun-mi riddled them with holes too.

It was over in moments. The AK-47s ceased firing and the courtyard in front of the postern gate was littered with bodies and spent cartridges.

"A most disagreeable instrument," Evelyn observed with a wry twist of her lip. "But highly efficient nevertheless."

Charm's girls cheered with joy.

"Nice one, whoever you are," Emma said, looking the pair of them up and down with a grimace and wondering which of them was the carer of the other.

"You really brought an army with you?" Conor asked, peering through the broken doorway.

"No, dear," Evelyn told him. "There's just a full car park out there, with a side order of orchestra pit."

"What, so there's just you two?"

"As you can see."

"No tanks, heavy artillery? No back-up?"

"Not so you'd notice, no. And I do so apologise for my tardiness. It's entirely Gerald's fault. Of all the vehicles he could have stolen, he selected one not worth the scrap value. We broke down twice getting here. If it wasn't for Eun-mi's mechanical expertise, we wouldn't have made it at all. I sincerely hope we're not too late!"

"Oh, brilliant," Emma snorted. "We've been rescued by some tacky Eurovision tribute act. This is not gonna end well."

"Now," Evelyn continued, "some of you will recognise this remarkable person from your time in North Korea. For the benefit of those who weren't there, this is Chung Eun-mi and I am Evelyn Hole, professor of music."

"Why'd she bleach her hair?" asked Blueberry Muffin.

"That's rather a protracted story."

"It looks better now."

"I like it too," added Chocolate Mousse.

"It's manga-ish."

"Why we wait here?" Eun-mi demanded, uncomfortable with the attention her abnormal hair was attracting. "We must complete mission."

"Look at the cranes!" Sandra cried, pointing up at the steel masts that were crackling with electricity. "What's happening?"

"Time for you to go!" Evelyn said sharply. "Get out of this terrible place. Take the little ones and get as far away from here as you can. The service roads are clear for the moment, but that could change at any time. Can any of you drive a motor car?"

"I can!" Lukas said, along with three of the shepherds.

"Splendid! Each of you take one of those vehicles out there and go."

"What'll you be doing?" Conor asked. "What's this mission?"

"Best leave that to Miss Chung and myself. Now hurry along. Don't worry about the lightning; a car is the safest place to be during a storm."

"I'll stop and help you if I can," the boy volunteered. "Got any spare guns?"

"Certainly not!"

"What's in that then?" Conor asked, nodding at the rolled-up blanket strapped to Eun-mi's back. "Looks like another rifle to me."

"He no come with us," Eun-mi said tersely. "He will get in way."

"Go protect the girls," Evelyn told him.

"I want to stay too," Maggie said quickly.

"Nooo!" the little sheep protested. "Come with us, Maggie! Come, be safe."

"Yes, you all go," Evelyn urged. "Leave it up to Eun-mi and I."

It was then the giant Christmas tree burst into flames. They saw its topmost branches burning behind the two inner walls, then flinched in fear as a glowing shape scaled the Keep beyond.

The children uttered shrieks of terror and their knees buckled. Shuddering, they fell to the ground. The many horrors they'd witnessed since *Dancing Jax* ruined their lives were as nothing compared to this. The mere sight of that bright figure filled them with a blind panic they'd never known before. Even Eun-mi felt her courage falter and, though she clenched her teeth and reproached herself, she could not bear to gaze on that evil vision and looked away sharply.

"What is that?" Emma cried, shaking her head, aghast.

"The Dawn Prince is here," Maggie whispered.

Ruddy light filled the courtyard, flaring over the dark pools of the Punchinellos' blood. Where it touched Conor's skin, it stung and his flesh crawled and pricked with sweat. It made him feel sick and he wanted to scrape it off or cut it away.

Only Evelyn could withstand the unholy glare of the power that ascended the throne without averting her eyes. The force that flowed from it made her gasp and catch her breath, but she was tough and stronger than Gerald would have been. Marshalling that strength, she passed among the petrified youngsters and gently encouraged them towards the gateway.

"Keep your heads down and don't look at that up there," she warned. "Get going. Now!"

Emma didn't need telling again.

"Be lucky, yeah," she said, running out of the postern gate.

Sandra thanked the two strangers for saving their lives and followed her.

"Lord be with you," Lukas told them, his head bowed, too afraid to raise his face.

"I'm not going," Maggie said stubbornly. "I'm coming with you. I can help!"

"So can I!" Conor insisted. "You don't know the layout of this place.

It's enormous. Where are you even trying to get to?"

"Best you don't know," Evelyn said. "And those young girls need you far more than us. Keep them safe and, if we somehow get out of this alive, we'll all have some of Gerald's chocolate mincies."

"His what?" Maggie asked with impatience.

Blueberry Muffin grabbed her hand to pull her towards the doorway.

"Eew – you're cold and clammy!" she cried.

Evelyn glanced again at the terrifying form upon the Waiting Throne. Closing her eyes, an expression of extreme sorrow passed over her face. Then she collected herself and tapped the fake magic wand on the ground decisively.

"Actually," she declared, "perhaps it would be best if Maggie were to come along. Now no argument, girls. You go with the others and no squabbling about who sits in what car. No, there isn't time to hug her. Be off with you! At once!"

The girls only obeyed because they knew it was Gerald under that get-up. Tearfully they ran into the car park, and the ones who were left heard car doors slamming.

"Now we go," Eun-mi said.

"And I'm coming as well," Conor told them. "You can't stop me. What you going to do, shoot me?"

"Shoot him in legs," Eun-mi suggested in irritation.

"What?" the boy cried.

"You might wish we had," Evelyn said gravely. "This is a one-way mission. We're not anticipating getting out alive."

Conor managed a grim smile. "I know. I might be blond, but I'm not dumb. If I can help stop this, it'll be worth it."

"We aren't even hoping we can achieve that," Evelyn told him. "It's just a little idea, but finding the lot of you has already made everything worthwhile. You really should go with the rest, while there's time."

"Why's it OK for her to stay?" he asked, meaning Maggie. "If she's stopping then so am I."

"Very well," Evelyn accepted. "Make yourself useful; can you show us the quickest way to the main gate?"

"But... that's where the Ismus is."

"Quite."

Conor shook his head. "Weapons won't work on him. You're wasting your time."

"If you're going to be this argumentative the whole way, I may very well shoot you after all."

"You're crazy."

"About many things, dear boy."

They heard engines starting in the car park and the vehicles pulled away, crunching over the gravel and up the service road.

Conor gave a grunt of resignation. "OK. This way."

Pausing to pick up his sword, he led them alongside the second curtain wall, then through an inner gate and on to the common lawn beyond. All the while they were acutely aware of the hellish light that shone on the roof of the Keep and tried to keep out of the glare as much as possible.

Keeping the safety catch of her rifle off, Eun-mi's eyes were constantly roving over the enclosing walls, searching and keeping lookout. Finally she found what she'd been seeking.

"Stop!" she shouted suddenly.

"What is it?" Evelyn asked.

"Listen to that," Conor said.

Outside the castle was a new and different sound – more chilling than any they had heard so far. The huge crowd was stirring, emerging from the dreadful nightmare of *Fighting Pax*. Their distraught wails and cries were heartbreaking. Beyond the moat a world in pain was awakening.

But that was not why Eun-mi had halted.

Gradually the others realised she had her Kalashnikov trained on them and was reaching into her holster for the pistol.

"This time I check it loaded," she told Evelyn as she pointed it at her head. "Put down rifle, please."

"What are you doing?" Evelyn asked in bewilderment.

"Rifle on ground, please. Do not force me to shoot. I am grateful for what you did, setting me free of... of that."

"It's all right to say her name. Estelle Winyard won't come back. You're rid of her now. If you want to talk about—"

"Rifle!" Eun-mi repeated more forcefully.

Evelyn placed the weapon down.

"I don't understand why you're doing this," she said. "You know what we must do."

"Isn't it obvious?" Conor blurted, glaring at Eun-mi with contempt. "She's selling you out."

"Eun-mi?" Evelyn asked in disbelief. "Is this true?"

"Stand over there, please," the Korean girl ordered.

Evelyn, Conor and Maggie obeyed and they finally saw what she'd been looking for: a remote camera fixed to the wall.

"Ismus!" Eun-mi yelled. "Ismus! I must speak with you. I want to do exchange."

"Don't do this," Evelyn pleaded. "Don't betray us, don't betray me."

The gun in Eun-mi's hand was trembling. The conflicting emotions were almost overwhelming and Evelyn couldn't help pitying her.

"I do not want to hurt you," Eun-mi said unhappily. "You kind, good person – man and lady."

"Then don't."

"But I made promise, to protect sister. Nabi more important. Forgive me."

A soft hiss issued from a speaker hidden somewhere above them, and then the Ismus spoke.

"What do you all look like?" his voice floated down. "A very odd assortment indeed. Just what were you hoping to achieve, sneaking about the castle like the noisiest burglars ever? Did you think I couldn't hear you? Assault rifles aren't renowned for their discretion. Poor Swazzle and his crew. An ignoble end, but there's always more vicious and deformed homunculi where they came from – plenty more. You've spoiled my Nativity scene though; where are all my shepherds and wise men and little sheep?"

"Ismus!" Eun-mi called to the camera. "I bring you gift and ask for bargain."

"A gift, for me? You really shouldn't have."

"This person has plan to destroy your machine," she said, waving her pistol at Evelyn. "I have stopped plan – and there is more..."

Evelyn hung her head and callous laughter sounded from the speaker.

"Do you honestly believe you could have got anywhere near me and my master console?" he asked. "There are cameras all over this castle.

You've already passed seven of them."

"My gift is..."

"I don't need your pathetic little act of treachery as an offering. Cast your eyes up to He who sits upon the Waiting Throne and see how insignificant you truly are. We are at the beginning of a new era – an age of despair and suffering and His Glorious Majesty shall dominate and rule every desolate thought, every tormented breath."

"My sister! A bargain – for my sister, I will give to you..."

"Chung Nabi?" the Ismus scoffed. "That adorable little Five of Spades? Why, she's probably dead already, throttled by someone who caught her spying once too often in *Fighting Pax*."

"No!"

"If only you'd been here half an hour earlier, you might have saved her."

Eun-mi stumbled back. "Is not true!" she said.

"But then it wouldn't be the first time you were too late to save a family member, would it? I've learned all about you. What a fascinating subject for study you are. You'd keep teams of psychiatrists tied up for years. Tell me, was that piano ever properly in tune after your mother put a razor to her wrists and leaked all over it? How did Chopsticks sound? A bit sploshy?"

"Stop!" she cried.

"If you'd returned from school a little earlier that day, if you hadn't dawdled, looking at the beauty of the sunlight on the stream, listened to the birds in the trees, watched the insects on the flowers, perhaps you even made eyes at a boy, do you think you could have prevented it?"

Eun-mi covered her face. "Yes," she murmured. "It was my fault. I was not there."

The girl lowered the rifle and dropped the pistol.

The camera lens zoomed in on her anguish and the Ismus drank it in.

After some moments, he said, "But the blame wasn't yours. Did you never question why she did it? Did your father, General Chung Kang-dae, never speak of it to you?"

Eun-mi shook her head.

"Of course he wouldn't. It was the great family shame. But the real reason is because he was the one who drove her to it."

"That is lie!" she shouted. "She loved him. My father was very great General. He was important man – much respect!"

"And how quickly he rocketed up the ranks," the Ismus chuckled coldly. "Why do you think that was? Not because of his abilities; he was a bit of a plodder from all accounts. No, he hopped up those rungs so fast because he made an... arrangement with the Chief of the General Staff."

"Arrangement? What is this?"

"Imagine, if you will, a private library with only one rare, beautiful and delicate book. Is it just coincidence that every time the book was borrowed, your father was promoted?"

Eun-mi took up the rifle once more and shot at the wall, in the direction of that filthy voice. The speaker squealed and was silenced. The girl sank to her knees in the grass, shaking.

"It was an arrangement your mother could not live with." The voice came drifting from another speaker some distance away. There was a slight echo to it now, making it worse somehow, more disembodied and insidious. Then it said, "And, of course, little Nabi is not the daughter of General Chung Kang-dae at all."

Eun-mi whirled about. "Is not true!" she wept. "My father, he loved Nabi!"

"Guilt works at a man in the strangest ways. He lavished on Nabi the pure, unselfish love he should have always given your mother. Whereas you... you looked back at him with her eyes, the eyes that accused and were full of the hurt he put there – or so he thought. You see, he was never sure what you knew. He suspected your mother spoke to you before she died, telling you what he had done, how dishonourably he had used her. He feared you and hated you for that. Everything you ever did, to try and impress him, only inflated his distrust and horror of you. You constantly reminded him exactly what he was."

Weeping helplessly, Eun-mi doubled over. The echoing laughter ricocheted around the walls, then was cut off as the Ismus's attention was drawn elsewhere. Outside the castle, the wretched sounds of awakening were changing to murderous shouts of hate and screams of pain as the killings began.

Evelyn crouched at Eun-mi's side. The Korean girl was inconsolable.

"Eun-mi," she said compassionately. "Remember, the Ismus lies."

The girl could not answer. Many things were beginning to make sense. She recalled how her grandfather had rowed with his son-in-law and was later taken to a labour camp. Now she knew what the argument had been about. Everything she had ever believed about the proud General Chung Kang-dae had been exploded. Her revered image of him was blown to atoms. The shock of the revelation left her breathless and reeling.

"Nabi may still be alive," Evelyn told her. "Do not give up hope."

"We should move," Conor said, glancing around cautiously. "He'll be sending something to get us. We don't have much time."

"Eun-mi," Evelyn tried again.

It was no use. Eun-mi could not even hear her.

Evelyn thought quickly. The boy was right; remaining here was insanely dangerous, but the necessary alternative was undoubtedly worse, on so many levels. Her face grew stern and resolute. Gerald might have wavered, but she had always been made of sterner stuff. That's why she was here. To perform the hardest tasks that he could not, to be tough and unyielding and not let judgement be clouded by sentiment. It had to be done, for everyone's sake.

"Stay with her," she told Conor. "Keep the rifle. Maggie and I will go on. We'll finish what we set out to do."

"What?" he cried. "You're still making for the gatehouse? But he knows that's where you were going! It was a crazy plan before, but now you're just being bloody stupid."

"It's still our only hope."

"Then I'll go with you. Don't make her go – it's certain death that way."

"I know I can trust Maggie," Evelyn said adamantly. "I'm sorry, but I don't know you."

Conor turned to Maggie. "Tell her I'm OK, she can trust me. You know I'm OK!"

"No," Evelyn said sharply.

"What's the matter with you?" Conor asked Maggie. "Say something! You don't have to do this, she can't make you go."

"Leave her alone!" Evelyn ordered. "I need Maggie with me. I won't be able to do this single-handedly – but you're not coming and that's final."

"I'm not stopping here, babysitting this snitching trash!"

"Don't condemn Eun-mi too harshly. You don't know what she's been through."

"Oh, come off it! Name one person who's had it easy!"

"She's a very damaged, troubled young woman, has been for a very long time – long before *Dancing Jax*. And she isn't a traitor, not really. She didn't tell the Ismus everything. She could have, there's a lot she might have said, but she didn't betray me completely. She didn't mention our secret weapon. There's still a chance and I've got to take it."

"What secret weapon?"

"I'm hardly going to tell you that, in front of so many cameras, am I, dear boy? Now, Maggie, will you accompany me? He's right, I can't make you."

"Of course I'll come," Maggie said brightly.

Evelyn smiled. "I'm so glad. Thank you, dear."

"You don't know the direct way," Conor interrupted.

"We'll manage. I think we'll be just fine from now on. You take care of Eun-mi. Get her out of here and tell her I understand. No, tell her... we both understand – and there's nothing to forgive."

Evelyn retrieved her rifle. Then she and Maggie skirted the wall, entered a colonnade and vanished from sight.

Angry at being left behind, Conor glowered down at the collapsed wreck that was Eun-mi.

"Snap out of it," he said harshly. "We're sitting ducks here. I'm not going to get killed because of you."

Every moment they remained in that spot brought danger ever closer. If he couldn't get her to move, he'd have to drag her. There were more howls and screams outside the castle walls now. He tried not to imagine what was happening and just hoped the service roads were still clear. If they could make it to the car park, he reckoned he could start a vehicle and get them away.

"Right," he said, reaching under her arms to hoist her to her feet.

The girl's reaction at being touched was astonishing. Before he knew what was happening, she'd lashed out, kicked his legs from under him, and had one hand round his throat, the other poised above his face, ready to smash down.

"Get off!" his strangled voice cried. "What are you doing? I was trying to help you, you daft cow! Don't freak out!"

Eun-mi breathed hard. Her training in Juche Kyuksul meant she could snap his neck easily if she wished. But at that moment she needed him.

"I must find sister," she said. "Dead or alive. I must find Nabi. Where will she be? Answer!"

Conor had no idea. She applied a little more pressure to his throat.

"All the courtiers are in the Great Hall," he spluttered. "If she's anywhere in the castle, she'll be there."

"You show," Eun-mi commanded, jumping up, grabbing her rifle and wrenching him to his feet.

"A please would be nice," he said ruefully.

The girl clutched at his arm and, when he saw the desperation burning in her eyes, he wished he hadn't been so unpleasant earlier.

"Please," she begged. "Nabi – she is only six."

Conor took up his sword. "Follow me."

Racing back the way they'd come, they used the royal gates that led directly to the inner ward. Passing through the final entrance, the awful spectacle of the Keep reared before them. The Christmas tree was still blazing and the infernal light that beat from the Waiting Throne made its flames appear pale and colourless. The shimmering figure of Lucifer was brighter and more intense now, drawing strength from the hate and violence of the awakened Jaxers around the world.

Shielding his eyes, Conor pointed at the Keep.

"The Great Hall is in there!" he shouted, above the din of the raging fire and the fury outside.

Eun-mi nodded in gratitude. "You not need to come further."

"I'm kind of committed now. Besides, playing the hero isn't an easy habit to kick – either that or I genuinely am dumb."

Running across the cobbled yard, into the full searing glare blasting down from high above, they reached the foot of the steps leading to the Great Hall. The hacked body of a knight lay at the bottom; his blood trail marked every step. From inside the hall came the clamour of battle: the clashing of steel against steel, bloodthirsty shrieks and screeches of death.

Without hesitation, Conor and Eun-mi rushed up and burst through the ornately carved doors.

A scene of carnage and barbarism awaited them. The members of the Court were slaughtering each other. The Royal Houses were at war: Under Kings fought one another and their households were engaged in bitter combat. Under Queens ran at their enemies with daggers, knights hewed their rivals with brutal blows, pages were choking the squires and serving wenches attacked the ladies-in-waiting.

The banqueting tables were now duelling platforms and obstacles to brawl across. Chairs had been smashed across heads, cutlery had become weapons, candlesticks were bludgeons and the tapestries were burning. Even the minstrels in the gallery were killing one another. Strewn across the floor, amid the debris of spilled food and golden dishes, the screens of the many discarded e-readers still displayed the text of *Fighting Pax*.

Dodging and ducking the riotous chaos, Eun-mi scanned the Great Hall for her sister. Nabi was nowhere to be seen.

"You take that side!" Conor shouted. "I'll go this – and we'll meet at the far end! She has to be in here!"

Eun-mi agreed. Dashing into the bloody conflict, she searched frantically. It wasn't easy. Jaxers barged in front and against her, blocking the way as they fought. But they were blind to her presence; she wasn't one of them and she could weave through unchallenged.

A number of bodies and severed limbs already littered the floor, but Nabi wasn't among them. Her sister checked every possible hiding place, without success. She wasn't cowering beneath the tables, or concealed inside the wooden chests beneath the windows. Where was she?

On the right-hand side of that enormous room, Conor's progress was hampered by his costume. Still dressed as the Jack of Clubs, he was fair game to any of the Court who had a quarrel with him after reading *Fighting Pax*. A man he recognised as Sir Darksilver roared across one of the tables and vowed to slice his head off, when he was done dispatching Sir Gorvain, whose armour he was currently belting with a mace and axe.

Diving under the arm of a lord who made a swipe at his head with a goblet, Conor stumbled over a body on the floor. Looking down, he saw it was a boy dressed in the same clothes as himself. Two daggers were in his chest. Beside him was the Jill of Spades' replacement and her throat had been cut. Conor lurched away.

The stained glass in the windows throbbed with the fiery light outside and lurid colours splashed across the uproar, heightening the confusion. Unbridled hate and savagery charged the air that was already thick with smoke from the burning wall hangings.

Suddenly Conor saw the wooden screen that covered the way to the kitchens and heard a young girl's voice crying out behind it. Leaping over upturned stools and a pile of broken earthenware, he threw himself round the screen, ready with his sword, hoping he wasn't too late.

No doubt about it, there was Eun-mi's sister, and Conor crashed in on a deadly confrontation between her and the Queen of Diamonds. One was prostrate on the floor, the other stood over her, a meat cleaver raised, about to swing down and chop.

But it was Nabi who was about to deliver the fatal blow. The cleaver was in her small hands and she was cackling malevolently. Conor snatched her backwards and knocked the weapon from her grasp. The little girl shrieked in protest and twisted round to scratch and bite him. Conor towed her into the Great Hall and Nabi resisted with every step. Then a new ferocious shout went up and Sir Darksilver vaulted over the tables to stand in their way.

He was the tallest of the knights and towered over Conor. The Jaxers who became that character were always thick-set and had spent too many hours in the gym flinging free weights about. As this man was the prime example of Sir Darksilver, he was burlier than most and, when he flexed his arms, the chain mail round his biceps strained and the leather straps bound about his thick wrists creaked. The heavy mace he wielded might have been made of balsa wood, for all the effort it took for him to spin it round.

"There are matters of honour between us that can only be settled by blood," he growled at Conor threateningly. "Thou art a craven deceiver. I was unhorsed at the tournament through perfidy. I have already slain mine esquire. Now I shall send thee galloping after him."

He swept the mace through a wide arc and brought it crunching down on the table. It splintered in two.

"That shall be the way of thine head," he swore, lumbering forward.

Conor was completely outmatched. He didn't have a hope of fighting this hulking giant. He wasn't sure he could bring himself to use his sword against a human being anyway. Jackals and Punchinellos were one thing, but this was a man, a person possessed by the power of the book, who didn't know what he was doing. But he knew he had to defend himself or die.

"Run for the door," he told Nabi as he released her. "Get out of here."

The girl shook her head vehemently. "I'm going to set fire to Lady Marlot's wimple!" she cried, springing away to seize a fallen candlestick. "I'm going to burn her hair off!"

The shadow of Sir Darksilver fell across Conor and the mace was ready to dash out his brains. The boy flinched at the sight of it and staggered backwards.

Suddenly there was a yell and Eun-mi came charging along the broken table. The knight turned, just as she launched herself at him, feet first. A perfectly aimed kick caught him on the jaw and his head whipped round, spitting teeth. He toppled like an oak tree and she landed on his breastplate to deliver a controlled, chopping blow to his neck.

The armour rattled and the knight went limp.

"Bullet would be quicker," Eun-mi said, "but I not enjoy it so much."

Her confidence restored, she looked at Conor with an expression of immense satisfaction.

"You killed him?" he asked.

"No, but maybe better if I do. He die in here soon."

Then she ran after little Nabi, who was just about to set a flame to the headdress of a woman who was strangling another.

Eun-mi swept her up in her arms and they hurried from the Great Hall.

"Let's grab a car!" Conor said as they ran down the steps outside.

Eun-mi hugged her struggling sister tightly, then handed her over.

"You go," she told him. "Take Nabi. Take her safe place."

"What?"

"Take this also," she said, giving him the Kalashnikov. "Protect Nabi."

"What's going on?" he demanded.

"I cannot leave," she said with iron resolve. "I made pledge. I must restore the true order. I must be a human rifle, a human bomb, a dagger in the hand of the Eternal President."

Conor couldn't believe what he was hearing.

"You're not serious!" he shouted. "You'll be dead is all you'll be! There's nothing you can do! It's the end of everything. Give up. It's over! Best we can hope for is to keep moving, try to find somewhere miles from anywhere – until they hunt us down."

Eun-mi raised her beautiful face. The evil that blazed on top of the Keep was more powerful than ever and the night sky burned the colour of dark blood. Again she felt her courage weaken, but she saw something else up there, something that gave her the slenderest of hopes and she knew she had to risk it.

Glowing cinders swirled through the air as the flames around the Christmas tree perished, leaving it a charred skeleton. Around the castle the sounds of death were beginning to change. Anguish and horror were taking their place as Jaxers began to remember their true selves and realise the atrocious crimes they had just committed. Despair and madness engulfed the world.

In every country, across every continent, people were stumbling and reeling backwards, their hands wet with blood, their bodies aching from desperate struggles. As the insanity that had seized mankind abated, they looked around them and were filled with loathing and disgust. Awakening from the power of *Fighting Pax*, they discovered their cities were burning; monstrous creatures crawled and stalked the streets and screeched in the sky above. The planet was in uproar, but, most hideous of all, everyone who stirred from the book's spell was confronted with the dreadful truth that they had just committed murder.

In every town and village, people were staggering away from what they had done. Bodies dressed as characters from that vile book, or merely with playing cards pinned to their clothes, lay at their feet. Billions were dead, most killed by members of their own family, or by friends or lovers. Tormented cries engulfed the world and, on every TV screen, every mobile device, the image of Lucifer upon the iron throne continued to shine, reigning supreme and presiding over their pain and desolation.

In Conor's arms, little Nabi had ceased kicking, her energies spent, and her head drooped. Then, groggily, she raised her face. When she saw Eun-mi, she cried out to her in Korean. Conor let her go and the sisters embraced.

"Enough," Eun-mi said shortly. "You must be brave and do as I say. This boy is a friend. Go with him. Do not question. There is no time. This is an order of Kim Il-sung."

Nabi gasped, then her small face crumpled in misery.

"No tears," Eun-mi commanded sternly. "The People's Army does not weep. You must be strong, have courage."

Kissing her forehead, she turned to Conor and urged him to leave.

"Come with us!" he begged her. "Please, Eun-mi, don't throw your life away."

Her features grew hard.

"Not Chung Eun-mi any more," she said. "I choose new name, one without disgrace of General Chung Kang-dae."

"I don't care what you call yourself. Just don't be bloody stupid. Come with us."

The girl wasn't listening. Turning back to the Keep, she stepped up to the scaffolding and began to climb.

"All you women are crazy!" Conor yelled. "Stubborn and crazy!"

Little Nabi fought back the tears. Picking her up, he ran across the courtyard, towards the inner gates and the car park beyond.

"Eun-mi!" Nabi wailed. "Eun-mi!"

Climbing swiftly, her sister shook her head with vigorous denial and lost the military cap of her uniform. In the baking, infernal winds that tore around the Keep, her unnaturally white hair came loose and streamed about her.

"Not Eun-mi," she proclaimed proudly. "I am Arirang!"

Evelyn and Maggie hadn't gone far when Evelyn put a hand to her forehead.

"Oh, gracious!" she exclaimed, halting in a short tunnel that cut through the inner curtain wall. Her voice bounced around the curved ceiling and she dabbed at her neck with a lace handkerchief.

"I'm rather too long in the tooth for this dashing about. In my vim and vigour days, when I was on tour with Bunty, my musical partner, I had to lug a cello, saxophone, harp and violin about, all in one go, from venue to venue. But the four-hundred-metre dash was never one of my triumphs."

Tucking the handkerchief in her sleeve, she looked at Maggie with concern.

"You feeling quite yourself, dear? You're most frightfully quiet."

The girl stirred. The hellish light flooding the castle reached even into this passageway and it threw a bloody cast on her young face.

"It's been a long night," she replied.

"Assuredly so," Evelyn agreed.

"What is this secret weapon?" Maggie asked curiously. "How can it possibly work?"

Evelyn turned a benign smile on her and was no longer out of breath, but calm and pragmatic as ever. "That was just a ruse to get you away from the others, dear," she said mildly. "Although I do have a couple of hand grenades tacked to my crinoline, but that's neither here nor there."

"Excuse me?"

"I had to keep the other children safe, you see. Just as I insisted the girls get away from you as soon as possible. I couldn't risk you harming them, now could I?"

The pretence of innocence slipped from Maggie's face.

"You've known since then?"

Evelyn nodded. "I suspected you weren't Maggie, as soon as I saw you. She and Gerald were very close, you see. He even daydreamed of adopting her, if the world ever returned to normal. Silly old fool that he is."

"Chocolate mincies," the girl declared with dawning realisation. "That was a test, wasn't it?"

"Yes, yes, it was. My lovely friend Maggie would have known what they were. That really did break my heart. I actually felt it tear in two; isn't that interesting?"

Evelyn paused and waited until she was sure she could continue without her voice cracking.

"She's gone, isn't she?" she said. "This isn't just temporary, Maggie is gone."

Speckles of black mould broke out over the girl's face and when she next spoke it was with the voice of Austerly Fellows.

"It takes time to absorb every memory," he explained. "And I'd only just moved in and taken root when you... gatecrashed. I am but a splinter after all – a seedling that hasn't yet reached its potential."

"I thought so, but I had to be certain."

Evelyn forced herself to look at the blooms of mould on that dear face. It made it easier to aim the Kalashnikov.

"Funny thing about the AK-47 assault rifle," Austerly remarked coolly. "The Russian factory that produces them is staffed almost entirely by women. They machine the parts and assemble them. In that way, I suppose, you could almost call it a woman's weapon. Ironic, isn't it? Considering both of us are merely masquerading as one."

Inside that tunnel, the single shot that followed thundered like a cannon blast.

Evelyn's eyelids fluttered as the pain registered. Uttering a small cry, she let the rifle fall and slid to the ground. A large bloodstain was already soaking through the gold silk of her bodice.

The mould flowed thickly over Maggie's features and Austerly Fellows chuckled softly. There was a smoking hole in the girl's shepherd robes. He removed Eun-mi's pistol from the pocket.

"Neither you nor my erstwhile Jack of Clubs saw me lift this from the grass," he chided Evelyn as she lay dying. "Most remiss of you both. Do you think it would be wittier to shoot him and the Chung girl with it, or with the rifle?"

"Go back to Hell," Evelyn whispered, her eyes dimming as they stared up at him.

"Look around you!" he answered, laughing. "We're already here. Every creature and comfort of home and, any moment now, your angry young friend Lee is going to kill the Bad Shepherd for me in Mooncaster – if your other friend, Martin, doesn't drive a dagger into his sleeping body here first. I'd prefer Lee to succeed, ideally, but either way I win. They're both damned."

Evelyn shook her head feebly. "They... they're better than that," she said, her voice growing weaker.

"Given the right inducement, humans are capable of the most depraved, corrupt and cruel acts. You're just beasts, chasing a mythical respectability you don't really want, not deep down. You think you're civilised, but every one of you cries out to be tempted back to your default factory settings. I rather think *Dancing Jax* proved that conclusively."

"It didn't work on Lee or Martin – or Maggie."

"Defectives, that's all you were. I knew there'd be some and incorporated you into my design."

Evelyn was fighting to keep conscious. "No," she said. "They're marvellous. Your dirt can't touch them, your shadow... won't darken them. Oh, yes, we're... we're weak, but we can also shine with such goodness it would dazzle you. Lee and Martin – they'll blind you yet, Austerly Fellows. That's... that's my faith – I believe in them – in their goodness."

Her breaths were quick and shallow. Her time was almost over.

"You're an imbecile," Austerly said caustically. "Now excuse me, I must run and tell those two out there about your most tragic accident, just before I kill them. No, I think I'll just kill the boy. Miss Chung's suffering is too delicious to extinguish quite so soon."

The mould receded from the face and Maggie's flesh was clear once more. The girl turned to leave the tunnel.

"There was... was one more," Evelyn said.

"One more what?"

"Reason why I knew... knew you weren't my Maggie. You see... almost the first thing M... Maggie would have asked... the fir... the first thing she'd have said..."

The girl returned and lifted the pistol a second time.

"Trouble with you third-rate music-hall types," Austerly Fellows complained, "you never know when to leave the stage."

A faint, victorious laugh left Evelyn's lips.

"Maggie would have asked... would have asked... where Spencer was..."

And her head fell forward.

Instead of firing, the girl pulled the gun up sharply. What did that mean? The dark eyes glared down, but it was too late. Evelyn and Gerald were dead and the wig had slipped forward. Yet there was a mysterious smile on that old face. Then, as the splinter of Austerly Fellows searched Maggie's memory, something rolled out of Evelyn's hand.

It was a grenade.

Austerly tried to escape, but, an instant later, the explosion brought the tunnel crashing down and that section of the castle wall caved in.

27

BY THE TIME Martin reached the top of the spiral stairs within the South Tower, he was totally out of breath. Resting against the curved wall, he put his head on the cold stone and wheezed down deep gulps of air.

A torch burned above him and the golden dagger in his hand gleamed in its flaring light. Martin kept repeating to himself he had to do this. For the sake of humanity, he couldn't shrink from this grisly responsibility. Lee had to die. The violent Peckham yob couldn't be allowed to kill the Bad Shepherd.

"Come on," the ex-teacher told himself. "Everything depends on this. You can do it. Just go out there and... It'll be quick. He won't even feel anything."

He tried to picture in his mind a character from his favourite movies, someone he could draw strength from. But it didn't help; his mind was a blank. There was no room for fantasy now. This one unbearably real moment was all that mattered.

Stepping out on to the roof of the tower, he wished desperately for it to be over. Then he saw the hospital bed, the medical equipment nearby – and Lee.

Overhead the cranes were bristling with electricity and lightning forked across the castle.

Martin approached the bed with leaden steps. His heart quailed. The dagger seemed to grow heavier in his hand as his sense of dread and horror mounted. And then he was looking down at Lee.

The boy appeared to be fast asleep – or dead. There wasn't even any movement beneath the eyelids. His face had lost the hard belligerence it displayed during his waking hours. Right now he looked like any other sixteen-year-old, someone with a whole life ahead of him. A life that Martin had to take.

Gazing down at that vulnerable face, Martin's resolve faltered. Could he seriously do this?

Around the castle the arc lights were exploding. At that moment the Christmas tree burst into flames. Martin raised his eyes. Across the battlements he saw it burning and wondered what it portended. Then he witnessed the harrowing sight of Lucifer rising through the fire, to scale the Keep. Martin watched the Harlequin Priests combust and the shining figure ascend the throne in a rippling heat haze. It was the most terrifying thing he had ever seen or imagined. He felt his spirit shrivel inside him. Nothing in any of his large collection of fantasy movies could ever have prepared him for this. The dagger almost fell from his fingers. He wanted to turn and run, to hide or hurl himself from the tower – anything to escape the tide of horror beating from that shimmering shape upon the throne. It was all he could do to remain standing, and he prayed that those pitiless, blazing eyes did not turn his way.

But the new lord of the earth was staring out, beyond the castle walls, at the world that was now his. Where his perilous gaze rested and he raised his left hand, pillars of flame leaped from the ground and soon the surrounding countryside was fenced with towering fires.

Martin heard the screams and dismal howling of the vast audience and, somehow, he gathered up the fragments of his courage to accomplish what he had come here to do. Those sounds of suffering swept aside any doubts, any anxieties. His fear and hesitation had already wasted too much time and probably cost countless lives.

But, when he raised the dagger over Lee's chest, his hands were still shaking, still sweating. "One forceful downward strike will be enough," he told himself. Two at the most. Martin tensed his shoulders and squeezed his eyes shut. Although he had to do it, he didn't have to look.

"Forgive me," he whispered.

"Martin!" a voice shouted suddenly. "Martin Baxter! Stay your hand!"

Martin stopped himself just in time and caught his breath. Opening his eyes, he turned stiffly and saw the Jockey skip out on to the roof behind him.

"Get away!" Martin yelled furiously. "Whatever trick you're playing, just go. Don't come any closer or I'll stick this in you as well."

"No trick, no game," the Jockey promised, holding up his hands. "Not against you, not this time."

"You'd say that anyway. Stand still! I mean it. I'll use this if you take another step. Why aren't you off reading *Fighting Pax*? Or have you finished it already?"

The Jockey gazed beyond Martin, towards the glorious spectacle of the Dawn Prince. He ached to go and worship Him. But first of all...

"One last naughtiness, Martin," he explained. "The Jockey must ride everyone of the Court, including the Ismus. That is why I am here, that is why I sent Nosy Posy to the Great Hall alone. I must play one final trick on the Holy Enchanter before I leave this dreary place for good."

Martin didn't understand.

"'Tis the way I am," the Jockey said simply. "'Tis the part I must play. I can be no otherwise. I am tasked to hinder and needle, thwart, upset and confound and now, at the very brink of the Ismus's triumph, I am compelled to meddle."

"Do it somewhere else!"

"The Ismus wishes the Castle Creeper's dreaming self to die here, and I must foil him if I may. But there is another reason, one that paws at me and that I strive to comprehend. Earlier this day, when I led you from the dungeons... those young aberrants, how they cheered. I had never heard such acclaim, save at the joust when a champion's praise is loud yet brief. Those children, Martin. They adored you, you were their king, their idol."

"Shut up."

"I confess I felt naught but envy. To be held in such esteem. 'Twas a thing new and excellent to me. Answer me truthfully: would those aberrants hold you in such high regard if they could see you now?"

"Don't you try that one on me!" Martin snapped. "There's no other choice! I'm doing it for the sake of everyone!"

The Jockey chortled. "Haw haw haw – is that so?"

"What do you mean? Of course it is! If Lee kills the Bad Shepherd then—"

"'If'?" the Jockey flung the word back at him. "Tell me, Martin, are you really going to murder the Creeper on the strength of such a meagre word as 'if'? Is there any doubt he will do what you fear so much?"

Martin struggled to answer. "Gerald thought he wouldn't do it," he said grudgingly.

"Ah, and you reckon his opinion so low? His judgement was not to be trusted?"

"No – just the opposite."

"Then what was his doubt founded upon?"

Martin frowned in annoyance. It sounded so stupid.

"Gerald believed in Lee," he muttered. "Because... a girl loved him. A dead girl called Charm. The one everyone cared so much for. Gerald said Lee couldn't be the scum I think he is because he'd won her love."

"Is love then so blind?"

"I... I don't know. It might be. She didn't sound very bright."

"So love is a measure of intellect?"

"No, but..."

"Art thou loved, Martin?"

Martin glanced over at the West Tower, where Carol and Paul were crouched down, protecting the baby from the intensity of Lucifer's infernal light. His pulse quickened and he wanted to charge across to them.

"Yes," he said. "Yes, I am."

"And do you return that love?"

"Oh, God, yes."

"With thy brain or with thine heart?"

"With everything. Absolutely everything – and more if I had it."

"Then answer me this, Martin," the Jockey asked curiously. "Why are you here, atop this tower? This is not the place for you, at this ultimate moment when your grey world is ending. Why is there a dagger in your hand? Why are you so impatient to plunge it into a defenceless boy's heart? Why are you not with your beloved? What keeps you from her – from them?"

Martin stared at him, guilty and ashamed. "The Ismus told me they'd be spared, and I could go to them if..."

"If you did this foul murder. Such a price, Martin, such a scarlet price. And would they still love you after that?"

"I... I don't know. Stop messing with my head! You're trying to confuse me, stopping me from what I should do."

"I am merely trying to make you see clearly."

"You? You've already fooled me twice. Last year, at school, when you pretended the book hadn't worked on you, then this week in North Korea. You don't get to do it a third time!"

"Did my easy teasings bruise your pride so much?" the Jockey asked. "If so then set that aside. It matters not that you believe me. Accept the words of the Ismus if you would rather, but ask yourself, which of us, he or I, placed that blade in your hand?"

Martin looked at the golden dagger and the fear and panic that clouded his reason drew aside. Finally his mind was crystal clear. Stripped of the horror and desperation, this was a simple choice between right and wrong. Suddenly he was overwhelmed by a violent sense of repulsion and he threw the weapon down. He was appalled by what he had almost done. Disgusted with himself, he held his head in his hands.

"I can't murder Lee!" he uttered. "I just can't. But what can I do? What about the people out there? What if Lee does kill the Bad Shepherd? What hope is there then?"

"I say to you, have faith in your friend's doubt and pay no heed to that mischievous 'if'."

"Entrust the lives of billions to the love of a dead girl I never even met? That's not faith, it's madness."

"Is it wisdom then to entrust the fate of your family to the mendacity of the Ismus?"

"I don't follow you."

"Know this, Martin Baxter: the Holy Enchanter has no intention of keeping his promise to you. There will be no reunion. In this wretched existence there can never be a happy ever after, especially for you and Carol. The Jockey uncloaks all perfidy and lays it bare. All this long night, the Ismus has played the world false. The votes shown during the entertainment were a deception. It was rigged. Manger won every instance, but my Lord Ismus was determined to deny him and hold him back, till the very end."

"But the broadcast is over."

"The entertainment is not. The Ismus is going to release Mauger and send him to the West Tower – to slay and devour your family, for his own amusement."

"What?" Martin cried, bolting to the top of the stairs. "Why didn't you tell me that straight away?"

"Ho ho ho. As I have said, 'tis my nature. Do not forget your dagger, Martin Baxter. You have better cause to use it now."

Martin rushed back for it. He glanced quickly at Lee's unconscious form and his guts clenched when he thought how close he had come to killing him.

"Thank you... Barry," he told the Jockey. "You saved me from making a horrible mistake."

"Haw haw haw, there is no Barry," the Jockey replied.

"Yeah, right," Martin shouted as he dashed down the stairs.

Alone with Lee, the Jockey chuckled to himself. He had made his last mischief here. Now it was time to enter the pages of *Fighting Pax* and commence the uninterrupted life in Mooncaster. Bowing to the Keep, he offered up praise to the fiery radiance of the Dawn Prince and reflected that, from now on, he would have to be extra cautious with his japes and tricks. It would not do to incur His wrath.

Singing softly, he began skipping down the stairs, passing empty chambers that, in the true Realm, belonged to the House of Clubs. Here, in this unfinished reconstruction, the rooms and apartments were bare and darkness filled the doorless doorways.

Suddenly a figure sprang from those shadows. With a demented yell, a wild-eyed Kate Kryzewski leaped on his back and looped a camera cable round his neck. Dropping down, she pulled it tight. Arching backwards, the Jockey choked and clawed at his throat.

"That's for your 'sport'!" she screamed, tying a knot in the cable. "Die gasping and in terror, the same as you left me."

With that, she shoved him away from her. Black in the face, the Jockey went crashing down the spiral stairs and was dead before he hit the bottom.

"I, Columbine," the woman boasted, "a lowly Two of Hearts, have rid the Court of your cruel trickery and care not what their

Lordships do to me!"

Throwing back her head, she laughed madly She was dressed in only her costume rags. The tambourine was at her hip. Hearing the metal discs rattle, she clutched it and the deranged laughter gave way to groggy confusion.

"How can this be?" she murmured. "How came it here, when that felon stole it away?"

Her eyes wandered, misting over and swimming in and out of focus. Then, abruptly, she stumbled back and screamed.

"What have I done?" Kate shrieked, as the memory of who she really was purged her mind of the Columbine delusion. "Oh, sweet God, what have I just done? No! No!"

Sick with fear and shock, she stared, aghast, down the spiral stairway and shook her head, refusing to accept it. Breathing hard, she descended, apprehensive and dreading what she might discover. With every step, she kept telling herself it couldn't possibly be true, it had to be part of the sick Mooncaster hallucination, she wasn't capable of such a brutal and abhorrent act. And then, when she reached the bottom, she saw the monstrous reality of what she had done.

The reporter stumbled away, running blindly back up the stairs. Overcome with remorse and despair, she rushed out on to the roof. Out there the sight of that shining being, high on the Keep, unleashed a scream from her lips that would not stop. Then those pitiless eyes turned to gaze at her and her mind collapsed.

Impelled by terror, Kate flung herself forward. She blundered against the hospital bed and knocked over Lee's saline drip, pulling the tube from his arm. Then she staggered to the edge of the tower and, without hesitation, threw herself off.

Martin didn't see her fall. He was already racing across plank bridges suspended between the concentric walls, cutting the corners to reach the West Tower as fast as he could.

From the front of the castle, he heard a bestial roar and recognised the voice of Mauger. He wondered if the demon was loose yet, if it too was speeding towards the West Tower.

On the gatehouse roof, the Ismus had watched the Jockey's intervention on the monitor and he cursed under his breath. It had been too much to expect that character to behave himself the whole night long. Still, it had been enjoyable to observe how close Martin had come to using the dagger on the Castle Creeper.

But now the final, and most gratifying, round of Flee the Beast was due to commence. The Ismus turned to the Black Face Dames, still grovelling on the floor, and ordered them to release Mauger.

The three men hurried to obey and the Ismus draped himself across the Bakelite console, face tilted towards the Keep. What a truly fantastic panorama. He'd never dreamed it would be so ravishing. Lucifer, in all His brilliant splendour, surveying the wretched world he, His humble servant, had wrought for His return. He could sense the satisfaction, the dark pleasure emanating from that lofty throne and, when the glare from those scalding eyes glanced across him, he felt a soaring pride. He had done well. No one had ever achieved more in His name. There had never been destruction and terror on such a scale as this. And there was still more to come.

Returning his attention to the controls, he flicked off a row of switches and waited.

Overhead, the lightning turned crimson, like gigantic veins and arteries, flaring in the broiling night. The invisible barriers he had raised and maintained, this final week, dissipated and the huge area round the construction site was now defenceless. The myriad creatures that had been drawn to this seething mass of people were free to move in and dine.

The Ismus stared out, over the horror-filled, burning landscape, where his former readers were either killing one another, or were consumed with despair and self-loathing and trying to kill themselves.

Almost immediately new sounds swelled that agonised cacophony. A hill of people lifted, as something immense burrowed up from below. A segmented back broke the surface, followed by a writhing mass of tentacles that snaked from its gaping mouth. It was the same species of nightmare that had appeared in the aberrant camp that summer, the thing Captain Swazzle had called a Marshwyrm. But this one was much larger.

Its massive bulk steered through the screaming multitude. The fleshy, worm-like tentacles snatched everything in their path and shovelled them into the hungry mouth. Then another of them burst up from the deep regions of the earth – and another.

"I saw three ships come sailing in," the Ismus sang, clapping his hands, rejoicing.

On the horizon, winged shapes were circling in the sky.

The scavengers of Hell had come to feed.

"Christmas dinner, with all the trimmings," he welcomed them. "Tuck in, my friends, no party hats or table manners required. Plenty for everyone. Make merry, indulge and be sated."

The Ismus breathed a gratified sigh. He who had been cast down was most pleased in him. He could feel the approval radiating from His Sovereign Majesty. It had been a difficult road, but the sacrifices had been worth it: the small defeats, the trials, the doubts, the long wait, the dangers and uncertainties that had so often threatened to upset the entire scheme. Finally each one had been overcome. His triumph was complete and total. It was a magnificent moment to savour.

"My Lord!" a voice interrupted.

Irritated, the Ismus turned his head and saw that two of his Black Face Dames had returned. Struggling between them, held fast, was a bespectacled teenage boy wearing a cowboy hat.

"What have we here?" the Ismus asked in amused surprise. "Why – it's the Milky Bar Kid! Ha ha!"

Spencer said nothing and the toes of his boots scraped the floor, as the bodyguards dragged him closer.

"When I said no party hats," the Ismus scolded, "that included Stetsons, not just paper ones from crackers. Are you feeble-minded, boy? This isn't a barn dance. Where can you have sprung from?"

Spencer refused to answer. The Ismus raised his eyebrows at the Black Face Dames.

"We found him skulking by the drawbridge," one of them reported. "When we went to release Mauger."

"Ah, yes," the Ismus said, studying the monitor. "Has the Growly Guardian been let out of his den?"

"Any moment now, my Lord."

The Ismus selected the camera in the archway of the gatehouse, the one pointing at a large, heavy door built from stout metal bars. He saw the third bodyguard attend to an iron padlock and begin drawing back the bolts.

The Ismus picked up the horn-shaped microphone.

"Mauger, my lovely pet," his voice broadcast over the speakers below. "The time has come for your grand finale – a solo spectacular. Out there in the castle is the man who evaded you once. His family is on top of the West Tower. Run, my favourite. Slay them first, then bring me back his head, or anything that's left over – I don't really care what."

A bellowing roar vibrated through the stones of the gatehouse. On the monitor, the Black Face Dame stepped back. The door flew open and Mauger came storming out. Its powerful jaws ripped through the man's throat and, with a shake of its great head, the two horns tore him in two.

Its mighty fists pounded the ground, until the flagstones cracked, and Mauger let out another ferocious roar. Then, tossing its head, it bounded away, across the courtyard – towards the West Tower.

The Ismus watched it charge through the castle. "How he loves to gambol and frolic," he remarked with affection, before giving the captured boy his full attention once more.

"I ask again," he demanded, now deadly serious and threatening. "Who are you and what were you doing? Where are you from and how did you get here?"

Spencer remained tight-lipped, but the awful vision of the entity that reigned supreme upon the Keep would have rendered any attempt to speak impossible. He was so petrified, he could scarcely breathe.

"He was carrying these, my Lord," one of the bodyguards said, holding out two hand grenades.

The Ismus took them and an ugly grin split his thin face as he realised.

"So that's who you are," he said. "You're Spencer, of course. That's what the old fairy meant. I should have remembered you from my days hiding inside Christina, back in the camp, and when we met at Malinda's cottage in Mooncaster. But then you're not exactly memorable, are you, boy? Takes more than a novelty hat to make you interesting. You're one of those grey-faced wallpaper people, forever unnoticed, always hovering in the background – being a bit creepy with nothing interesting to say for yourself. At least the zits have cleared up."

Removing the pins, he threw the grenades into the moat, where they exploded with great spouts of water.

"Let him go," he instructed. "I don't think there's any fight left, if indeed there was any to begin with. What a specimen. He can hardly stand up unaided. The resplendence of the Dawn Prince is too much for him to bear."

The Black Face Dames released Spencer and took a step back. The boy wilted and almost fell among the cables that trailed from the back of the console.

"Were you seriously planning on blowing this up?" the Ismus asked in bemused disbelief. "You? On your own? Were Old Mother Riley and Miss Sour Noodle supposed to be some sort of diversion? That really is the most ludicrous plan I've ever heard. I'm almost insulted! If I'd known they had plotted something so cretinously pathetic, I'd have made them suffer a lot more before they died."

Spencer winced and his mouth quivered.

"Oh, yes," the Ismus assured him. "Your hapless little band of outlaws are all dead and dying. The pensioner has worn his last frock, the Korean girl is a gibbering wreck, soon to be picked clean by my Christmas guests, the cars containing the little sheep won't get far, they'll be opened up like tin cans, and my bloodthirsty demon is just about to rend Martin Baxter limb from limb. It's been a highly satisfying, productive night. I'm so very lucky. Merry Christmas to one and all – but especially me!"

A choked, crushed cry sounded in Spencer's throat and his tormentor laughed viciously as he turned to the monitor to watch Mauger closing in on Martin Baxter.

"They really do show the best telly over the festive season. This is my all-time favourite programme!"

Austerly Fellows was triumphant.

28

THE ADRENALIN PUMPING through Martin's system had brought him to the West Tower ahead of Mauger. He could hear the demon stampeding through the castle, smashing its way in this direction. It wouldn't be long now. Sweat was running down his face, washing clean rivers through the smeared filth, and steam rose from his stinking rags.

Standing on the battlements, he stared up at the tower. From here he could see only one corner of the Nativity roof. Was there time to run inside and climb the winding stairs to be with Carol and Paul? Or should he deal with Mauger first, down here?

Looking at the golden dagger in his hand, he knew it was too paltry a weapon to inflict any harm on that monster. He remembered their last encounter, when it pursued him from Fellows End. Mauger was going to make very short work of him. Martin cast around to see if there was anything else he could use against it. He pulled at the scaffold poles round the tower, but they were fixed firmly in place and there was no time to unfasten the couplers to release one.

Another roar resounded across the castle walls. Mauger was closing. Martin didn't know what to do. And then he heard a snicker behind him.

"Kizka smell scared Mauger meat," a voice said.

Martin jumped round. Emerging from the darkness of the tower entrance was the Punchinello that had been guarding the Nativity scene. A spear and sword were in his gnarled hands, but he hadn't come down to attack; he wanted to watch the fun.

"Mauger make much mess!" the Punchinello gurgled in excited anticipation. "Your guts will be strung like bunting, your bloody bones..."

His gloating ended abruptly when a length of timber walloped him across the shoulders. The guard whirled round furiously and was clobbered by the same piece of wood across the face.

While he tottered in stunned surprise, he was robbed of his weapons and pitched over the edge of the high walkway.

"That's for threatening my baby," Carol spat when his tumbling body hit the ground. "Yeah – and everything else!"

"Carol!" Martin yelled.

The woman threw the timber on the floor and rushed to him.

"Oh, Martin!" she cried joyously. "Martin, Martin..."

Despite everything, she couldn't help laughing. "You really do stink. You never did know how to dress."

Clutching her face in his hands, he kissed her passionately on the mouth. Standing in the tower entrance, cradling the baby, Paul grinned.

"We smashed up the manger," the boy said, nudging the wood with his foot. "Perfect for thwacking!"

Martin hugged him and gazed down at his infant son.

"I think he's got your nose," Paul said.

"Poor thing," his mother added.

Martin wanted to take the baby in his arms, but was so dirty he didn't dare touch him. He was a beautiful child. Large hazel eyes stared up at him and he giggled, wrinkling his nose.

"What's his name?" Martin asked.

"Hasn't got one," Carol told him. "Not a real name, not from this world. I want you to choose it for him... but try to resist Spock or Bilbo."

At that moment Mauger came rampaging into the courtyard below. The repulsive head turned and twisted as the nostrils flared. Prowling over the cobbles, the demon approached the Punchinello's body. With a casual shake of its curved horns, it flung the guard against the far wall.

Then the yellow eyes slid upwards and fixed on the humans gathered upon the battlements. Mauger's jagged teeth crunched together. Then it let loose a chilling roar.

Martin took the spear and sword from Carol.

"Get back inside the tower," he told her and Paul sharply. "Go right to the top and wait for me there."

"Oh, no," she refused, making a grab to get the sword back. "I'm not leaving your side ever again!"

Martin recognised that obstinate, belligerent tone and knew it was pointless trying to argue.

"All right, you madwoman," he said, keeping the sword and giving her the dagger instead. "But stay behind me. Don't do anything reckless."

"Bit late to tell me that," she replied. "I moved in with you, didn't I?"

Then Carol turned to Paul and urged him to take the baby up to the top of the tower. The boy didn't want to leave them, but he knew he had

542

to take care of his little brother now. Carol and Martin embraced him. Paul took one last look at them, preparing to fight a demon they didn't have a hope of defeating, and hurried away.

With a lumbering gait, and a percolating growl vibrating in its throat, Mauger stalked towards the courtyard steps that led to the battlements. The powerful, gorilla-like shoulders rolled as it lumbered forward. Then, with a sudden spurt of speed, it sprang up the steps, six at a time.

Martin's sweat had turned cold. Mauger had grown since their last meeting. Against that ferocious horror, what could one middle-aged man, with a spear and a sword, hope to accomplish? He would be as effective as a figure made from straw. He would be dashed aside with a single swipe of those mighty claws.

Despairing for those he loved most more than for himself, he watched the demon race up on to the high walkway and turn towards them. Digging the tip of one of its horns into the stonework, it gouged a deep trench along the wall as it advanced.

This was it.

Carol reached forward and touched Martin's hand.

That simple gesture, a pure demonstration of love, here at this deadly finale to the night's entertainment, made the hairs on the back of Martin's neck rise. Suddenly the fear, the nervous dread and doubt left him completely. Anger and determination rushed in to replace them. His courage soared. That foul creature wasn't going to find it so easy to get past him. Even if it was as unstoppable as an express train, he'd make it tremble whenever it recalled this second encounter – and he'd make sure there were plenty of deep scars to keep those memories fresh and stinging.

Gripping the sword and spear firmly, he marched along the walkway to meet the demon head on.

"Come on, you great ugly mongrel!" he yelled, cutting the air with the blade. "I'm going to give you a lesson in fractions you won't ever forget!"

Mauger threw back its head and its bellow was augmented by an explosion somewhere in the castle. Then it charged straight for him.

On the gatehouse roof, Spencer hung his head. There had never been much hope for this suicidal operation, but to hear the news of Gerald's death, delivered in so off-hand a fashion, was a grievous shock. He couldn't bear it and could no longer look at that shining being up on the Keep. The boy tried to blot it out, forget it was there, concentrate on what was directly in front of him. But wave upon wave of terror flowed out from the new ruler of the world and Spencer couldn't master himself. Gerald and Eun-mi shouldn't have put their faith in him. He was letting them down. Why did he ever dare think he could accomplish this? From the moment that unspeakable horror had ascended the Waiting Throne, they should have abandoned their foolish plan and crept away, to die in the darkness somewhere.

And who was he anyway? The Ismus had described him with painful accuracy. He was just a nerdy loner who didn't have any friends, long before *Dancing Jax* trashed the world.

But, since that book had surfaced and its poison had spread, he had made true friends – the very best.

Spencer scowled and ground his teeth, furious with himself. Eun-mi had been right too: he was weak. But, standing there, steeped in the effulgence of Hell, his hands began to clench into fists. He wasn't going to cheapen those friendships and the memories of those amazing, courageous people by giving up, here at the very end of everything.

"Who am I?" he found himself whispering. "I'm Herr Spenzer, that's who."

Taking heart from the name Marcus had called him in the camp, he went on to recall a favourite quote – uttered by the greatest Western hero of them all.

Courage is being scared to death, but saddling up anyway.

Well, here he was, scared to death, so he told himself it was time to saddle up.

Spencer raised his head defiantly and brushed his fingers across the brim of his Stetson in a salute to 'the Duke'. There was a bold new gleam in his eye. For the next five minutes, in all probability the last of his young life, he was going to be John Wayne.

"Think you're pretty smart, don't ya?" he said in a bellicose drawl to the Ismus. "Well, let me tell you somethin', tenderfoot. We already blew up your homestead, with all those other fancy doodads in it. You shoulda patented them as a cure for bad skin, cos that's all they is good fer."

The Ismus was so taken aback by this unexpected display of spirit, he gave a snort of laughter, thinking the boy had lost his wits entirely.

"How the blazing glory of His Radiant Majesty afflicts them," he observed. "How His presence shrivels their insect minds. Do you think, boy, that I was unaware of what you did in Fellows End? For almost eighty years, my essence saturated every stone, seeped through every fibre of that house and, after I departed, echoes of my thought and being remained. Not a mote of dust floated through those hallways that I was not cognisant of. The moment Miss Winyard, my bright little protégée, guided you over the threshold, I knew of it. Such a pity you razed the old place, but it had served its purpose. I was never going to return. And, as for my special room, the bridging devices there had only a very localised field of influence. Their destruction didn't even register on this master console. You achieved nothing."

Spencer breathed deeply and adopted the famous John Wayne stance he had practised so often before. He wasn't going to let the Ismus distract him. Grasping the crown of his Stetson, he lifted the hat from his head carefully and held it against his chest.

"Now you might think you got it all figured out," he said, mangling lines from the classic movie *McLintock!* with his own words. "But you caused a whole mess o' trouble here today and got folks killed, and somebody oughta whup ya real good and belt you in the mouth. But I won't, I won't..."

Spencer glanced down at his Stetson and reached inside. With a brazen grin, he looked up again, stared the Ismus square in the eyes and snarled, "The hell I won't!"

Taking the grenade that had been concealed under his hat, and from which he'd just ripped the pin, he dropped it into one of the vents at the back of the master console.

The Ismus took a moment to comprehend what he'd done. Then he yelled at the Black Face Dames, who sprang forward. One of them pulled at the back panel, while the other hurled the Ismus to the floor and dived on top of him.

Whooping, Spencer ran for the steps. He never reached them. The explosion blew him from the gatehouse roof. Before he blacked out, he smiled. One more cliff jump.

In the realm of Mooncaster, Lee looked up. The talking fox had bid him adieu some moments ago. The cave entrance was ahead, through the trees, and his horse would go no further. A foul stench of death flowed from that rocky mouth.

The boy slid from the saddle and drew the back of his hand across his nose in revulsion.

"Why does even the bad stuff have to smell twice as strong in this damn place?" he grumbled.

Leaving the horse behind, he made his way up the forest slope. The reek of decay and rottenness grew worse and the air was thick with bluebottles, drawn to the tantalising scents of corruption.

"That is hummin'!" Lee said, coughing. "And I guess it's gonna get a whole lot worse, cos real soon there's gonna be one more dead thing stinking that hole out."

He reached for the long knife at his side and gazed around warily. He didn't want to be pounced on by that Cinnamon Bear – or anything else. Nothing better try and get between him and the Bad Shepherd. If it did, it wouldn't live long enough to apologise.

The early rays of dawn streamed through the leaf canopy, dappling and dancing over the bracken. It flashed and winked across the burnished blade in Lee's hand and reflected back into his eyes.

"Yeah," he said bitterly. "You dazzle all you want, but you won't never light up the darkness I got in me. I ain't gonna turn back now. This party is on."

Pressing further, he reached an outcrop of rock, a little distance from the cave mouth, and paused.

"Hey!" he shouted. "You in there – shepherd guy. I know you're hidin' out in that dump. Don't make me come in there and get you – stinks bad enough out here."

He waited a few minutes, but there was no answer.

"You me gotta talk," he called. "Got things we need to chew over."

There was no sign of him. Lee swore under his breath. The Bad Shepherd wasn't going to show himself.

"Guess he ain't so crazy after all."

Muttering and batting the flies away, he pushed through the undergrowth and continued on to the cave.

Sucking the air sharply through his teeth, he slapped his arm and rolled back the shirt sleeve. One of those hungry insects must have bitten him. Examining the bead of blood, he wiped it with his thumb. The small wound looked more like the mark a needle might make if it was dragged roughly out of the skin.

Lee scowled, realising his unconscious body back home had suffered some injury. He clenched his jaw and hoped whatever was happening back there would allow him enough time to do what he'd come here for.

Suddenly a face appeared in the craggy entrance. It darted from the shadows so quickly, it startled Lee and made him cry out.

The last time he'd seen the Bad Shepherd that ragged terror had been a frightening sight, a sinister force, whose eyes blazed with hate. He was a psychotic madman who'd swung one of the village boys around by his feet and had attacked Lee with an axe.

Now a terrible change had come over him. The gaunt face was even thinner and those rancorous eyes were sunken in deep hollows. The grubby flesh was stretched tissue-thin over the skull and had a sickly, yellowish pallor. The long, matted hair was even dirtier than before and the straggly beard was clogged with dried gobbets of bile, phlegm and blood.

"Jesus, you look bad," Lee uttered honestly.

The figure at the cave snarled back, steadying himself against the rock because he was so frail. The shepherd's robes were tattered and slashed and hung loosely off his skeletal frame. Lee caught a glimpse of ribs and a distended stomach and wondered when he'd last eaten any sort of meal. That guy was beyond starving.

But the hatred was still there, in those staring eyes. He glared at Lee and clawed the air with bony fingers. The bearded mouth parted and unintelligible curses poured out.

"Yeah?" Lee goaded. "You come here and say that."

The Bad Shepherd took several shambling steps forward, then staggered back. He was too weak to stand, never mind walk. Spitting and wheezing, he leaned against the rock and the shaggy brows scrunched together.

"That all you got?" Lee demanded ruthlessly. "This won't take no time at all."

The boy advanced with slow, measured steps and raised the knife in readiness.

He saw the unhinged rage and malice in those eyes dissolve into fear and the Bad Shepherd let out a dismal wail. With the rocky wall against his shoulders, he scrambled out of sight, back into the cave.

"Hell," Lee hissed.

But the scourge of Mooncaster wasn't going to come out again. Lee was going to have to go in after him, into that stinking den.

"If that's where this has gotta happen," he said grimly. "Don't make no odds to me." He just hoped he wasn't going to find the Bad Shepherd cowering behind a ferocious Cinnamon Bear.

Lee approached the entrance. The early sunlight blinded his eyes to the gloom inside. He felt the sun's warmth on the back of his neck and lingered briefly. What he was about to do was going to be a crucial turning point – a genuine moment in history. He felt there should be a fanfare or a drum roll to see him across that dank threshold. But there was only the buzz of bluebottles.

"That'll have to do," he said and he stepped into the shadow of the rocky entrance.

Keeping a fierce grip on the knife, in case a savage bear came lunging at him, he waited for his eyes to adjust. Then he shuddered at what he saw.

The cave wasn't large. It didn't reach far back into the wooded hill and, although the shadows were deep, it wasn't in total darkness.

In the centre, lying on the earthen floor, was the Cinnamon Bear. But it was long dead and its dilapidated carcass had been gnawed clean. Every bone had been broken and sucked dry and the hide had been chewed of every last scrap of nourishment. This was why the Bad Shepherd hadn't been glimpsed since the spring: he'd been living off the bear's corpse all that time, until there was nothing left to leach out of it and, judging by the state of him, that was quite a while ago.

The cave echoed with rattling breaths and Lee looked beyond the heap of fur and bones to where the ragged man was cringing behind a boulder.

Lee waved the knife through the shadows. Even in there it gleamed.

The Bad Shepherd's eyes were locked on it and he was shivering.

"You ain't nuthin' like the paintin' my gran'ma had of you," Lee said, taking a step nearer.

"You at Heart's Door, it was called. But you looked a whole lot better in them days. Nice shiny robe, hair by L'Oréal or somethin' like that. Never thought you'd stink so bad. You and Yogi bones there in competition?"

He took another step.

"And your eyes ain't blue neither. What's that about? Man, you is a wreck and a disappointment."

The boy spread his arms wide. "So here we is," he said. "Just you an' me – and I got me a damn big blade and I'm the Castle Creeper, the one who can take you out, both here and in the real place, and make it like you never was."

The Bad Shepherd's eyes darted towards the sunlight.

"Oh, no," Lee warned. "Don't you get no ideas about runnin'. You is too weak to go anyplace an', if you try before I've said my piece, I'll cut you deep and let that Holy Spirit right outta there."

The man bared his broken teeth at him and snarled like a cornered beast.

"Right back at ya," Lee said.

He took another step closer.

"Let me take a minute to tell you 'bout my gran'ma," he began. "She believed in you all her life, sang your songs, lived by your words, dressed up real extra nice to go your places on Sunday and gave them money she couldn't afford. And what did she get out of it? What was it for? Being all wiseass one day, I aksed her and she sat me down and told me, 'Faith ain't no easy thing.'"

He grinned at the memory.

"I didn't know what she meant by that so she said, 'Lee Jules Sherlon Charles, when you think about it, really sit and think real hard, faith is batshit scary.' Yeah, she said it just like that – had a spicy vocab, my gran'ma. Then she told me you pile every hope, every dream, your whole sorry-ass life on what could be the biggest con ever – and you bet the whole damn lot on it. If that ain't mad scary I don't know what is."

The grin faded.

"I told her that weren't scary, just plain stupid, and she'd been scammed by a book of lies, written by white guys with twisted agendas, too long ago for it to matter no more, and you know what she said back? She told me that, cos I didn't believe in nuthin', I wasn't scared of nuthin'. But when the time was right, and I found my own faith, somethin' I could believe in, I'd understand."

Lee took a breath and moistened his lips.

"Well," he continued, "I guess this must be that time, cos right now I is the scaredest I ever was. I dunno if I'm dumb, crazy or both, but more than all that, Lee Jules Sherlon Charles is terrified."

Looking down, he ran his fingers along the sharp blade.

The Bad Shepherd spat at him.

"See," Lee said. "I could take this and carve you a Peckham smile and tailor you right outta your skin. But... my special girl, my Charm, she had the sweetest nature I ever met. She wouldn't want me to do that. I knowed just what she'd say. I hear her – all the damn time."

He thumped his fist against his chest.

"In here!" he said. "She's with me in here. She makes my heart so big I don't know how it stays inside. But it hurts like nuthin' I ever knowed before, and here's the thing – I don't never want that pain to stop. Cos that pain is proof my feelin's for her is real and that's my reason for everything."

Lee snorted and shook his head. "I don't trust that Ismus psycho," he said. "Not for one minute. That weren't my Charm lying on that pimped-out bed he showed me. That were just some painted doll and all that bull about the ruby thing – more dreams, more lies. My special girl is gone and he can't bring her back. Maybe you could, back in the day, I dunno, but not him. I made a promise to her one time: I wouldn't let her be turned into no freak in this world if anything happened. So that's why – I ain't gonna do what the Ismus wants."

The Bad Shepherd glared at him suspiciously.

"So why am I here, right?" Lee said. "Little while back, a good friend of mine called Maggie, she aksed what my favourite Christmas carol was. I told her to shove it. Yeah, I so do not deserve no friends. But there is one – about the snow an' frost an' ice an' stuff – in the winter. My gran'ma used to love that – she even used to sing it in July to cool herself down. That carol said it don't matter if you don't have nuthin' to give, no sheep, no wise man gold and stuff..."

The boy frowned as he concentrated, trying to remember the words.

"What can I give him? Give my heart. Yeah, that's how it went."

Lee turned the knife about, with the hilt towards the trembling man crouching before him.

"And that's it," he explained. "That's why I'm here. I weren't never gonna stick you. If you're really who the Ismus says you is, and you're all inside out and opposite, cos that's the way you have to be in this world, then here I am, givin' you my everything, givin' you my life –

and I don't know what else. This is what my gran'ma was talkin' about. This here blade is how much trust I got in you. This is the batshit-scary faith part. I'm gonna hand this over to you now. Take it and do whatever, cos I am done here. I wanna be with my girl again, but not his way. If you really are who he says then I'll take your way, if it's still available. Please?"

Leaning forward, his own hands were rock steady, but the emaciated, dirt-encrusted fingers of the Bad Shepherd were shaking when they came reaching. Then, as they closed round the hilt, the murderous fire was rekindled in those sunken eyes.

The haggard face contorted with a sneer and angry, malignant sounds, that weren't words, spewed from his bearded lips. Rising, he seemed to draw strength from the dagger in his grasp and he turned on Lee.

The boy didn't move. He didn't try to escape, or defend himself; he offered no resistance. He merely stood there, calm and ready, with his hands clasped tightly behind his back. Total surrender. He'd been waiting for this for too long. Closing his eyes, he summoned his favourite memory of Charm in his mind's eye and he smiled.

The knife came stabbing down. It sliced through his shirt and into his chest. The Bad Shepherd shrieked with vicious joy. Again and again the steel slashed and cut through Lee's flesh until he slumped to the floor.

Then the starving man, the bane of Mooncaster, the haunter of nightmares, knelt beside him, carved out his beating heart and devoured it.

29

IN THAT TORMENTED other world, at the construction site of the White Castle replica, the Ismus stirred on top of the gatehouse.

The dead weight of a Black Face Dame was on top of him. The Ismus heaved the body off and raised his head.

The master console was destroyed and the second bodyguard had been flung from the roof in splattered pieces.

The lightning was fizzling from the sky. The steel cranes were no longer crackling with electricity and, as he stared out over the surrounding landscape, he saw the huge predators sputter and vanish. Across the castle, by the West Tower, Mauger's attacking roar was already fading on the air and a bloody Martin Baxter was being nursed by Carol.

Anxious, the Ismus turned to look at the Keep. To his unbounded relief he saw his Sovereign Prince was still presiding there. The destruction of the Bakelite device had not diminished His brilliance. But the Ismus could sense displeasure. The fierce intensity of those eyes beat down upon him and he scrambled to his knees to bow his head and offer his sincere apology and to implore His indulgence and forgiveness.

"The way shall be opened again!" he vowed. "I can build a new transmitter. There are already many lesser devices in this world. This is only a brief hiatus. Within a week, all shall be as it was and Your gates will be cast down forever more."

That colossal, mordant anger was not appeased and he felt shrivelled and scorched by it. Then, suddenly, the baleful stare shifted away from him. It was like the door of a furnace closing.

The Ismus straightened his back and was alarmed to see the Dawn Prince rising from the throne. Immense fiery wings unfurled and the huge arms covered His face, shielding Himself.

In disbelief, the Ismus turned his gaze to see what could possibly be assailing his Sovereign Lord.

Up on the South Tower, where Lee's dead body lay on the hospital bed, a tall figure was now standing beside him. The man's head was bowed in humble prayer, and he gave thanks to the boy for releasing him.

It was the shepherd.

But now that face was no longer withered and skull-like, as it had been in Mooncaster, and the wild, uncontrolled savagery had left those eyes. It was the face of one at peace.

"You don't belong here!" the Ismus screamed, jumping to his feet. "You have no part to play now."

The shepherd looked over with the gentlest of smiles.

"My place is always here," the warmest of voices said.

"No!" the Ismus screeched. "There's nothing you can do. It's too late!"

"Have you forgotten?" the shepherd asked. "I too am an isthmus."

Looking down at Lee, he reached into the horrific wounds in the boy's chest and his hand closed round an object that shone and sparkled through his fingers.

There was the Healing Ruby, where it had always been.

The shepherd raised it above his head as a beacon. Its pure, steady light pierced the oppressive glare of Lucifer's wrathful fire. On the Keep, He let out a deafening roar of pain and defiance that rolled under the sky and boomed beneath the oceans of the world. His flames ripped up into the dark clouds.

The Healing Ruby shone even brighter.

Outstretching His great wings, Lucifer rose into the night.

"You shall have no dominion here," the shepherd said. "Our strength has been renewed."

A flash of violet light rippled out across the heavens, accompanied by an almighty clap of thunder that shook the castle walls, and three towers split apart.

The Ismus recoiled and covered his eyes. A violent tremor tore through the earth and the air was shredded by a piercing scream.

When he removed his hands and blinked away the dots that popped around his vision, the Ismus saw shreds of red flame falling out of the sky, on to the melted wreckage of the Waiting Throne.

A cold December wind blew across the castle and silence descended. The top of the South Tower was deserted. The shepherd had gone – and the hospital bed was empty.

"No!" the Ismus raged. "This does not end here! I am Austerly Fellows. I go on! I am not defeated! I am—"

Before he could finish, he heard a different voice raised in righteous condemnation.

The Ismus looked back at the Keep. Something was rushing towards him, flying through the air at tremendous speed. He saw a golden star, glimmering above a halo of streaming white hair, as a figure came swooping down over the battlements. He thought it was an avenging angel until he saw the uniform and heard those proclaiming words.

"I am a human rifle. A human bomb, a dagger of your hand!"

With one hand holding on to witchcam, the girl who now called herself Arirang came shooting across the castle like a rocket on a wire. In her other hand she held the thing she had smuggled out of the mountain base wrapped in a blanket. It was the real wand of Malinda.

When the Ismus recognised the danger, he turned to run, but it was too late.

Zooming towards the gatehouse, Arirang let go of witchcam and jumped, wielding the wand like a spear.

"I strike at the diseased heart of the Western enemy!" she yelled, lunging with all her strength.

The Ismus arched his back and swallowed a cry as the wand's silver shaft skewered him. Staggering forward, he clutched the gleaming tip jutting from his chest and tried in vain to push it back. Behind him, the amber star burst into coruscating flames. They fizzed and crackled along the silver rod and leaped into his body.

The Ismus threw back his head, shrieking in agony. His face frothed and blistered with black mould. Branching growths surged swiftly from his mouth, trying to escape the magick, cauterising fires. But the might of the wand consumed every writhing strand, every pulsing bloom, every ejected spore. They spat and glittered around his flailing form, sizzling and smoking, until every unholy trace of Austerly Fellows had been destroyed.

And because the wand had been brought from that other Realm, where its power was even greater, striding among the smoking carnage of Mooncaster, looking with satisfaction on the corpses of the guards and courtiers strewn around the castle, their Holy Enchanter felt the death blow strike through his own chest. Sparks and flames erupted from his ribs. There was no time to cry out. As his hands reached to clutch the crackling wound, they crumbled to dust and cinders. His stricken body toppled, but was blown away as smoke and ash before it ever reached the ground.

On top of the gatehouse, Arirang surveyed what she had done and grunted with the satisfaction of a mission accomplished. She stared at the charred and burned husk of the man once called Jezza, impaled by the wand that still blazed with supernatural golden flames.

The Korean girl strode round the edge of the gatehouse roof and gazed out across a wilderness of death and horror that would take many lifetimes to repair. By the West Tower, she saw Martin Baxter with his arms round a woman. A boy carrying an infant was running to join them and they held each other desperately.

As her white hair whipped about her beautiful face, Arirang heard countless voices weeping in the wind. Throughout the world, the survivors of *Fighting Pax* were struggling to come to terms with what had happened. But now their despair and mourning would not be so impenetrably dark. There was light, if they chose to reach for it.

Arirang held her head high. For her, this was merely the beginning; she still had much to achieve. First she would find little Nabi. Then they would return home, where the greater, more difficult mission would commence.

"Hey!" a familiar voice called up from the courtyard below. "Anyone there? Can anyone hear me? Er... I think, ow – I think I busted some bones – ow!"

An uncharacteristic grin, the first of many, lit up her face as she sought the stairs and ran to attend to Spencer.

Snow began to fall.

Free will was re-established across the globe. 2.47 minutes later, the first murder, unrelated to *Dancing Jax*, was committed.

IN THE YEARS that followed, Grumbles the Conservius trotted up and down the tower steps more times than there were stars in the sky over Mooncaster – or so he muttered to himself. Gazing out over Battle Wood, towards the castle in the distance, he often wondered what had happened to the Ismus, for he never returned, and he thought that was a strange thing.

The unknown answers to many other questions irked Grumbles greatly. Just what had occurred on that night of smoke and turmoil? The ornate bed, with its beautiful occupant, disappeared from the tower that very same night and he found himself sighing wistfully at the remembrance of her lovely face. He should like to look on it again one day, but of course that was impossible.

It was all very vexing and if Them Upstairs knew those answers, they weren't about to tell him. The eternal game of cards continued as it had ever done and, down in the tower's bottom-most chamber, the piles of unused decks dwindled daily. The final end was creeping closer and that troubled Grumbles deeply. He also suspected that those diminishing stacks concealed one or two more gilt-edged cards to trouble the world and a growing unease crept over him.

Now, when he stood on the tower's lofty roof and stared out at the hills and fields of Mooncaster, his horned brows creased with anxiety and he no longer paused to muse on why the White Castle had been painted a different colour, or tried to guess what was happening within its walls or down in the village.

"Some new trouble is brewing, that's for sure," he told himself. "I can smell it on the wind and my hooves do itch, which is as certain a sign as any. Oh, yes, some new awfulness is hatching, somewhere, someplace."

Shaking his head with worry, he hopped down into the hatch and descended the steps. Beneath the great lantern, the four robed players continued the game. A skeletal hand placed the latest card on the stone table.

The Spectre from the Ashes.

11.53am, the Head Office of PlayKing Toys Corp, Chicago

Everyone in the boardroom was keyed up. They'd been looking forward to this meeting for three months. They didn't mind that their celebrity guest was already fifty minutes late. They had spent that extra time going over the proposal and making sure they were all on message. They also spent a lot of that time discussing the controversy surrounding the new blockbuster movie that had premiered in New York earlier that week.

"So do we mention it, or do we not mention it?" Constance Trask, head of the creative team, asked.

"It's like a huge elephant in the room if we don't," said Brayden, one of the two designers present.

"So we get it out of the way at the start, yeah?" Constance suggested.

Madison Page, the marketing director, tapped her wedding ring against her coffee cup for attention and peered sternly over the rim of her owlish spectacles.

"I don't care if that elephant takes a two-hundred-pound dump in the middle of this table," she said severely. "If our guest doesn't want to talk about the movie, or anything else, we keep our lips zipped – got that? You know how tough it is to even get through to her people? I don't want any of you to screw this up. This deal is going to be worth a lot of dollars. The company can't afford to lose this endorsement."

"No wonder they all distanced themselves from it," Brayden mused, returning to the subject of the movie. "The liberties they took with the characters..."

"Real people, Brayden. They were real people."

"I know."

"Is it true they wanted to make the Lee boy white?"

"As if making him come from Queens wasn't bad enough."

"So my cousin named her son after him. She was beyond mad at what they've done. She joined the protesters outside the movie theatre and got arrested."

"That was a pretty violent protest," Madison observed.

"It was hijacked by a militant denier group. They were the ones throwing tear gas at the red carpet.

"Beats me how anyone can deny all that," Brayden muttered.

"They're mostly teens," Madison commented. "Either too young to remember what really happened or too screwed up to want to be reminded. Hell, who here hasn't spent the last five years in therapy or woken up drenched in sweat every night? We've been close to fighting three wars about it, and each religion blames another."

"You got to be real dumb to believe it was down to psychotropic drugs and LSD in the food chain though."

"I dunno," Constance said. "Wish I could blame it on chemicals and global government conspiracies, 'stead of having these images lodged in my head. I just don't wanna think about it, period. At least two billion dead, total number unknown. So many cities still like ghost towns and an economy so far down the toilet, it can wave at China."

"Markets are the healthiest they've been," Olivia, the other designer, interrupted. "They say in three years' time it'll get back to normal."

"Normal?" Brayden said incredulously. "There'll never be 'normal' again. We're all only here today cos we survived it and we only survived it cos each of us kil—"

"That's enough," Madison snapped. "That kind of talk is against company policy, you know that. Survivor guilt, murder guilt have no place in the office. Save it for your support-group sessions, in your own time – and keep taking the meds."

"Yeah," Brayden said. "Those pharmaceutical companies are the only ones making the big bucks now. I know I couldn't sleep without my yellow pill every night."

"You think the rest of us can?"

"So," Constance put in. "They're still finding nests of those spider things and other nasties, and that minchet weed still hasn't been eradicated. You reckon there really are some of those old-time radio gizmos out there? And what about the cult of Austerly Fellows? That Inner Circle is still supposed to be active."

"You really have to stop reading *The Enquirer*," Olivia told her. "It's turning your brains to mush."

The boardroom door opened and Elliot King, the chairman, entered. His craggy face was wreathed in his most professional smile as he ushered the special guest inside.

"And here is our team," he said proudly.

Everyone rose and greeted the celebrity with the most reverential welcomes, as polite introductions were made.

Madison Page studied the slim young woman, with a keen eye to the marketing angle. The brand recognition was impeccable, couldn't be better. Here was one of those amazing young people who had actually been at the castle site that Christmas Eve, one of the most famous of all those aberrants, and she was the most camera-shy of the lot, building up a huge mystique around herself. Maybe they could hype that Garbo angle and make it work for them.

She looked fabulous. That was at least a 400-dollar haircut, and the shoes alone could bankroll someone through their first college semester. As for the suit, Madison had never seen an Alexander McQueen sharper and better fitted. The Moss Lipow sunglasses dripped class and there was the silver-topped black walking cane that had become such a trademark with her.

Elliot showed her to a seat. The limp wasn't too noticeable. Might have been a lot worse, considering she'd been trapped under rubble for four days until the rescue.

"Before we begin," the stylish young woman said, in a firm and businesslike, no-nonsense tone, "let's get a few things straight, so we can move on to why I'm here. First off, I don't want to be called Maggie. My name is Margaret, but I prefer 'Miss Blessing'; let's not get too familiar, I'm not looking for friends here and small talk is for small minds. This is strictly business. You all got that? However, I can see you're bursting to ask a lot of questions, so I'll do a pre-emptive strike. No, I haven't seen the movie.

"From what I gather, the actor playing Marcus is far too buff, the girl playing me is nowhere near fat enough and they made Charm into some posh stoner. Spencer might have his own movie career now, but back then he looked like a pizza – and the way they camped up Gerald's character is an offence to his memory. He was never a hissy diva. This is the man Britain changed a law for, so they could award a posthumous knighthood. He should have got a damehood too, in my opinion. He deserved better than to be reduced to some limp-wristed, prancing stereotype that stopped being amusing twenty years ago. Oh, and apparently the guy they got to be Martin is up for the next James Bond; now that really is a joke. The less said about Lee, the better."

"Hollywood never did let facts stand in its way," Elliot ventured, not wanting to prolong this. "Doesn't seem to have gotten any better since it happened. Holding the premiere on the same date as World Memorial Day was a cheap stunt."

The woman wasn't quite done.

"Just so you all know, I don't see the others. After I got Charm's girls reunited with what was left of their families, I needed to get my head together, far away from all those reminders and the press intrusion. So I can't tell you any more than you probably know already. Martin is busy running his centres for disturbed kids. I think Emma and Sandra are still working with him, though I don't know how Sandra finds time to write her novels. Conor is never off British TV and, well, you know about Spencer, single-handedly resurrecting the Western genre. He does look good on a horse – and he's insured that hat for millions. As for what's happened in North Korea, I have no way of knowing if Eun-mi, or Arirang, or whatever she's calling herself now, is responsible."

Looking round the table, she saw there were questions still aching to be asked. Madison noticed it too and gave the staff a sharp reprimanding glance. She was a tough-nosed, corporate career woman, who wasn't afraid to kick ass, both metaphorically and literally, if need be.

Their guest stiffened with irritation.

"No," she told them, predicting those annoying questions with 100 per cent accuracy and firing off the answers with impatience. "I don't know why they didn't find Lee's body, or Gerald's, or some of the others who died in the castle that night. Could be any number of mundane reasons. What it doesn't mean is that they were taken to Mooncaster as some sort of reward. I don't care what Martin's stepson, Paul, said in the media about that recurring dream he has, or what any number of weirdos have contributed since. There's no way back to that place, whatever it was – and saying he saw the White Castle painted pink is just wishful thinking. Same applies to the Loch Ness Monster and UFOs. Now can we start?"

"By all means," Elliot agreed. "Our creative team have worked up a lot of initial concepts for your approval. They're early stages yet, but we wanted—"

"Excuse me? Concepts?"

"Designs for the plush characters you're going to endorse," Constance said, reaching for the presentation folder.

"Wait a minute, I think there's been a misunderstanding here. This range of toys is my idea. I approached your company. I'm not looking to endorse or promote anything you may come up with."

There was an awkward silence round the table.

"So you do or don't want to see the concepts?" Constance asked.

"I don't. We're going to use my ideas or I've had a wasted journey."

"Your ideas?"

Madison groaned inwardly. Yet another celebrity who thought they could tell professionals how to do their jobs. Marketing the crap these amateurs came up with wasn't impossible, but it wasn't enjoyable either. Still, her fame was the selling point so it didn't really matter how bad her ideas were. They could still shift plenty on the back of who she was and that's what the company needed most of all. They'd have to insist she wore her George Medal for the publicity though. Everyone adores a hero.

"Even after five years, the world is still grieving," Miss Blessing said. "So many loved ones lost, and so brutally, so needlessly. What I want to do is help heal those hurts. My concept has been designed specifically to do just that."

She turned to Elliot and asked him to open the door.

The chairman obliged and was surprised to see an Arab servant waiting outside, bearing a large box.

"Bring it in, Abdul-Sabur," Miss Blessing instructed. "Put them on the table."

The Arab came in and took three soft toys from the box, which he placed on the highly polished surface. Then he bowed and retreated to stand against the wall.

The staff of PlayKing Toys Corp stared at the stuffed characters in surprise. They weren't expecting her to bring in her own samples. But they were beautifully made, the best prototypes they'd ever seen, and unlike other plush designs. They weren't overtly cute, but they had masses of character and those soft faces expressed a hopeless and forlorn quality that made you want to hold and protect them.

"Neat," Brayden commented.

"Who are these little guys?" Constance asked. "They're adorable."

Miss Blessing nodded. "They're refugees, like I was once," she said. "But these are from the happy land of Huggumee, which has recently been despoiled by drought and tempests, flood and forest fires. So many tribes have been displaced from their ancient homes and many beloved family members didn't make it."

To her astonishment, Madison felt a sob rising in her throat.

"I know what that's like," she murmured, gazing at the small, imploring faces on those strange dolls, and thinking about things she hadn't even got around to mentioning in therapy yet.

"These are from the hill tribes of Cubblebub, Pumpleshin and Thrump," Miss Blessing continued. "Three of the most badly affected communities in the land."

"Oh, that's brilliant," Brayden said, marvelling. "There's a backstory and everything worked out for these dudes. There's your marketing strategy, Madison."

They looked to the marketing director. The usually terse, sceptical woman was absorbed in caressing one of those sad faces.

"Madison?" Elliot said.

Looking round at Miss Blessing, Madison asked, "Who's this guy? He reminds me of... someone I lost."

"He's called Orphan Mewly, and that's Patch Doosome and she's Mawny Sal."

"I... I want to take him home."

"He needs a home. They all desperately need to be taken care of, nurtured and cherished. It's the only way to heal their profound sorrow and maybe, by loving them, they can help the rest of us."

Madison picked up Orphan Mewly and cradled him in her arms.

"Hey there, little buddy," she cooed. "Think you could be happy with a big grown-up person like me? I could be your new mommy."

Her colleagues stared at her, dumbfounded.

"Godsakes!" she cried. "Did he just smile at me?"

"Madison, you OK?" Elliot asked in concern.

"It's the stitching," Miss Blessing explained, amused. "I discovered a way of rucking the fabric in subtle ways, so when the light falls on it, even slightly differently, it causes an illusion of movement. He didn't really smile at you."

Madison shook herself and gave an embarrassed laugh. "Thought I was losing it there," she said. "Thought I'd have to move on to the green pills."

"Wait," Brayden broke in. "You saying you made these yourself, Miss Blessing?"

"Yes. I used to make dolls out of scraps for the others, when we were in that mountain. They seemed to help then, and these can help now."

"Amazing."

"These are so much better than what we came up with," Constance agreed. "I love Mawny Sal. I had a sister..."

"Is there a faint musty smell?" Olivia interjected.

"They've been stored in my basement and I had a boiler leak. I was thinking about impregnating the cloth with some kind of scent anyway, vanilla, chocolate or gingerbread – something cosy to snuggle up to."

"Great idea!"

"Hey, did you make the eyes too? Wow. You got real talent. It's like they're looking right at me."

Elliot found himself drawn to Patch Doosome. Something about that face...

"This could be big," he said, pulling himself together. "I mean real big. Everybody is gonna want one of these guys. I love this fella already."

"They're for everyone who ever lost somebody close or dear," Miss Blessing told him. "They're not just for children."

"You don't say. Well, our distribution is second to none and our product lines speak for themselves. You got that information already, right? We get all our plush made out in Asia. I want to see how well they can copy these."

"Oh, they're all unique. No two characters are the same."

"That simply isn't viable."

"I believe I've found a way. Tell me more about your Asian operation."

Elliot wasn't sure there could be a way, but that was something they could tackle later. He wanted to get these into production right away. They'd revitalise the fortunes of the entire company.

"We only use plush factories with good safety records, where they do needle tracking – the whole bit," he said. "Our products totally meet the code. Course, it hikes up the unit price. Can't get around that one..."

"These are not 'units'."

"Oh, no offence intended," he said, and for some reason found himself addressing that apology to Patch Doosome instead of her.

"And what about child labour?"

Elliot shifted uncomfortably.

"Well, that's a real big issue and one that our culture doesn't properly understand. We have to wink at some of the practices out there, same as everyone else who does business with them, specially nowadays. Hey, it's the only way those people can get by. Otherwise what else are those kids gonna do? Get sent out begging on the streets by gang lords who'll chop some limbs off them so they can earn a few extra rupees? Believe me, child labour is a good alternative. We're saving lives there."

He couldn't tell if the look she gave him was condemning or approving.

"Can I really take Orphan Mewly home with me?" Madison asked.

"Once you've signed the contract of care," Miss Blessing told her. "Of course."

"The what?"

"I must ensure that every refugee goes to a responsible carer. Each one comes with a contract that must be signed."

"Hey, sort of adoption papers?" asked Brayden.

"No, not a bit like that. This is far more... binding."

"Cool."

"Well, Miss Blessing," Elliot declared, "it's going to be swell doing business with you. Is there a unifying name we can put these critters out under?"

"Huggumee Kids?" Olivia proposed.

"Lost Tribes?" Brayden added.

"Wait," Constance said enthusiastically. "How about... 'Little Blessings'?"

"I like that!" Elliot congratulated her. "This is why I pay you, Connie."

"They already have a name," Miss Blessing said. "It's non-negotiable, I'm afraid."

"What is it?" Elliot asked.

"Good Intentions."

There was a silence. They didn't like it. Then Madison suggested thoughtfully, "We could change the dots above the 'i's into little pink hearts..."

Visit the chilling, fantastical world of
the *WYRD MUSEUM* in this
spell-binding trilogy.